BASIC
WRITINGS
OF
KANT

BASIC
WRITINGS
OF
KANT

Edited and with an Introduction
by Allen W. Wood

THE MODERN LIBRARY

NEW YORK

2001 Modern Library Paperback Edition

Introduction copyright © 2001 by Allen W. Wood

LIBRARY OF CONGRESS CATALOGING-IN-PUBLICATION DATA
Kant, Immanuel, 1724–1804.
Basic writings of Kant / edited and with an introduction by Allen W. Wood.
p.   cm.
ISBN 0-375-75733-3
1. Philosophy. I. Wood, Allen W. II. Title.
B2758 .B352   2001
193—dc21   2001018303

Modern Library website address: www.modernlibrary.com

Printed in the United States of America

CONTENTS

INTRODUCTION

Allen W. Wood

Immanuel Kant's conception of man and his relationship to the world is the pivotal event in the history of modern philosophy. It not only transformed the way philosophers since have thought about human knowledge, the reality of the world, and the foundations of morality, but also significantly impacted the history of the natural sciences and virtually laid the foundation for the way people in the last two centuries have confronted such widely differing subjects as the experience of beauty and the meaning of human history.

Kant changed the very meaning of "metaphysics" or "first philosophy" from the first-order study of the supernatural or incorporeal realm of being to the second-order study of the way human inquiry itself makes possible its access to whatever subject matter it studies. He revolutionized the foundations of philosophical ethics, changing it from a science directed toward achieving a pre-given good, or a study of the way human actions and evaluations are controlled by natural sentiments, into an inquiry into the way free agents govern their own lives according to self-given rational principles. In so doing, he brought the critical spirit of the eighteenth-century Enlightenment—the spirit of radical questioning and self-reflection that demands every human activity justify itself before the court of reason—to every area of life: to the sciences, to personal morality, to the criticism of works of art, to politics, to religion. Like the Enlightenment itself, Kant's philosophy spawned a bewildering variety of thinkers and movements claiming either to be its heirs or to have exposed and corrected its fundamental errors. The story of the battle over Kant's legacy and of the struggle to transcend Kant's standpoint amounts to the intellectual history of the entire nineteenth and twentieth centuries, and these same conflicts promise to characterize the future in the same way for as long as we can now foresee.

The writings in which Kant worked this influence contain, in their superficial literary form, nothing attractive or inspiring, and would seem the very reverse of anything that might promise such influence and inspiration. Kant usually wrote in the dry, cumbersome scholastic jargon he learned in an eighteenth-century German university whose intellectual life was firmly under the tutelage of the pedantic polymath Christian Wolff. He deliberately avoided a popular style, thinking that popularity is incompatible with rigorous thinking about the foundations of the sciences. The originality of his thought often only adds to the obscurity of his writing style, in which traditional terms drawn from the scholastic tradition are used to express new thoughts and a revolutionary program, so that their familiar meanings are constantly being placed under stress. It is difficult not to find Kant's way of writing a deterrent to studying his philosophy, and more than a little of the controversy his philosophy provokes has no doubt been due to the fact that readers have been frustrated to the point of exasperation by prose that seems gratuitously uninviting or even deliberately repellent.

Yet in most of his philosophical works, the ponderousness of his prose is above all a result of the fact that he sees himself as a serious scientific laborer with an important job to do, which denied him the luxury of the literary time and space to interrupt his intellectual workmanship merely for the sake of literary effects that might ingratiate him with a larger audience. Moreover, there is a sense in which Kant was right in seeing his way of writing as a way of preserving philosophical rigor. For when Kant forces himself (and his readers) to follow new thoughts expressed in a set of traditional terms, he leaves behind a graphic record of the process through which the entire philosophical tradition is being radically transformed. The infamous length and complexity of Kant's sentences challenges the reader to participate in the struggle for critical reflection required for the intellectual revolution that is being accomplished in them.

———

Immanuel Kant was born April 22, 1724, in Königsberg, East Prussia. At that time the city was an isolated eastern outpost of German culture (though it was briefly occupied by Russian troops during Kant's lifetime); since its conquest by the Allies in 1945, it has been renamed Kaliningrad and is now an isolated western outpost of Russian culture. Kant was the sixth of nine children born to Johann Georg Kant, a humble saddler (or leather-worker), and Anna Regina Reuter. Both Kant's parents were devout Pietists. Pietism was a revivalist movement that arose in the seventeenth century and had a great impact on German culture throughout the eighteenth century; it is comparable to other contemporary religious movements such as Quakerism or Methodism in England or Hassidism among central-European Jews. The family pastor, Franz Albert Schulz, was also rector of the newly founded *Collegium Fredericianum,* and noticing signs of exceptional intellect in the young Immanuel, arranged for him an educational opportunity that was surely rare for children of his parents' social class.

Kant entered the University of Königsberg in 1740, the same year in which Frederick the Great became King of Prussia—a significant date in the intellectual life of Germany. One of Frederick's first acts was to recall Christian Wolff to his professorship at the University of Halle, thus offering symbolic support to the intellectual movement known as the *Aufklärung* (Enlightenment), of which Wolff was considered the father. Seventeen years earlier, Frederick's father had exiled Wolff from Prussian territories (he then took up residence in Marburg) under the influence of Pietists in the

Prussian court, who objected to the way the Enlightenment had made the German universities places of dry scholastic reasoning rather than religious inspiration and moral exhortation. They also found Wolff's fascination with pagan thought objectionable (he was, for instance, one of the first Europeans to undertake the philosophical study of Confucian writings, which he treated sympathetically) and protested some of his philosophical doctrines, such as that the human will is subject to causal determination under the principle of sufficient reason. The struggle, both within the universities and in intellectual life generally, between Wolffianism and Pietism was decisive for the intellectual environment in which Kant came of age.

At the university, Kant first studied Latin literature, which left its mark in the form of the quotations from Latin poets that constitute almost the only literary adornments of Kant's writings. But soon he came under the influence of a brilliant young teacher of mathematics and natural science, Martin Knutzen (1713–1751), whose early death (it is sometimes speculated) might have deprived him of some of the philosophical influence later exercised by his most famous student. Knutzen found it possible to be both a Wolffian and a Pietist, and under his guidance Kant directed his attention to questions of natural science.

Kant left the university in 1744, at the age of twenty, to earn a living as a private tutor in various households in East Prussia. In the next few years, he was twice engaged to marry but both times postponed the nuptials on the grounds that he was not financially solvent enough to support a family, and both times his fiancée tired of waiting and married someone else. It was eleven years before he could return to university life, receiving in 1755 the degrees of Master and Doctor of Philosophy, and obtaining a position as privatdocent. He was licensed to teach at the university but was paid no salary, earning his living from fees paid to him by students for his lectures. Since his livelihood depended on teaching whatever students wanted to learn, Kant found himself lecturing not only on logic, metaphysics, ethics, natural theology, and the natural sciences—including physics, chemistry, and physical geography, but also on related practical subjects, such as military fortification and pyrotechnics.

As a researcher, for a time Kant devoted his intellectual labors mainly to questions of natural science: mathematical physics, chemistry, astronomy, and the discipline (of which he is now considered the founder) of "physical geography"—what we would now call "earth sciences." This work culminated in *Universal Natural History and Theory of the Heavens* (1755), in which Kant was the first to propound the nebular hypothesis of the origin of the solar system. In the same year, however, he also began to engage in critical philosophical reflections on the foundations of knowledge and the first principles of Wolffian metaphysics in his Latin treatise *New Elucidation of the First Principles of Metaphysical Cognition.* Here he subjected central propositions and arguments of Wolffian metaphysics and theory of knowledge to searching criticism, and we find the earliest statements concerning Kant's characteristic thoughts about causality, mind-body interaction, and the traditional metaphysical proofs for God's existence. The early appearance of these writings illustrates the fact that the emergence of the "critical philosophy" in Kant's great work the *Critique of Pure Reason* was a protracted process that occupied his entire youth and most of his middle age. But we can see already in the *New Elucidation* that there never was a time in Kant's career as a philosopher in which he was an uncritical Wolffian.

Kant first attracted the attention of a wider philosophical audience in 1762, when he entered a prize essay competition on the foundations of metaphysics. The competition was won by Moses Mendelssohn, but Kant's essay, *On the Distinctness of the Principles of Natural Theology and Morals,* won second prize, was published in 1764 along with Mendelssohn's winning essay, and received compliments from Mendelssohn. Kant's interest in moral philosophy developed relatively late. In the prize essay as well as his earliest lectures on ethics, he seems to have been attracted by the moral sense theory of Francis Hutcheson. But he was soon to become convinced that a theory based on feelings was inadequate to capture the universal validity and unconditional bindingness of a moral law that must often challenge and overrule corrupt human feelings and desires. His thinking about ethics was dramatically changed in about 1762 by his acquaintance with the newly published writings of Jean-Jacques Rousseau: *Emile, Or on Education* and *Of the Social Contract.* Pietism had already taught him to believe in the equality of all human beings and the moral ideal of the church universal encompassing the priesthood of all believers, which is to be pursued in a sinful world of spiritual division and inequality. These convictions now took the more rationalistic form of Rousseau's vision of human beings, free and equal by nature, who find themselves in a social world of unfreedom and unjust inequality. Soon Kant began defining his own ethical position through emphasis on the sovereignty of reason, associating his moral philosophy with the title "metaphysics of morals." However, it was another twenty years before Kant brought his ethical theory to maturity. In the meantime, the task to which he devoted his principal labor was that of reforming the foundations of the sciences and discovering the proper relation within them between empirical science and the claims of a priori or metaphysical knowledge.

Kant's academic career was almost as slow in developing as were the thoughts for which we now most remember him. Professorships in logic and metaphysics opened at the University of Königsberg in 1756 and 1758. Kant did not even apply for the first, and with his still very limited qualifications he was routinely passed over for the second. After the recognition he received from Mendelssohn and the Prussian academy, he was offered the position of professor of poetry at the university in 1764, but declined it in order to continue to devote himself to natural science and philosophy. In 1766 he did accept a position as sublibrarian at the university, providing him with his first regular academic salary. But he declined opportunities for professorships at Jena and Erlangen in 1769, no doubt in part because of his reluctance to leave East Prussia, but probably chiefly because he knew that the professorship of logic at Königsberg would be available to him the following year. In subsequent years he had other opportunities (for instance, he was offered a professorship at Halle in 1778), but chose never to leave Königsberg. (Just as Beethoven wrote some of his greatest music after he was totally deaf, so the most cosmopolitan of all philosophers was a man from an isolated province who never traveled farther than thirty miles from the place of his birth.)

In the Latin inaugural dissertation, *On the Forms and Principles of the Sensible and Intelligible World,* which Kant wrote upon assuming his professorship at Königsberg, Kant took several important steps in the direction we can now see eventually led him to the "critical philosophy" of the 1780s and 1790s. By 1772, Kant told his friend and former student Marcus Herz that he was at work on a major philosophical treatise, to be entitled *The Limits of Sensibility and Reason,* and expected to finish it within a year. But it was nearly a decade more, during which Kant wrote and published very little, before Kant published the *Critique of Pure Reason.* Despite his elevation to a professorship, Kant continued to live in furnished rooms on the island in the river Pregel on which stood both the university building and the cathedral in which its library was housed. It would be another thirteen years before he would be able to purchase a house of his own.

During the 1770s, however, Kant began lecturing on the subject of anthropology, stimulated (or provoked) by Ernst Platner's *Anthropology for Physicians and Philosophers* (1772). Kant rejected Platner's "physiological" reductivism in favor of an approach that emphasized the practical experience of human interaction and the historicity of human beings. Kant was, however, always deeply skeptical of the capacity of human beings to gain anything like a scientific knowledge of their own nature, and he was especially dissatisfied with the entire state of the study of human nature up to now, looking forward to a future scientific revolution in this area of study (which he himself did not pretend to be able to accomplish). He lectured in a popular style on anthropology, however, for the next twenty-five years, and these lectures were the most frequently given and the most well attended of any he gave during his teaching career.

———

Kant finally published the *Critique of Pure Reason* in 1781. He believed he had made an important contribution to the foundations of human knowledge. He was therefore disappointed when his book did not immediately make the impact on the learned world that he expected. Early reviews seemed both cool and uncomprehending. Particularly annoying was a prominent review in the *Göttingen Learned Notices,* written by Christian Garve, a man Kant respected (though the review was apparently revised extensively by the editor of the journal, J. G. Feder, whose attitude toward Kant was far less sympathetic and respectful). This review interpreted Kant's transcendental idealism as agreeing with Berkeley that the sensible world lacks true reality and consists only of the ideas in individual minds. Both in order to correct what he regarded as fundamental misinterpretations of his position and to make it more readily intelligible to his audience, Kant wrote the *Prolegomena to Any Future Metaphysics* (1783). But Kant's complex treatment of the traditional problems of philosophy did not lend itself well to popularization (and simplification). It would be several more years before Kant's critical philosophy achieved the influence he hoped for.

Kant was born poor, and throughout most of his life he was a struggling academic, too indigent to marry or raise a family. But his appointment to a professorship finally gave him a comfortable living, and his eventual fame made him one of the highest paid professors in the Prussian educational system by the early 1790s. In 1783, at age fifty-nine, through the help and influence of his friend J. G. Hippel, the mayor of Königsberg, Kant finally bought a home of his own—a large, comfortable house on Prinzessinstraße in the center of town, almost in the shadow of the royal castle that gave the city its name. (Hippel was not only active politically, but also intellectually. He was a learned and intelligent man, the author of satirical novels and progressive political treatises defending the civil equality of Jews and advocating a quite radical position on the emancipation of women and the reform of marriage to insure their equality with men in all spheres of life. His views were far in advance of Kant's own, even though rumor had it that Kant shared in the authorship of his feminist writings.) The first floor of Kant's house contained a hall in which he gave his lectures, and the kitchen where food was prepared by a cook of his own, which he now could afford to hire; on the second floor were Kant's bedroom, his study (where there reportedly hung the only decoration he permitted in the house—a portrait of Rousseau), a sitting room, and a dining room. The third floor was occupied by Kant's personal servant Lampe (who, however, was apparently given to drink, and was eventually discharged in the late 1790s when he reportedly attacked his frail and aging master during a quarrel).

In the second floor dining room Kant enjoyed his only real meal of the day, a dinner at which he usually entertained several guests. Königsberg was a seaport, and although Kant never himself ventured far from it, he took the opportunity to acquaint himself with many of the distinguished foreigners who passed through. By the time of these banquets (in the early afternoon), Kant had usually completed his main academic work. He rose regularly at 5:00 A.M., having only a cup of tea and a pipe of tobacco for breakfast. Then he prepared for his lectures, which he delivered five or six days a week, beginning at seven or eight in the morning. After them, he would go to his study and write until it was time for dinner. After his guests had departed, Kant often would take a nap in an easy chair in his sitting room (sometimes a good friend, such as the English merchant Green, would nap in the chair next to him). At 5:00 P.M. the philosopher would take his constitutional walk, the timing of which was reputedly so precise that the housewives of Königsberg would set their clocks according to the time Professor Kant walked past their windows. The regularity of Kant's schedule, as well as his various crotchets about diet (he believed in eating a lot of carrots, and drank wine but never beer) probably resulted less from a compulsive personality than from the necessity of an aging man, who had never been in the best of health, to keep himself strong enough to complete philosophical labors that he had not been properly able to begin until he was far into middle age.

———

In the middle of the 1780s, Kant laid the foundation for much of the nineteenth-century philosophy of history in several brief occasional essays. To a significant degree, Kant's thinking about history was excited by the work of his sometime student J. G. Herder, the installments of whose multivolume *Ideas Toward a Philosophy of the History of Humanity* (1785–1787) Kant reviewed. Herder saw himself as a critic of the Enlightenment rationalism Kant defended, and Kant's contributions to the philosophy of history were in part an attempt to vindicate the cause of Enlightenment in that debate. The earliest and most methodologically self-conscious of Kant's essays on the philosophy of history, however, was an attempt to articulate the *historical* presuppositions of what one of Kant's followers had called his "favorite idea": that the final end of the human race consists in the attainment of the most perfect political constitution. Kant's *Idea for a Universal History with a Cosmopolitan Intent* (1784) sketches a way of making human history theoretically intelligible to us, based on the idea of the human race as an animal species. Kant's philosophy of history is based on a collective finality that is neither intended nor known by the human agents who carry it out. It is the prototype for Hegel's conception of history as the working out of the "cunning of reason." Kant's conception of the growth of human capacities as the fundamental tendency leading to historical progress is also the prototype for the "historical materialism" of Marx. We will also see presently that Kant's philosophy of history plays an important role in his ethical theory by motivating the theory of human nature that serves as its background.

Another important short essay displaying the historical conception of Kant's philosophy was prompted by the published remark of a conservative cleric who dismissed the call for greater enlightenment in religious and political matters with the comment that no one had yet been able to say what was meant by the term "enlightenment." Kant's response was the short essay *Answer to the Question: What is Enlightenment?* (1784). Kant refuses to identify *enlightenment* with mere learning or the acquisition of knowledge (which he thinks is at most a consequence of that to which the term genuinely refers). Instead, Kant regards enlightenment as the act of leaving behind a condition of immaturity, in which a person's intelligence must be guided by another. To be enlightened is therefore to have the courage and energy to be self-directing in one's thinking, to *think for oneself*. Kant also emphasizes that enlightenment must be regarded as a social and historical process. Throughout humanity's past, most people have been accustomed to having their thinking directed by others (by paternalistic governments, by the authority of old books, most of all, and most degrading of all, in Kant's view, by the priestcraft of religious authorities who usurp the role of individual conscience). Becoming enlightened is hard to do for an isolated individual, but it becomes possible when the practice of thinking critically becomes prevalent in an entire public which insists on free and open communication between its members. Kant's proposals concerning freedom of communication in *What is Enlightenment?* are tailored to his own time and place, and designed to encourage the growth of an enlightened public.

Since the mid-1760s, Kant had intended to develop a system of moral philosophy under the title "metaphysics of morals." It is probably no accident that he began to fulfill this intention only after he had been provoked into thinking about human history and the moral predicament in which the natural progress of the human species places its individual members. Early on, Kant observes that human reason, arising in conjunction with an "unsociable sociability" that brings people into conflict, making them both evil and miserable, cannot serve the natural end of making people happy. Instead, he argues, the aim of reason must be to develop a good will, which enables human beings to be self-governing under common laws as members of a shared realm of ends, and thus finally to turn against the natural conditions of its own origin, overcoming the competitiveness and antagonism through which it arose.

In 1786 Kant's philosophy was suddenly thrust into prominence by the favorable discussion of it presented in a series of articles in Christoph Wieland's widely read publication *Deutsche Merkur* (called "Letters on the Kantian Philosophy") by the Jena philosopher Karl Leonard Reinhold. Reinhold's presentations of Kant did very suddenly what Kant's own works had thus far failed to do—namely, make the theories of the *Critique* into the principal focus of philosophical discussion in Germany. Soon the critical philosophy came to be seen as a revolutionary new standpoint; the main philosophical questions to be answered were whether one should adopt the Kantian position, and if one did, exactly what version or interpretation of it one should adopt. Soon there also arose a new kind of critic of Kant—a "post-Kantian" philosopher whose criticisms of Kant were motivated by alleged unclarities and tensions within Kant's philosophy itself, and who sought to absorb the lessons of the Kantian philosophy and yet also to "go beyond" it.

Kant decided to produce a second edition of the *Critique*, in which he could present his position more clearly. At first he thought he would add a section on *practical* (or moral) reason, following up his treatment in the *Fundamental Principles* of 1785 (and also replying to critical discussions of that work that had appeared). In 1787 the new and improved version of the *Critique of Pure Reason* did appear, but by then Kant had decided that his discussion of practical reason would have to be too lengthy to be added to what was already a very long book, so he decided to publish it separately as a second "critique."

Almost immediately Kant was working on a third project that was to bear a similar title. But it was never part of his systematic project to write three Critiques. His reasons for writing the *Critique of Judgment* were complex and a bit inscrutable, as is the work itself. Kant had been thinking for a long time about the topic of taste and judgments of taste, and wanted to come to terms with the modern tradition of thinking about these matters found in such philosophers as Hutcheson, Baumgarten, Hume, and Mendelssohn. But to analyze the judgment of taste was far from being the whole motivation behind the third Critique. The two main themes dealt with in this work—aesthetic experience and natural teleology—were both preoccupations of the Enlightenment's critics, such as Herder. Kant also needed to clarify and explicate his own thinking about the status of teleological thinking in relation to natural science, a subject that had engaged him both in previous essays about natural theology and the philosophy of history. If we are to take him at his word, the main motive for writing the *Critique of Judgment* was to deal with the "immense gulf" that he saw between the theoretical use of reason in knowledge of the natural world and its practical use in morality and moral faith in God. It remains to this day a subject of controversy exactly how Kant hoped to bridge this gulf in the third Critique and how far he was successful. But the *Critique of Judgment* reveals Kant, now in his late sixties, as a philosopher who is still willing to question and even revise the fundamental tenets of his system. And to his idealist followers, Fichte, Schelling, and Hegel, it was the *Critique of Judgment* that seemed to them to portray Kant as open to the kind of radical speculative philosophy in which they were interested.

———

The final decade of Kant's activity as a philosopher was one beset with conflict. As the critical philosophy became increasingly prominent in German intellectual life, and as it came to be variously interpreted by different proponents and would-be reformers of it, Kant found himself defending his position on several sides, against the attacks of Wolffians such as J. A. Eberhard, Lockeans such as J. G. Feder and C. G. Selle, popular Enlightenment rationalists such as Garve, religious fideists such as Wizenmann and Jacobi, or against a new kind of "Kantian" speculative philosopher, such as the brilliant and eccentric Salomon Maimon. Kant's larger-scale published works during the nineties, however, were devoted to applying the critical philosophy to matters of general human concern, especially in the practical sphere—to religion, political philosophy, and to the completion of the ethical system he had for thirty years called the "metaphysics of morals."

Kant also came into conflict with the political authorities over his views on religion. From the beginning of Kant's academic career until 1786, the Prussian monarch had been Frederick the Great. Frederick may have been a military despot, but his views on matters of religion favored tolerance and theological liberalism (some of his enemies considered him to be privately a "freethinker" or even an unbeliever). Frederick's death in 1786 brought to the throne a very different monarch, his nephew Friedrich Wilhelm III, for whom religion was a very serious matter and who had long been shocked by the wide variety of unorthodoxy, skepticism, and irreligion that his uncle had permitted to flourish within the Prussian state and even within the Lutheran state church. Two years after coming to power, he removed Baron von Zedlitz (the man to whom Kant had dedicated the *Critique of Pure Reason*) from the position of Minister of Education, replacing him with J. C. Wöllner (whom Frederick the Great had described as a "deceitful, scheming parson"). Both the king and his new minister believed that the stability of the state depended directly on correct religious beliefs among its subjects, and hence that those who questioned Christian orthodoxy were directly threatening the foundations of civil peace. To them, Kant's attack on objective proofs for God's existence, and his denial of knowledge to make room for faith, seemed dangerously subversive. And his "enlightenment principles"—that all individuals have not only a right but even a duty to think for themselves in religious matters, and that the state should encourage such free thought by protecting a "public" realm of discourse from all state interference—seemed like recipes for civil anarchy.

Wöllner soon issued two "religious edicts" intending to reverse the effects of Enlightenment thinking on both the church and the universities, by subjecting clergy and academics to tests of religious orthodoxy concerning both what they published and what they taught from the pulpit or the lectern. The edicts put many liberal pastors in the position of choosing between their livelihood and teaching what they regarded as a set of outdated superstitions. Action was taken against some academics as well (especially critical biblical scholars), who had either to recant what they had said in their writings (which usually discredited them among their colleagues) or lose their university positions (and thus opportunity to teach their views). Writings on religious topics were also to be submitted to a board of censorship, which had to approve the orthodoxy of what they taught before they could be published.

By 1791 Kant learned from his former student J. G. Kiesewetter, who was a royal tutor in Berlin, that the decision had been taken to forbid him to write anything further on religious subjects. But by this time Kant's prominence was such that this would not be an easy or a comfortable action for the reactionary ministers to take. Kant had planned to write a book on religion and did not let word of these threats dissuade him. But he very much wanted to avoid confrontation with the authorities, both in order to protect himself and on sincerely held moral grounds.

In fact, Kant was far from being a political radical on matters such as this. His political thought is strongly impacted by the Hobbesian view that the state is needed to protect both individuals and the basic institutions of society against the human tendencies to violent infringement of rights, and that in order to prevent civil disorder, the state must have considerable power to regulate the lives of individuals. *What is Enlightenment?* teaches that it is entirely legitimate for freedom of communication to be regulated in matters that are "private," dealing with a person's professional responsibilities. This principle might have been used to justify the very actions that had been taken by the Prussian government against pastors and even professors. He deplored Wöllner's edicts, of course, and regarded their application to the clergy only as having the effect of making hypocrisy a necessary qualification for ecclesiastical office. But it is not at all clear whether he regarded these measures as any more than a disastrously unwise abuse of powers the state can legitimately claim. Kant sincerely believed that it is morally wrong to disobey even the unjust commands of a legitimate authority, and even before anything was done to him he had made his decision that he would comply with whatever commands were given. This is all quite clear in Kant's first extensive presentation of his philosophy of the state in the second part of the three-part essay he wrote on the common saying: "That may be correct in theory but it does not work in practice." There he outlines a theory of political right that sees the state as the protector of the freedom, equality, and independence of citizens. He also defends (against Hobbes) the position that the subjects of a state have some rights against the state that are binding on the government but not enforceable against the head of state. This means that there can be no right of insurrection, and that even the unjust commands of a legitimate authority must be obeyed by its subjects (so long as these do not directly command the subject to do something that is in itself wrong or evil). The application of this last principle to Kant's own situation is obvious: He had decided that when the Prussian authorities commanded him to cease writing or teaching on religious subjects, he would obey them.

But of course Kant had no intention of anticipating such commands or doing anything merely to please authorities he regarded as unenlightened, unwise, and unjust. And he was determined to use all the legal devices at his disposal to thwart their intentions. In 1792 he gave his essay on radical evil (which later became Part One of *Religion Within the Limits of Reason Alone*) to the *Berlin Monthly* for publication. He insisted on its being submitted to the censorship; when it was rejected, he submitted the entirety of *Religion* to the academic faculty of philosophy in Jena, which under the law was an alternative to the official state censorship. A first edition appeared in 1793, and a second (expanded) edition in 1794. Kant's evasion angered the censors in Berlin, however, and led them finally to take action against him. In October, Wöllner sent Kant a letter expressing in the King's name the royal displeasure with his writings on religion and commanding him neither to teach nor write on religious subjects until he was able to conform his opinions to the tenets of Christian orthodoxy. In his reply, Kant defended both his opinions and the legitimacy of his writing about them but did solemnly promise to the King that he would obey the royal command.

Kant had been forbidden by the authorities to write on religious topics, but he had no intention of keeping quiet on other matters of general human concern, even when his views were likely to be unpopular with the government. In March 1795, a period of war between France and the First Coalition of monarchical states was brought to a close by the Peace of Basel between France and Prussia. Kant's essay *To Eternal Peace* should be read as an expression of support not only for this treaty but also for the First French Republic, since it declares that the constitution of every state should be republican and also conjectures that peace between nations might be furthered if one enlightened nation transformed itself into a republic and then through treaties became the focal point for a federal union between other states. *To Eternal Peace* is the chief statement by a major figure in the history of philosophy that addresses the issues of war, peace, and international relations that have been central concerns of humanity during the two centuries since it was written. It is perhaps Kant's most genuine attempt to address a universal enlightened public concerning issues of importance not only to scientists and philosophers but vital to all humanity.

Kant retired from university lecturing in 1796. Soon afterward his difficulties with the religious authorities were resolved. King Friedrich Wilhelm died in 1797, and Kant, regarding his promise as a personal one made to the monarch, considered himself free to publish again on the subject of religion—which he did in his treatise *Conflict of the Faculties* (1798). He then devoted himself to three principal tasks. The first was the completion of his system of ethics, the *Metaphysics of Morals*, consisting of a Doctrine of Right (covering philosophy of law and the state) and a Doctrine of Virtue (dealing with the system of voluntary moral duties of individuals). The first part was published in 1797 and the whole in 1798. Kant's second task was the publication of materials from the lectures he had given over many years. He himself published a text based on his popular lectures on anthropology in 1798. Declining powers led him to consign to others the task of publishing his lectures on logic, pedagogy, and physical geography that appeared during his lifetime. Kant's third project after his retirement is the most extraordinary. He set out to write a new work centering on the transition between transcendental philosophy and empirical science. In it Kant was responding creatively both to recent developments in the sciences themselves (such as the revolution in chemistry initiated by Lavoisier's investigation of combustion) and to the work of younger philosophers who took their inspiration from the Kantian philosophy itself (such as the "philosophy of nature" of F. W. J. Schelling, who was still in his early twenties). Kant's failing powers prevented him from completing this work, but from the fragments he produced (first published in the early twentieth century under the title *Opus Postumum*), we can see that even in his late seventies, Kant took a critical attitude toward every philosophical question and entertained fundamental revisions in the philosophical system that had been the labor of his entire life. He died early in 1804, a few months short of his eightieth birthday.

———

If there is a basic theme in Kant's philosophy, perhaps it is the portrayal of our problematic condition as beings who must learn to live by a reason that is limited in what it can achieve and that develops along with a propensity to evil against which it is our task to endlessly struggle. No philosopher has laid more stress on the limitations of human reason, especially in the conduct of inquiry and formation of beliefs. At the same time, no philosopher ever asserted more ardently the absolute title of reason to govern human thought and action, or gave us sterner warnings concerning both the inherent evil and the disastrous consequences of permitting human passions, enthusiasms, or inspirations, or the supernatural deliverances of authority or tradition, to overrule reason or even to usurp its authority. Human nature is torn between a natural competitiveness rooted in self-conceit and a moral esteem for rational nature rooted in the equal dignity of all rational beings and the ideal of a realm of ends in which their aims are brought into harmony.

Reason thus marks out for us both theoretical and practical ideals. We can never hope to achieve these ideals in their entirety, and we are still far from having done what we can to approach them. Kant thinks we must learn to live with our painful limitations, resisting the illusion that we might be able to transcend them either through our own heroic efforts or through some kind of incomprehensible supernatural assistance. The limitedness of reason would be an argument for challenging its authority only if we knew we had something more reliable and less limited to fall back on. We could know this, however, only if reason were capable of certifying such a higher source. But this is precisely what its limitations prevent it from doing.

Our condition, then, must be one of ceaseless striving and restless dissatisfaction. It is a condition more of striving than attainment, more of self-dissatisfaction than of complacency, and more of self-alienation than of happiness. But the beings who occupy it possess the only kind of self-worth or dignity of which we can form any conception—the self-worth of beings who can understand their own limitations and the dignity of beings who can turn their limitations into self-limitations by exercising the rational capacity of self-legislation and self-government.

—

ALLEN W. WOOD is a professor of philosophy at Stanford University. He is the author of *Kant's Rational Theology* and *Kant's Ethical Thought* and, with Paul Guyer, general editor of the *Cambridge Edition of the Works of Kant*.

GUIDE TO THE
MARGINAL NOTATIONS

Given in the margins of the texts that follow are numbers that refer to the original German versions as found in *Kants Schriften,* Ausgabe der königlich preussischen Akademie der Wissenschaften (Berlin: Walter de Gruyter, 1902–). The first number indicates the volume, and the second gives the page number. However, in the case of *Critique of Pure Reason,* "A" indicates the first edition of the text, followed by its page number, and "B" the second edition, with its corresponding page.

SELECTIONS FROM

CRITIQUE OF
PURE REASON

[1781, 1787]

Translated by F. Max Müller

PREFACE

[to the First Edition, 1781]

Our reason (*Vernunft*) has this peculiar fate that, with reference to one class of its knowledge, it is always troubled with questions which cannot be ignored, because they spring from the very nature of reason, and which cannot be answered, because they transcend the powers of human reason.

Nor is human reason to be blamed for this. It begins with principles which, in the course of experience, it *must* follow, and which seem sufficiently confirmed by experience. With these again, according to the necessities of its nature, it rises higher and higher to more remote conditions. But when it perceives that in this way its work remains for ever incomplete, because the questions never cease, it finds itself constrained to take refuge in principles which exceed every possible experimental application, and nevertheless seem so unobjectionable that even ordinary common sense agrees with them. Thus reason becomes involved in darkness and contradictions, from which, no doubt, it may conclude that errors must be lurking somewhere, but without being able to discover them, because the principles which it follows transcend all the limits of experience and withdraw themselves from all experimental tests. It is the battle-field of these endless controversies which is called *Metaphysic.*

There was a time when Metaphysic held a royal place among all the sciences, and, if the will were taken for the deed, the exceeding importance of her subject might well have secured to her that place of honour. At present it is the fashion to despise metaphysic, and the poor matron, forlorn and forsaken, complains like Hecuba, *Modo maxima rerum, tot generis natisque potens—nunc trahor exul, inops* (Ovid, Metam. xiii. 508).

Aix At first the rule of Metaphysic, under the dominion of the dogmatists, was despotic. But as the laws still bore the traces of an old barbarism, intestine wars and complete anarchy broke out, and the sceptics, a kind of nomads, despising all settled culture of the land, broke up from time to time all civil society. Fortunately their number was small, and they could not prevent the old settlers from returning to cultivate the ground afresh, though without any fixed plan or agreement. Not long ago one might have thought, indeed, that all these quarrels were to have been settled and the legitimacy of her claims decided once for all through a certain physiology of the human understanding, the work of the celebrated *Locke.* But, though the descent of that royal pretender, traced back as it had been to the lowest mob of common experience, ought to have rendered her claims very suspicious, yet, as that genealogy turned out to be in reality a false invention, the old queen (metaphysic) con-

Ax tinued to maintain her claims, everything fell back into the old rotten dogmatism, and the contempt from which metaphysical science was to have been rescued, remained the same as ever. At present, after everything has been tried, so they say, and tried in vain, there reign in philosophy weariness and complete indifferentism, the mother of chaos and night, though, at the same time, we perceive the spring or, at least, the prelude of a near reform and of a new light, after an ill-applied study has rendered everything dark, confused, and useless.

It is in vain to assume a kind of artificial indifferentism in respect to inquiries the object of which cannot be indifferent to human nature. Nay, those pretended indifferentists (however they may try to disguise themselves by changing scholastic terminology into popular language), if they think at all, fall back inevitably into those very metaphysical dogmas which they profess to despise. Nevertheless this indifferentism, showing itself in the very midst of the most flourishing state of all sciences, and affecting those very sciences the teachings of which, if they could be had, would be the last to be surrendered, is a phenomenon well worthy of our attention and consideration. It is clearly the result, not of the carelessness, but of the matured judgment[1] of our age, which will no longer Axi rest satisfied with the mere appearance of knowledge. It is, at the same time, a powerful appeal to reason to undertake anew the most difficult of its duties, namely, self-knowledge, and to institute a court of appeal which should protect the just rights of reason, but dismiss all groundless claims, and should do this not by means of irresponsible decrees, but according to the eternal and unalterable laws of reason. This court of appeal is no other but the *Critique of* Axii *Pure Reason.*

I do not mean by this a criticism of books and systems, but of the faculty of reason in general, touching that whole class of knowledge which it may strive after, unassisted by experience. This must decide the question of the possibility or impossibility of metaphysic in general, and the determination of its sources, its extent and its limits—and all this according to fixed principles.

This, the only way that was left, I have followed, and I flatter myself that I have thus removed all those errors which have hitherto brought reason, being unassisted by experience, into conflict with itself. I have not evaded its questions by pleading the insufficiency of human reason, but I have classified them according to principles,

---

1 We often hear complaints against the shallowness of thought in our own time, and the decay of sound knowledge. But I do not see that sciences which rest on a solid foundation, such as mathematics, physics, etc. deserve this reproach in the least. On the contrary, they maintain their old reputation of solidity, and with regard to physics, even surpass it. The same spirit would manifest itself in other branches of knowledge, if only their principles had first been properly determined. Till that is done, indifferentism and doubt, and ultimately severe criticism, are rather signs of honest thought. Our age is, in every sense of the word, the age of criticism, and everything must submit to it. Religion, on the strength of its sanctity, and law, on the strength of its majesty, try to withdraw themselves from it; but by so doing they arouse just suspicions, and cannot claim that sincere respect which reason pays to those only who have been able to stand its free and open examination.

and, after showing the point where reason begins to misunderstand itself, solved them satisfactorily. It is true that the answer of those questions is not such as a dogma-enamoured curiosity might wish for, for such curiosity could not have been satisfied except by juggling tricks in which I am no adept. But this was not the natural intention of our reason, and it became the duty of philosophy to remove the deception which arose from a false interpretation, even though many a vaunted and cherished dream should vanish at the same time. In this work I have chiefly aimed at completeness, and I venture to maintain that there ought not to be one single metaphysical problem that has not been solved here, or to the solution of which the key at least has not been supplied. In fact Pure Reason is so perfect a unity that, if its principle should prove insufficient to answer any one of the many questions started by its very nature, one might throw it away altogether, as insufficient to answer the other questions with perfect certainty.

While I am saying this I fancy I observe in the face of my readers an expression of indignation, mixed with contempt, at pretensions apparently so self-glorious and extravagant; and yet they are in reality far more moderate than those made by the writer of the commonest essay professing to prove the simple nature of the soul or the necessity of a first beginning of the world. For, while he pretends to extend human knowledge beyond the limits of all possible experience, I confess most humbly that this is entirely beyond my power. I mean only to treat of reason and its pure thinking, a knowledge of which is not very far to seek, considering that it is to be found within myself. Common logic gives an instance how all the simple acts of reason can be enumerated completely and systematically. My question is, what we can hope to achieve with reason, when all the material and assistance of experience is taken away.

So much with regard to the completeness in our laying hold of every single object, and the thoroughness in our laying hold of all objects, as the material of our critical inquiries—a completeness determined, not by a casual idea, but by the nature of our knowledge itself.

PREFACE

[to the Second Edition, 1787]

Whether the treatment of that class of knowledge with which reason is occupied, follows the secure method of a science or not, can easily be determined by the result. If, after repeated preparations, it comes to a standstill, as soon as its real goal is approached, or is obliged, in order to reach it, to retrace its steps again and again, and strike into fresh paths; again, if it is impossible to produce unanimity among those who are engaged in the same work, as to the manner in which their common object should be obtained, we may be convinced that such a study is far from having attained to the secure method of a science, but is groping only in the dark. In that case we are conferring a great benefit on reason, if we only find out the right method, though many things should have to be surrendered as useless, which were comprehended in the original aim that had been chosen without sufficient reflection.

That *Logic*, from the earliest times, has followed that secure method, may be seen from the fact that since *Aristotle* it has not had to retrace a single step, unless we choose to consider as improvements the removal of some unnecessary subtleties, or the clearer definition of its matter, both of which refer to the elegance rather than to the solidity of the science. It is remarkable also, that to the present day, it has not been able to make one step in advance, so that, to all appearance, it may be considered as completed and perfect. If some modern philosophers thought to enlarge it, by introducing *psychological* chapters on the different faculties of knowledge (faculty of imagination, wit, &c.), or *metaphysical* chapters on the origin of knowledge, or the different degrees of certainty according to the difference of objects (idealism, scepticism, &c.), or lastly, *anthropological* chapters on prejudices, their causes and remedies, this could only arise from their ignorance of the peculiar nature of logical science. We do not enlarge, but we only disfigure the sciences, if we allow their respective limits to be confounded: and the limits of logic are definitely fixed by the fact, that it is a science

Bix which has nothing to do but fully to exhibit and strictly to prove all formal rules of thought (whether it be *a priori* or empirical, whatever be its origin or its object, and whatever be the impediments, accidental or natural, which it has to encounter in the human mind).

That logic should in this respect have been so successful, is due entirely to its limitation, whereby it has not only the right, but the duty, to make abstraction of all the objects of knowledge and their differences, so that the understanding has to deal with nothing beyond itself, and its own forms. It was far more difficult, of course, for reason to enter on the secure method of science, considering that it has to deal not with itself only, but also with objects. Logic, therefore, as a kind of preparation (propædeutic) forms, as it were, the vestibule of the sciences only, and where real knowledge is concerned, is presupposed for critical purposes, while the acquisition of knowledge must be sought for in the sciences themselves, properly and objectively so called.

If there is to be in those sciences an element of reason, something in them must be known *a priori*, and knowledge may stand in

Bx a twofold relation to its object, by either simply *determining* it and its concept (which must be supplied from elsewhere), or by making it *real* also. The former is *theoretical*, the latter *practical knowledge* of reason. In both the *pure* part, namely, that in which reason determines its object entirely *a priori* (whether it contain much or little), must be treated first, without mixing up with it what comes from other sources; for it is bad economy to spend blindly whatever comes in, and not to be able to determine, when there is a stoppage, which part of the income can bear the expenditure, and where reductions must be made.

Mathematics and *physics* are the two theoretical sciences of reason, which have to determine their *objects a priori;* the former quite purely, the latter partially so, and partially from other sources of knowledge besides reason. *Mathematics,* from the earliest times to which the history of human reason can reach, has followed, among that wonderful people of the Greeks, the safe way of a science. But it must not be supposed that it was as easy for mathematics as for logic, in which reason is concerned with itself alone, to find, or rather to make for itself that royal road. I believe, on the contrary, that there was a long period of tentative work (chiefly still among Bxi the Egyptians), and that the change is to be ascribed to a *revolution,* produced by the happy thought of a single man, whose experiment pointed unmistakably to the path that had to be followed, and opened and traced out for the most distant times the safe way of a science. The history of that intellectual revolution, which was far more important than the discovery of the passage round the celebrated Cape of Good Hope, and the name of its fortunate author, have not been preserved to us. But the story preserved by Diogenes Laertius, who names the reputed author of the smallest elements of ordinary geometrical demonstration, even of such as, according to general opinion, do not require to be proved, shows, at all events, that the memory of the revolution, produced by the very first traces of the discovery of a new method, appeared extremely important to the mathematicians, and thus remained unforgotten. A new light flashed on the first man who demonstrated the properties of the isosceles triangle (whether his name was *Thales* or any other name), for he found that he had not to investigate what he saw in Bxii the figure, or the mere concept of that figure, and thus to learn its properties; but that he had to produce his knowledge by means of what he had himself, according to concepts *a priori,* placed into that figure, and represented (by construction), so that, in order to know anything with certainty *a priori*, he must not attribute to that figure anything beyond what necessarily follows from what he has himself placed into it, in accordance with the concept.

It took a much longer time before physics entered on the high way of science: for no more than a century and half has elapsed, since the ingenious proposal of Bacon partly initiated that discovery, partly, as others were already on the right track, gave a new impetus to it,—a discovery which, like the former, can only be explained by a rapid intellectual revolution. In what I have to say, I shall confine myself to natural science, so far as it is founded on *empirical* principles.

When Galilei let balls of a particular weight, which he had determined himself, roll down an inclined plain, or Torricelli made the air carry a weight, which he had previously determined to be equal to that of a definite volume of water; or when, in later times, Stahl[2] changed metal into lime, and lime again into metals, by withdrawing and restoring something, a new light flashed on all students of nature. They comprehended that reason has insight into that only, which she herself produces on her own plan, and that she must move forward with the principles of her judgments, according to fixed law, and compel nature to answer her questions, but not let herself be led by nature, as it were in leading strings, because otherwise, accidental observations, made on no previously fixed plan, will never converge towards a necessary law, which is the only thing that reason seeks and requires. Reason, holding in one hand its principles, according to which concordant phenomena alone can be admitted as laws of nature, and in the other hand the experiment, which it has devised according to those principles, must approach nature, in order to be taught by it: but not in the character of a pupil, who agrees to everything the master likes, but as an appointed judge, who compels the witnesses to answer the questions which he himself proposes. Therefore even the science of physics entirely owes the beneficial revolution in its character to

Bxiii

---

2 I am not closely following here the course of the history of the experimental method, nor are the first beginnings of it very well known.

the happy thought, that we ought to seek in nature (and not import
into it by means of fiction) whatever reason must learn from nature,
and could not know by itself, and that we must do this in accordance with what reason itself has originally placed into nature.
Thus only has the study of nature entered on the secure method of
a science, after having for many centuries done nothing but grope
in the dark.

Metaphysic, a completely isolated and speculative science of reason, which declines all teaching of experience, and rests on concepts only (not on their application to intuition, as mathematics), in
which reason therefore is meant to be her own pupil, has hitherto
not been so fortunate as to enter on the secure path of a science, although it is older than all other sciences, and would remain, even if
all the rest were swallowed up in the abyss of an all-destroying barbarism. In metaphysic, reason, even if it tries only to understand *a
priori,* (as it pretends to do,) those laws which are confirmed by the
commonest experience, is constantly brought to a standstill, and we
are obliged again and again to retrace our steps, because they do
not lead us where we want to go; while as to any unanimity among
those who are engaged in the same work, there is so little of it in
metaphysic, that it has rather become an arena, specially destined,
it would seem, for those who wish to exercise themselves in mock
fights, and where no combatant has, as yet, succeeded in gaining an
inch of ground that he could call permanently his own. It cannot be
denied, therefore, that the method of metaphysic has hitherto consisted in groping only, and, what is the worst, in groping among
mere concepts.

What then can be the cause that hitherto no secure method of
science has been discovered? Shall we say that it is impossible?
Then why should nature have visited our reason with restless aspi-
ration to look for it, as if it were its most important concern? Nay
more, how little should we be justified in trusting our reason if,
with regard to one of the most important objects we wish to know,
it not only abandons us, but lures us on by vain hopes, and in the
end betrays us! Or, if hitherto we have only failed to meet with the
right path, what indications are there to make us hope that, if we

renew our researches, we shall be more successful than others before us?

The examples of mathematics and natural science, which by one
Bxvi revolution have become what they now are, seem to me sufficiently
remarkable to induce us to consider, what may have been the essential element in that intellectual revolution which has proved so
beneficial to them, and to make the experiment, at least, so far as
the analogy between them, as sciences of reason, with metaphysic
allows it, of imitating them. Hitherto it has been supposed that all
our knowledge must conform to the objects: but, under that supposition, all attempts to establish anything about them *a priori,* by
means of concepts, and thus to enlarge our knowledge, have come
to nothing. The experiment therefore ought to be made, whether
we should not succeed better with the problems of metaphysic, by
assuming that the objects must conform to our mode of cognition,
for this would better agree with the demanded possibility of an *a
priori* knowledge of them, which is to settle something about objects, before they are given us. We have here the same case as with
the first thought of Copernicus, who, not being able to get on in the
explanation of the movements of the heavenly bodies, as long as he
assumed that all the stars turned round the spectator, tried,
whether he could not succeed better, by assuming the spectator to
be turning round, and the stars to be at rest. A similar experiment
Bxvii may be tried in metaphysic, so far as the *intuition* of objects is concerned. If the intuition had to conform to the constitution of objects, I do not see how we could know anything of it *a priori;* but if
the object (as an object of the senses) conform to the constitution of
our faculty of intuition, I can very well conceive such a possibility.
As, however, I cannot rest in these intuitions, if they are to become
knowledge, but have to refer them, as representations, to something
as their object, and must determine that object by them, I have the
choice of admitting, either that the *concepts,* by which I carry out
that determination, conform to the object, being then again in the
same perplexity on account of the manner how I can know anything about it *a priori;* or that the objects, or what is the same, the experience in which alone they are known (as given objects), must

conform to those concepts. In the latter case, the solution becomes more easy, because experience, as a kind of knowledge, requires understanding, and I must therefore, even before objects are given to me, presuppose the rules of the understanding as existing within me *a priori,* these rules being expressed in concepts *a priori,* to which all objects of experience must necessarily conform, and with which they must agree. With regard to objects, so far as they are conceived by reason only, and conceived as necessary, and which can never be given in experience, at least in that form in which they are conceived by reason, we shall find that the attempts at conceiving them (for they must admit of being conceived) will furnish afterwards an excellent test of our new method of thought, according to which we do not know of things anything *a priori,* except what we ourselves put into them.[3] Bxviii

This experiment succeeds as well as we could desire, and promises to metaphysic, in its first part, which deals with concepts *a priori,* of which the corresponding objects may be given in experience, the secure method of a science. For by thus changing our point of view, the possibility of knowledge *a priori* can well be explained, and, what is still more, the laws which *a priori* lie at the foundation of nature, as the sum total of the objects of experience, may be supplied with satisfactory proofs, neither of which was possible with the procedure hitherto adopted. But there arises from this deduction of our faculty of knowing *a priori,* as given in the first part of metaphysic, a somewhat startling result, apparently most detri- Bxix

3 This method, borrowed from the student of nature, consists in our looking for the elements of pure reason in that *which can be confirmed or refuted by experiment.* Now it is impossible, in order to test the propositions of pure reason, particularly if they venture beyond all the limits of possible experience, to make any experiment with their *objects* (as in natural science); we can therefore only try with *concepts* and *propositions* which we admit *a priori,* by so contriving that the same objects may be considered on one side as objects of the senses and of the understanding in experience, and, on the *other,* as objects which are only thought, intended, it may be, for the isolated reason which strives to go beyond all the limits of experience. This gives us two different sides to be looked at; and if we find that, by looking on things from that twofold point of view, there is an agreement with the principle of pure reason, while by admitting one point of view only, there arises an inevitable conflict with reason, then the experiment decides in favour of the correctness of that distinction.

mental to the objects of metaphysic that have to be treated in the second part, namely the impossibility of going with it beyond the frontier of possible experience, which is precisely the most essen-

Bxx tial purpose of metaphysical science. But here we have exactly the experiment which, by disproving the opposite, establishes the truth of our first estimate of the knowledge of reason *a priori*, namely, that it can refer to phenomena only, but must leave the thing by itself as unknown to us, though as existing by itself. For that which impels us by necessity to go beyond the limits of experience and of all phenomena, is the *unconditioned*, which reason postulates in all things by themselves, by necessity and by right, for everything conditioned, so that the series of conditions should thus become complete. If then we find that, under the supposition of our experience conforming to the objects as things by themselves, it is *impossible to conceive* the unconditioned *without contradiction*, while, under the supposition of our representation of things, as they are given to us, not conforming to them as things by themselves, but, on the contrary, of the objects conforming to our mode of representation, that *contradiction vanishes*, and that therefore the unconditioned must not be looked for in things, so far as we know them (so far as they are given to us), but only so far as we do not know them (as things by themselves), we clearly perceive that, what we at first assumed ten-

Bxxi tatively only, is fully confirmed.[4]

But, after all progress in the field of the supersensuous has thus been denied to speculative reason, it is still open to us to see, whether in the practical knowledge of reason data may not be found which enable us to determine that transcendent concept of the unconditioned which is demanded by reason, in order thus, according to the wish of metaphysic, to get beyond the limits of all

---

4 This experiment of pure reason has a great similarity with that of the *chemists*, which they sometimes call the experiment of *reduction*, or the *synthetical process* in general. The *analysis* of the *metaphysician* divided pure knowledge *a priori* into two very heterogeneous elements, namely, the knowledge of things as phenomena, and of things by themselves. *Dialectic* combines these two again, to bring them into *harmony* with the necessary idea of the *unconditioned*, demanded by reason, and then finds that this harmony can never be obtained, except through the above distinction, which therefore must be supposed to be true.

possible experience, by means of our knowledge *a priori*, which is possible to us for practical purposes only. In this case, speculative reason has at least gained for us room for such an extension of knowledge, though it had to leave it empty, so that we are not only at liberty, but are really called upon to fill it up, if we are able, by *practical* data of reason.[5]

The very object of the critique of pure speculative reason consists in this attempt at changing the old procedure of metaphysic, and imparting to it the secure method of a science, after having completely revolutionized it, following the example of geometry and physical science. That critique is a treatise on the method (*Traité de la méthode*), not a system of the science itself; but it marks out nevertheless the whole plan of that science, both with regard to its limits, and to its internal organisation. For pure speculative rea-

son has this peculiar advantage that it is able, nay bound to measure its own powers, according to the different ways in which it chooses its own objects, and to completely enumerate the different ways of choosing problems; thus tracing a complete outline of a system of metaphysic. This is due to the fact that, with regard to the first point, nothing can be attributed to objects in knowledge *a priori*, except what the thinking subject takes from within itself; while, with regard to the second point, reason, so far as its principles of cognition are concerned, forms a separate and independent unity, in which, as in an organic body, every member exists for the sake of all others, and all others exist for the sake of the one, so that no principle can be safely applied in *one* relation, unless it has been care-

---

5 In the same manner the laws of gravity, determining the movements of the heavenly bodies, imparted the character of established certainty to what Copernicus had assumed at first as an hypothesis only, and proved at the same time the invisible force (the Newtonian attraction) which holds the universe together, which would have remained for ever undiscovered, if Copernicus had not dared, by an hypothesis, which, though contradicting the senses, was yet true, to seek the observed movements, not in the heavenly bodies, but in the spectator. I also propose in this preface my own view of metaphysics, which has so many analogies with the Copernican hypothesis, as an hypothesis only, though, in the Critique itself, it is proved by means of our representations of space and time, and the elementary concepts of the understanding, not hypothetically, but apodictically; for I wish that people should observe the first attempts at such a change, which must always be hypothetical.

fully examined in *all* its relations, to the whole employment of pure reason. Hence, too, metaphysic has this singular advantage, an advantage which cannot be shared by any other science, in which reason has to deal with objects (for *Logic* deals only with the form of thought in general) that, if it has once attained, by means of this critique, to the secure method of a science, it can completely comprehend the whole field of knowledge pertaining to it, and thus finish its work and leave it to posterity, as a capital that can never be added to, because it has only to deal with principles and the limits of their employment, which are fixed by those principles themselves. And this completeness becomes indeed an obligation, if it is to be a fundamental science, of which we must be able to say, *"nil actum reputans, si quid superesset agendum."*

Bxxiv

But it will be asked, what kind of treasure is it which we mean to bequeath to posterity in this metaphysic of ours, after it has been purified by criticism, and thereby brought to a permanent condition? After a superficial view of this work, it may seem that its advantage is *negative* only, warning us against venturing with speculative reason beyond the limits of experience. Such is no doubt its primary use: but it becomes *positive*, when we perceive that the principles with which speculative reason ventures beyond its limits, lead inevitably, not to an *extension,* but, if carefully considered, to a *narrowing* of the employment of reason, because, by indefinitely extending the limits of sensibility, to which they properly belong, they threaten entirely to supplant the pure (practical) employment of reason. Hence our *critique,* by limiting speculative reason to its proper sphere, is no doubt *negative,* but by thus removing an impediment, which threatened to narrow, or even entirely to destroy its practical employment, it is in reality of *positive,* and of very important use, if only we are convinced that there is an absolutely necessary practical use of pure reason (the moral use), in which reason must inevitably go beyond the limits of sensibility, and though not requiring for this purpose the assistance of speculative reason, must at all events be assured against its opposition, lest it be brought in conflict with itself. To deny that this service, which is rendered by criticism, is a *positive* advantage, would be the same as to deny that

Bxxv

the police confers upon us any positive advantage, its principal occupation being to prevent violence, which citizens have to apprehend from citizens, so that each may pursue his vocation in peace and security. We had established in the analytical part of our critique the following points:—First, that space and time are only forms of sensuous intuition, therefore conditions of the existence of things, as phenomena only; Secondly, that we have no concepts of the understanding, and therefore nothing whereby we can arrive at the knowledge of things, except in so far as an intuition corresponding to these concepts can be given, and consequently that we cannot have knowledge of any object, as a thing by itself, but only in so far as it is an object of sensuous intuition, that is, a phenomenon. This proves no doubt that all speculative knowledge of reason is limited to objects of *experience;* but it should be carefully borne in mind, that this leaves it perfectly open to us, to *think* the same objects as things by themselves, though we cannot *know* them.[6] For otherwise we should arrive at the absurd conclusion, that there is phenomenal appearance without something that appears. Let us suppose that the necessary distinction, established in our critique, between things as objects of experience and the same things by themselves, had not been made. In that case, the principle of causality, and with it the mechanism of nature, as determined by it, would apply to all things in general, as efficient causes. I should then not be able to say of one and the same being, for instance the human soul, that its will is free, and, at the same time, subject to the necessity of nature, that is, not free, without involving myself in a palpable contradiction: and this because I had taken the soul, in both propositions, in *one and the same sense,* namely, as a thing in general (as

Bxxvi

Bxxvii

6 In order to *know* an object, I must be able to prove its possibility, either from its reality, as attested by experience, or *a priori,* by means of reason. But I can *think* whatever I please, provided only I do not contradict myself, that is, provided my conception is a possible thought, though I may be unable to answer for the existence of a corresponding object in the sum total of all possibilities. Before I can attribute to such a concept objective reality (real possibility, as distinguished from the former, which is purely logical), something more is required. This something more, however, need not be sought for in the sources of theoretical knowledge, for it may be found in those of practical knowledge also.

something by itself), as, without previous criticism, I could not but take it. If, however, our criticism was true, in teaching us to take an object in two senses, namely, either as a phenomenon, or as a thing by itself, and if the deduction of our concepts of the understanding was correct, and the principle of causality applies to things only, if taken in the first sense, namely so far as they are objects of experience, but not to things, if taken in their second sense, we can, without any contradiction, think the same will as phenomenal (in visible Bxxviii actions) as necessarily conforming to the law of nature, and so far, *not free*, and yet, on the other hand, if belonging to a thing by itself, as not subject to that law of nature, and therefore *free*. Now it is quite true, that I may not *know* my soul, as a thing by itself, by means of speculative reason (still less through empirical observation), and consequently may not know freedom either, as the quality of a being to which I attribute effects in the world of sense, because, in order to do this, I should have to know such a being as existing, and yet as not determined in time (which, as I cannot provide my concept with any intuition, is impossible). This, however, does not prevent me from *thinking* freedom; that is, my representation of it contains at least no contradiction within itself, if only our critical distinction of the two modes of representation (the sensible and the intelligible), and the consequent limitation of the concepts of the pure understanding, and of the principles based on them, has been properly carried out. If, then, morality necessarily presupposes freedom (in the strictest sense) as a property of our will, producing, as *a priori data* of it, practical principles, belonging originally to our reason, which, without freedom, would be absolutely impossible, Bxxix while speculative reason proves that such a freedom cannot even be thought, the former supposition, namely, the moral one, would necessarily have to yield to another, the opposite of which involves a palpable contradiction, so that *freedom*, and with it morality (for its opposite contains no contradiction, unless freedom is presupposed), would have to make room for the *mechanism* of nature. Now, however, as morality requires nothing but that freedom should only not contradict itself, and that, though unable to understand, we should at least be able to think it, there being no reason why freedom should interfere with the natural mechanism of the same act (if only taken in a different sense), the doctrine of morality may well hold its place, and the doctrine of nature may hold its place too, which would have been impossible, if our critique had not previously taught us our inevitable ignorance with regard to things by themselves, and limited everything, which we are able to *know* theoretically, to mere phenomena.

The same discussion as to the positive advantage to be derived from the critical principles of pure reason, might be repeated with regard to the concept of *God,* and of the *simple nature* of our *soul;* but, for the sake of brevity, I shall pass this by. We have seen, therefore, that I am not allowed even to *assume,* for the sake of the necessary Bxxx practical employment of my reason, *God, freedom,* and *immortality,* if I cannot *deprive* speculative reason of its pretensions to transcendent insights, because reason, in order to arrive at these, must use principles which are intended originally for objects of possible experience only, and which, if in spite of this, they are applied to what cannot be an object of experience, really change this into a phenomenon, thus rendering all *practical extension* of pure reason impossible. I had therefore to remove *knowledge,* in order to make room for *belief.* For the dogmatism of metaphysic, that is, the presumption that it is possible to achieve anything in metaphysic without a previous criticism of pure reason, is the source of all that unbelief, which is always very dogmatical, and wars against all morality.

If then, it may not be too difficult to leave a bequest to posterity, in the shape of a systematical metaphysic, carried out according to the critique of pure reason, such a bequest is not to be considered therefore as of little value, whether we regard the improvement which reason receives through the secure method of a science, in place of its groundless groping and uncritical vagaries, or whether Bxxxi we look to the better employment of the time of our enquiring youth, who, if brought up in the ordinary dogmatism, are early encouraged to indulge in easy speculations on things of which they know nothing, and of which they, as little as anybody else, will ever understand anything; neglecting the acquirement of sound knowledge, while bent on the discovery of new metaphysical thoughts and opinions. The greatest benefit however will be, that such a work will enable us to put an end for ever to all objections to morality and religion, according to the Socratic method, namely, by the clearest proof of the ignorance of our opponents. Some kind of metaphysic has always existed, and will always exist, and with it a dialectic of pure reason, as being natural to it. It is therefore the first and most important task of philosophy to deprive metaphysic, once for all, of its pernicious influence, by closing up the sources of its errors.

In spite of these important changes in the whole field of science, and of the *losses* which speculative reason must suffer in its fancied Bxxxii possessions, all general human interests, and all the advantages which the world hitherto derived from the teachings of pure reason, remain just the same as before. The loss, if any, affects only the *monopoly of the schools,* and by no means the *interests* of *humanity.* I appeal to the staunchest dogmatist, whether the proof of the continued existence of our soul after death, derived from the simplicity of the substance, or that of the freedom of the will, as opposed to the general mechanism of nature, derived from the subtle, but inefficient, distinction between subjective and objective practical necessity, or that of the existence of God, derived from the concept of an Ens realissimum (the contingency of the changeable, and the necessity of a prime mover), have ever, after they had been started by the schools, penetrated the public mind, or exercised the slightest influence on its convictions? If this has not been, and in fact could not be so, on account of the unfitness of the ordinary understanding for such subtle speculations; and if, on the contrary, with regard to the first point, the hope of a *future life* has chiefly rested on that peculiar character of human nature, never to be satisfied by what is merely temporal (and insufficient, therefore, for the character of its whole destination); if with regard to the second, the clear con- Bxxxiii sciousness of *freedom* was produced only by the clear exhibition of duties, in opposition to all the claims of sensuous desires; and if, lastly, with regard to the third, the belief in a great and wise *Author of the world* has been supported entirely by the wonderful beauty, order, and providence, everywhere displayed in nature, then this possession remains not only undisturbed, but acquires even greater authority, because the schools have now been taught, not to claim for themselves any higher or fuller insight on a point which concerns general human interests, than what is equally within the reach of the great mass of men, and to confine themselves to the elaboration of these universally comprehensible, and, for moral purposes, quite sufficient proofs. The change therefore affects the arrogant pretensions of the schools only, which would fain be considered as the only judges and depositaries of such truth (as they are, no doubt, with regard to many other subjects), allowing to the public its use only, and trying to keep the key to themselves, *quod mecum nescit, solus vult scire videri.* At the same time full satisfaction is given to the more moderate claims of speculative philosophers. Bxxxii They still remain the exclusive depositors of a science which benefits the masses without their knowing it, namely the critique of reason. That critique can never become popular, nor does it need to be so, because, if on the one side the public has no understanding for the fine-drawn arguments in support of useful truths, it is not troubled on the other by the equally subtle objections. It is different with the schools which, in the same way as every man who has once risen to the height of speculation, must know both the pro's and the con's, and are bound, by means of a careful investigation of the rights of speculative reason, to prevent, once for all, the scandal which, sooner or later, is sure to be caused even to the masses, by the quarrels in which metaphysicians (and, as such, theologians also) become involved, if ignorant of our critique, and by which their doctrine becomes in the end entirely perverted. Thus, and thus alone, can the very root be cut off of *materialism, fatalism, atheism, free-thinking unbelief, fanaticism,* and *superstition,* which may become universally injurious, and finally of *idealism* and *scepticism* also, which are dangerous rather to the schools, and can scarcely ever penetrate into the public. If governments think proper ever to Bxxxv interfere with the affairs of the learned, it would be far more consistent with their wise regard for science as well as for *society,* to favour the freedom of such a criticism by which alone the labours of reason can be established on a firm footing, than to support the ridiculous despotism of the schools, which raise a loud clamour of public danger, whenever the cobwebs are swept away of which the public has never taken the slightest notice, and the loss of which it can therefore never perceive.

Our critique is not opposed to the *dogmatical procedure* of reason, as a science of pure knowledge (for this must always be dogmatical, that is, derive its proof from sure principles *a priori*), but to *dogmatism* only, that is, to the presumption, that it is possible to make any progress with pure (philosophical) knowledge, consisting of concepts, and guided by principles, such as reason has long been in the habit of employing, without first enquiring in what way, and by what right, it has come possessed of them. Dogmatism is therefore the dogmatical procedure of pure reason, *without a previous criticism of its own powers;* and our opposition to this is not intended to defend either that loquacious shallowness which arrogates to itself the good name of popularity, much less that scepticism which makes short work with the whole of metaphysic. On the contrary, our critique is meant to form a necessary preparation in support of a thoroughly scientific system of metaphysic, which must necessarily be carried out dogmatically and strictly systematically, so as to satisfy all the demands, not so much of the public at large, as of the schools, this being an indispensable condition, as it has undertaken to carry out its work entirely *a priori,* and thus to the complete satisfaction of speculative reason. In the execution of this plan, as traced out by the critique, that is, in a future system of metaphysic, we shall have to follow in the strict method of the celebrated Wolf, the greatest of all dogmatic philosophers, who first showed (and by his example called forth, in Germany, that spirit of thoroughness, which is not yet extinct) how the secure method of a science could be attained only by a legitimate establishment of principles, a clear definition of concepts, an attempt at strictness of proof, and an avoidance of all bold combinations in concluding. He was therefore most eminently qualified to raise metaphysics to the dignity of a science, if it had only occurred to him, by criticism of the organum, namely of pure reason itself, first to prepare his field,—an omission to be ascribed, not so much to himself as to the dogmatical spirit of his age, and with regard to which the philosophers of his own, as well as of all previous times, have no right to reproach each other. Those who reject, at the same time, the method of Wolf, and the procedure of the critique of pure reason, can have no other aim but to shake off the fetters of *science* altogether, and thus to change work into play, conviction into opinion, and philosophy into philodoxy.

INTRODUCTION.

I.

Of the Difference between pure and empirical Knowledge.

That all our knowledge begins with experience there can be no doubt. For how should the faculty of knowledge be called into activity, if not by objects which affect our senses, and which either produce representations by themselves, or rouse the activity of our understanding to compare, to connect, or to separate them; and thus to convert the raw material of our sensuous impressions into a knowledge of objects, which we call experience? In respect of time, therefore, no knowledge within us is antecedent to experience, but all knowledge begins with it.

But although all our knowledge begins with experience, it does not follow that it arises from experience. For it is quite possible that even our empirical experience is a compound of that which we receive through impressions, and of that which our own faculty of knowledge (incited only by sensuous impressions), supplies from itself, a supplement which we do not distinguish from that raw material, until long practice has roused our attention and rendered us capable of separating one from the other.

It is therefore a question which deserves at least closer investigation, and cannot be disposed of at first sight, whether there exists a knowledge independent of experience, and even of all impressions of the senses? Such *knowledge* is called *a priori*, and distinguished from *empirical* knowledge, which has its sources *a posteriori*, that is, in experience.

This term *a priori*, however, is not yet definite enough to indicate the full meaning of our question. For people are wont to say, even with regard to knowledge derived from experience, that we have it, or might have it, *a priori*, because we derive it from experience, not *immediately*, but from a general rule, which, however, has itself been derived from experience. Thus one would say of a person who undermines the foundations of his house, that he might have known *a priori* that it would tumble down, that is, that he need not wait for the experience of its really tumbling down. But still he could not know this entirely *a priori*, because he had first to learn from experience that bodies are heavy, and will fall when their supports are taken away.

We shall therefore, in what follows, understand by knowledge *a priori* knowledge which is *absolutely* independent of all experience, and not of this or that experience only. Opposed to this is empirical knowledge, or such as is possible *a posteriori* only, that is, by experience. Knowledge *a priori*, if mixed up with nothing empirical, is called *pure*. Thus the proposition, for example, that every change has its cause, is a proposition *a priori*, but not pure: because change is a concept which can only be derived from experience. B3

II.

We are in possession of certain Cognitions a priori, *and even the ordinary understanding is never without them.*

All depends here on a criterion, by which we may safely distinguish between pure and empirical knowledge. Now experience teaches us, no doubt, that something is so or so, but not that it cannot be different. *First,* then, if we have a proposition, which is thought, together with its necessity, we have a judgment *a priori;* and if, besides, it is not derived from any proposition, except such as is itself again considered as necessary, we have an absolutely *a priori* judgment. *Secondly,* experience never imparts to its judgments true or strict, but only assumed or relative universality (by means of induction), so that we ought always to say, so far as we have observed hitherto, there is no exception to this or that rule. If, therefore, a judgment is thought with strict universality, so that no exception is admitted as possible, it is not derived from experience, but valid absolutely *a priori*. Empirical universality, therefore, is only an arbitrary extension of a validity which applies to most cases, to one that applies to all: as, for instance, in the proposition, all bodies are heavy. If, on the contrary, strict universality is essential to a judgment, this always points to a special source of knowledge, namely, a faculty of knowledge *a priori*. Necessity, therefore, and strict universality are safe criteria of knowledge *a priori*, and are inseparable one from the other. As, however, in the use of these criteria, it is sometimes easier to show the empirical limitation than the contingency of judgments, and as it is sometimes more convincing to prove the unlimited universality which we attribute to a judgment than its necessity, it is advisable to use both criteria separately, each being by itself infallible.

That there really exist in our knowledge such necessary, and in the strictest sense universal, and therefore, pure judgments *a priori*, is easy to show. If we want a scientific example, we have only to look to any of the propositions of mathematics; if we want one from the sphere of the ordinary understanding, such a proposition as that each change must have a cause, will answer the purpose; nay, in the latter case, even the concept of cause contains so clearly the concept of the necessity of its connection with an effect, and of the strict universality of the rule, that it would be destroyed altogether if we attempted to derive it, as Hume does, from the frequent concomitancy of that which happens with that which precedes, and from a habit arising thence,—therefore from a purely subjective necessity of connecting representations. It is possible even, without having recourse to such examples in proof of the reality of pure propositions *a priori* within our knowledge, to prove their indispensability for the possibility of experience itself, thus proving it *a priori*. For whence should experience take its certainty, if all the rules which it follows were always again and again empirical, and therefore contingent and hardly fit to serve as first principles? For the present, however, we may be satisfied for having shown the pure employment of the faculty of our knowledge as a matter of fact, with the criteria of it.

Not only in judgments, however, but even in certain concepts, can we show their origin *a priori*. Take away, for example, from the concept of body, as supplied by experience, everything that is empirical, one by one; such as colour, hardness, or softness, weight, and even impenetrability, and there still remains the space which the body (now entirely vanished) occupied: that you cannot take away. And in the same manner, if you remove from your empirical concept of any object, corporeal or incorporeal, all properties which experience has taught you, you cannot take away from it that property by which you conceive it as a substance, or inherent in a substance (although such a concept contains more determinations than that of an object in general). Convinced, therefore, by the necessity with which that concept forces itself upon you, you will have to admit that it has its seat in your faculty of knowledge *a priori*. B6

III.

Philosophy requires a science to determine a priori *the possibility, the principles, and the extent of all Knowledge.*

But what is still more extraordinary is this, that certain kinds of knowledge leave the field of all possible experience, and seem to enlarge the sphere of our judgments beyond the limits of experience by means of concepts to which experience can never supply any corresponding objects. A3

And it is in this very kind of knowledge which transcends the world of the senses, and where experience can neither guide nor correct us, that reason prosecutes its investigations, which by their importance we consider far more excellent and by their tendency far more elevated than anything the understanding can find in the sphere of phenomena. Nay, we risk rather anything, even at the peril of error, than that we should surrender such investigations, B7 either on the ground of their uncertainty, or from any feeling of indifference or contempt.

"These inevitable problems of pure reason itself are, *God, Freedom,* and *Immortality.*" The science which with all its apparatus is really intended for the solution of these problems, is called *Metaphysic.* Its procedure is at first *dogmatic,* i.e. unchecked by a previous examination of what reason can and cannot do, before it engages confidently in so arduous an undertaking.

Now it might seem natural that, after we have left the solid ground of experience, we should not at once proceed to erect an edifice with knowledge which we possess without knowing whence it came, and trust to principles the origin of which is unknown, without having made sure of the safety of the foundations by means of careful examination. It would seem natural, I say, that we should first of all have asked the question how the mere understanding could arrive at all this knowledge *a priori,* and what extent, what truth, and what value it could possess. If we take natural to mean what is just and reasonable, then indeed nothing could be more natural. But if we understand by natural what takes place ordinarily, then, on the contrary, nothing is more natural and more intelligible than that this examination should have been neglected for so long a time. For one part of this knowledge, namely, the mathematical, has always been in possession of perfect trustworthiness; and thus produces a favourable presumption with regard to other parts also, although these may be of a totally different nature. Besides, once beyond the precincts of experience, and we are certain that experience can never contradict us, while the charm of enlarging our knowledge is so great that nothing will stop our progress until we encounter a clear contradiction. This can be avoided if only we are cautious in our imaginations, which nevertheless remain what they are, imaginations only. How far we can advance independent of all experience in *a priori* knowledge is shown by the brilliant example of mathematics. It is true they deal with objects and knowledge so far only as they can be represented in intuition. But this is easily overlooked, because that intuition itself may be given *a priori,* and be difficult to distinguish from a pure concept. Thus inspirited by a splendid proof of the power of rea-

son, the desire of enlarging our knowledge sees no limits. The light
dove, piercing in her easy flight the air and perceiving its resistance, B9
imagines that flight would be easier still in empty space. It was thus
that Plato left the world of sense, as opposing so many hindrances
to our understanding, and ventured beyond on the wings of his
ideas into the empty space of pure understanding. He did not perceive that he was making no progress by these endeavours, because
he had no resistance as a fulcrum on which to rest or to apply his
powers, in order to cause the understanding to advance. It is indeed
a very common fate of human reason first of all to finish its speculative edifice as soon as possible, and then only to inquire whether
the foundation be sure. Then all sorts of excuses are made in order
to assure us as to its solidity, or to decline altogether such a late and
dangerous inquiry. The reason why during the time of building we
feel free from all anxiety and suspicion and believe in the apparent
solidity of our foundation, is this:—A great, perhaps the greatest
portion of what our reason finds to do consists in the analysis of our
concepts of objects. This gives us a great deal of knowledge which, A6
though it consists in no more than in simplifications and explanations of what is comprehended in our concepts (though in a confused manner), is yet considered as equal, at least in form, to new
knowledge. It only separates and arranges our concepts, it does not B10
enlarge them in matter or contents. As by this process we gain a
kind of real knowledge *a priori,* which progresses safely and use-
fully, it happens that our reason, without being aware of it, appro-
priates under that pretence propositions of a totally different
character, adding to given concepts new and strange ones *a priori,*
without knowing whence they come, nay without even thinking of
such a question. I shall therefore at the very outset treat of the distinction between these two kinds of knowledge.

IV.

*Of the distinction between analytical and
synthetical Judgments.*

In all judgments in which there is a relation between subject and
predicate (I speak of affirmative judgments only, the application to

negative ones being easy), that relation can be of two kinds. Either
the predicate B belongs to the subject A as something contained
(though covertly) in the concept A; or B lies outside the sphere of
the concept A, though somehow connected with it. In the former
case I call the judgment analytical, in the latter synthetical. Analyt-
A7 ical judgments (affirmative) are therefore those in which the connection of the predicate with the subject is conceived through
identity, while others in which that connection is conceived with-
B11 out identity, may be called synthetical. The former might be called
illustrating, the latter expanding judgments, because in the former
nothing is added by the predicate to the concept of the subject, but
the concept is only divided into its constituent concepts which
were always conceived as existing within it, though confusedly;
while the latter add to the concept of the subject a predicate not
conceived as existing within it, and not to be extracted from it by
any process of mere analysis. If I say, for instance, All bodies are extended, this is an analytical judgment. I need not go beyond the
concept connected with the name of body, in order to find that extension is connected with it. I have only to analyse that concept and
become conscious of the manifold elements always contained in it,
in order to find that predicate. This is therefore an analytical judgment. But if I say, All bodies are heavy, the predicate is something
quite different from what I think as the mere concept of body. The
addition of such a predicate gives us a synthetical judgment.

Empirical judgments, as such, are all synthetical; for it would be
absurd to found an analytical judgment on experience, because, in
order to form such a judgment, I need not at all step out of my concept, or appeal to the testimony of experience. That a body is extended, is a proposition perfectly certain *a priori*, and not an
B12 empirical judgment. For, before I call in experience, I am already in
possession of all the conditions of my judgment in the concept of
body itself. I have only to draw out from it, according to the principle of contradiction, the required predicate, and I thus become
conscious, at the same time, of the necessity of the judgment,
which experience could never teach me. But, though I do not include the predicate of gravity in the general concept of body, that

concept, nevertheless, indicates an object of experience through one of its parts: so that I may add other parts also of the same experience, besides those which belonged to the former concept. I may, first, by an analytical process, realise the concept of body, through the predicates of extension, impermeability, form, &c., all of which are contained in it. Afterwards I expand my knowledge, and looking back to the experience from which my concept of body was abstracted, I find gravity always connected with the before mentioned predicates, and therefore I add it synthetically to that concept as a predicate. It is, therefore, experience on which the possibility of the synthesis of the predicate of gravity with the concept of body is founded: because both concepts, though neither of them is contained in the other, belong to each other, though accidentally only, as parts of a whole, namely, of experience, which is itself a synthetical connection of intuitions.

In synthetical judgments *a priori*, however, that help is entirely wanting. If I want to go beyond the concept A in order to find another concept B, connected with it, where is there anything on which I may rest and through which a synthesis might become possible, considering that I cannot have the advantage of looking about in the field of experience? Take the proposition that all which happens has its cause. In the concept of something that happens I no doubt conceive of something existing preceded by time, and from this certain analytical judgments may be deduced. But the concept of cause is entirely outside that concept, and indicates something different from that which happens, and is by no means contained in that representation. How can I venture then to predicate of that which happens something totally different from it, and to represent the concept of cause, though not contained in it, as belonging to it, and belonging to it by necessity? What is here the unknown *x*, on which the understanding may rest in order to find beyond the concept A a foreign predicate B, which nevertheless is believed to be connected with it? It cannot be experience, because the proposition that all which happens has its cause represents this second predicate as added to the subject not only with greater generality than experience can ever supply, but also with a character of necessity,

and therefore purely *a priori*, and based on concepts. All our specu-
A10 lative knowledge *a priori* aims at and rests on such synthetical, i.e.
expanding propositions, for the analytical are no doubt very important and necessary, yet only in order to arrive at that clearness of
B14 concepts which is requisite for a safe and wide synthesis, serving as
a really new addition to what we possess already.

V.

In all theoretical Sciences of reason synthetical Judgments a priori *are contained as principles.*

1. All mathematical judgments are synthetical. This proposition,
though incontestably certain, and very important to us for the future, seems to have hitherto escaped the observation of those who
are engaged in the anatomy of human reason: nay, to be directly
opposed to all their conjectures. For as it was found that all mathematical conclusions proceed according to the principle of contradiction (which is required by the nature of all apodictic certainty),
it was supposed that the fundamental principles of mathematics
also rested on the authority of the same principle of contradiction.
This, however, was a mistake: for though a synthetical proposition
may be understood according to the principle of contradiction, this
can only be if another synthetical proposition is presupposed, from
which the latter is deduced, but never by itself. First of all, we
ought to observe, that mathematical propositions, properly so
B15 called, are always judgments *a priori*, and not empirical, because
they carry along with them necessity, which can never be deduced
from experience. If people should object to this, I am quite willing
to confine my statement to pure mathematics, the very concept of
which implies that it does not contain empirical, but only pure
knowledge *a priori*.

At first sight one might suppose indeed that the proposition $7 + 5 = 12$ is merely analytical, following, according to the principle of
contradiction, from the concept of a sum of 7 and 5. But, if we look
more closely, we shall find that the concept of the sum of 7 and 5
contains nothing beyond the union of both sums into one, whereby

nothing is told us as to what this single number may be which combines both. We by no means arrive at a concept of Twelve, by thinking that union of Seven and Five; and we may analyse our concept of such a possible sum as long as we will, still we shall never discover in it the concept of Twelve. We must go beyond these concepts, and call in the assistance of the intuition corresponding to one of the two, for instance, our five fingers, or, as Segner does in his B16 arithmetic, five points, and so by degrees add the units of the Five, given in intuition, to the concept of the Seven. For I first take the number 7, and taking the intuition of the fingers of my hand, in order to form with it the concept of the 5, I gradually add the units, which I before took together, to make up the number 5, by means of the image of my hand, to the number 7, and I thus see the number 12 arising before me. That 7 should be added to 5 was no doubt implied in my concept of a sum $7 + 5$, but not that the sum should be equal to 12. An arithmetical proposition is, therefore, always synthetical, which is seen more easily still by taking larger numbers, where we clearly perceive that, turn and twist our conceptions as we may, we could never, by means of the mere analysis of our concepts and without the help of intuition, arrive at the sum that is wanted.

Nor is any proposition of pure geometry analytical. That the straight line between two points is the shortest, is a synthetical proposition. For my concept of *straight* contains nothing of magnitude (quantity), but a quality only. The concept of the *shortest* is, therefore, purely adventitious, and cannot be deduced from the concept of the straight line by any analysis whatsoever. The aid of intuition, therefore, must be called in, by which alone the synthesis is possible.

It is true that some few propositions, presupposed by the geometrician, are really analytical, and depend on the principle of contradiction: but then they serve only, like identical propositions, to form the chain of the method, and not as principles. Such are the propositions, $a = a$, the whole is equal to itself, or $(a + b) > a$, that the B17 whole is greater than its part. And even these, though they are valid according to mere concepts, are only admitted in mathematics, because they can be represented in intuition. What often makes us believe that the predicate of such apodictic judgments is contained in our concept, and the judgment therefore analytical, is merely the ambiguous character of the expression. We are told that we *ought* to join in thought a certain predicate to a given concept, and this necessity is inherent in the concepts themselves. But the question is not what we *ought* to join to the given concept, but what we *really think* in it, though confusedly only, and then it becomes clear that the predicate is no doubt inherent in those concepts by necessity, not, however, as thought in the concept itself, but by means of an intuition, which must be added to the concept.

2. *Natural science (physica) contains synthetical judgments* a priori *as principles.* I shall adduce, as examples, a few propositions only, such as, that in all changes of the material world the quantity of matter always remains unchanged: or that in all communication of motion, action and reaction must always equal each other. It is clear not only that both convey necessity, and that, therefore, their origin is *a priori,* but also that they are synthetical propositions. For in the concept of matter I do not conceive its permanency, but only its presence in the space which it fills. I therefore go beyond the concept of matter in order to join something to it *a priori,* which I did not before conceive *in it.* The proposition is, therefore, not analytical, but synthetical, and yet *a priori,* and the same applies to the other propositions of the pure part of natural science.

3. *Metaphysic,* even if we look upon it as hitherto a tentative science only, which, however, is indispensable to us, owing to the very nature of human reason, is meant to *contain synthetical knowledge a priori.* Its object is not at all merely to analyse such concepts as we make to ourselves of things *a priori,* and thus to explain them analytically, but to expand our knowledge *a priori.* This we can only do by means of concepts which add something to a given concept that was not contained in it; nay, we even attempt, by means of synthetical judgments *a priori,* to go so far beyond a given concept that experience itself cannot follow us: as, for instance, in the proposition that the world must have a first beginning. Thus, according at least to its intentions, metaphysic consists merely of synthetical propositions *a priori.*

VI.

The General Problem of Pure Reason.

Much is gained if we are able to bring a number of investigations under the formula of one single problem. For we thus not only facilitate our own work by defining it accurately, but enable also everybody else who likes to examine it to form a judgment, whether we have really done justice to our purpose or not. Now the real problem of pure reason is contained in the question, *How are synthetical judgments* a priori *possible?*

That metaphysic has hitherto remained in so vacillating a state of ignorance and contradiction is entirely due to people not having thought sooner of this problem, or perhaps even of a distinction between *analytical* and *synthetical* judgments. The solution of this problem, or a sufficient proof that a possibility which is to be explained does in reality not exist at all, is the question of life or death to metaphysic. *David Hume*, who among all philosophers approached nearest to that problem, though he was far from conceiving it with sufficient definiteness and universality, confining his attention only to the synthetical proposition of the connection of an effect with its causes (*principium causalitatis*), arrived at the conclusion that such a proposition *a priori* is entirely impossible. According to his conclusions, everything which we call metaphysic would turn out to be a mere delusion of reason, fancying that it knows by itself what in reality is only borrowed from experience, and has assumed by mere habit the appearance of necessity. If he had grasped our problem in all its universality, he would never have thought of an assertion which destroys all pure philosophy, because he would have perceived that, according to his argument, no pure mathematical science was possible either, on account of its certainly containing synthetical propositions *a priori;* and from such an assertion his good sense would probably have saved him.

On the solution of our problem depends, at the same time, the possibility of the pure employment of reason, in establishing and carrying out all sciences which contain a theoretical knowledge *a priori* of objects, i.e. the answer to the questions

How is pure mathematical science possible?

How is pure natural science possible?

As these sciences really exist, it is quite proper to ask, *How* they are possible? for *that* they must be possible, is proved by their reality.[7]

But as to *metaphysic,* the bad progress which it has hitherto made, and the impossibility of asserting of any of the metaphysical systems yet brought forward that it really exists, so far as its essential aim is concerned, must fill every one with doubts as to its possibility.

Yet, in a certain sense, this *kind of knowledge* also must be looked upon as given, and though not as a science, yet as a natural disposition (*metaphysica naturalis*) metaphysic is real. For human reason, without being moved merely by the conceit of omniscience, advances irresistibly, and urged on by its own need, to questions such as cannot be answered by any empirical employment of reason, or by principles thence derived, so that we may really say, that all men, as soon as their reason became ripe for speculation, have at all times possessed some kind of metaphysic, and will always continue to possess it. And now it will also have to answer the question,

How is metaphysic possible, as a natural disposition? that is, how does the nature of universal human reason give rise to questions which pure reason proposes to itself, and which it is urged on by its own need to answer as well as it can?

As, however, all attempts which have hitherto been made at answering these natural questions (for instance, whether the world has a beginning, or exists from all eternity), have always led to inevitable contradictions, we cannot rest satisfied with the mere natural disposition to metaphysic, that is, with the pure faculty of reason itself, from which some kind of metaphysic (whatever it

B21   7 One might doubt this with regard to pure natural science; but one has only to consider the different propositions which stand at the beginning of real (empirical) physical science, those, for example, relating to the permanence of the same quantity of matter to the vis inertiæ, the equality of action and reaction, &c., in order to become convinced that they constitute a physica pura, or rationalis, which well deserves to stand by itself as an independent science, in its whole extent, whether narrow or wide.

may be) always arises; but it must be possible to arrive with it at some certainty as to our either knowing or not knowing its objects; that is, we must either decide that we can judge of the objects of these questions, and of the power or want of power of reason, in deciding anything upon them,—therefore that we can either enlarge our pure reason with certainty, or that we have to impose on it fixed and firm limits. This last question, which arises out of the former more general problem, would properly assume this form,

How is metaphysic possible, as a science?

The critique of reason leads, therefore, necessarily, to true science, while its dogmatical use, without criticism, lands us in groundless assertions, to which others, equally specious, can always B23 be opposed, that is, in *scepticism*.

Nor need this science be very formidable by its great prolixity, for it has not to deal with the objects of reason, the variety of which is infinite, but with reason only, and with problems, suggested by reason and placed before it, not by the nature of things, which are different from it, but by its own nature; so that, if reason has only first completely understood its own power, with reference to objects given to it in experience, it will have no difficulty in determining completely and safely the extent and limits of its attempted application beyond the limits of all experience.

We may and must therefore regard all attempts which have hitherto been made at building up a metaphysic dogmatically, as *non-avenu*. For the mere analysis of the concepts that dwell in our reason *a priori*, which has been attempted in one or other of those metaphysical systems, is by no means the aim, but only a preparation for true metaphysic, namely, the answer to the question, how we can enlarge our knowledge *a priori* synthetically; nay, it is utterly useless for that purpose, because it only shows what is contained in those concepts, but not by what process *a priori* we arrive at them, in order thus to determine the validity of their employment with reference to all objects of knowledge in general. Nor does it require much self-denial to give up these pretensions, con- B24 sidering that the undeniable and, in the dogmatic procedure, inevitable contradictions of reason with itself, have long deprived every system of metaphysic of all authority. More firmness will be required in order not to be deterred by difficulties from within and resistance from without, from trying to advance a science, indispensable to human reason, (a science of which we may lop off every branch, but will never be able to destroy the root,) by a treatment entirely opposed to all former treatments, which promises, at last, to ensure the successful and fruitful growth of metaphysical science.

VII.

The Idea and Division of a Special Science under the Name of a Critique of Pure Reason.

It will now be seen how there can be a special science serving as a critique of pure reason. Reason is the faculty which supplies the principles of knowledge *a priori.* Pure reason therefore is that faculty which supplies the principles of knowing anything entirely *a priori.* An Organum of pure reason ought to comprehend all the principles by which pure knowledge *a priori* can be acquired and fully established. A complete application of such an Organum would give us a System of Pure Reason. But as that would be a difficult task, and as at present it is still doubtful whether such an expansion of our knowledge is here possible, we may look on a mere criticism of pure reason, its sources and limits, as a kind of preparation for a complete system of pure reason. It should be called a critique, not a doctrine, of pure reason. Its usefulness would be negative only, serving for a purging rather than for an expansion of our reason, and, what after all is a considerable gain, guarding reason against errors.

I call all knowledge *transcendental* which is occupied not so much with objects, as with our *a priori* concepts of objects.[8] A system of such concepts might be called Transcendental Philosophy. But for the present this is again too great an undertaking. We should have

---

8 "As with our manner of knowing objects, so far as this is meant to be possible *a priori.*" Second Edition.

to treat therein completely both of analytical knowledge, and of synthetical knowledge *a priori,* which is more than we intend to do, being satisfied to carry on the analysis so far only as is indispensably necessary in order to understand in their whole extent the principles of synthesis *a priori,* which alone concern us. This inves- B26 tigation which should be called a transcendental critique, but not a systematic doctrine, is all we are occupied with at present. It is not meant to extend our knowledge, but only to rectify it, and to become the test of the value of all *a priori* knowledge. Such a critique therefore is a preparation for a New Organum, or, if that should not be possible, for a Canon at least, according to which hereafter a complete system of a philosophy of pure reason, whether it serve for an expansion or merely for a limitation of it, may be carried out, both analytically and synthetically. That such a system is possible, nay that it need not be so comprehensive as to prevent the hope of its completion, may be gathered from the fact that it would have to deal, not with the nature of things, which is endless, but with the understanding which judges of the nature of things, and this again A13 so far only as its knowledge *a priori* is concerned. Whatever the understanding possesses, as it has not to be looked for without, can B27 hardly escape our notice, nor is there any reason to suppose that it will prove too extensive for a complete inventory, and for such a valuation as shall assign to it its true merits or demerits.

Still less ought we to expect here a criticism on the books and systems treating of pure reason, but only on the faculty of pure reason itself. It is only if we are in possession of this, that we possess a safe criterion for estimating the philosophical value of old and new works on this subject. Otherwise, an unqualified historian and judge does nothing but criticise the groundless assertions of others by means of his own, which are equally groundless.

Transcendental Philosophy is with us an idea (of a science) only, for which the critique of pure reason should trace, according to fixed principles, an architectonic plan, guaranteeing the completeness and certainty of all parts of which the building consists. (It is a system of all principles of pure reason.) The reason why we do not call such a critique a transcendental philosophy in itself is simply

this, that in order to be a complete system, it ought to contain likewise a complete analysis of the whole of human knowledge *a priori*.
It is true that our critique must produce a complete list of all the
fundamental concepts which constitute pure knowledge. But it
need not give a detailed analysis of these concepts, nor a complete
A14 list of all derivative concepts. Such an analysis would be out of
B28 place, because it is not beset with the doubts and difficulties which
are inherent in synthesis, and which alone necessitate a critique of
pure reason. Nor would it answer our purpose to take the responsibility of the completeness of such an analysis and derivation. This
completeness of analysis, however, and of derivation from such *a
priori* concepts as we shall have to deal with presently, may easily be
supplied, if only they have first been laid down as perfect principles
of synthesis, and nothing is wanting to them in that respect.

All that constitutes transcendental philosophy belongs to the
critique of pure reason, nay it is the complete idea of transcendental philosophy, but not yet the whole of that philosophy itself, because it carries the analysis so far only as is requisite for a complete
examination of synthetical knowledge *a priori*.

The most important consideration in the arrangement of such a
science is that no concepts should be admitted which contain anything empirical, and that the *a priori* knowledge shall be perfectly
pure. Therefore, although the highest principles of morality and
A15 their fundamental concepts are *a priori* knowledge, they do not belong to transcendental philosophy, because the concepts of plea-
B29 sure and pain, desire, inclination, free-will, etc., which are all of
empirical origin, must here be presupposed. Transcendental philosophy is the wisdom of pure speculative reason. Everything practical, so far as it contains motives, has reference to sentiments, and
these belong to empirical sources of knowledge.

If we wish to carry out a proper division of our science systematically, it must contain first *a doctrine of the elements*, secondly, *a doctrine of the method* of pure reason. Each of these principal divisions
will have its subdivisions, the grounds of which cannot however be
explained here. So much only seems necessary for previous information, that there are two stems of human knowledge, which per-

haps may spring from a common root, unknown to us, viz. *sensibility* and the *understanding,* objects being given by the former and thought by the latter. If our sensibility should contain *a priori* representations, constituting conditions under which alone objects can B30 be given, it would belong to transcendental philosophy, and the doctrine of this transcendental sense-perception would necessarily A16 form the first part of the doctrine of elements, because the conditions under which alone objects of human knowledge can be given must precede those under which they are thought.

THE TRANSCENDENTAL
DOCTRINE OF ELEMENTS

FIRST PART.
TRANSCENDENTAL ÆSTHETIC.

§ 1.

Whatever the process and the means may be by which knowledge reaches its objects, there is one that reaches them directly, and forms the ultimate material of all thought, viz. intuition (*Anschauung*). This is possible only when the object is given, and the object can be given only (to human beings at least) through a certain affection of the mind (*Gemüth*).

This faculty (receptivity) of receiving representations (*Vorstellungen*), according to the manner in which we are affected by objects, is called sensibility (*Sinnlichkeit*).

Objects therefore are given to us through our sensibility. Sensibility alone supplies us with intuitions (*Anschauungen*). These intuitions become thought through the understanding (*Verstand*), and hence arise conceptions (*Begriffe*). All thought therefore must, directly or indirectly, go back to intuitions (*Anschauungen*), i.e. to our sensibility, because in no other way can objects be given to us.

The effect produced by an object upon the faculty of represen-

tation (*Vorstellungsfähigkeit*), so far as we are affected by it, is called   B34
sensation (*Empfindung*). An intuition (*Anschauung*) of an object, by
means of sensation, is called empirical. The undefined object of
such an empirical intuition is called phenomenon (*Erscheinung*).

In a phenomenon I call that which corresponds to the sensation
its *matter*; but that which causes the manifold matter of the phenomenon to be perceived as arranged in a certain order, I call its
form.

Now it is clear that it cannot be sensation again through which
sensations are arranged and placed in certain forms. The matter
only of all phenomena is given us *a posteriori*; but their form must be
ready for them in the mind (*Gemüth*) *a priori*, and must therefore be
capable of being considered as separate from all sensations.

I call all representations in which there is nothing that belongs to
sensation, *pure* (in a transcendental sense). The pure form therefore
of all sensuous intuitions, that form in which the manifold elements
of the phenomena are seen in a certain order, must be found in the
mind *a priori*. And this pure form of sensibility may be called the
pure intuition (*Anschauung*).

Thus, if we deduct from the representation (*Vorstellung*) of a   B35
body what belongs to the thinking of the understanding, viz. substance, force, divisibility, etc. and likewise what belongs to sensation, viz. impermeability, hardness, colour, etc., there still remains   A21
something of that empirical intuition (*Anschauung*), viz. extension
and form. These belong to pure intuition, which *a priori*, and even
without a real object of the senses or of sensation, exist in the mind
as a mere form of sensibility.

The science of all the principles of sensibility *a priori* I call
Transcendental Æsthetic[9] There must be such a science, forming the

---

9 The Germans are the only people who at present (1781) use the word *æsthetic* for what   A21
others call criticism of taste. There is implied in that name a false hope, first conceived by   B35
the excellent analytical philosopher, Baumgarten, of bringing the critical judgment of the
beautiful under rational principles, and to raise its rules to the rank of a science. But such endeavours are vain. For such rules or criteria are, according to their principal sources, empirical only, and can never serve as definite *a priori* rules for our judgment in matters of taste; on   B36
the contrary, our judgment is the real test of the truth of such rules. It would be advisable

B36 first part of the Elements of Transcendentalism, as opposed to that which treats of the principles of pure thought, and which should be called *Transcendental Logic.*

A22   In Transcendental Æsthetic therefore we shall first isolate sensibility, by separating everything which the understanding adds by means of its concepts, so that nothing remains but empirical intuition (*Anschauung*).

Secondly, we shall separate from this all that belongs to sensation (*Empfindung*), so that nothing remains but pure intuition (*reine Anschauung*) or the mere form of the phenomena, which is the only thing which sensibility *a priori* can supply. In the course of this investigation it will appear that there are, as principles of *a priori* knowledge, two pure forms of sensuous intuition (*Anschauung*), namely, *Space* and *Time.* We now proceed to consider these more in detail.

FIRST SECTION OF THE TRANSCENDENTAL ÆSTHETIC.

Of Space.

§ 2.

By means of our external sense, a property of our mind (*Gemüth*), we represent to ourselves objects as external or outside ourselves, and all of these in space. It is within space that their form, size, and relative position are fixed or can be fixed. The internal sense by means of which the mind perceives itself or its internal state, does A23 not give an intuition (*Anschauung*) of the soul (*Seele*) itself, as an object, but it is nevertheless a fixed form under which alone an intuition of its internal state is possible, so that whatever belongs to its internal determinations (*Bestimmungen*) must be represented in relations of time. Time cannot be perceived (*angeschaut*) externally, as little as space can be perceived as something within us.

---

therefore to drop the name in that sense, and to apply it to a doctrine which is a real science, thus approaching more nearly to the language and meaning of the ancients with whom the division into αἰσθητὰ καὶ νοητά was very famous, (or to share that name in common with speculative philosophy, and thus to use æsthetic sometimes in a transcendental, sometimes in a psychological sense).

What then are space and time? Are they real beings? Or, if not that, are they determinations or relations of things, but such as would belong to them even if they were not perceived? Or lastly, are they determinations and relations which are inherent in the form of intuition only, and therefore in the subjective nature of our B38 mind, without which such predicates as space and time would never be ascribed to anything?

In order to understand this more clearly, let us first consider space.

1. Space is not an empirical concept which has been derived from external experience. For in order that certain sensations should be referred to something outside myself, i.e. to something in a different part of space from that where I am; again, in order that I may be able to represent them (*vorstellen*) as side by side, that is, not only as different, but as in different places, the representation (*Vorstellung*) of space must already be there. Therefore the representation of space cannot be borrowed through experience from relations of external phenomena, but, on the contrary, those external phenomena become possible only by means of the representation of space.

2. Space is a necessary representation *a priori*, forming the very foundation of all external intuitions. It is impossible to imagine A24 that there should be no space, though one might very well imagine that there should be space without objects to fill it. Space is therefore regarded as a condition of the possibility of phenomena, not as a determination produced by them; it is a representation *a priori* which necessarily precedes all external phenomena.

3. Space is not a discursive or so-called general concept of the A25 relations of things in general, but a pure intuition. For, first of all, we can imagine one space only, and if we speak of many spaces, we mean parts only of one and the same space. Nor can these parts be considered as antecedent to the one and all-embracing space and, as it were, its component parts out of which an aggregate is formed, but they can be thought of as existing within it only. Space is essentially one; its multiplicity, and therefore the general concept of spaces in general, arises entirely from limitations. Hence it follows

that, with respect to space, an intuition *a priori*, which is not empirical, must form the foundation of all conceptions of space. In the same manner all geometrical principles, e.g. "that in every triangle two sides together are greater than the third," are never to be derived from the general concepts of side and triangle, but from an intuition, and that *a priori*, with apodictic certainty.

4. Space is represented as an infinite given quantity. Now it is B40 quite true that every concept is to be thought as a representation, which is contained in an infinite number of different possible representations (as their common characteristic), and therefore comprehends them: but no concept, as such, can be thought, as if it contained in itself an infinite number of representations. Nevertheless, space is so thought, (for all parts of space exist simultaneously ad infinitum). Consequently, the original representation of space is an *intuition a priori*, and not a concept.

§ 3.

Transcendental Exposition of the concept of space.

I understand by transcendental *exposition* (*Erörterung*), the explanation of a concept, as of a principle by which the possibility of other synthetical kinds of knowledge *a priori* can be understood. For this purpose it is necessary, 1. That such kinds of knowledge really do flow from the given concept. 2. That they are possible only under the presupposition of a given mode of explanation of such concept.

Geometry is a science which determines the properties of space synthetically, and yet *a priori*. What then must be the representation of space, to render such a knowledge of it possible? It must be orig-B41 inally intuitive; for it is impossible from a mere concept to deduce propositions which go beyond that concept, as we do in geometry. That intuition, however, must be *a priori*, that is, it must exist within us before any perception of the object, and must therefore be pure, not empirical intuition. For all geometrical propositions are apodictic, that is, connected with the consciousness of their necessity, as for instance the proposition, that space has only three dimensions; and such propositions cannot be empirical judgments, nor conclusions from them.

How then can an external intuition dwell in the mind anterior to the objects themselves, and in which the concept of objects can be determined *a priori?* Evidently not otherwise than so far as it has its seat in the subject only, as the formal condition under which the subject is affected by the objects, in receiving an *immediate representation,* that is, *intuition* of them; therefore as a form of the external *sense* in general.

It is therefore by our explanation only that the *possibility* of *geometry* as a synthetical science *a priori* becomes intelligible. Every other explanation, which fails to account for this possibility, can best be distinguished from our own by that criterion, although it may seem to have some similarity with it.

Conclusions from the foregoing concepts. A26

a. Space does not represent any quality of objects by themselves, or objects in their relation to one another; i.e. space does not repre- B42 sent any determination which is inherent in the objects themselves, and would remain, even if all subjective conditions of intuition were removed. For no determinations of objects, whether belonging to them absolutely or in relation to others, can enter into our intuition before the actual existence of the objects themselves, that is to say, they can never be intuitions *a priori.*

b. Space is nothing but the form of the phenomena of all external senses; it is a subjective condition of our sensibility, without which no external intuition is possible for us. If then we consider that the receptivity of the subject, its capacity of being affected by objects, must necessarily precede all intuition of objects, we shall understand how the form of all phenomena may be given before all real perceptions, may be, in fact, *a priori* in the soul, and may, as a pure intuition, by which all objects must be determined, contain, prior to all experience, principles regulating their relations.

It is therefore from the human standpoint only that we can speak of space, extended objects, etc. If we drop the subjective condition under which alone we can gain external intuition, according as we ourselves may be affected by objects, the representation of space means nothing. For this predicate is applied to objects only in so far A27 as they appear to us, and are objects of our senses. The constant B43 form of this receptivity, which we call sensibility, is a necessary condition of all relations in which objects, as without us, can be perceived; and, when abstraction is made of these objects, what remains is that pure intuition which we call space. As the peculiar conditions of our sensibility cannot be looked upon as conditions of the possibility of the objects themselves, but only of their appearance as phenomena to us, we may say indeed that space comprehends all things which may appear to us externally, but not all things by themselves, whether perceived by us or not, or any subject whatsoever. We cannot judge whether the intuitions of other thinking beings are subject to the same conditions which determine our intuition, and which for us are generally binding. If we add the limitation of a judgment to a subjective concept, the judgment gains absolute validity. The proposition "all things are beside each other in space," is valid only under the limitation that things are taken as objects of our sensuous intuition (*Anschauung*). If I add that limitation to the concept and say "all things, as external phenomena, are beside each other in space," the rule obtains universal and A28 unlimited validity. Our discussions teach therefore the reality, i.e. B44 the objective validity, of space with regard to all that can come to us externally as an object, but likewise the *ideality* of space with regard to things, when they are considered in themselves by our reason, and independent of the nature of our senses. We maintain the empirical reality of space, so far as every possible external experience is concerned, but at the same time its transcendental ideality; that is to say, we maintain that space is nothing, if we leave out of consideration the condition of a possible experience, and accept it as something on which things by themselves are in any way dependent.

With the exception of space there is no other subjective repre-
B45 sentation (*Vorstellung*) referring to something external, that would be called *a priori* objective.

With the exception of space there is no other subjective representation, referring to something external, that could be called *a priori* objective. For from none of them can we derive synthetical propositions *a priori*, as we can from the intuition in space § 3. Strictly speaking, therefore, they can claim no ideality at all, though

they agree with the representa
only to the subjective nature (
hearing, and feeling, through t
heat. All these, however, being
do not help us by themselves to

My object in what I have sai
from imagining that they can pr
tions which are altogether insu
which should never be considere
fications of the subject, and whi
different people. For in this case
nomenon only, as for instance, a ro
standing for a thing by itself, w
colour, may appear different to e
ception, on the contrary, of all phe
ing that nothing which is seen in sp
form of things supposed to belong t
jects by themselves are not known to
ternal objects are nothing but repre
of which is space, and the true corr
by itself, is not known, nor can be kno
do we care to know anything about i

SECOND SECTION OF THE
ÆSTHET

Of Tim

1. Time is not an empirical conce
ence, for neither coexistence nor suc
perception, if the representation of
Only when this representation *a priori*
certain things happen at the same tim
ferent times (successively).

2. Time is a necessary representatio
pend. We cannot take away time fro
though we can well take away phenome
fore is given *a priori*. In time alone is rea

...tion of space in this, that they belo...
...f sensibility, for instance, of sight...
...he sensations of colours, sounds,...
...sensations only, and not intuit...
...know any object, least of all *a*...
...d just now is only to prevent...
...ove the ideality of space by il...
...fficient, such as colour, tas...
...d as qualities of things, but...
...ch therefore may be diffe...
...hat which originally is its...
...se, is taken by the empir...
...hich nevertheless, with...
...very eye. The transcer...
...nomena in space, is a...
...ace is a thing by itse...
...o them by themselv...
...us at all, and that...
...sentations of our...
...elative of which...
...wn by these re...
...t in our daily e...

E TRANSCE...
IC.

A32

B48

e.

pt ded...
...cessio...
time
is gi...
e (...

...de-
...cal,
...nedi-
...d
...ary def-
...at...ne time
...ini...presenta-
whi...when the
...tion...be repre-
...part...resentation
...sent...l representa-
...cann...e intuition.
...tions

of time.

...sake of brevity, I
I can h...under the head of
have p...hat the concept of
metaph...

they agree with the representation of space in this, that they belong only to the subjective nature of sensibility, for instance, of sight, of hearing, and feeling, through the sensations of colours, sounds, and heat. All these, however, being sensations only, and not intuitions, do not help us by themselves to know any object, least of all *a priori.*

My object in what I have said just now is only to prevent people from imagining that they can prove the ideality of space by illustrations which are altogether insufficient, such as colour, taste, etc., which should never be considered as qualities of things, but as modifications of the subject, and which therefore may be different with different people. For in this case that which originally is itself a phenomenon only, as for instance, a rose, is taken by the empirical understanding for a thing by itself, which nevertheless, with regard to colour, may appear different to every eye. The transcendental conception, on the contrary, of all phenomena in space, is a critical warning that nothing which is seen in space is a thing by itself, nor space a form of things supposed to belong to them by themselves, but that objects by themselves are not known to us at all, and that what we call external objects are nothing but representations of our senses, the form of which is space, and the true correlative of which, that is the thing by itself, is not known, nor can be known by these representations, nor do we care to know anything about it in our daily experience. A30

SECOND SECTION OF THE TRANSCENDENTAL ÆSTHETIC.

B46

Of Time.

1. Time is not an empirical concept deduced from any experience, for neither coexistence nor succession would enter into our perception, if the representation of time were not given *a priori.* Only when this representation *a priori* is given, can we imagine that certain things happen at the same time (simultaneously) or at different times (successively). A31

2. Time is a necessary representation on which all intuitions depend. We cannot take away time from phenomena in general, though we can well take away phenomena out of time. Time therefore is given *a priori.* In time alone is reality of phenomena possible.

All phenomena may vanish, but time itself (as the general condition of their possibility) cannot be done away with.

B47   3. On this *a priori* necessity depends also the possibility of apodictic principles of the relations of time, or of axioms of time in general. Time has one dimension only; different times are not simultaneous, but successive, while different spaces are never successive, but simultaneous. Such principles cannot be derived from experience, because experience could not impart to them absolute universality nor apodictic certainty. We should only be able to say that common experience teaches us that it is so, but not that it must be so. These principles are valid as rules under which alone experience is possible; they teach us before experience, not by means of experience.

4. Time is not a discursive, or what is called a general concept, but a pure form of sensuous intuition. Different times are parts
A32 only of one and the same time. Representation, which can be produced by a single object only, is called an intuition. The proposition that different times cannot exist at the same time cannot be deduced from any general concept. Such a proposition is synthetical, and cannot be deduced from concepts only. It is contained immediately in the intuition and representation of time.

5. To say that time is infinite means no more than that every definite quantity of time is possible only by limitations of one time
B48 which forms the foundation of all times. The original representation of time must therefore be given as unlimited. But when the parts themselves and every quantity of an object can be represented as determined by limitation only, the whole representation cannot be given by concepts (for in that case the partial representations come first), but it must be founded on immediate intuition.

§ 5.

Transcendental Exposition of the concept of time.

I can here refer to No. III. p. 27, where, for the sake of brevity, I have placed what is properly transcendental under the head of metaphysical exposition. Here I only add that the concept of change, and with it the concept of motion (as change of place), is possible only through and in the representation of time; and that, if this representation were not intuitive (internal) *a priori*, no concept, whatever it be, could make us understand the possibility of a change, that is, of a connection of contradictorily opposed predicates (for instance, the being and not-being of one and the same thing in one and the same place) in one and the same object. It is only in time that both contradictorily opposed determinations can be met with in the same object, that is, one after the other. Our concept of time, therefore, exhibits the possibility of as many synthetical cognitions *a priori* as are found in the general doctrine of motion, which is very rich in them.

B49

Conclusions from the foregoing concepts. A32

a. Time is not something existing by itself, or inherent in things as an objective determination of them, something therefore that might remain when abstraction is made of all subjective conditions of intuition. For in the former case it would be something real, without being a real object. In the latter it could not, as a determination or order inherent in things themselves, be antecedent to things as their condition, and be known and perceived by means of synthetical propositions *a priori*. All this is perfectly possible if time is nothing but a subjective condition under which all intuitions take place within us. For in that case this form of internal intuition can be represented prior to the objects themselves, that is, *a priori*.

A33

b. Time is nothing but the form of the internal sense, that is, of our intuition of ourselves, and of our internal state. Time cannot be a determination peculiar to external phenomena. It refers neither to their shape, nor their position, etc., it only determines the relation of representations in our internal state. And exactly because this internal intuition supplies no shape, we try to make good this deficiency by means of analogies, and represent to ourselves the succession of time by a line progressing to infinity, in which the manifold constitutes a series of one dimension only; and we conclude from the properties of this line as to all the properties of time, with one exception, i.e. that the parts of the former are simul-

B50

taneous, those of the latter successive. From this it becomes clear also, that the representation of time is itself an intuition, because all its relations can be expressed by means of an external intuition.

c. Time is the formal condition, *a priori,* of all phenomena what-
A34 soever. Space, as the pure form of all external intuition, is a condi-
tion, *a priori,* of external phenomena only. But, as all representations, whether they have for their objects external things or not, belong by themselves, as determinations of the mind, to our inner state, and as this inner state falls under the formal conditions of internal intu-ition, and therefore of time, time is a condition, *a priori,* of all phe-nomena whatsoever, and is so directly as a condition of internal phenomena (of our mind) and thereby indirectly of external phe-nomena also. If I am able to say, *a priori,* that all external phenomena are in space, and are determined, *a priori,* according to the relations
B51 of space, I can, according to the principle of the internal sense, make the general assertion that all phenomena, that is, all objects of the senses, are in time, and stand necessarily in relations of time.

If we drop our manner of looking at ourselves internally, and of comprehending by means of that intuition all external intuitions also within our power of representation, and thus take objects as they may be by themselves, then time is nothing. Time has objec-tive validity with reference to phenomena only, because these are
A35 themselves things which we accept as objects of our senses; but time is no longer objective, if we remove the sensuous character of our intuitions, that is to say, that mode of representation which is peculiar to ourselves, and speak of things in general. Time is there-fore simply a subjective condition of our (human) intuition (which is always sensuous, that is so far as we are affected by objects), but by itself, apart from the subject, nothing. Nevertheless, with respect to all phenomena, that is, all things which can come within our ex-
B52 perience, time is necessarily objective. We cannot say that all things are in time, because, if we speak of things in general, nothing is said about the manner of intuition, which is the real condition under which time enters into our representation of things. If therefore this condition is added to the concept, and if we say that all things as phenomena (as objects of sensuous intuition) are in time, then

such a proposition has its full objective validity and *a priori* universality.

What we insist on therefore is the empirical reality of time, that is, its objective validity, with reference to all objects which can ever come before our senses. And as our intuition must at all times be sensuous, no object can ever fall under our experience that does not come under the conditions of time. What we deny is, that time has any claim on absolute reality, so that, without taking into account A36 the form of our sensuous condition, it should by itself be a condition or quality inherent in things; for such qualities which belong to things by themselves can never be given to us through the senses. This is what constitutes the transcendental ideality of time, so that, if we take no account of the subjective conditions of our sensuous intuitions, time is nothing, and cannot be added to the objects by themselves (without their relation to our intuition) whether as subsisting or inherent. This ideality of time, however, as well as that of space, should not be confounded with the deceptions of our sensations, because in their case we always suppose that the phenomenon to which such predicates belong has objective reality, which is B53 not at all the case here, except so far as the phenomenon is purely empirical, that is, so far as the object itself is looked upon as a mere phenomenon. On this subject see a previous note, in section i, on Space.

TRANSCENDENTAL ANALYTIC
ANALYTIC OF CONCEPTS.

CHAPTER I.
METHOD OF DISCOVERING ALL PURE
CONCEPTS OF THE UNDERSTANDING.

When we watch any faculty of knowledge, different concepts, characteristic of that faculty, manifest themselves according to different circumstances, which, as the observation has been carried on for a longer or shorter time, or with more or less accuracy, may be gathered up into a more or less complete collection. Where this collection will be complete, it is impossible to say beforehand, when we follow this almost mechanical process. Concepts thus dis-
covered fortuitously only, possess neither order nor systematic unity, but are paired in the end according to similarities, and, according to their contents, arranged as more or less complex in various series, which are nothing less than systematical, though to a certain extent put together methodically.

Transcendental philosophy has the advantage, but also the duty of discovering its concepts according to a fixed principle. As they spring pure and unmixed from the understanding as an absolute unity, they must be connected with each other, according to *one* concept or idea. This connection supplies us at the same time with a rule, according to which the place of each pure concept of the understanding and the systematical completeness of all of them can be determined *a priori*, instead of being dependent on arbitrary choice or chance.

TRANSCENDENTAL METHOD OF THE DISCOVERY OF ALL PURE CONCEPTS OF THE UNDERSTANDING.

SECTION I.

Of the Logical Use of the Understanding in general.

We have before defined the understanding negatively only, as a non-sensuous faculty of knowledge. As without sensibility we can- A68 not have any intuition, it is clear that the understanding is not a faculty of intuition. Besides intuition, however, there is no other kind of knowledge except by means of concepts. The knowledge B93 therefore of every understanding, or at least of the human under-standing, must be by means of concepts, not intuitive, but discur-sive. All intuitions, being sensuous, depend on affections, concepts on functions. By this function I therefore mean the unity of the act of arranging different representations under one common repre-sentation. Concepts are based therefore on the spontaneity of thought, sensuous intuitions on the receptivity of impressions. The only use which the understanding can make of these concepts is to form judgments by them. As no representation, except the in-tuitional, refers immediately to an object, no concept is ever re-ferred to an object immediately, but to some other representation of it, whether it be an intuition, or itself a concept. A judgment is therefore a mediate knowledge of an object, or a representation of a representation of it. In every judgment we find a concept apply-ing to many, and comprehending among the many one single rep-resentation, which is referred immediately to the object. Thus in the judgment that all bodies are divisible, the concept of divisible applies to various other concepts, but is here applied in particular

to the concept of body, and this concept of body to certain phe-
A69   nomena of our experience. These objects therefore are represented mediately by the concept of divisibility. All judgments
B94   therefore are functions of unity among our representations, the
knowledge of an object being brought about, not by an immediate
representation, but by a higher one, comprehending this and several others, so that many possible cognitions are collected into one.
As all acts of the understanding can be reduced to judgments, the
understanding may be defined as *the faculty of judging*. For we saw
before that the understanding is the faculty of thinking, and thinking is knowledge by means of concepts, while concepts, as predicates of possible judgments, refer to some representation of an
object yet undetermined. Thus the concept of body means something, for instance, metal, which can be known by that concept. It
is only a concept, because it comprehends other representations,
by means of which it can be referred to objects. It is therefore the
predicate of a possible judgment, such as, that every metal is a
body. Thus the functions of the understanding can be discovered
in their completeness, if it is possible to represent the functions of
unity in *judgments*. That this is possible will be seen in the following section.

A70/   **METHOD OF THE DISCOVERY OF ALL PURE CONCEPTS OF**
B95   **THE UNDERSTANDING.**

SECTION II.

Of the Logical Function of the Understanding in Judgments.

If we leave out of consideration the contents of any judgment and
fix our attention on the mere form of the understanding, we find
that the function of thought in a judgment can be brought under
four heads, each of them with three subdivisions. They may be represented in the following table—

ranging different representations together, and of comprehending what is manifold in them under one form of knowledge. Such a synthesis is pure, if the manifold is not given empirically, but *a priori* (as in time and space). Before we can proceed to an analysis of our representations, these must first be given, and, as far as their contents are concerned, no concepts can arise analytically. Knowledge is first produced by the synthesis of what is manifold (whether given empirically or *a priori*). That knowledge may at first be crude and confused and in need of analysis, but it is synthesis which really collects the elements of knowledge, and unites them to a certain extent. It is therefore the first thing which we have to consider, if we want to form an opinion on the first origin of our knowledge.

A78

We shall see hereafter that synthesis in general is the mere result of what I call the faculty of imagination, a blind but indispensable function of the soul, without which we should have no knowledge whatsoever, but of the existence of which we are scarcely conscious. But to reduce this synthesis to concepts is a function that belongs to the understanding, and by which the understanding supplies us for the first time with knowledge properly so called.

B104

Pure synthesis in its most general meaning gives us the pure concept of the understanding. By this pure synthesis I mean that which rests on the foundation of what I call synthetical unity *a priori*. Thus our counting (as we best perceive when dealing with higher numbers) is a synthesis according to concepts, because resting on a common ground of unity, as for instance, the decade. The unity of the synthesis of the manifold becomes necessary under this concept.

B105

By means of analysis different representations are brought under one concept, a task treated of in general logic; but how to bring, not the representations, but the pure synthesis of representations, under concepts, that is what transcendental logic means to teach. The first that must be given us for the sake of knowledge of all objects *a priori*, is the manifold in pure intuition. The second is,

A79 the synthesis of the manifold by means of imagination. But this does not yet produce true knowledge. The concepts which impart unity to this pure synthesis and consist entirely in the representation of this necessary synthetical unity, add the third contribution towards the knowledge of an object, and rest on the understanding.

The same function which imparts unity to various representations in one judgment imparts unity likewise to the mere synthesis of various representations in one intuition, which in a general way may be called the pure concept of the understanding. The same understanding, and by the same operations by which in concepts it achieves through analytical unity the logical form of a judgment, introduces also, through the synthetical unity of the manifold in intuition, a transcendental element into its representations. They are therefore called pure concepts of the understanding, and they refer *a priori* to objects, which would be quite impossible in general logic. A80

In this manner there arise exactly so many pure concepts of the understanding which refer *a priori* to objects of intuition in general, as there were in our table logical functions in all possible judgments, because those functions completely exhaust the understanding and comprehend every one of its faculties. Borrowing a term of Aristotle, we shall call these concepts *categories*, our intention being originally the same as his, though widely diverging from it in its practical application.

TABLE OF CATEGORIES.

B106

I.

Of Quantity.

Unity.

Plurality.

Totality.

II

Of Quality.

Reality.

Negation.

Limitation.

III.

Of Relation.

Of Inherence and Subsistence
(substantia et accidens).

Of Causality and Dependence
(cause and effect).

Of Community
(reciprocity between
the active and the passive).

IV.

Of Modality.

Possibility.   Impossibility.

Existence.   Non-existence.

Necessity.   Contingency.

CHAPTER II.
OF THE DEDUCTION OF THE PURE CONCEPTS OF THE UNDERSTANDING.

§ 13.

Of the Principles of a Transcendental Deduction in general.

Jurists, when speaking of rights and claims, distinguish in every lawsuit the question of right (*quid juris*) from the question of fact (*quid facti*), and in demanding proof of both they call the former, which is to show the right or, it may be, the claim, the *deduction*. We, not being jurists, make use of a number of empirical concepts, without opposition from anybody, and consider ourselves justified, without any deduction, in attaching to them a sense or imaginary meaning, because we can always appeal to experience to prove their objective reality. There exist however illegitimate concepts also, such as, for instance, chance, or fate, which through an almost general indulgence are allowed to be current, but are yet from time to time challenged by the question quid juris. In that case we are greatly embarrassed in looking for their deduction, there being no clear legal title, whether from experience or from reason, on which their claim to employment could be clearly established.

Among the many concepts, however, which enter into the complicated code of human knowledge, there are some which are destined for pure use *a priori*, independent of all experience, and such a claim requires at all times a deduction, because proofs from experience would not be sufficient to establish the legitimacy of such a use, though it is necessary to know how such concepts can refer to objects which they do not find in experience. I call the explanation of the manner how such concepts can *a priori* refer to objects their transcendental deduction, and distinguish it from the empirical deduction which shows the manner how a concept may be gained by experience and by reflection on experience; this does not touch the legitimacy, but only the fact whence the possession of the concept arose.

We have already become acquainted with two totally distinct classes of concepts, which nevertheless agree in this, that they both refer *a priori* to objects, namely, the concepts of space and time as forms of sensibility, and the categories as concepts of the under- B118 standing. It would be labour lost to attempt an empirical deduction of them, because their distinguishing characteristic is that they refer to objects without having borrowed anything from experience A86 for their representation. If therefore a deduction of them is neces- sary, it can only be transcendental.

It is possible however with regard to these concepts, as with re- gard to all knowledge, to try to discover in experience, if not the principle of their possibility, yet the contingent causes of their production. And here we see that the impressions of the senses give the first impulse to the whole faculty of knowledge with re- spect to them, and thus produce experience which consists of two very heterogeneous elements, namely, matter for knowledge, de- rived from the senses, and a certain form according to which it is arranged, derived from the internal source of pure intuition and pure thought, first brought into action by the former, and then producing concepts. Such an investigation of the first efforts of our faculty of knowledge, beginning with single perceptions and rising to general concepts, is no doubt very useful, and we have to thank the famous Locke for having been the first to open the way B119 to it. A deduction of the pure concepts *a priori*, however, is quite impossible in that way. It lies in a different direction, because, with reference to their future use, which is to be entirely independent of experience, a very different certificate of birth will be required from that of mere descent from experience. We may call this at- tempted physiological derivation (which cannot properly be called A87 deduction, because it refers to a quaestio facti), the explanation of the possession of pure knowledge. It is clear therefore that of these pure concepts *a priori* a transcendental deduction only is possible, and that to attempt an empirical deduction of them is mere waste of time, which no one would think of except those who have never understood the very peculiar nature of that kind of knowledge.

But though it may be admitted that the only possible deduction B120 of pure knowledge *a priori* must be transcendental, it has not yet been proved that such a deduction is absolutely necessary. We have before, by means of a transcendental deduction, followed up the concepts of space and time to their very sources, and explained and defined their objective validity *a priori*. Geometry, however, moves along with a steady step, through every kind of knowledge *a priori*, without having to ask for a certificate from philosophy as to the pure legitimate descent of its fundamental concept of space. But it should be remarked that in geometry this concept is used with reference to the outer world of sense only, of which space is the pure form of intuition, and where geometrical knowledge, being based on *a priori* intuition, possesses immediate evidence, the objects being given through their very knowledge, and, so far as A88 their form is concerned, *a priori* in intuition. When we come however to the pure concepts of the understanding, it becomes absolutely necessary to look for a transcendental deduction, not only for them, but for space also, because they speak of objects, not through predicates of intuition and sensibility, but of pure thought *a priori*, and apply to objects generally, without any of the conditions of sensibility. Again, as these concepts of the pure understanding are not founded on experience, nor able to produce in intuition *a priori* any object on which, previous to all experience, their synthesis was founded, they not only excite suspicion with regard to the objective validity and the limits of their own applica- B121 tion, but render even the concept of space equivocal, because of an inclination to apply it beyond the conditions of sensuous intuition, which was the very reason that made a transcendental deduction of it, such as we gave before, necessary. Before the reader has made a single step in the field of pure reason, he must be convinced of the inevitable necessity of such a transcendental deduction, otherwise he would walk on blindly and, after having strayed in every direction, he would only return to the same ignorance from which he started. He must at the same time perceive the inevitable difficulty of such a deduction, so that he may not complain about obscurity A89 where the object itself is obscure, or weary too soon with our removal of obstacles, the fact being that we have either to surrender altogether all claims to the knowledge of pure reason—the most favourite field of all philosophers, because extending beyond the limits of all possible experience—or to bring this critical investigation to perfection.

It was easy to show before, when treating of the concepts of space and time, how these, though being knowledge *a priori*, refer necessarily to objects, and how they make a synthetical knowledge of them possible, which is independent of all experience. For, as no object can appear to us, that is, become an object of empirical intuition, except through such pure forms of sensibility, space and time are pure intuitions which contain *a priori* the conditions of the possibility of objects as phenomena, and the synthesis in these intuitions possesses objective validity.

B122

The categories of the understanding, on the contrary, are not conditions under which objects can be given in intuition, and it is quite possible therefore that objects should appear to us without any necessary reference to the functions of the understanding, thus showing that the understanding contains by no means any of their conditions *a priori*. There arises therefore here a difficulty, which we did not meet with in the field of sensibility, namely, how subjective conditions of thought can have objective validity, that is, become conditions of the possibility of the knowledge of objects. It cannot be denied that phenomena may be given in intuition without the functions of the understanding. For if we take, for instance, the concept of cause, which implies a peculiar kind of synthesis, consisting in placing according to a rule after something called A something totally different from it, B, we cannot say that it is *a priori* clear why phenomena should contain something of this kind. We cannot appeal for it to experience, because what has to be proved is the objective validity of this concept *a priori*. It would remain therefore *a priori* doubtful whether such a concept be not altogether empty, and without any corresponding object among phenomena. It is different with objects of sensuous intuition. They must conform to the formal conditions of sensibility existing *a priori* in the mind, because otherwise they could

A90

B123

in no way be objects to us. But why besides this they should conform to the conditions which the understanding requires for the
synthetical operations of thought, does not seem to follow quite
so easily. For we could quite well imagine that phenomena might
possibly be such that the understanding should not find them
conforming to the conditions of its synthetical unity, and all
might be in such confusion that nothing should appear in the succession of phenomena which could supply a rule of synthesis,
and correspond, for instance, to the concept of cause and effect,
so that this concept would thus be quite empty, null and mean-
A91 ingless. With all this phenomena would offer objects to our intuition, because intuition by itself does not require the functions of
thought.

It might be imagined that we could escape from the trouble of
these investigations by saying that experience offers continually
examples of such regularity of phenomena as to induce us to abstract from it the concept of cause, and it might be attempted to
prove thereby the objective validity of such a concept. But it
ought to be seen that in this way the concept of cause cannot possibly arise, and that such a concept ought either to be founded *a
priori* in the understanding or be surrendered altogether as a mere
B124 hallucination. For this concept requires strictly that something, A,
should be of such a nature that something else, B, follows from it
necessarily and according to an absolutely universal rule. Phenomena no doubt supply us with cases from which a rule becomes
possible according to which something happens usually, but never
so that the result should be necessary. There is a dignity in the
synthesis of cause and effect which cannot be expressed empirically, for it implies that the effect is not only an accessory to the
cause, but given by it and springing from it. Nor is the absolute
A92 universality of the rule a quality inherent in empirical rules,
which by means of induction cannot receive any but a relative
universality, that is, a more or less extended applicability. If we
were to treat the pure concepts of the understanding as merely
empirical products, we should completely change their character
and their use.

Transition to a Transcendental Deduction of the Categories.

Two ways only are possible in which synthetical representations and their objects can agree, can refer to each other with necessity, B125 and so to say meet each other. Either it is the object alone that makes the representation possible, or it is the representation alone that makes the object possible. In the former case their relation is empirical only, and the representation therefore never possible *a priori*. This applies to phenomena with reference to whatever in them belongs to sensation. In the latter case, though representation by itself (for we do not speak here of its causality by means of the will) cannot produce its object so far as its existence is concerned, nevertheless the representation determines the object *a priori*, if through it alone it is possible to know anything as an object. To know a thing as an object is possible only under two conditions. First, there must be intuition by which the object is given us, though as a phenomenon A93 only, secondly, there must a concept by which an object is thought as corresponding to that intuition. From what we have said before it is clear that the first condition, namely, that under which alone objects can be seen, exists, so far as the form of intuition is concerned, in the soul *a priori*. All phenomena therefore must conform to that formal condition of sensibility, because it is through it B126 alone that they appear, that is, that they are given and empirically seen.

Now the question arises whether there are not also antecedent concepts *a priori*, forming conditions under which alone something can be, if not seen, yet thought as an object in general; for in that case all empirical knowledge of objects would necessarily conform to such concepts, it being impossible that anything should become an object of experience without them. All experience contains, besides the intuition of the senses by which something is given, a concept also of the object, which is given in intuition as a phenomenon. Such concepts of objects in general therefore must form conditions *a priori* of all knowledge produced by experience, and the objective validity of the categories, as being such concepts *a priori*, rests on this very fact that by them alone, so far as the form of thought is concerned, experience becomes possible. If by them only it is possible to think any object of experience, it follows that they refer by necessity and *a priori* to all objects of experience.

A94   There is therefore a principle for the transcendental deduction of all concepts *a priori* which must guide the whole of our investigation, namely, that all must be recognised as conditions *a priori* of the possibility of experience, whether of intuition, which is found in it, or of thought. Concepts which supply the objective ground of the possibility of experience are for that very reason necessary. An analysis of the experience in which they are found would not be a deduction, but a mere illustration, because they would there have an accidental character only. Nay, without their original relation to

B127 all possible experience in which objects of knowledge occur, their relation to any single object would be quite incomprehensible.

A98

Preliminary Remark.

The deduction of the categories is beset with so many difficulties and obliges us to enter so deeply into the first grounds of the possibility of our knowledge in general, that I thought it more expedient, in order to avoid the lengthiness of a complete theory, and yet to omit nothing in so essential an investigation, to add the following four paragraphs with a view of preparing rather than instructing the reader. After that only I shall in the third section proceed to a systematical discussion of these elements of the understanding. Till then the reader must not allow himself to be frightened by a certain amount of obscurity which at first is inevitable on a road never trodden before, but which, when we come to that section, will give way, I hope, to a complete comprehension.

I.

Of the Synthesis of Apprehension in Intuition.

Whatever the origin of our representations may be, whether they be due to the influence of external things or to internal causes, whether they have arisen *a priori* or empirically as phenomena, as

A99 modifications of the mind they must always belong to the internal sense, and all our knowledge must therefore finally be subject to the formal condition of that internal sense, namely, time, in which they are all arranged, joined, and brought into certain relations to each other. This is a general remark which must never be forgotten in all that follows.

Every representation contains something manifold, which could not be represented as such, unless the mind distinguished the time in the succession of one impression after another; for as contained in one moment, each representation can never be anything but absolute unity. In order to change this manifold into a unity of intuition (as, for instance, in the representation of space), it is necessary first to run through the manifold and then to hold it together. It is this act which I call the synthesis of apprehension, because it refers directly to intuition which no doubt offers something manifold, but which, without a synthesis, can never make it such, as it is contained in *one* representation.

This synthesis of apprehension must itself be carried out *a priori* also, that is, with reference to representations which are not empirical. For without it we should never be able to have the representations either of space or time *a priori*, because these cannot be A100 produced except by a synthesis of the manifold which the senses offer in their original receptivity. It follows therefore that we have a pure synthesis of apprehension.

II.

Of the Synthesis of Reproduction in Imagination.

It is no doubt nothing but an empirical law according to which representations which have often followed or accompanied one another, become associated in the end and so closely united that, even without the presence of the object, one of these representations will, according to an invariable law, produce a transition of the mind to the other. This law of reproduction, however, presupposes that the phenomena themselves are really subject to such a rule, and that there is in the variety of these representations a sequence and concomitancy subject to certain rules; for without this the faculty of empirical imagination would never find anything to do that it is able to do, and remain therefore buried within our mind as a dead faculty, unknown to ourselves. If cinnabar were sometimes red and sometimes black, sometimes light and sometimes heavy, if a man could be changed now into this, now into another animal

A101 shape, if on the longest day the fields were sometimes covered with fruit, sometimes with ice and snow, the faculty of my empirical imagination would never be in a position, when representing red colour, to think of heavy cinnabar. Nor, if a certain name could be given sometimes to this, sometimes to that object, or if the same object could sometimes be called by one, and sometimes by another name, without any rule to which representations are subject by themselves, would it be possible that any empirical synthesis of reproduction should ever take place.

There must therefore be something to make this reproduction of phenomena possible by being itself the foundation *a priori* of a necessary synthetical unity of them. This becomes clear if we only remember that all phenomena are not things by themselves, but only the play of our representations, all of which are in the end determinations only of the internal sense. If therefore we could prove that even our purest intuitions *a priori* give us no knowledge, unless they contain such a combination of the manifold as to render a constant synthesis of reproduction possible, it would follow that this synthesis of the imagination is, before all experience, founded on principles *a priori,* and that we must admit a pure transcendental synthesis of imagination which alone forms the founda-

A102 tion of the possibility of all experience, such experience being impossible without the reproductibility of phenomena. Now, when I draw a line in thought, or if I think the time from one noon to another, or if I only represent to myself a certain number, it is clear that I must first necessarily apprehend one of these manifold representations after another. If I were to lose from my thoughts what precedes, whether the first parts of a line or the antecedent portions of time, or the numerical unities represented one after the other, and if, while I proceed to what follows, I were unable to reproduce what came before, there would never be a complete representation, and none of the before-mentioned thoughts, not even the first and purest representations of space and time, could ever arise within us.

The synthesis of apprehension is therefore inseparably connected with the synthesis of reproduction, and as the former constitutes the transcendental ground of the possibility of all knowledge (not only of empirical, but of pure *a priori* knowledge), it follows that a reproductive synthesis of imagination belongs to the transcendental acts of the soul. We may therefore call this faculty the transcendental faculty of imagination.

III.

Of the Synthesis of Recognition in Concepts. A103

Without our being conscious that what we are thinking now is the same as what we thought a moment before, all reproduction in the series of representations would be vain. Each representation would, in its present state, be a new one, and in no wise belonging to the act by which they are to be produced one after the other, and the manifold in it would never form a whole, because deprived of that unity which consciousness alone can impart to it. If in counting I forget that the unities which now present themselves to my mind have been added gradually one to the other, I should not know the production of a quantity by the successive addition of one to one, I should know nothing of number, this being a concept consisting entirely in the consciousness of that unity of synthesis.

The very word of concept (*Begriff*) could have suggested this remark, for it is the *one* consciousness which unites the manifold that has been perceived successively, and afterwards reproduced into one representation. This consciousness may often be very faint, and we may connect it in the effect only, and not in the act itself, with A104 the production of a representation. But in spite of this, that consciousness, though deficient in pointed clearness, must always be there, and without it, concepts, and with them, knowledge of objects are perfectly impossible.

B129

OF THE DEDUCTION OF THE PURE CONCEPTS OF THE UNDERSTANDING.

SECOND SECTION.

TRANSCENDENTAL DEDUCTION OF THE PURE CONCEPTS OF THE UNDERSTANDING.

§ 15.

Of the possibility of connecting (conjunctio) in general.

The manifold of representations may be given in an intuition which is purely sensuous, that is, nothing but receptivity, and the form of that intuition may lie *a priori* in our faculty of representation, without being anything but the manner in which a subject is affected. But the connection (conjunctio) of anything manifold can never enter into us through the senses, and cannot be contained, B130 therefore, already in the pure form of sensuous intuition, for it is a spontaneous act of the power of representation; and as, in order to distinguish this from sensibility, we must call it understanding, we see that all connecting, whether we are conscious of it or not, and whether we connect the manifold of intuition or several concepts together, and again, whether that intuition be sensuous or not sensuous, is an act of the understanding. This act we shall call by the general name of *synthesis,* in order to show that we cannot represent to ourselves anything as connected in the object, without having previously connected it ourselves, and that of all representations *connection* is the only one which cannot be given through the objects, but must be carried out by the subject itself, because it is an act of its spontaneity. It can be easily perceived that this act must be originally one and the same for every kind of connection, and that its dissolution, that is, the *analysis,* which seems to be its opposite, does always presuppose it. For where the understanding has not previously connected, there is nothing for it to disconnect, because, as connected, it could only be given by the understanding through the faculty of representation.

But the concept of connection includes, besides the concept of the manifold and the synthesis of it, the concept of the unity of the manifold also. Connection is representation of the *synthetical* unity of the manifold.[10]

The representation of that unity cannot therefore be the result B131 of the connection; on the contrary, the concept of the connection becomes first possible by the representation of unity being added to the representation of the manifold. And this unity, which precedes *a priori* all concepts of connection, must not be mistaken for that category of unity of which we spoke on p.[A68]; for all categories depend on logical functions in judgments, and in these we have already connection, and therefore unity of given concepts. The category, therefore, presupposes connection, and we must consequently look still higher for this unity as qualitative in that, namely, which itself contains the ground for the unity of different concepts in judgment, and therefore of the very possibility of the understanding in its logical employment.

§ 16.

The original synthetical unity of Apperception.

It must be *possible* that the *I think* should accompany all my representations: for otherwise something would be represented within B132 me that could not be thought, in other words, the representation would either be impossible or nothing, at least so far as I am concerned. That representation which can be given before all thought, is called *intuition*, and all the manifold of intuition has therefore a necessary relation to the *I think* in the same subject in which that manifold of intuition is found. That representation, however (intuition), is an act of *spontaneity*, that is, it cannot be considered as belonging to sensibility. I call it *pure apperception*, in order to distinguish it from empirical apperception, or *original apperception* also,

---

10 Whether the representations themselves are identical, and whether therefore one can B131 be thought analytically by the other, is a matter of no consequence here. The *consciousness* of the one has always to be distinguished from the consciousness of the other, so far as the manifold is concerned; and everything here depends on the synthesis only of this (possible) consciousness.

because it is that self-consciousness which by producing the representation, *I think*, which must accompany all others, and is one and the same in every act of consciousness, cannot itself be accompanied by any other. I also call the unity of it the transcendental unity of self-consciousness, in order to indicate that it contains the possibility of knowledge *a priori*. For the manifold representations in any given intuition would not all be in my representations, if they did not all belong to one self-consciousness. What I mean is that, as my representations (even though I am not conscious of them as such), they must be in accordance with that condition, under which alone they can stand together in one common self-consciousness, because otherwise they would not all belong to me. Much may be deduced from this original connection.

B133

Thus the unbroken identity of apperception of the manifold that is given in intuition contains a synthesis of representations, and is possible only through the consciousness of that synthesis. The empirical consciousness, which accompanies various representations, is itself various and disunited, and without reference to the identity of the subject. Such a relation takes place, not by my simply accompanying every relation with consciousness, but by my *adding* one to the other and being conscious of that act of adding, that is, of that synthesis. Only because I am able to connect the manifold of given representations in *one consciousness*, is it possible for me to represent to myself the *identity* of the *consciousness* in these *representations*, that is, only under the supposition of some synthetical unity of apperception does the analytical unity of apperception become possible.[11]

B134

11 This analytical unity of consciousness belongs to all general concepts, as such. If, for instance, I think *red* in general, I represent to myself a property, which (as a characteristic mark) may be found in something, or can be connected with other representations; that is to say, only under a presupposed possible synthetical unity can I represent to myself the ana-
B134 lytical. A representation which is to be thought as common to *different* representations, is looked upon as belonging to such as possess, besides it, something *different*. It must therefore have been thought in synthetical unity with other (though only possible) representations, before I can think in it that analytical unity of consciousness which makes it a conceptus communis. The synthetical unity of apperception is, therefore, the highest point with which all employment of the understanding, and even the whole of logic, and afterwards the whole of transcendental philosophy, must be connected; ay, that faculty is the understanding itself.

The thought that the representations given in intuition belong all of them to me, is therefore the same as that I connect them in one self-consciousness, or am able at least to do so; and though this is not yet the *consciousness* of the *synthesis* of representations, it nevertheless presupposes the possibility of the latter. In other words, it is only because I am able to comprehend the manifold of representations in one consciousness, that I call them altogether my representations, for otherwise, I should have as manifold and various a self as I have representations of which I am conscious. The synthetical unity of the manifold of intuitions as given *a priori* is therefore the ground also of the identity of that apperception itself which precedes *a priori* all definite thought. Connection, however, B135 does never lie in the objects, and cannot be borrowed from them by perception, and thus be taken into the understanding, but it is always an act of the understanding, which itself is nothing but a faculty of connecting *a priori*, and of bringing the manifold of given representations under the unity of apperception, which is, in fact, the highest principle of all human knowledge.

It is true, no doubt, that this principle of the necessary unity of apperception is itself identical, and therefore an analytical proposition; but it shows, nevertheless, the necessity of a synthesis of the manifold which is given in intuition, and without which it would be impossible to think the unbroken identity of self-consciousness. For through the Ego, as a simple representation, nothing manifold is given; in the intuition, which is different from that, it can be given only, and then, by *connection*, be thought in one consciousness. An understanding in which, by its self-consciousness, all the manifold would be given at the same time, would possess *intuition;* our understanding can do nothing but think, and must seek for its intuition in the senses. I am conscious, therefore, of the identical self with respect to the manifold of the representations, which are given to me in an intuition, because I call them, altogether, my representations, as constituting *one.* This means, that I am conscious of a necessary synthesis of them *a priori,* which is called the original synthetical unity of apperception under which all representations given to me must stand, but have to be brought there, first, by means of a synthesis. B136

§ 17.

The principle of the synthetical unity of Apperception is the highest principle of all employment of the Understanding.

The highest principle of the possibility of all intuition, in relation to sensibility, was, according to the Transcendental Æsthetic, that all the manifold in it should be subject to the formal conditions of space and time. The highest principle of the same possibility in relation to the understanding is, that all the manifold in intuition must be subject to the conditions of the original synthetical unity of apperception.[12]

All the manifold representations of intuition, so far as they are *given* us, are subject to the former, so far as they must admit of being connected in one consciousness, to the latter; and without that nothing can be thought or known, because the given representations would not share the act of apperception (I think) in common, and could not be comprehended in one self-consciousness.

The *understanding* in its most general sense is the faculty of *cognitions*. These consist in a definite relation of given representations to an object; and an *object* is that in the concept of which the manifold of a given intuition is *connected*. All such connection of representations requires of course the unity of the consciousness in the synthesis: consequently, the unity of consciousness is that which alone constitutes the relation of representations to an object, that is, their objective validity, and consequently their becoming cognitions, so that the very possibility of the understanding depends on it.

The first pure cognition of the understanding, therefore, on which all the rest of its employment is founded, and which at the

B137

---

12 Space and time, and all portions thereof, are *intuitions*, and consequently single representations with the manifold for their content. (See the Transcendental Æsthetic.) They are not, therefore, mere concepts, through which the same consciousness, as existing in many representations, but through which many representations, as contained in one, and in its consciousness (therefore as compounded) are brought to us; thus representing the unity of consciousness as *synthetical*, but yet as primitive. This character of *singleness* in them is practically of great importance.

same time is entirely independent of all conditions of sensuous intuition, is this very principle of the original synthetical unity of apperception. Space, the mere form of external sensuous intuition, is not yet cognition: it only supplies the manifold of intuition *a priori* for a possible cognition. In order to know anything in B138 space, for instance, a line, I must *draw* it, and produce synthetically a certain connection of the manifold that is given, so that the unity of that act is at the same time the unity of the consciousness (in the concept of a line), and is thus only known, for the first time, as an object (a determinate space). The synthetical unity of consciousness is, therefore, an objective condition of all knowledge; a condition, not necessary for myself only, in order to know an object, but one to which each intuition must be subject, in order to become an *object* for me, because the manifold could not become connected in one consciousness in any other way, and without such a synthesis.

No doubt, that proposition, as I said before, is itself analytical, though it makes synthetical unity a condition of all thought, for it really says no more than that all my representations in any given intuition must be subject to the condition under which alone I can ascribe them, as my representations, to the identical self, and therefore comprehend them, as synthetically connected, in one apperception through the general expression, *I think*.

And yet this need not be a principle for every possible understanding, but only for that which gives nothing manifold through its pure apperception in the representation, *I am*. An understanding B139 which through its self-consciousness could give the manifold of intuition, and by whose representation the objects of that representation should at the same time exist, would not require a special act of the synthesis of the manifold for the unity of its consciousness, while the human understanding, which possesses the power of thought only, but not of intuition, requires such an act. To the human understanding that first principle is so indispensable that it really cannot form the least concept of any other possible understanding, whether it be intuitive by itself, or possessed of a sensuous intuition, different from that in space and time.

§ 18.

What is the objective unity of Self-consciousness?

The transcendental *unity* of apperception connects all the manifold given in an intuition into a concept of an object. It is therefore called *objective*, and must be distinguished from the *subjective unity* of consciousness, which is a form of the *internal sense*, by which the manifold of intuition is empirically given, to be thus connected. Whether I can become *empirically* conscious of the manifold, as either simultaneous or successive, depends on circumstances, or empirical conditions. The empirical unity of consciousness, therefore, through the association of representations, is itself phenomenal and wholly contingent, while the pure form of intuition in time, merely as general intuition containing the manifold that is given, is subject to the original unity of the consciousness, through the necessary relation only of the manifold of intuition to the one, *I think*,—that is, through the pure synthesis of the understanding, which forms the *a priori* ground of the empirical synthesis. That unity alone is, therefore, valid objectively; the empirical unity of apperception, which we do not consider here, and which is only derived from the former, under given conditions in concreto, has subjective validity only. One man connects the representation of a word with one thing, another with another, and the unity of consciousness, with regard to what is empirical, is not necessary nor universally valid with reference to that which is given.

§ 19.

The logical form of all Judgments consists in the objective unity of Apperception of the concepts contained therein.

I could never feel satisfied with the definition of a judgment in general, given by our logicians, who say that it is the representation of a relation between two concepts. Without disputing with them in this place as to the defect of that explanation, which may possibly apply to categorical, but not to hypothetical and disjunctive judgments (the latter containing, not a relation of concepts, but of judgments themselves),—though many tedious consequences have arisen from this mistake of logicians,—I must at least make this observation, that we are not told in what that *relation* consists.[13]

But, if I examine more closely the relation of cognitions in every judgment, and distinguish it, as belonging to the understanding, from the relation according to the rules of reproductive imagination (which has subjective validity only), I find that a judgment is nothing but the mode of bringing given cognitions into the *objective* unity of apperception. This is what is intended by the copula *is*, B142 which is meant to distinguish the objective unity of given representations from the subjective. It indicates their relation to the original apperception, and their necessary *unity*, even though the judgment itself be empirical, and therefore contingent; as, for instance, bodies are heavy. By this I do not mean to say that these representations belong *necessarily* to each other, in the empirical intuition, but that they belong to each other by means of the *necessary unity* of apperception in the synthesis of intuitions, that is, according to the principles of the objective determination of all representations, so far as any cognition is to arise from them, these principles being all derived from the principle of the transcendental unity of apperception. Thus, and thus alone, does the relation become a *judgment*, that is, a relation that is valid objectively, and can thus be kept sufficiently distinct from the relation of the same representations, if it has subjective validity only, for instance, according to the laws of association. In the latter case, I could only say, that if I carry a body I feel the pressure of its weight, but not, that it, the body, is heavy, which is meant to say that these two representations are connected together, in the object, whatever the

13 The lengthy doctrine of the four syllogistic figures concerns categorical syllogisms only, and though it is really nothing but a trick for obtaining the appearance of more modes of concluding than that of the first figure, by secretly introducing immediate conclusions (consequentiæ immediatæ) among the premisses of a pure syllogism, this would hardly have secured its great success, had not its authors succeeded, at the same time, in establishing the exclusive authority of categorical judgments, as those to which all others must be referred. This, as we showed in § 9, p. 62, is wrong. [This passage, found at A73/B98–99, is not included in the present selections.]

PRINCIPLES OF PURE UNDERSTANDING

I.

AXIOMS OF INTUITION.

Their principle is: All intuitions are extensive quantities.

Proof.

All phenomena contain, so far as their form is concerned, an intuition in space and time, which forms the *a priori* foundation of all of them. They cannot, therefore, be apprehended, that is, received into empirical consciousness, except through the synthesis of the manifold, by which the representations of a definite space or time are produced, i.e. through the synthesis of the homogeneous, and the consciousness of the synthetical unity of that manifold (homogeneous). Now the consciousness of the manifold and homogeneous in intuition, so far as by it the representation of an object is first rendered possible, is the concept of quantity (quantum). Therefore even the perception of an object as a phenomenon is possible only through the same synthetical unity of the manifold of the given sensuous intuition, by which the unity of the composition of the manifold and homogeneous is conceived in the concept of a *quantity;* that is, phenomena are always quantities, and *extensive quantities;* because as intuitions in space and time, they must be represented through the same synthesis through which space and time in general are determined.

II.

ANTICIPATIONS OF PERCEPTION.

Their principle is: In all *phenomena* the *Real,* which is the *object of a sensation, has intensive quantity,* that is, a degree.

Proof.

Perception is empirical consciousness, that is, a consciousness in which there is at the same time sensation. Phenomena, as objects of perception, are not pure (merely formal) intuitions, like space and time (for space and time can never be perceived by themselves). They contain, therefore, over and above the intuition, the material for some one object in general (through which something existing in space and time is represented); that is, they contain the real of sensation, as a merely subjective representation, which gives us only the consciousness that the subject is affected, and which is referred to some object in general. Now there is a gradual transition possible from empirical to pure consciousness, till the real of it vanishes completely and there remains a merely formal consciousness (*a priori*) of the manifold in space and time; and, therefore, a synthesis also is possible in the production of the quantity of a sensation, from its beginning, that is, from the pure intuition = 0, onwards to any quantity of it. As sensation by itself is no objective representation, and as in it the intuition of neither space nor time can be found, it follows that though not an extensive, yet some kind of quantity must belong to it (and this through the apprehension of it, in which the empirical consciousness may grow in a certain time from nothing = 0 to any amount). That *quantity* must be *intensive*, and corresponding to it, an intensive quantity, i.e. a degree of influence upon the senses, must be attributed to all objects of perception, so far as it contains sensation.

III.

ANALOGIES OF EXPERIENCE.

Their principle is: Experience is possible only through the representation of a necessary connection of perceptions.

Proof.

Experience is empirical knowledge, that is, knowledge which determines an object by means of perceptions. It is, therefore, a synthesis of perceptions, which synthesis itself is not contained in the perception, but contains the synthetical unity of the manifold of the perceptions in a consciousness, that unity constituting the essential of our knowledge of the objects of the senses, i.e. of experience (not only of intuition or of sensation of the senses). In experience perceptions come together contingently only, so that no necessity of their connection could be discovered in the perceptions themselves, apprehension being only a composition of the manifold of empirical intuition, but containing no representation of the necessity of the connected existence of phenomena which it places together in space and time. Experience, on the contrary, is a knowledge of objects by perceptions, in which therefore the relation in the existence of the manifold is to be represented, not as it is put together in time, but as it is in time, objectively. Now, as time itself cannot be perceived, the determination of the existence of objects in time can take place only by their connection in time in general, that is, through concepts connecting them *a priori*. As these concepts always imply necessity, we are justified in saying that experience is possible only through a representation of the necessary connection of perceptions.

A. FIRST ANALOGY.   B224

Principle of the Permanence of Substance.

In all changes of phenomena the substance is permanent, and
its quantum is neither increased nor diminished in nature.

Proof.

All phenomena exist in time, and in it alone, as the substratum (as permanent form of the internal intuition) can *simultaneousness* as well as *succession* be represented. Time, therefore, in which all change of phenomena is to be thought, does not change, for it is that in which simultaneousness and succession can be represented as determinations of it. As time by itself cannot be perceived, it follows that the substratum which represents time in general, and in which all change or simultaneousness can be perceived in apprehension, through the relation of phenomena to it, must exist in the objects of perception, that is, in the phenomena. Now the substratum of all that is real, that is of all that belongs to the existence of things, is the *substance*, and all that belongs to existence can be conceived only as a determination of it. Consequently the permanent, in reference to which alone all temporal relations of phenomena can be determined, is the substance in phenomena, that is, what is real in them, and, as the substratum of all change, remains always the same. As therefore substance cannot change in existence, we were justified in saying that its quantum can neither be increased nor diminished in nature.

B232

B. SECOND ANALOGY.

Principle of the Succession of Time, according to the Law of Causality.

All changes take place according to the law of connection between cause and effect.

Proof.

(It has been shown by the preceding principle, that all phenomena in the succession of time are *changes* only, i.e. a successive being and not-being of the determinations of the substance, which is permanent, and consequently that the being of the substance itself, which follows upon its not-being, and its not-being, which follows on its being,—in other words, that an arising or perishing of the sub-

B233 stance itself is inadmissible. The same principle might also have been expressed thus: *all change [succession] of phenomena consists in modification only*, for arising and perishing are no modifications of the substance, because the concept of modification presupposes the same subject as existing with two opposite determinations, and therefore as permanent. After this preliminary remark, we shall proceed to the proof.)

I perceive that phenomena succeed each other, that is, that there is a state of things at one time the opposite of which existed at a previous time. I am therefore really connecting two perceptions in time. That connection is not a work of the senses only and of intuition, but is here the product of a synthetical power of the faculty of imagination, which determines the internal sense with reference to relation in time. Imagination, however, can connect those two states in two ways, so that either the one or the other precedes in time: for time cannot be perceived by itself, nor can we determine in the object empirically and with reference to time, what precedes and what follows. I am, therefore, conscious only that my imagina- B234 tion places the one before, the other after, and not, that in the object the one state comes before the other. In other words, the objective relation of phenomena following upon each other remains unde-termined by mere perception. In order that this may be known as determined, it is necessary to conceive the relation between the two states in such a way that it should be determined thereby with necessity, which of the two should be taken as coming first, and which as second, and not conversely. Such a concept, involving a necessity of synthetical unity, can be a pure concept of the under-standing only, which is not supplied by experience, and this is, in this case, the concept of the *relation of cause and effect*, the former de-termining the latter in time as the consequence, not as something that by imagination might as well be antecedent, or not to be per-ceived at all. Experience itself, therefore, that is, an empirical knowledge of phenomena, is possible only by our subjecting the succession of phenomena, and with it all change, to the law of causality, and phenomena themselves, as objects of experience, are consequently possible according to the same law only.

C. THIRD ANALOGY. B256

Principle of Coexistence, according to the Law of Reciprocity or Community.

All substances, so far as they can be perceived as coexistent in space, are always affecting each other reciprocally.

Proof.

Things are coexistent when, in empirical intuition, the perception of the one can follow upon the perception of the other, and *vice versa*, which, as was shown in the second principle, is impossible in B257

the temporal succession of phenomena. Thus I may first observe the moon and afterwards the earth, or, conversely also, first the earth and afterwards the moon, and because the perceptions of these objects can follow each other in both ways, I say that they are coexistent. Now coexistence is the existence of the manifold in the same time. Time itself, however, cannot be perceived, so that we might learn from the fact that things exist in the same time that their perceptions can follow each other reciprocally. The synthesis of imagination in apprehension would therefore, give us each of these perceptions as existing in the subject, when the other is absent, and *vice versa:* it would never tell us that the objects are coexistent, that is, that if the one is there, the other also must be there in the same time, and this by necessity, so that the perceptions may follow each other reciprocally. Hence we require a concept of the reciprocal sequence of determinations of things existing at the same time, but outside each other, in order to be able to say, that the reciprocal sequence of the perceptions is founded in the object, and thus to represent their coexistence as objective. The relation of substances, however, of which the first has determinations the ground of which is contained in the other, is the relation of influ-
B258 ence, and if, conversely also, the first contains the ground of determinations in the latter, the relation is that of community or reciprocity. Hence the coexistence of substances in space cannot be known in experience otherwise but under the supposition of reciprocal action: and this is therefore the condition also of the possibility of things as objects of experience.

B274 An important protest, however, against these rules for proving existence mediately is brought forward by *Idealism,* and this is therefore the proper place for its refutation.

Refutation of Idealism.

Idealism (I mean *material* idealism) is the theory which declares the existence of objects in space, without us, as either doubtful only and not demonstrable, or as false and impossible. The *former* is the *problematical* idealism of Descartes, who declares one empirical assertion only to be undoubted, namely, that of *I am;* the *latter* is the *dogmatical* idealism of Berkeley, who declares space and all things to which it belongs as an inseparable condition, as something impossible in itself, and, therefore, the things in space as mere imaginations. Dogmatic idealism is inevitable, if we look upon space as a property belonging to things by themselves, for in that case space and all of which it is a condition, would be a non-entity. The ground on which that idealism rests has been removed by us in the Transcendental Æsthetic. Problematical idealism, which asserts nothing, but only pleads our inability of proving any existence except our own by means of immediate experience, is reasonable and in accordance with a sound philosophical mode of thought, which allows of no decisive judgment, before a sufficient proof has been found. The required proof will have to demonstrate that we may have not only an *imagination,* but also an *experience* of external things, and this it seems can hardly be effected in any other way except by proving that even our internal experience, which Descartes considers as undoubted, is possible only under the supposition of external experience. B275

Theorem.

The simple, but empirically determined Consciousness of my own existence, proves the Existence of objects in space outside myself.

Proof.

I am conscious of my own existence as determined in time, and all determination in time presupposes something *permanent* in the perception. That *permanent,* however, cannot be an intuition within me, because all the causes which determine my existence, so far as they can be found within me, are representations, and as such require themselves something permanent, different from them, in reference to which their change, and therefore my existence in the time in which they change, may be determined. The perception of this permanent, therefore, is possible only through a thing *outside* me, and not through the mere *representation* of a thing outside me, and

B276 the determination of my existence in time is, consequently, possible only by the existence of real things, which I perceive outside me. As therefore the consciousness in time is necessarily connected with the consciousness of the possibility of that determination of time, it is also necessarily connected with the existence of things outside me, as the condition of the determination of time. In other words, the consciousness of my own existence is, at the same time, an immediate consciousness of the existence of other things.

NOTE 1.—It will have been perceived that in the foregoing proof the trick played by idealism has been turned against it, and with greater justice. Idealism assumed that the only immediate experience is the internal, and that from it we can no more than *infer* external things, though in an untrustworthy manner only, as always happens if from given effects we infer *definite* causes: it being quite possible that the cause of the representations, which are ascribed

B277 by us, it may be wrongly, to external things, may lie within ourselves. We, however, have proved that external experience is really immediate[14], and that only by means of it, though not the consciousness of our own existence, yet its determination in time, that is, internal experience, becomes possible. No doubt the representation of *I am*, which expresses the consciousness that can accompany all thought, is that which immediately includes the existence of a subject: but it does not yet include a *knowledge* of it, and therefore no empirical knowledge, that is, experience. For that we require, besides the thought of something existing, intuition also, and in this case internal intuition, in respect to which, that is, to time, the subject must be determined. For that purpose external objects are ab-

---

B276   14 The *immediate* consciousness of the existence of external things is not simply assumed in the preceding theorem, but proved, whether we can understand its possibility or not. The question with regard to that possibility would come to this, whether we have an internal

B277 sense only, and no external sense, but merely an external imagination. It is clear, however, that, even in order to imagine only something as external, that is, to represent it to the senses in intuition, we must have an external sense, and thus distinguish immediately the mere receptivity of an external intuition from that spontaneity which characterizes every act of imagination. For only to imagine an external sense would really be to destroy the faculty of intuition, which is to be determined by the faculty of imagination.

solutely necessary, so that internal experience itself is possible, mediately only, and through external experience.

NOTE 2.—This view is fully confirmed by the empirical use of our faculty of knowledge, as applied to the determination of time. Not only are we unable to perceive any determination of time, except through a change in external relations (motion) with reference to what is permanent in space (for instance, the movement of the B278 sun with respect to terrestrial objects), but we really have nothing permanent to which we could refer the concept of a substance, as an intuition, except *matter* only: and even this permanence is not derived from external experience, but presupposed *a priori* as a necessary condition of all determination of time, and therefore also as the determination of the internal sense with respect to our own existence through the existence of external things. The consciousness of myself, in the representation of the ego, is not an intuition, but a merely *intellectual* representation of the spontaneity of a thinking subject. Hence that ego has not the slightest predicate derived from intuition, which, as *permanent*, might serve as the correlate of the determination of time in the internal sense: such as *impermeability*, for instance, is with regard to matter, as an *empirical* intuition.

NOTE 3.—Because the existence of external objects is required for the possibility of a definite consciousness of ourselves, it does not follow that every intuitional representation of external things involves, at the same time, their existence; for such a representation may well be the mere effect of the faculty of imagination (in dreams as well as in madness), and is possible only through the reproduction of former external perceptions, which, as we have shown, is impossible without the reality of *external* objects. What we wanted to prove here was only that internal experience in general B279 is possible only through external experience in general. Whether this or that supposed experience be purely imaginary, must be settled according to its own particular determinations, and through a comparison with the criteria of all real experience.

THE ANTINOMY

FIRST CONFLICT OF THE

Thesis.

The world has a beginning in time, and is limited also with regard to space.

Proof.

For if we assumed that the world has no beginning in time, then an eternity must have elapsed up to every given point of time, and therefore an infinite series of successive states of things must have passed in the world. The infinity of a series, however, consists in this, that it never can be completed by means of a successive synthesis. Hence an infinite series of past worlds is impossible, and the beginning of the world a necessary condition of its existence. This was what had to be proved first.

With regard to the second, let us assume again the opposite. In that case the world would be given as an infinite whole of co-existing things. Now we cannot conceive in any way the extension of a quantum, which is not given within certain limits to every intuition,[15] except through the synthesis of its parts, nor the total of such a quantum in any way, except through a completed synthesis,

(continued on page 90)

15 We may perceive an indefinite quantum as a whole, if it is included in limits, without having to build up its totality by means of measuring, that is, by the successive synthesis of its parts. The limits themselves determine its completeness, by cutting off everything beyond.

OF PURE REASON.

TRANSCENDENTAL IDEAS.

Antithesis.

The world has no beginning and no limits in space, but is infinite, in respect both to time and space.

Proof.

For let us assume that it has a beginning. Then, as beginning is an existence which is preceded by a time in which the thing is not, it would follow that antecedently there was a time in which the world was not, that is, an empty time. In an empty time, however, it is impossible that anything should take its beginning, because of such a time no part possesses any condition of existence or non-existence to distinguish it from another (whether produced by itself or through another cause). Hence, though many a series of things may take its beginning in the world, the world itself can have no beginning, and in reference to time past is infinite.

With regard to the second, let us assume again the opposite, namely, that the world is finite and limited in space. In that case the world would exist in an empty space without limits. We should therefore have not only a relation of things *in space,* but also of things *to space.* As however the world is an absolute whole, outside
of which no object of intuition, and therefore no correlate of the world can be found, the relation of the world to empty space would

(continued on page 91)

Thesis.

or by the repeated addition of unity to itself.[16] In order therefore to conceive the world, which fills all space, as a whole, the successive synthesis of the parts of an infinite world would have to be looked upon as completed; that is, an infinite time would have to be looked upon as elapsed, during the enumeration of all co-existing things. This is impossible. Hence an infinite aggregate of real things cannot be regarded as a given whole, nor as a whole given at the same time. Hence it follows that the world is not infinite, as regards extension in space, but enclosed in limits. This was the second that had to be proved.

---

16 The concept of totality is in this case nothing but the representation of the completed synthesis of its parts, because, as we cannot deduce the concept from the intuition of the whole (this being in this case impossible), we can conceive it only through the synthesis of its parts, up to the completion of the infinite, at least in the idea.

Antithesis.

be a relation to *no object.* Such a relation, and with it the limitation of the world by empty space, is nothing, and therefore the world is not limited with regard to space, that is, it is unlimited in extension.[17]

17 Space is merely the form of external intuition (formal intuition) and not a real object that can be perceived prior to all things which determine it (fill or limit it), or rather which give an empirical intuition determined by its form. Space, under the name of absolute space, is nothing but a mere possibility of external phenomena, so far as they either exist by themselves, or can be added to given phenomena. Empirical intuition, therefore, is not a compound of phenomena and of space (perception and empty intuition). The one is not a correlate of the other in a synthesis, but the two are only connected as matter and form in one and the same empirical intuition. If we try to separate one from the other, and to place space outside all phenomena, we arrive at a number of empty determinations of external intuition, which, however, can never be possible perceptions; for instance, motion or rest of the world in an infinite empty space, or a determination of the mutual relation of the two, which can never be perceived, and is therefore nothing but the predicate of a mere idea.

OBSERVATIONS ON THE

I.

On the Thesis.

In exhibiting these conflicting arguments I have not tried to avail myself of mere sophisms for the sake of what is called special pleading, taking advantage of the want of caution of the opponent, and gladly allowing his appeal to a misunderstood law, in order to establish my own illegitimate claims on its refutation. Every one of our proofs has been deduced from the nature of the case, and no advantage has been taken of the wrong conclusions of dogmatists on either side.

I might have apparently proved my thesis too by putting forward, as is the habit of dogmatists, a wrong definition of the infinity of a given quantity. I might have said that the quantity is *infinite*, if no greater quantity (that is, greater than the number of given units contained in it) is possible. As no number is the greatest, because one or more units can always be added to it, I might have argued that an infinite given quantity, and therefore also an infinite world (infinite as regards both the past series of time and extension in space) is impossible, and therefore the world limited in space and time. I might have done this, but, in that case, my definition would not have agreed with the true concept of an infinite whole. We do not represent by it how large it is, and the concept of it is not therefore the concept of a *maximum*, but we conceive by it its relation only to any possible unit, in regard to which it is greater than any number. According as this unit is either greater or smaller, the infinite would be greater or smaller, while infinity, consisting in the relation only to this given unit, would always remain the same, although the absolute quantity of the whole would not be known by it. This, however, does not concern us at present.

(continued on page 94)

FIRST ANTINOMY.

II.

On the Antithesis.

The proof of the infinity of the given series, and of the totality of the world, rests on this, that in the opposite case an empty time, and likewise an empty space, would form the limits of the world. Now I am quite aware that people have tried to escape from this conclusion by saying that a limit of the world, both in time and space, is quite possible, without our having to admit an absolute time before the beginning of the world or an absolute space outside the real world, which is impossible. I have nothing to say against the latter part of this opinion, held by the philosophers of the school of Leibniz. Space is only the form of external intuition, and not a real object that could be perceived externally, nor is it a correlate of phenomena, but the form of phenomena themselves. Space, therefore, cannot exist absolutely (by itself) as something determining the existence of things, because it is no object, but only the form of possible objects. Things, therefore, as phenomenal, may indeed determine space, that is, impart reality to one or other of its predicates (quantity and relation); but space, on the other side, as something existing by itself, cannot determine the reality of things in regard to quantity or form, because it is nothing real in itself. Space therefore (whether full or empty[18]) may be limited by phenomena, but phenomena cannot be limited *by empty space* outside them. The same applies to time. But, granting all this, it cannot be

(continued on page 95)

---

18 It is easily seen that what we wish to say is that empty space, so far as limited *by phenomena*, that is, space *within* the world, does not at least contradict transcendental principles, and may be admitted, therefore, so far as they are concerned, though by this its possibility is not asserted.

Thesis.

The true transcendental concept of infinity is, that the successive synthesis of units in measuring a quantum, can never be completed.[19] Hence it follows with perfect certainty, that an eternity of real and successive states cannot have elapsed up to any given (the present) moment, and that the world therefore must have a beginning.

With regard to the second part of the thesis, the difficulty of an endless and yet past series does not exist; for the manifold of a world, infinite in extension, is given at *one and the same time.* But, in order to conceive the totality of such a multitude of things, as we cannot appeal to those limits which in intuition produce that totality by themselves, we must render an account of our concept, which in our case cannot proceed from the whole to the determined multitude of the parts, but has to demonstrate the possibility of a whole by the successive synthesis of the parts. As such a synthesis would constitute a series that would never be completed, it is impossible to conceive a totality either before it, or through it. For the concept of totality itself is in this case the representation of a completed synthesis of parts, and such a completion, and therefore its concept also, is impossible.

19 This quantum contains therefore a multitude (of given units) which is greater than any number; this is the mathematical concept of the infinite.

Antithesis.

denied that we should be driven to admit these two monsters, empty space outside, and empty time before the world, if we assumed the limit of the world, whether in space or time.

For as to the plea by which people try to escape from the conclusion, that if the world has limits in time or space, the infinite void would determine the existence of real things, so far as their dimensions are concerned, it is really no more than a covered attempt at putting some unknown *intelligible* world in the place of our *sensuous* world, and an existence in general, which *presupposes no other condition* in the world, in the place of a first beginning (an existence preceded by a time of non-existence), and *boundaries* of the universe in place of the limits of extension,—thus getting rid of time and space. But we have to deal here with the *mundus phænomenon* and its quantity, and we could not ignore the conditions of sensibility, without destroying its very essence. The world of sense, if it is limited, lies necessarily within the infinite void. If we ignore this, and with it, space in general, as an *a priori* condition of the possibility of phenomena, the whole world of sense vanishes, which alone forms the object of our enquiry. The *mundus intelligibilis* is nothing but the general concept of any world, which takes no account of any of the conditions of intuition, and which therefore admits of no synthetical proposition, whether affirmative or negative.

THE ANTINOMY

THIRD CONFLICT OF THE

Thesis.

Causality, according to the laws of nature, is not the only causality from which all the phenomena of the world can be deduced. In order to account for these phenomena it is necessary also to admit another causality, that of freedom.

Proof.

Let us assume that there is no other causality but that according to the laws of nature. In that case everything that *takes place,* presupposes an anterior state, on which it follows inevitably according to a rule. But that anterior state must itself be something which has taken place (which has come to be in time, and did not exist before), because, if it had always existed, its effect too would not have only just arisen, but have existed always. The causality, therefore, of a cause, through which something takes place, is itself an *event,* which again, according to the law of nature, presupposes an anterior state and its causality, and this again an anterior state, and so on. If, therefore, everything takes place according to mere laws of nature, there will always be a secondary only, but never a primary beginning, and therefore no completeness of the series, on the side of successive causes. But the law of nature consists in this, that nothing takes place without a cause sufficiently determined *a priori.* Therefore the proposition that all causality is possible according to the laws of nature only, contradicts itself, if taken in unlimited generality, and it is impossible, therefore, to admit that causality as the only one.

(continued on page 98)

OF PURE REASON.

TRANSCENDENTAL IDEAS.

Antithesis.

There is no freedom, but everything in the world takes place entirely according to the laws of nature.

Proof.

If we admit that there is *freedom*, in the transcendental sense, as a particular kind of causality, according to which the events in the world could take place, that is a faculty of absolutely originating a state, and with it a series of consequences, it would follow that not only a series would have its absolute beginning through this spontaneity, but the determination of that spontaneity itself to produce the series, that is, the causality, would have an absolute beginning, nothing preceding it by which this act is determined according to permanent laws. Every beginning of an act, however, presupposes a state in which the cause is not yet active, and a dynamically primary beginning of an act presupposes a state which has no causal connection with the preceding state of that cause, that is, in no wise follows from it. Transcendental freedom is therefore opposed to the law of causality, and represents such a connection of successive
states of effective causes, that no unity of experience is possible with it. It is therefore an empty fiction of the mind, and not to be met with in any experience.

We have, therefore, nothing but *nature*, in which we must try to find the connection and order of cosmical events. Freedom (independence) from the laws of nature is no doubt a *deliverance* from restraint, but also from the *guidance* of all rules. For we cannot say

(continued on page 99)

Thesis.

We must therefore admit another causality, through which something takes place, without its cause being further determined according to necessary laws by a preceding cause, that is an *absolute spontaneity* of causes, by which a series of phenomena, proceeding according to natural laws, begins by itself; we must consequently admit transcendental freedom, without which, even in the course of nature, the succession of phenomena on the side of causes, can never be perfect.

Antithesis.

that, instead of the laws of nature, laws of freedom may enter into the causality of the course of the world, because, if determined by laws, it would not be freedom, but nothing else but nature. Nature, therefore, and transcendental freedom differ from each other like legality and lawlessness. The former, no doubt, imposes upon the understanding the difficult task of looking higher and higher for the origin of events in the series of causes, because their causality is always conditioned. In return for this, however, it promises a complete and well-ordered unity of experience; while, on the other side, the fiction of freedom promises, no doubt, to the enquiring mind, rest in the chain of causes, leading him up to an unconditioned causality, which begins to act by itself, but which, as it is blind itself, tears the thread of rules by which alone a complete and coherent experience is possible.

OBSERVATIONS ON THE

I.

On the Thesis.

The transcendental idea of freedom is far from forming the whole content of the psychological concept of that name, which is chiefly empirical, but only that of the absolute spontaneity of action, as the real ground of imputability; it is, however, the real stone of offence in the eyes of philosophy, which finds its unsurmountable difficulties in admitting this kind of unconditioned causality. That element in the question of the freedom of the will, which has always so much embarrassed speculative reason, is therefore in reality *transcendental* only, and refers merely to the question whether we must admit a faculty of *spontaneously* originating a series of successive things or states. How such a faculty is possible need not be answered, because, with regard to the causality, according to the laws of nature also, we must be satisfied to know *a priori* that such a causality has to be admitted, though we can in no wise understand the possibility how, through one existence, the existence of another is given, but must for that purpose appeal to experience alone. The necessity of a first beginning of a series of phenomena from freedom has been proved so far only as it is necessary in order to comprehend an origin of the world, while all successive states may be regarded as a result in succession according to mere laws of nature.

But as thus the faculty of originating a series in time by itself has been proved, though by no means understood, it is now permitted also to admit, within the course of the world, different series, beginning by themselves, with regard to their causality, and to attribute to their substances a faculty of acting with freedom. But we must not allow ourselves to be troubled by a misapprehension,

(continued on page 102)

THIRD ANTINOMY.

II.

On the Antithesis.

He who stands up for the omnipotence of nature (transcendental *physiocracy*), in opposition to the doctrine of freedom, would defend his position against the sophistical conclusions of that doctrine in the following manner. *If you do not admit something mathematically the first in the world with reference to time, there is no necessity why you should look for something dynamically the first with reference to causality.* Who has told you to invent an absolutely first state of the world, and with it an absolute beginning of the gradually progressing series of phenomena, and this solely for the sake of giving to your imagination something to rest on, and to set limits to unlimited nature? As substances have always existed in the world, or as the unity of experience renders at least such a supposition necessary, there is no difficulty in assuming that a change of their states, that is, a series of their changes, has always existed, so that there is no necessity for looking for a first beginning either mathematically or dynamically. It is true we cannot render the possibility of such an infinite descent comprehensible without the first member to which everything else is subsequent. But, if for this reason you reject this riddle of nature, you will feel yourselves constrained to reject many synthetical fundamental properties (natural forces), which you cannot comprehend any more, nay, the very possibility of change in general would be full of difficulties. For if you did not know from experience that change exists, you would never be able to conceive *a priori* how such a constant succession of being and not being is possible.

And, even if the transcendental faculty of freedom might some-

(continued on page 103)

Thesis.

namely that, as every successive series in the world can have only a relatively primary beginning, some other state of things always preceding in the world, therefore no absolutely primary beginning of different series is possible in the course of the world. For we are speaking here of the absolutely first beginning, not according to time, but according to causality. If, for instance, at this moment I rise from my chair with perfect freedom, without the necessary determining influence of natural causes, a new series has its absolute beginning in this event, with all its natural consequences ad infinitum, although, with regard to time, this event is only the continuation of a preceding series. For this determination and this act do not belong to the succession of merely natural effects, nor are they a mere continuation of them, but the determining natural causes completely stop before it, so far as this event is concerned, which no doubt follows them, but does not *result* from them, and may therefore be called an absolutely first beginning in a series of phenomena, not with reference to time, but with reference to causality.

This requirement of reason to appeal in the series of natural causes to a first and free beginning is fully confirmed if we see that, with the exception of the Epicurean school, all philosophers of antiquity have felt themselves obliged to admit, for the sake of explaining all cosmical movements, a *prime mover*, that is, a freely acting cause which, first and by itself, started this series of states. They did not attempt to make a first beginning comprehensible by an appeal to nature only.

Antithesis.

how be conceded, to start the changes of the world, such faculty would at all events have to be outside the world, though it would always remain a bold assumption to admit, outside the sum total of all possible intuitions, an object that cannot be given in any possible experience. But to attribute in the world itself such a faculty to substances can never be allowed, because in that case the connection of phenomena determining each other by necessity and according to general laws, which we call nature, and with it the test of empirical truth, which distinguishes experience from dreams, would almost entirely disappear. For by the side of such a lawless faculty of freedom, nature could hardly be conceived any longer, because the laws of the latter would be constantly changed through the influence of the former, and the play of phenomena which, according to nature, is regular and uniform, would become confused and incoherent.

THE ANTINOMY OF PURE REASON.

Section IX.

Of the empirical use of the regulative Principle of Reason with regard to all Cosmological Ideas.

No transcendental use, as we have shown on several occasions, can be made of the concepts either of the understanding or of reason; and the absolute totality of the series of conditions in the world of sense is due entirely to a transcendental use of reason, which demands this unconditioned completeness from what it presupposes as a thing by itself. As no such thing by itself is contained in the world of sense, we can never speak again of the absolute quantity of different series in it, whether they be limited or in themselves unlimited; but the question can only be, how far, in the empirical regressus, we may go back in tracing experience to its conditions, in order to stop, according to the rule of reason, at no other answer of its questions but such as is in accordance with the object.

What therefore remains to us is only the *validity of the principle of reason,* as a rule for the continuation and for the extent of a possible experience, after its invalidity, as a constitutive principle of phenomena by themselves, has been sufficiently established. If we have clearly established that invalidity, the conflict of reason with itself will be entirely finished, because not only has the illusion which led to that conflict been removed through critical analysis, but in its place the sense in which reason agrees with itself and the misapprehension of which was the only cause of conflict, has been clearly exhibited, and a principle formerly *dialectical* changed into a *doctrinal* one. In fact, if that principle, according to its subjective meaning, can be proved fit to determine the greatest possible use of the understanding in experience, as adequate to its objects, this
would be the same as if it determined, as an axiom, (which is impossible from pure reason) the objects themselves *a priori:* for this also could not, with reference to the object of experience, exercise

a greater influence on the extension and correction of our knowledge, than proving itself efficient in the most extensive use of our understanding, as applied to experience.

I.

Solution of the Cosmological Idea of the totality of the composition of phenomena in an universe.

Here, as well as in the other cosmological problems, the regulative principle of reason is founded on the proposition that, in the empirical regressus, *no experience of an absolute limit,* that is, of any condition as such, which *empirically is absolutely unconditioned,* no quantity in the object, can clearly enough be distinguished from the regressus in infinitum.

I cannot say therefore that, as to time past or as to space, the world is infinite. For such a concept of quantity, as a given infinity, is empirical, and therefore, with reference to the world as an object of the senses, absolutely impossible. Nor shall I say that the regressus, beginning with a given perception, and going on to everything that limits it, as a series both in space and in time past, goes on *in infinitum,* because this would presuppose an infinite quantity of the world. Nor can I say again that it is *finite,* for the absolute limit is likewise empirically impossible. Hence it follows that I shall not be able to say anything of the whole object of experience (the world of sense), but only of the rule, according to which experience can take place and be continued in accordance with its object.

To the cosmological question, therefore, respecting the quantity of the world, the first and negative answer is, that the world has no first beginning in time, and no extreme limit in space.

For, in the contrary case, the world would be limited by empty time and empty space. As however, as a phenomenon, it cannot, by itself, be either,—a phenomenon not being a thing by itself,—we should have to admit the perception of a limitation by means of absolute empty time or empty space, by which these limits of the world could be given in a possible experience. Such an experience, however, would be perfectly void of contents, and therefore impossible. Consequently an absolute limit of the world is impossible empirically, and therefore absolutely also.[20]

From this follows at the same time the affirmative answer, that the regressus in the series of the phenomena of the world, intended as a determination of the quantity of the world, goes on in indefinitum, which is the same, as if we say, that the world of sense has no absolute quantity, but that the empirical regressus (through which alone it can be given on the side of its conditions) has its own rule, namely, to advance from every member of the series, as conditioned, to a more distant member, whether by our own experience, or by the guidance of history, or through the chain of causes and their effects; and never to dispense with the extension of the possible empirical use of the understanding, this being the proper and really only task of reason and its principles.

A522/
B550

We do not prescribe by this a definite empirical regressus advancing without end in a certain class of phenomena; as, for instance, that from a living person one ought always to ascend in a series of ancestors, without ever expecting a first pair; or, in the series of cosmical bodies, without admitting in the end an extremest sun. All that is demanded is a progressus from phenomena to phenomena, even if they should not furnish us with a real perception (if it is too weak in degree to become experience in our consciousness), because even thus they belong to a possible experience.

Every beginning is in time, and every limit of extension in space. Space and time, however, exist in the world of sense only. Hence phenomena only are limited *in the world* conditionally, the *world* itself, however, is limited neither conditionally nor unconditionally.

For the same reason, and because the world can never be given *complete*, and even the series of conditions of something given as conditioned cannot, as a cosmical series, *be given as complete*, the

20 It will have been observed that the argument has here been carried on in a very different way from the dogmatical argument, which was presented before, in the antithesis of the first antinomy. There we took the world of sense, according to the common and dogmatical view, as a thing given by itself, in its totality, before any regressus: and we had denied to it, if it did not occupy all time and all space, any place at all in both. Hence the conclusion also was different from what it is here, for it went to the real infinity of the world.

concept of the quantity of the world can be given through the re- A523/
gressus only, and not before it in any collective intuition. That re- B551
gressus, however, consists only in the *determining* of the quantity,
and does not give, therefore, any *definite* concept, nor the concept of
any quantity which, with regard to a certain measure, could be called
infinite. It does not therefore proceed to the infinite (as if given), but
only into an indefinite distance, in order to give a quantity (of experience) which has first to be realised by that very regressus.

II.

Solution of the Cosmological Idea of the totality of the division of a whole given in intuition.

If I divide a whole, given in intuition, I proceed from the conditioned to the conditions of its possibility. The division of the parts
(subdivisio or decompositio) is a regressus in the series of those conditions. The absolute totality of *this series* could only be given, if the
regressus could reach the *simple* parts. But if all parts in a continu-
ously progressing decomposition are always divisible again, then the
division, that is, the regressus from the conditioned to its conditions,
goes on in infinitum; because the conditions (the parts) are contained in the conditioned itself, and as that is given as complete in an A524/
intuition enclosed within limits, are all given with it. The regressus B552
must therefore not be called a regressus in indefinitum, such as was
alone allowed by the former cosmological idea, where from the conditioned we had to proceed to conditions outside it, and therefore
not given at the same time through it, but first to be added in the empirical regressus. It is not allowed, however, even in the case of a
whole that is divisible in infinitum, to say, *that it consists of infinitely
many parts.* For although all parts are contained in the intuition of
the whole, yet the *whole division* is not contained in it, because it
consists in the continuous decomposition, or in the regressus itself,
which first makes that series real. As this regressus is infinite, all
members (parts) at which it arrives, are contained, no doubt, in the
given whole as *aggregates;* but not so the *whole series of the division,*
which is successively infinite and never complete, and cannot,

therefore, represent an infinite number, or any comprehension of it as a whole.

It is easy to apply this remark to space. Every space, perceived within its limits, is such a whole the parts of which, in spite of all A525/ decomposition, are always spaces again, and therefore divisible *in* B553 *infinitum*.

From this follows, quite naturally, the second application to an external phenomenon, enclosed within its limits (body). The divisibility of this is founded on the divisibility of space, which constitutes the possibility of the body, as an extended whole. This is therefore divisible *in infinitum*, without consisting, however, of an infinite number of parts.

It might seem indeed, as a body must be represented as a substance in space, that, with regard to the law of the divisibility of space, it might differ from it, for we might possibly concede, that in the latter case decomposition could never do away with all composition, because in that case all space, which besides has nothing independent of its own, would cease to be (which is impossible), while, even if all composition of matter should be done away with in thought, it would not seem compatible with the concept of a substance that nothing should remain of it, because substance is meant to be the subject of all composition, and ought to remain in its elements, although their connection in space, by which they become a body, should have been removed. But, what applies to a thing by itself, represented by a pure concept of the understanding, does not apply to what is called substance, as a phenomenon. This is not an absolute subject, but only a permanent image of sensibil- A526/ ity, nothing in fact but intuition, in which nothing unconditioned B554 can ever be met with.

But although this rule of the progress *in infinitum* applies without any doubt to the subdivision of a phenomenon, as a mere occupant of space, it does not apply to the number of the parts, separated already in a certain way in a given whole, which thus constitute a *quantum discretum*. To suppose that in every organised whole every part is again organised, and that by thus dissecting the parts *in infinitum* we should meet again and again with new organised parts, in fact that the whole is organised *in infinitum*, is a thought difficult to think, though it is possible to think that the parts of matter decomposed *in infinitum* might become organised. For the infinity of the division of a given phenomenon in space is founded simply on this, that by it *divisibility* only, that is, an entirely indefinite number of parts, is given, while the parts themselves can only be given and determined through the subdivision, in short, that the whole is not itself already divided. Thus the division can determine a number in it, which goes so far as we like to go, in the regressus of a division. In an organic body, on the contrary, organised *in infinitum* the whole is by that very concept represented as divided, and a number of parts, definite in itself, and yet infinite, is found in it, before every regressus of division. This would be self-contradictory, because we should have to consider this infinite convolute as a never-to-be-completed series (infinite), and yet as complete in its (organised) comprehension. Infinite division takes the phenomenon only as a *quantum continuum*, and is inseparable from the occupation of space, because in this very occupation lies the ground of endless divisibility. But as soon as anything is taken as a *quantum discretum*, the number of units in it is determined, and therefore at all times equal to a certain number. How far the organisation in an organised body may go, experience alone can show us; but though it never arrived with certainty at any unorganised part, they would still have to be admitted as lying within possible experience. It is different with the transcendental division of a phenomenon. How far that may extend is not a matter of experience, but a principle of reason, which never allows us to consider the empirical regressus in the decomposition of extended bodies, according to the nature of these phenomena, as at any time absolutely completed.

A527/
B555

Concluding Remarks on the Solution of the Transcendental-mathematical Ideas, and Preliminary Remark for the Solution of the Transcendental-dynamical Ideas.

A528/
B556

When exhibiting in a tabular form the antinomy of pure reason, through all the transcendental ideas, and indicating the ground of the conflict and the only means of removing it, by declaring both contradictory statements as false, we always represented the conditions as belonging to that which they conditioned, according to relations of space and time, this being the ordinary supposition of the common understanding, and in fact the source from which that conflict arose. In that respect all dialectical representations of the totality in a series of conditions of something given as conditioned were always of the *same character*. It was always a series in which the condition was connected with the conditioned, as members of the same series, both being thus *homogeneous*. In such a series the regressus was never conceived as completed, or, if that had to be done, one of the members, being in itself conditioned, had wrongly to be accepted as the first, and therefore as unconditioned. If not always the object, that is, the conditioned, yet the series of its conditions was always considered according to quantity only, and then the difficulty arose (which could not be removed by any compromise, but only by cutting the knot), that reason made it either *too long or too short* for the understanding, which could in neither case come up to the idea.

But in this we have overlooked an essential distinction between the objects, that is, the concepts of the understanding, which reason tries to raise into ideas. Two of them, according to the above table of the categories, imply a *mathematical*, the remaining two a *dynamical* synthesis of phenomena. Hitherto this overlooking was of no great importance, because, in the general representation of all transcendental ideas, we always remained under *phenomenal* conditions, and with regard to the two transcendental-mathematical ideas also, we had to do with no object but the phenomenal only. Now, however, as we have come to consider the *dynamical* concepts of the understanding, so far as they should be rendered adequate to the idea of reason, that distinction becomes important, and opens to us an entirely new insight into the character of the suit in which reason is implicated. That suit had before been dismissed, as resting on both sides on wrong presuppositions. Now, however, as there seems to be in the dynamical antinomy such a presupposition as may be compatible with the pretensions of reason, and as the

A529/
B557

A530/
B558

judge himself supplies perhaps the deficiency of legal grounds, which had been misunderstood on both sides, the suit may possibly be adjusted, from this point of view, to the satisfaction of both parties, which was impossible in the conflict of the mathematical antinomy.

If we merely look to the extension of the series of conditions, and whether they are adequate to the idea, or whether the idea is too large or too small for them, the series are no doubt all homogeneous. But the concept of the understanding on which these ideas are founded contains either a *synthesis* of the *homogeneous* only (which is presupposed in the composition as well as the decomposition of every quantity), or of the *heterogeneous* also, which must at least be admitted as possible in the dynamical synthesis, both in a causal connection, and in the connection of the necessary with the contingent.

Thus it happens that none but sensuous conditions can enter into the mathematical connection of the series of phenomena, that is, conditions which themselves are part of the series; while the dynamical series of sensuous conditions admits also of a heterogeneous condition, which is not a part of the series, but, as merely intelligible, outside it; so that a certain satisfaction is given to reason by the unconditioned being placed before the phenomena, without disturbing the series of the phenomena, which must always be conditioned, or breaking it off, contrary to the principles of the understanding.

A531 / B559

Owing to the dynamical ideas admitting of a condition of the phenomena outside their series, that is, a condition which itself is not a phenomenon, something arises which is totally different from the result of the mathematical[21] antinomy. The result of that antinomy was, that both the contradictory dialectical statements had to be declared false. The throughout conditioned character, however, of the dynamical series, which is inseparable from them as phenomena, if connected with the empirically unconditioned, but at the same time *not sensuous* condition, may give satisfaction to the

21 Mathematical, omitted in the First and Second Editions.

understanding on one, and the *reason* on the other side,[22] because the dialectical arguments which, in some way or other, required unconditioned totality in mere phenomena, vanish; while the propositions of reason, if thus amended, may *both be true*. This cannot be the case with the cosmological ideas, which refer only to a mathematically unconditioned unity, because with them no condition can be found in the series of phenomena which is not itself a phenomenon, and as such constitutes one of the links of the series.

III.

Solution of the Cosmological Ideas with regard to the totality of the derivation of Cosmical Events from their cause.

We can conceive two kinds of causality only, with reference to events, causality either of *nature* or of *freedom*. The former is the connection of one state in the world of sense with a preceding state, on which it follows according to a rule. As the *causality* of phenomena depends on conditions of time, and as the preceding state, if it had always existed, could not have produced an effect, which first takes place in time, it follows that the causality of the cause of that which happens or arises must, according to the principle of the understanding, have itself *arisen* and require a cause.

By freedom, on the contrary, in its cosmological meaning, I understand the faculty of beginning a state *spontaneously*. Its causality, therefore, does not depend, according to the law of nature, on another cause, by which it is determined in time. In this sense freedom is a purely transcendental idea, which, first, contains nothing derived from *experience*, and, secondly, the object of which cannot be determined in any *experience*; because it is a general rule, even of the possibility of all *experience*, that everything which happens has a

---

22 The understanding admits of no condition *among phenomena*, which should itself be empirically unconditioned. But if we might conceive an *intelligible condition*, that is to say, a condition, not belonging itself as a link to the series of phenomena, of something conditioned (as a phenomenon) without in the least interrupting the series of empirical conditions, such a condition might be admitted as *empirically unconditioned*, without interfering with the empirical continuous regressus.

cause, and that therefore the causality also of the cause, which *itself has happened* or arisen, must again have a cause. In this manner the whole field of experience, however far it may extend, has been changed into one great whole of nature. As, however, it is impossible in this way to arrive at an absolute totality of conditions in their causal connection, reason creates for itself the idea of spontaneity, or the power of beginning by itself, without an antecedent cause determining it to action, according to the law of causal connection.

It is extremely remarkable, that the practical concept of freedom is founded on the *transcendental idea of freedom*, which constitutes indeed the real difficulty which at all times has surrounded the question of the possibility of freedom. *Freedom*, in its *practical sense*, is the independence of our (arbitrary) will from the *coercion* through sensuous impulses. Our (arbitrary) will is *sensuous*, so far as it is *affected pathologically* (by sensuous impulses); it is called animal (*arbitrium brutum*), if *necessitated* pathologically. The human will is certainly sensuous, an *arbitrium sensitivum*, but not *brutum*, but *liberum*, because sensuous impulses do not necessitate its action, but there is in man a faculty of determination, independent of the necessitation through sensuous impulses. A534/ B562

It can easily be seen that, if all causality in the world of sense belonged to nature, every event would be determined in time through another, according to necessary laws. As therefore the phenomena, in determining the will, would render every act necessary as their natural effect, the annihilation of transcendental freedom would at the same time destroy all practical freedom. Practical freedom presupposes that, although something has not happened, it *ought* to have happened, and that its cause therefore had not that determining force among phenomena, which could prevent the causality of our will from producing, independently of those natural causes, and even contrary to their force and influence, something determined in the order of time, according to empirical laws, and originating *by itself* a series of events.

What happens here is what happens generally in the conflict of reason venturing beyond the limits of possible experience, namely, that the problem is not *physiological*, but *transcendental*. Hence the A535/ B563 question of the possibility of freedom concerns no doubt psychology; but its solution, as it depends on dialectical arguments of pure reason, belongs entirely to transcendental philosophy. In order to enable that philosophy to give a satisfactory answer, which it cannot decline to do, I must first try to determine more accurately its proper procedure in this task.

If phenomena were things by themselves, and therefore space and time forms of the existence of things by themselves, the conditions together with the conditioned would always belong, as members, to one and the same series, and thus in our case also, the antinomy which is common to all transcendental ideas would arise, namely, that that series is inevitably too large or too small for the understanding. The dynamical concepts of reason, however, which we have to discuss in this and the following section, have this peculiarity that, as they are not concerned with an object, considered as a quantity, but only with its *existence,* we need take no account of the quantity of the series of conditions. All depends here only on the dynamical relation of conditions to the conditioned, so that in the question on nature and freedom we at once meet with the difficulty, whether freedom is indeed possible, and whether, if it is possible, it can exist together with the universality of the natural law of causality. The question in fact arises, whether it is a proper disjunctive proposition to say, that every effect in the world must arise, *either* from nature, *or* from freedom, or whether *both* cannot coexist in the same event in different relations. The correctness of the principle of the unbroken connection of all events in the world of sense, according to unchangeable natural laws, is firmly established by the transcendental Analytic, and admits of no limitation. The question, therefore, can only be whether, in spite of it, freedom also can be found in the same effect which is determined by nature; or whether freedom is entirely excluded by that inviolable rule? Here the common but fallacious supposition of the *absolute reality* of phenomena shows at once its pernicious influence in embarrassing reason. For if phenomena are things by themselves, freedom cannot be saved. Nature in that case is the complete and sufficient cause determining every event, and its condition is always contained in that series of phenomena only which, together with their effect, are necessary under the law of nature. If, on the contrary, phenomena are taken A537/ for nothing except what they are in reality, namely, not things by B565 themselves, but representations only, which are connected with each other according to empirical laws, they must themselves have causes, which are not phenomenal. Such an intelligible cause, however, is not determined with reference to its causality by phenomena, although its effects become phenomenal, and can be determined by other phenomena. That intelligible cause, therefore, with its causality, is outside the series, though its effects are to be found in the series of empirical conditions. The effect therefore can, with reference to its intelligible cause, be considered as free, and yet at the same time, with reference to phenomena, as resulting from them according to the necessity of nature; a distinction which, if thus represented, in a general and entirely abstract form, may seem extremely subtle and obscure, but will become clear in its practical application. Here I only wished to remark that, as the unbroken *connection* of all phenomena in the context (woof) of nature, is an unalterable law, it would necessarily destroy all freedom, if we were to defend obstinately the reality of phenomena. Those, therefore, who follow the common opinion on this subject, have never been able to reconcile nature and freedom.

IDEA FOR A UNIVERSAL HISTORY WITH COSMOPOLITAN INTENT

[1784]

Translated by Carl J. Friedrich

No matter what conception one may form of the freedom of the will in metaphysics, the phenomenal appearances of the will, i.e., human actions, are determined by general laws of nature like any other event of nature. History is concerned with telling about these events. History allows one to hope that when history considers *in the large* the play of the freedom of human will, it will be possible to discover the regular progressions thereof. Thus (it is to be hoped) that what appears to be complicated and accidental in individuals, may yet be understood as a steady, progressive, though slow, evolution of the original predispositions of the entire species. Thus marriages, the consequent births and the deaths, since the free will seems to have such a great influence on them, do not seem to be subject to any law according to which one could calculate their number beforehand. Yet the annual (statistical) tables about them in the major countries show that they occur according to stable natural laws. It is like the erratic weather the occurrence of which cannot be determined in particular instances, although it never fails in maintaining the growth of plants, the flow of streams, and other of nature's arrangements at a uniform, uninterrupted pace. Individual human beings, each pursuing his own ends according to his inclination and often one against another (and even one entire people against another) rarely unintentionally promote, as if it were their guide, an end of nature which is unknown to them. They thus work to promote that which they would care little for if they knew about it.

Since men in their endeavors do not act like animals merely according to instinct, nor like rational citizens of the world according to an agreed plan, no planned history seems to be possible (as in the case of bees and beavers). It is hard to suppress a certain disgust 8:18 when contemplating men's action upon the world stage. For one finds, in spite of apparent wisdom in detail that everything, taken as a whole, is interwoven with stupidity, childish vanity, often with childish viciousness and destructiveness. In the end, one does not know what kind of conception one should have of our species which is so conceited about its superior qualities. Since the philosopher must assume that men have a flexible *purpose of their own,* it is left to him to attempt to discover an end of nature in this senseless march of human events. A history of creatures who proceed without a plan would be possible in keeping with such an end; the history would proceed according to such an end of nature.

We shall see whether we can succeed in discovering a guide to such a history. We shall leave it to nature to produce a man who would be capable of writing history in accordance with such an end. Thus nature produced a *Kepler* who figured out an unexpected way of subsuming the eccentric orbits of the planets to definite laws, and a *Newton* who explained these laws by a general cause of nature.

FIRST PROPOSITION

All natural predispositions of a creature are destined to unfold completely and according to their end. External observation and analysis confirms this proposition concerning all authority. An organ which is not to be used, a regulation which does not accomplish its purpose, these are self-contradictions in the teleological theory of nature. If we abandon this principle, we no longer have a nature working according to laws, but an aimlessly playing nature. Then the hapless accident takes the place of reason as guide.

SECOND PROPOSITION

In man (as the only rational creature on earth) those natural predispositions which aim at the use of reason shall be fully developed in the species, not in the individual. Reason in a creature is the capacity to enlarge the rules and purposes of the use of his resources far beyond natural
8:19   instinct. It does not recognize any boundary to its projects. It does not develop instinctively but requires trials, experience and infor-

mation in order to progress gradually from one level of understanding to the next. Therefore every man would have to live excessively long in order to learn how to make full use of all his faculties. Or, if nature has set man a short term of life (as is, in fact, the case), then (perhaps) nature requires a endless procession of begettings of which one transmits its enlightenment to another, in order finally to push the genus of human kind to that level of development which is appropriate to the purpose of nature. This time must, at least theoretically, be the target of the endeavors of man, because otherwise the natural faculties would have to be considered largely pointless and in vain. This would vitiate all practical principles, as it would suggest that nature, the wisdom of which serves as a principle in judging all other natural arrangements, would have to be suspected of childish play when it comes to man.

THIRD PROPOSITION

Nature has intended that man develop everything which transcends the mechanical ordering of his animal existence, entirely by himself and that he does not partake of any other happiness or perfection except that which he has secured himself by his own reason and free of instinct. Nature does not do things superfluously and is not extravagant in the employment of its means to its end. Since nature gave man reason and the freedom of will which rests upon reason, that serves to show clearly nature's purpose in regard to man's equipment. He must namely do it not led by instinct or provided and instructed by innate knowledge; but rather he must produce all this out of himself. The discovery of his food, of his clothing, of his external security and defense (for which nature gave man neither the horns of the bull, nor the claws of the lion, nor the teeth of the dog, but only hands), all pleasures that can make life agreeable, even his insight and intelligence, indeed, the kindness of his will should be achieved by man's own work. Nature 8:20 seems to have delighted in the greatest parsimony; she seems to have barely provided man's animal equipment and limited it to the most urgent needs of a beginning existence, as if nature intended that man should owe all to himself, as though he should eventually struggle up from the greatest backwardness to the greatest skills, to inner perfection of mind, and (as far as it is possible on earth) to blessed happiness. Man alone should have the credit (for having accomplished this), as if nature were more concerned with man's rational *self-esteem* than with his well-being. In the course of human affairs a vast amount of hardship awaits man. It seems as though nature had not cared that man live well, but that by progressing thus far man would prove himself through his conduct worthy of life and well-being. However, it remains perplexing that earlier generations seem to do their laborious work for the sake of later generations, in order to provide a foundation from which the latter can advance the building which nature has intended. Only later generations will have the good fortune to live in the building. But however mysterious this may be, it is nevertheless necessary, if one assumes that an animal species is to have reason, and is to arrive at a complete development of its faculties as a class of reasonable beings who die while their species is immortal.

FOURTH PROPOSITION

The means which nature employs to accomplish the development of all faculties is the antagonism of men in society, since this antagonism becomes, in the end, the cause of a lawful order of this society. I mean by antagonism the unsociable sociability of man, i.e., the propensity of men to enter into a society, which propensity is, however, linked to a constant mutual resistance which threatens to dissolve this society. This propensity apparently is innate in man. Man has an inclination to *associate* himself, because in such a state he feels himself more like a man capable of developing his natural faculties. Man has also a marked propensity to *isolate* himself, because he finds in himself the unsociable quality to want to arrange everything according to his own ideas. He therefore expects resistance everywhere, just as he knows of himself that he is inclined to resist others. This resistance awakens all the latent forces in man which drive him to overcome his propensity to be lazy, and so, impelled by vainglory, ambition and avarice, he seeks to achieve a standing among his fellows, whom he does not suffer gladly, but whom he cannot *leave*. Thus the first steps from bar-

8:21

barism to culture are achieved; for culture actually consists in the social value of man. All man's talents are gradually unfolded, taste is
developed. Through continuous enlightenment the basis is laid for a
frame of mind which, in the course of time, transforms the raw natural faculty of moral discrimination into definite practical principles. Thus a *pathologically* enforced co-ordination of society finally
transforms it into a *moral* whole. Without these essentially unlovely
qualities of unsociability, from which springs the resistance which
everyone must encounter in his egoistic pretensions, all talents
would have remained hidden germs. If man lived an Arcadian shep-
herd's existence of harmony, modesty and mutuality, man, good-
natured like the sheep he is herding, would not invest his existence
with greater value than that his animals have. Man would not fill the
vacuum of creation as regards his end, rational nature. Thanks are
due to nature for his quarrelsomeness, his enviously competitive
vanity, and for his insatiable desire to possess or to rule, for without
them all the excellent natural faculties of mankind would forever remain undeveloped. Man wants concord, but nature knows better
what is good for his kind; nature wants discord. Man wants to live
comfortably and pleasurably but nature intends that he should raise
himself out of lethargy and inactive contentment into work and
trouble and then he should find means of extricating himself
adroitly from these latter. The natural impulses, the sources of unsociability and continuous resistance from which so many evils spring,
but which at the same time drive man to a new exertion of his pow- 8:22
ers and thus to a development of his natural faculties, suggest the
arrangement of a wise creator and not the hand of an evil spirit who
might have ruined this excellent enterprise or spoiled it out of envy.

FIFTH PROPOSITION

*The latest problem for mankind, the solution of which nature forces him to
seek, is the achievement of a civil society which administers right* (Recht)
generally. Nature can achieve its other intentions regarding mankind
only through the solution and fulfilment of this task, for a completely *just civil constitution* is the highest task nature has set

mankind. This is because only under such a constitution can there be achieved the supreme objective of nature, namely, the development of all the faculties of man by his own effort. It is also nature's intent that man should secure all these ends by himself only in a society which not only possesses the greatest freedom and hence a very general antagonism of its members but also possesses the most precise determination and enforcement of the limit of this freedom so that it can coexist with the freedom of other societies: this will serve the highest purpose of nature.

In other words, a society in which *freedom under external laws* is found combined in the highest degree with irresistible force, that is to say, a perfectly *just civil constitution*, must be the supreme task nature has set for mankind. Only through the solution and fulfilment of this task can nature hope to achieve its other objectives concerning man. Want forces man, who so greatly inclines toward unrestricted freedom, to enter into this state of constraint. It takes the greatest want of all to bring men to the point where they cannot live alongside each other in wild freedom but within such an enclosure as the civil association provides. These very same inclinations afterwards have a very good effect. It is like the trees in a forest which, since each seeks to take air and sun away from the other, compel each other to seek both and thus they achieve a beautiful straight growth. Whereas those that develop their branches as they please, in freedom and apart from each other, grow crooked and twisted. All culture and art which adorn mankind, the most beautiful social order, are the fruits of unsociability which is self-compelled to discipline itself and thus through a derived art to fulfill completely the germs of its nature.

8:23

SIXTH PROPOSITION

This problem is the most difficult and at the same time the one which mankind solves last. The difficulty which even the mere idea of this task clearly reveals is the following: Man is an animal who, if he lives among others of his kind, *needs a master*, for man certainly misuses his freedom in regard to others of his kind and, even though as a rational being he desires a law which would provide limits for the freedom of all, his egoistic animal inclination misguides him into excluding himself where he can. Man therefore *needs* a master who can break man's will and compel him to obey a general will under which every man could be free. But where is he to get this master? Nowhere else but from mankind. But then this master is in turn an animal who needs a master. Therefore one cannot see how man, try as he will, could secure a master maintaining public justice who would be himself just. This is true whether one seeks to discover such a master in a single person or in a group of elected persons. For each of these will always abuse his freedom if he has no one over him who wields power according to the laws. Yet the highest master is supposed to be *just in himself* and yet a *man*. The task involved is therefore most difficult; indeed, a complete solution is impossible. One cannot fashion something absolutely straight from wood which is as crooked as that of which man is made. Nature has imposed upon us the task of approximating this idea.[1] That his task should be the latest that man achieves follows from yet another consideration: the *right conceptions* regarding the nature of a possible constitution. Great *experience* in many activities and a *good will* which is prepared to accept such a constitution are all required. Obviously it will be very difficult, and if it happens it will be very late and after many unsuccessful attempts that three such things are found together.

SEVENTH PRINCIPLE   8:24

The problem of the establishment of a perfect civil constitution depends upon the problem of a lawful external relationship of the states and cannot be solved without the latter. What use is it to work out a lawful civil constitution among individual men, that is, to order a commonwealth?

1 The rule of man is therefore very artificial. We do not know how things are arranged with the inhabitants of other planets and their nature but if we execute this mandate of nature well we may properly flatter ourselves that we occupy a not inconsiderable position among our neighbors in the cosmos. Perhaps with these neighbors an individual can achieve his destiny in his own life. With us mortals it is different: only the species can hope to do so.

For the very same unsociability which compelled man to do this is again the cause of the fact that each commonwealth in its external relations, that is to say, as a state in relation to other states, is in a condition of unrestricted freedom. Consequently, one commonwealth must expect from the others the very same evils which oppress individual human beings and which compelled them to enter into a lawful civil state. Nature has again used incompatibility in this case that of the great societies and states, as a means for discovering a condition of quiet and security through the very *antagonism* inevitable among them. That is to say, wars, the excessive and never-ending preparation for wars, and the want which every state even in the midst of peace must feel—all these are means by which nature instigates attempts, which at first are inadequate, but which, after many devastations, reversals and a very general exhaustion of the states' resources, may accomplish what reason could have suggested to them without so much sad experience, namely; to leave the lawless state of savages and to enter into a union of nations wherein each, even the smallest state, could expect to derive its security and rights—not from its own power or its own legal judgment—but only from this great union of nations (*Foedus Amphictyonum*) and from united power and decisions according to the united will of them all. However fanciful this idea may seem and as such may have been ridiculed when held by the Abbé St. Pierre and Rousseau (perhaps because they believed the idea to be too near its realization), it is, nevertheless, the inevitable escape from the destitution into which human beings plunge each other. It is this which must compel states to the resolution to seek quiet and security through a lawful constitution (however hard it may be for them) and to do that which the wild man is so very reluctantly forced to do, namely, to give up his brutal freedom.

8:25   All wars are therefore so many attempts (not in the intention of men, but in the intention of nature) to bring about new relations among the states and to form new bodies by the breakup of the old states to the point where they cannot again maintain themselves alongside each other and must therefore suffer revolutions until finally, partly through the best possible arrangement of the civil constitution internally, and partly through the common agreement and legislation externally, there is created a state which, like a civil commonwealth, can maintain itself automatically.

(The question) whether one should expect that, from an Epicurean influence of efficient causes, the states, like small fragments of matter, by their accidental collision, make all kinds of formations which are destroyed again by a new impact until eventually and *accidentally* there occurs a formation which can maintain itself in its form (by a lucky accident which will hardly ever occur!); or whether one should rather assume that nature follows a regular sequence to lead our species from the lowest level of animality gradually to the highest level of humanity by man's own, though involuntary, effort and that thus nature is unfolding in this seemingly wild disorder man's original faculties quite according to rule; or whether one prefers to assume that all these effects and countereffects will in the long run result in nothing, or at least nothing sensible, and that things will remain as they always have been and therefore one cannot predict that the discord which is natural to the species is in the end preparing for us a hell of evils, evil in an ever so civilized state because perhaps nature will destroy, by barbaric devastation, this state and all advances of culture (a fate which one may well suffer with the government of blind accident which is indeed identical with lawless freedom if no wisely conceived direction of nature is imputed thereto)—these three alternatives, in the last analysis, amount to the question: Whether it be reasonable to assume that nature is purposive in its parts but (as a whole) unpurposive to its end?

Therefore, the feckless condition of the savages did in holding 8:26 back all the natural predispositions of our species, but which finally forced them, through the ill into which this placed them, of coming out of this state and entering into a civil constitution on which all their germs could be developed, what is also being effected by the barbarian freedom of the states which have been instituted; by the employment of all the resources of the commonwealth for armaments against one another, by the devastation which war is causing, but even more by the necessity of being constantly prepared for war. The full development of man's natural predispositions is being inhibited by the evils which spring from these conditions which compel our species to discover a counter-balance to the intrinsically healthy resistance of many states against each other resulting from their freedom and to introduce a united power which will give support to this balance. In other words these conditions compel our species to introduce a cosmopolitical state of public security which is not without all *danger*, [for we must see to it] that neither the vitality of mankind goes to sleep nor these states destroy each other as they might without a principle of balance of *equality* in their mutual *effects* and *counter-effects*. Before this last step, namely, the joining of the states, is taken, in other words, the half-way mark of mankind's development is reached; human nature is enduring the worst hardships under the guise of external welfare and *Rousseau* was not so very wrong when he preferred the condition of savages; provided one omits this last stage which our species will have to reach. We are highly civilized by art and science, we are civilized in all kinds of social graces and decency to the point where it becomes exasperating, but much (must be discarded) before we can consider ourselves truly ethicized. For the idea of morality is part of culture by the use that has been made of this idea which amounts only to something similar to ethics in the form of a love of honor and external decency (which) constitutes civilization. As long as states will use all their resources for their vain and violent designs for expansion and thus will continually hinder the slow efforts toward the inner shaping of the minds of their citizens, and even withdraw from their citizens all encouragement in this respect, we cannot hope for much because a great exertion by each commonwealth on behalf of the education of their citizens is required for this goal. Every pretended good that is not grafted upon a morally good frame of mind is nothing more than a pretense and glittering misery. Mankind will probably remain in this condition until, as I have said, it has struggled out of the chaotic condition of the relations among its states.

8:27

EIGHTH PROPOSITION

The history of mankind could be viewed on the whole as the realization of a hidden plan of nature in order to bring about an internally—and for this purpose also externally—perfect constitution; since this is the only state in which nature can develop all predispositions of mankind. This principle is a conclusion drawn from the previous principle. We can see that philosophy may also have its expectation of a millennium, but this millennium would be one for the realization of which philosophical ideas themselves may be helpful although only from afar. Therefore this expectation is hardly utopian. What matters is whether experience can discover some such progress of nature's intention. I would say *some small part;* for this revolution seems to require so much time that from the small distance which man has so far traversed one can judge only uncertainly the shape of the revolution's course and the relation of the parts to the whole. The situation is similar to that in astronomy where it is likewise difficult to determine from all the observations of the heavens up till now the course which our sun, with all its swarm of satellites, occupies in the system of fixed stars. But when one takes into account the general premise that the world is constituted as a system and considers what little has been observed one can say that the indications are sufficiently reliable to enable us to conclude that such a revolution is real. Our human nature has this aspect that it cannot be indifferent to even the most remote epoch at which our species may arrive if only that epoch may be expected with certainty. Furthermore, it is less feasible in our particular case since it seems that we could hasten by our own rational efforts the time when this state might occur which would be so enjoyable for our descendants. For that reason even feeble traces of an approach to this state become very important. The states are (now) on such artificial terms toward each other that not one of them can relax its efforts at internal development without losing, in comparison to the others, in power and influence. Thus if not progress then at least the maintenance of this end of nature (namely, culture) is safeguarded by the ambitions of those states to some extent. Furthermore, civil freedom cannot now be interfered with without the state feeling the disadvantage of such interference in all trades, primarily foreign commerce, and as a result (there is) a decline of 8:28 the power of the state in its foreign relations. Therefore this freedom is gradually being extended. If one obstructs the citizen in seeking his welfare in any way he chooses, as long as (his way) can coexist with the freedom of others, one also hampers the vitality of all business and the strength of the whole (state). For this reason restrictions of personal activities are being increasingly lifted and general freedom granted and thus enlightenment is gradually developing with occasional nonsense and freakishness. Enlightenment is a great good which must ever draw mankind away from the egoistic expansive tendencies of its rulers once they understand their own advantage. This enlightenment and along with it a certain participation of the heart (are things) which the enlightened man cannot fail to feel for the good which he fully understands must by and by reach the thrones and have influence upon the principles of government. For example, although our governors have no money to spare for public education nor for anything else that concerns the best interests of the world because all the money has in advance been budgeted for the coming war, they will nevertheless find it to their own advantage at least not to hinder the weak and slow independent efforts of their people in this regard. Eventually, even war will become a very dubious enterprise, not only because its result on both sides is so uncertain and artificial, but because in its aftermath the state consequently finds itself saddled with a growing debt the repayment of which becomes undeterminable. At the same time the effect of each impact of a government upon other governments in our continent, where the states have become so very much linked through commerce, will become so noticeable that the other states, compelled by their own danger, even when lacking a legal basis, will offer themselves as arbiters and thus start a future great government of which there is no previous example in history. Even though this body-politic at present is discernible only in its broadest outline, a feeling (for it) is rising in all member states since each is interested in the maintenance of the whole; and this provides the hope that after many revolutions, the transformation will finally come about of that which nature has as its highest intent, namely a general *cosmopolitan condition* as the womb to which all the original predispositions of the human species will be developed.

NINTH PROPOSITION

8:29

A philosophical attempt to write a general world history according to a plan of nature which aims at a perfect civil association of mankind must be considered possible and even helpful to this intention of nature. It is a strange and apparently paradoxical project to write a history according to an idea as to how the world should develop if its development is to have an appropriate rational end. It would seem that such a purpose could only produce a *novel*, but this idea might yet be usable if one could assume that nature and even the play of human freedom does not proceed without plan and intended end. Even though we are too shortsighted to perceive the secret mechanism of nature's plan an otherwise planless *conglomeration* of human activities could be used as a guide when presented as a *system*. If one starts with *Greek* history as the (one) through which all older and contemporary history has been preserved or at least certified,[2] one may trace the influence (of Greek history) upon the formation and malformation of the body-politic of the Roman people who devoured the Greek state. Again, (if one traces) down to our time the influence of 8:30 *Rome* upon the *Barbarian* who destroyed the empire; if one then periodically adds the history of the state of other peoples as knowledge of them has come to us through these enlightened nations; then one will discover a regular procession of improvements in constitutional government in our part of the world which will probably give laws to all other (states) eventually. By concentrating primarily on the civil constitution and its laws and on the relations among states, because both served to raise nations, their arts and sciences, one may discover a guide to explain the chaotic play of human affairs or to the art of political soothsaying regarding future changes in the state (a utility that has already been drawn from

2 Only a *learned public* which has continued from the beginning uninterruptedly to our time can certify to ancient history. Beyond that all is *terra incognita* and the history of nations which lived beyond that frame can only be started with the time when they entered it. For the *Jewish* people that happened in the time of the Ptolemies through the Greek translation of the Bible without which one would give little credence to their *isolated* reports. But one can trace backward from this event once it is adequately ascertained and thus with all peoples. The first page of *Thucydides*, says Hume, is the real beginning of history.

human history even if it was seen as the disconnected effect of an irregular freedom!); rather, it would open up a consoling vision of the future (which one has no ground from presupposing without a plan of nature), in which the human species is represented in the distant future as working itself up to the full development of all the germs that nature has laid in it, and as fulfilling its vocation here on earth. Such a *justification* of nature, or perhaps one should say of providence, is a not unimportant reason for selecting a particular outlook for observing the world. For what good is it to praise the majesty and wisdom of creation in the realm of nature, which is without reason, and to recommend contemplating them if that part of the great arena of supreme wisdom which above all contains that purpose, namely, the history of mankind, remains as a constant objection because its spectacle compels us to turn away our eyes in disgust and as we despair of ever encountering therein a completed rational end causes us to expect such perfection only in another world? It would be a misinterpretation of my intention to maintain that I wished to displace the work on true empirical history by this idea of a universal history which contains a principle *a priori.* This idea is only a notion of what a philosophical mind, who would have to be very knowledgeable in history, could attempt from another standpoint. Furthermore, the complexity, in many ways praiseworthy, with which the history of an age is now composed, naturally causes everyone to worry as to how our later descendants are going

8:31 to cope with the burden of history which, after some centuries, we are going to leave them. Without doubt they will care for the history of the most ancient period, for which the documents would have long perished, only from the standpoint (which) interests them, namely, what nations and governments have contributed toward world government or how they have damaged it. We may be concerned with this and may also consider (that) the ambition of rulers and their servants (should) be directed toward the only means which could secure a glorious reputation for them in later ages. These considerations may also offer a small reason for attempting such a philosophical history.

Answer to the Question: What Is Enlightenment?

[1784]

Translated by Thomas K. Abbott

Enlightenment is man's exit from his self-incurred minority. Minority is the incapacity to use one's intelligence without the guidance of another. Such minority is self-incurred if it is not caused by lack of intelligence, but by lack of determination and courage to use one's intelligence without being guided by another. *Sapere Aude!* Have the courage to use your own intelligence! is therefore the motto of the enlightenment.

Through laziness and cowardice a large part of mankind, even after nature has freed them from alien guidance, gladly remain in minority. It is because of laziness and cowardice that it is so easy for others to usurp the role of guardians. It is so comfortable to be a minor! If I have a book which provides meaning for me, a pastor who has conscience for me, a doctor who will judge my diet for me and so on, then I do not need to exert myself. I do not have any need to think; if I can pay, others will take over the tedious job for me. The guardians who have kindly undertaken the supervision will see to it that by far the largest part of mankind, including the entire "fair sex," should consider the step into maturity, not only as difficult but as very dangerous.

After having made their domestic animals dumb and having carefully prevented these quiet creatures from daring to take any step beyond the lead-strings to which they have fastened them, these guardians then show them the danger which threatens them, should they attempt to walk alone. Now this danger is not really so very great; for they would presumably learn to walk after some stumbling. However, an example of this kind intimidates and frightens people out of all further attempts.

It is difficult for the isolated individual to work himself out of the minority which has become almost natural for him. He has even become fond of it and for the time being is incapable of employing his own intelligence, because he has never been allowed to make the attempt. Statutes and formulas, these mechanical tools of a serviceable use, or rather misuse, of his natural faculties, are the ankle-chains of a perpetual minority. Whoever threw it off would make an uncertain jump over the smallest trench because he is not accustomed to such free movement. Therefore there are only a few who have pursued a firm path and have succeeded in escaping from minority by their own cultivation of the mind.

But it is more nearly possible for a public to enlighten itself: this is even inescapable if only the public is given its freedom. For there will always be some people who think for themselves, even among the self-appointed guardians of the great mass who, after having thrown off the yoke of minority themselves, will spread about them the spirit of a reasonable estimate of their own value and of the need for every man to think for himself. It is strange that the very public, which had previously been put under this yoke by the guardians, forces the guardians thereafter to keep it there if it is stirred up by a few of its guardians who are themselves incapable of all enlightenment. It is thus very harmful to plant prejudices, because they come back to plague those very people who themselves (or whose predecessors) have been the originators of these prejudices. Therefore a public can only arrive at enlightenment slowly. Through revolution, the abandonment of personal despotism may be engendered and the end of profit-seeking and domineering oppression may occur, but never a true reform of the state of mind. Instead, new prejudices, just like the old ones, will serve as the guiding reins of the great, unthinking mass.

All that is required for this enlightenment is *freedom*; and particularly the least harmful of all that may be called freedom, namely, the freedom for man to make *public use* of his reason in all matters. But I hear people clamor on all sides: Don't argue! The officer says: Don't argue, drill! The tax collector: Don't argue, pay! The pastor: Don't argue, believe! (Only a single lord in the world says: *Argue*, as much as you want to and about what you please, *but obey!*) Here we have restrictions on freedom everywhere. Which restriction is hampering enlightenment, and which does not, or even promotes it? I answer: The *public use* of a man's reason must be free at all times, and this alone can bring enlightenment among men: while the private use of a man's reason may often be restricted rather narrowly without thereby unduly hampering the progress of enlightenment.

I mean by the public use of one's reason, the use which a scholar makes of it before the entire reading public. Private use I call the use which he may make of this reason in a civic post or office. For some affairs which are in the interest of the commonwealth a certain mechanism is necessary through which some members of the commonwealth must remain purely passive in order that an artificial agreement with the government for the public good be maintained or so that at least the destruction of the good be prevented. In such a situation it is not permitted to argue; one must obey. But in so far as this unit of the machine considers himself as a member of the entire commonwealth, in fact even of world society; in other words, he considers himself in the quality of a scholar who is addressing the true public through his writing, he may indeed argue without the affairs suffering for which he is employed partly as a passive member. Thus it would be very harmful if an officer who, given an order by his superior, should start, while in the service, to argue concerning the utility or the appropriateness of that command. He must obey, but he cannot equitably be prevented from making observations as a scholar concerning the mistakes in the military service nor from submitting these to the public for its judgment. The citizen cannot refuse to pay the taxes imposed upon him. Indeed, a rash criticism of such taxes, if they are the ones to be paid by him, may be punished as a scandal which might cause general resistance. But the same man does not act contrary to the duty of a citizen if, as a scholar, he utters publicly his thoughts against 8:38 the undesirability or even the injustice of such taxes. Likewise a clergyman is obliged to teach his pupils and his congregation according to the creed of the church which he serves, for he has been accepted on that condition. But as a scholar, he has full freedom, in fact, even the obligation, to communicate to the public all his diligently examined and well-intentioned thoughts concerning erroneous points in that doctrine and concerning proposals regarding the better institution of religious and ecclesiastical matters. There is nothing in this for which the conscience could be blamed. For what he teaches according to his office as one authorized by the church, he presents as something in regard to which he has no latitude to teach according to his own preference.... He will say: Our church teaches this or that, these are the proofs which are employed for it. In this way he derives all possible practical benefit for his congregation from rules which he would not himself subscribe to with full conviction. But he may nevertheless undertake the presentation of these rules because it is not entirely inconceivable that the truth may be contained in them. In any case, there is nothing directly contrary to inner religion to be found in such doctrines. For, should he believe that the latter was not the case he could not administer his office in good conscience; he would have to resign it. Therefore the use which an employed teacher makes of his reason before his congregation is merely a private use since such a gathering is always only domestic, no matter how large. As a priest (a member of an organization) he is not free and ought not to be, since he is executing someone else's mandate. On the other hand, the scholar speaking through his writings to the true public which is the world, like the clergyman making public use of his reason, enjoys an unlimited freedom to employ his own reason and to speak in his own person. For to suggest that the guardians of the people in spiritual matters should always be immature minors is a nonsense which would mean perpetuating forever existing non-sense.

But should a society of clergymen, for instance an ecclesiastical assembly, be entitled to commit itself by oath to a certain unalterable doctrine in order to perpetuate an endless guardianship over each of its members and through them over the people? I answer that this is quite inconceivable. Such a contract which would be concluded in order to keep humanity forever from all further enlightenment is absolutely impossible, even should it be confirmed by the highest authority through parliaments and the most solemn peace treaties. An age cannot conclude a pact and take an oath upon it to commit the succeeding age to a situation in which it would be impossible for the latter to enlarge even its most important knowledge, to eliminate error and altogether to progress in enlightenment. Such a thing would be a crime against human nature, the original destiny of which consists in such progress. Succeeding generations are entirely justified in discarding such decisions as unauthorized and criminal. The touchstone of all this to be agreed upon as a law for people is to be found in the question whether a people could impose such a law upon itself. Now it might be possible to introduce a certain order for a definite short period as if in anticipation of a better order. This would be true if one permitted at the same time each citizen and especially the clergyman to make his criticisms in his quality as a scholar, i.e., through writings that make remarks about what is defective in the current arrangements. In the meantime, the provisional order might continue until the insight into the particular matter in hand has publicly progressed to the point where through a combination of voices (although not, perhaps, of all) a proposal may be brought to the crown. Thus those congregations would be protected which had agreed to (a changed religious institution) according to their own ideas and better understanding, without hindering those who desired to allow the old institutions to continue. But to unite on a persisting constitution that is not to be publicly doubted by anyone, even within the lifetime of a human being, and thereby to prevent the progress of humanity, this can only be disadvantageous to posterity, and is absolutely impermissible.

A man may postpone for himself, but only for a short time, enlightening himself regarding what he ought to know. But to resign from such enlightenment altogether either for his own person or even more for his descendants means to violate and to trample underfoot the sacred rights of mankind. Whatever a people may not decide for themselves, a monarch may even less decide for the people, for his legislative reputation rests upon his uniting the entire people's will in his own. If the monarch will only see to it that every true or imagined reform (of religion) fits in with the civil order, he had best let his subjects do what they consider necessary for the sake of their salvation; that is not his affair. His only concern is to prevent one subject from hindering another by force, to work according to each subject's best ability to determine and to promote his salvation. In fact, it detracts from his majesty if he interferes in such matters and subjects to governmental supervision the writings by which his subjects seek to clarify their ideas (concerning religion). This is true whether he does it from his own highest insight, for in this case he exposes himself to the reproach: *Caesar non est supra grammaticos;* it is even more true when he debases his highest power to support the spiritual despotism of some tyrants in his state against the rest of his subjects.

The question may now be put: Do we live at present in an enlightened age? The answer is: No, but in an age of enlightenment. Much still prevents men from being placed in a position or even being placed into position to use their own minds securely and well in matters of religion. But we do have very definite indications that this field of endeavor is being opened up for men to work freely and reduce gradually the hindrances preventing a general enlightenment and an escape from self-caused immaturity. In this sense, this age is the age of enlightenment and the age of Frederick (the Great).

A prince should not consider it beneath him to declare that he believes it to be his *duty* not to prescribe anything to his subjects in matters of religion but to leave to them complete freedom in such things. In other words, a prince who refuses the conceited title of being "tolerant," is himself enlightened. He deserves to be praised by his grateful contemporaries and descendants as the man who first freed humankind of minority, at least as far as the government is concerned and who permitted everyone to use his own reason in all matters of conscience. Under his rule, venerable clergymen could, regardless of their official duty, set forth their opinions and 8:41 views even though they differ from the accepted creed here and there; they could do so in the quality of scholars, freely and publicly. The same holds even more true of every other person who is not thus restricted by official duty. This spirit of freedom is spreading even outside (the country of Frederick the Great) to places where it has to struggle with the external hindrances imposed by a government which misunderstands its own position. For an example is illuminating them which shows that such freedom (public discussion) need not cause the slightest worry regarding public security and the unity of the commonwealth. Men raise themselves by and by out of backwardness if one does not purposely invent artifices to keep them down.

I have emphasized the main point of enlightenment, that is of man's release from his self-incurred minority, primarily *in matters of religion.* I have done this because our rulers have no interest in playing the guardian of their subjects in matters of arts and sciences. Furthermore minority in matters of religion is not only most noxious but also most dishonorable. But the point of view of a head of state who favors freedom in the arts and sciences goes even farther; for he understands that there is no danger in legislation permitting his subjects to make *public* use of their own reason and to submit *publicly* their thoughts regarding a better framing of such laws together with a frank criticism of existing *legislation.* We have a shining example of this; no prince excels him whom we admire. Only he who is himself enlightened does not fear spectres when he at the same time has a well-disciplined army at his disposal as a guarantee of public peace. Only he can say what (the ruler of a) free state dare not say: *Argue as much as you want and about whatever you want but obey!* Thus we see here as elsewhere an unexpected turn in human affairs just as we observe that almost everything therein is paradoxical. A great degree of civil freedom seems to be advantageous for the freedom of the *spirit* of the people and yet it establishes impassable limits. A lesser degree of such civil freedom provides additional space in which the spirit of a people can develop to its full capacity. Therefore nature has cherished, within its hard shell, the germ of the inclination and need for free *thought.* This free thought gradually acts upon the mind of the people and they gradually become more capable of acting in freedom. Eventually, the *government* is also influenced by this free thought and thereby it treats man, 8:42 who is now more than a machine, according to his dignity.

Koenigsberg, September 30, 1784

FUNDAMENTAL PRINCIPLES OF THE METAPHYSICS OF MORALS

[1785]

Translated by Thomas K. Abbott

ble of demonstration. Natural and moral philosophy, on the contrary, can each have their empirical part, since the former has to determine the laws of nature as an object of experience; the latter the laws of the human will, so far as it is affected by nature: the former, however, being laws according to which everything does happen; the latter, laws according to which everything ought to happen. Ethics, however, must also consider the conditions under which what ought to happen frequently does not.

4:388

We may call all philosophy *empirical*, so far as it is based on grounds of experience: on the other hand, that which delivers its doctrines from *a priori* principles alone we may call *pure* philosophy. When the latter is merely formal it is *logic;* if it is restricted to definite objects of the understanding it is *metaphysic.*

In this way there arises the idea of a two-fold metaphysic—a *metaphysic of nature* and a *metaphysic of morals.* Physics will thus have an empirical and also a rational part. It is the same with Ethics; but here the empirical part might have the special name of *practical anthropology*, the name *morality* being appropriated to the rational part.

All trades, arts, and handiworks have gained by division of labour, namely, when, instead of one man doing everything, each confines himself to a certain kind of work distinct from others in the treatment it requires, so as to be able to perform it with greater facility and in the greatest perfection. Where the different kinds of work are not so distinguished and divided, where everyone is a jack-of-all-trades, there manufactures remain still in the greatest barbarism. It might deserve to be considered whether pure philosophy in all its parts does not require a man specially devoted to it, and whether it would not be better for the whole business of science if those who, to please the tastes of the public, are wont to blend the rational and empirical elements together, mixed in all sorts of proportions unknown to themselves, and who call themselves independent thinkers, giving the name of minute philosophers to those who apply themselves to the rational part only—if these, I say, were warned not to carry on two employments together which differ widely in the treatment they demand, for each of which perhaps a special talent is required, and the combination of which in one person only produces bunglers. But I only ask here whether the nature of science does not require that we should always carefully separate the empirical from the rational part, and prefix to Physics proper (or empirical physics) a metaphysic of nature, and to practical anthropology a metaphysic of morals, which must be carefully cleared of everything empirical, so that we may know how much can be accomplished by pure reason in both cases, and from what sources it draws this its *a priori* teaching, and that whether the latter inquiry is conducted by all moralists (whose name is legion), or only by some who feel a calling thereto.

4:389

As my concern here is with moral philosophy, I limit the question suggested to this: Whether it is not of the utmost necessity to construct a pure moral philosophy, perfectly cleared of everything which is only empirical, and which belongs to anthropology? for that such a philosophy must be possible is evident from the common idea of duty and of the moral laws. Everyone must admit that if a law is to have moral force, *i.e.* to be the basis of an obligation, it must carry with it absolute necessity; that, for example, the precept, "Thou shalt not lie," is not valid for men alone, as if other rational beings had no need to observe it; and so with all the other moral laws properly so called; that, therefore, the basis of obligation must not be sought in the nature of man, or in the circumstances in the world in which he is placed, but *a priori* simply in the conceptions of pure reason; and although any other precept which is founded on principles of mere experience may be in certain respects universal, yet in as far as it rests even in the least degree on an empirical basis, perhaps only as to a motive, such a precept, while it may be a practical rule, can never be called a moral law.

Thus not only are moral laws with their principles essentially distinguished from every other kind of practical knowledge in which there is anything empirical, but all moral philosophy rests wholly on its pure part. When applied to man, it does not borrow the least thing from the knowledge of man himself (anthropology), but gives laws *a priori* to him as a rational being. No doubt these laws require a judgment sharpened by experience, in order on the one hand to distinguish in what cases they are applicable, and on the other to procure for them access to the will of the man, and effectual influence on conduct; since man is acted on by so many inclinations that, though capable of the idea of a practical pure reason, he is not so easily able to make it effective *in concreto* in his life.

4:390   A metaphysic of morals is therefore indispensably necessary, not merely for speculative reasons, in order to investigate the sources of the practical principles which are to be found *a priori* in our reason, but also because morals themselves are liable to all sorts of corruption, as long as we are without that clue and supreme canon by which to estimate them correctly. For in order that an action should be morally good, it is not enough that it *conform* to the moral law, but it must also be done *for the sake of the law,* otherwise that conformity is only very contingent and uncertain; since a principle which is not moral, although it may now and then produce actions conformable to the law, will also often produce actions which contradict it. Now it is only in a pure philosophy that we can look for the moral law in its purity and genuineness (and, in a practical matter, this is of the utmost consequence): we must, therefore, begin with pure philosophy (metaphysic), and without it there cannot be any moral philosophy at all. That which mingles these pure principles with the empirical does not deserve the name of philosophy (for what distinguishes philosophy from common rational knowledge is, that it treats in separate sciences what the latter only comprehends confusedly); much less does it deserve that of moral philosophy, since by this confusion it even spoils the purity of morals themselves, and counteracts its own end.

Let it not be thought, however, that what is here demanded is already extant in the propædeutic prefixed by the celebrated Wolf to his moral philosophy, namely, his so-called *general practical philosophy,* and that, therefore, we have not to strike into an entirely new field. Just because it was to be a general practical philosophy, it has not taken into consideration a will of any particular kind—say one which should be determined solely from *a priori* principles without any empirical motives, and which we might call a pure will, but volition in general, with all the actions and conditions which belong to it in this general signification. By this it is distinguished from a metaphysic of morals, just as general logic, which treats of the acts and canons of thought *in general,* is distinguished from transcen-

dental philosophy, which treats of the particular acts and canons of
pure thought, *i.e.* that whose cognitions are altogether *a priori.* For
the metaphysic of morals has to examine the idea and the princi- 4:391
ples of a possible *pure* will, and not the acts and conditions of
human volition generally, which for the most part are drawn from
psychology. It is true that moral laws and duty are spoken of in the
general practical philosophy (contrary indeed to all fitness). But
this is no objection, for in this respect also the authors of that science remain true to their idea of it; they do not distinguish the motives which are prescribed as such by reason alone altogether *a
priori*, and which are properly moral, from the empirical motives
which the understanding raises to general conceptions merely by
comparison of experiences; but without noticing the difference of
their sources, and looking on them all as homogeneous, they consider only their greater or less amount. It is in this way they frame
their notion of *obligation*, which, though anything but moral, is all
that can be asked for in a philosophy which passes no judgment at
all on the *origin* of all possible practical concepts, whether they are
a priori, or only *a posteriori.*

Intending to publish hereafter a metaphysic of morals, I issue in
the first instance these fundamental principles. Indeed there is
properly no other foundation for it than the *critical examination of a
pure practical reason;* just as that of metaphysics is the critical examination of the pure speculative reason, already published. But in the
first place the former is not so absolutely necessary as the latter, because in moral concerns human reason can easily be brought to a
high degree of correctness and completeness, even in the commonest understanding, while on the contrary in its theoretic but
pure use it is wholly dialectical; and in the second place if the critique of a pure practical reason is to be complete, it must be possible at the same time to show its identity with the speculative reason
in a common principle, for it can ultimately be only one and the
same reason which has to be distinguished merely in its application.
I could not, however, bring it to such completeness here, without
introducing considerations of a wholly different kind, which would
be perplexing to the reader. On this account I have adopted the title

of *Fundamental Principles of the Metaphysic of Morals,* instead of that of a *Critical Examination of the pure practical Reason.*

4:392 But in the third place, since a metaphysic of morals, in spite of the discouraging title, is yet capable of being presented in a popular form, and one adapted to the common understanding, I find it useful to separate from it this preliminary treatise on its fundamental principles, in order that I may not hereafter have need to introduce these necessarily subtle discussions into a book of a more simple character.

The present treatise is, however, nothing more than the investigation and establishment of *the supreme principle of morality,* and this alone constitutes a study complete in itself, and one which ought to be kept apart from every other moral investigation. No doubt my conclusions on this weighty question, which has hitherto been very unsatisfactorily examined, would receive much light from the application of the same principle to the whole system, and would be greatly confirmed by the adequacy which it exhibits throughout; but I must forego this advantage, which indeed would be after all more gratifying than useful, since the easy applicability of a principle and its apparent adequacy give no very certain proof of its soundness, but rather inspire a certain partiality, which prevents us from examining and estimating it strictly in itself, and without regard to consequences.

I have adopted in this work the method which I think most suitable, proceeding analytically from common knowledge to the determination of its ultimate principle, and again descending synthetically from the examination of this principle and its sources to the common knowledge in which we find it employed. The division will, therefore, be as follows:—

1. *First section.*—Transition from the common rational knowledge of morality to the philosophical.
2. *Second section.*—Transition from popular moral philosophy to the metaphysic of morals.
3. *Third section.*—Final step from the metaphysic of morals to the critique of the pure practical reason.

FIRST SECTION.

TRANSITION FROM THE COMMON RATIONAL KNOWLEDGE OF MORALITY TO THE PHILOSOPHICAL.

Nothing can possibly be conceived in the world, or even out of it, which can be called good without qualification, except a Good Will. Intelligence, wit, judgment, and the other *talents* of the mind, however they may be named, or courage, resolution, perseverance, as qualities of temperament, are undoubtedly good and desirable in many respects; but these gifts of nature may also become extremely bad and mischievous if the will which is to make use of them, and which, therefore, constitutes what is called *character*, is not good. It is the same with the *gifts of fortune*. Power, riches, honour, even health, and the general well-being and contentment with one's condition which is called *happiness*, inspire pride, and often presumption, if there is not a good will to correct the influence of these on the mind, and with this also to rectify the whole principle of acting, and adapt it to its end. The sight of a being who is not adorned with a single feature of a pure and good will, enjoying unbroken prosperity, can never give pleasure to an impartial rational spectator. Thus a good will appears to constitute the indispensable condition even of being worthy of happiness.

4:394 There are even some qualities which are of service to this good will itself, and may facilitate its action, yet which have no intrinsic unconditional value, but always presuppose a good will, and this qualifies the esteem that we justly have for them, and does not permit us to regard them as absolutely good. Moderation in the affections and passions, self-control and calm deliberation are not only good in many respects, but even seem to constitute part of the intrinsic worth of the person; but they are far from deserving to be called good without qualification, although they have been so unconditionally praised by the ancients. For without the principles of a good will, they may become extremely bad, and the coolness of a villain not only makes him far more dangerous, but also directly makes him more abominable in our eyes than he would have been without it.

A good will is good not because of what it performs or effects, not by its aptness for the attainment of some proposed end, but simply by virtue of the volition, that is, it is good in itself, and considered by itself is to be esteemed much higher than all that can be brought about by it in favour of any inclination, nay, even of the sum total of all inclinations. Even if it should happen that, owing to special disfavour of fortune, or the niggardly provision of a stepmotherly nature, this will should wholly lack power to accomplish its purpose, if with its greatest efforts it should yet achieve nothing, and there should remain only the good will (not, to be sure, a mere wish, but the summoning of all means in our power), then, like a jewel, it would still shine by its own light, as a thing which has its whole value in itself. Its usefulness or fruitlessness can neither add to nor take away anything from this value. It would be, as it were, only the setting to enable us to handle it the more conveniently in common commerce, or to attract to it the attention of those who are not yet connoisseurs, but not to recommend it to true connoisseurs, or to determine its value.

There is, however, something so strange in this idea of the absolute value of the mere will, in which no account is taken of its utility, that notwithstanding the thorough assent of even common reason to the idea, yet a suspicion must arise that it may perhaps really be the product of mere high-flown fancy, and that we may have misunderstood the purpose of nature in assigning reason as the governor of our will. Therefore we will examine this idea from this point of view.

4:395

In the physical constitution of an organized being, that is, a being adapted suitably to the purposes of life, we assume it as a fundamental principle that no organ for any purpose will be found but what is also the fittest and best adapted for that purpose. Now in a being which has reason and a will, if the proper object of nature were its *conservation*, its *welfare*, in a word, its *happiness*, then nature would have hit upon a very bad arrangement in selecting the reason of the creature to carry out this purpose. For all the actions which the creature has to perform with a view to this purpose, and the whole rule of its conduct, would be far more surely prescribed to it by instinct, and that end would have been attained thereby much more certainly than it ever can be by reason. Should reason have been communicated to this favoured creature over and above, it must only have served it to contemplate the happy constitution of its nature, to admire it, to congratulate itself thereon, and to feel thankful for it to the beneficent cause, but not that it should subject its desires to that weak and delusive guidance, and meddle bunglingly with the purpose of nature. In a word, nature would have taken care that reason should not break forth into *practical exercise*, nor have the presumption, with its weak insight, to think out for itself the plan of happiness, and of the means of attaining it. Nature would not only have taken on herself the choice of the ends, but also of the means, and with wise foresight would have entrusted both to instinct.

And, in fact, we find that the more a cultivated reason applies itself with deliberate purpose to the enjoyment of life and happiness, so much the more does the man fail of true satisfaction. And from this circumstance there arises in many, if they are candid enough to confess it, a certain degree of *misology*, that is, hatred of reason, especially in the case of those who are most experienced in the use of it, because after calculating all the advantages they derive, I do not say from the invention of all the arts of common luxury, but even from the sciences (which seem to them to be after all only a luxury of the understanding), they find that they have, in fact, only 4:396 brought more trouble on their shoulders, rather than gained in happiness; and they end by envying, rather than despising, the more common stamp of men who keep closer to the guidance of mere instinct, and do not allow their reason much influence on their conduct. And this we must admit, that the judgment of those who would very much lower the lofty eulogies of the advantages which reason gives us in regard to the happiness and satisfaction of life, or who would even reduce them below zero, is by no means morose or ungrateful to the goodness with which the world is governed, but that there lies at the root of these judgments the idea that our existence has a different and far nobler end, for which, and not for happiness, reason is properly intended, and which must, therefore, be regarded as the supreme condition to which the private ends of man must, for the most part, be postponed.

For as reason is not competent to guide the will with certainty in regard to its objects and the satisfaction of all our wants (which it to some extent even multiplies), this being an end to which an implanted instinct would have led with much greater certainty; and since, nevertheless, reason is imparted to us as a practical faculty, *i.e.* as one which is to have influence on the *will,* therefore, admitting that nature generally in the distribution of her capacities has adapted the means to the end, its true destination must be to produce a *will,* not merely good as a *means* to something else, but *good in itself,* for which reason was absolutely necessary. This will then, though not indeed the sole and complete good, must be the supreme good and the condition of every other, even of the desire of happiness. Under these circumstances, there is nothing inconsistent with the wisdom of nature in the fact that the cultivation of the reason, which is requisite for the first and unconditional purpose, does in many ways interfere, at least in this life, with the attainment of the second, which is always conditional, namely, happiness. Nay, it may even reduce it to nothing, without nature thereby failing of her purpose. For reason recognises the establishment of a good will as its highest practical destination, and in attaining this purpose is capable only of a satisfaction of its own proper kind, namely, that from the attainment of an end, which end again is determined by reason only, notwithstanding that this may involve many a disappointment to the ends of inclination.

We have then to develop the notion of a will which deserves to be highly esteemed for itself, and is good without a view to anything further, a notion which exists already in the sound natural understanding, requiring rather to be cleared up than to be taught, and which in estimating the value of our actions always takes the first place, and constitutes the condition of all the rest. In order to do this we will take the notion of duty, which includes that of a good will, although implying certain subjective restrictions and hindrances. These, however, far from concealing it, or rendering it unrecognisable, rather bring it out by contrast, and make it shine forth so much the brighter. 4:397

I omit here all actions which are already recognised as inconsistent with duty, although they may be useful for this or that purpose, for with these the question whether they are done *from duty* cannot arise at all, since they even conflict with it. I also set aside those actions which really conform to duty, but to which men have *no* direct *inclination*, performing them because they are impelled thereto by some other inclination. For in this case we can readily distinguish whether the action which agrees with duty is done *from duty*, or from a selfish view. It is much harder to make this distinction when the action accords with duty, and the subject has besides a *direct* inclination to it. For example, it is always a matter of duty that a dealer should not overcharge an inexperienced purchaser, and wherever there is much commerce the prudent tradesman does not overcharge, but keeps a fixed price for everyone, so that a child buys of him as well as any other. Men are thus *honestly* served; but this is not enough to make us believe that the tradesman has so acted from duty and from principles of honesty: his own advantage required it; it is out of the question in this case to suppose that he might besides have a direct inclination in favour of the buyers, so that, as it were, from love he should give no advantage to one over another. Accordingly the action was done neither from duty nor from direct inclination, but merely with a selfish view.

On the other hand, it is a duty to maintain one's life; and, in addition, every one has also a direct inclination to do so. But on this account the often anxious care which most men take for it has no intrinsic worth, and their maxim has no moral import. They preserve their life *as duty requires,* no doubt, but not *because duty requires.* On the other hand, if adversity and hopeless sorrow have completely taken away the relish for life; if the unfortunate one, strong in mind, indignant at his fate rather than desponding or dejected, wishes for death, and yet preserves his life without loving it—not from inclination or fear, but from duty—then his maxim has a moral worth.

To be beneficent when we can is a duty; and besides this, there are many minds so sympathetically constituted that, without any other motive of vanity or self-interest, they find a pleasure in spreading joy around them, and can take delight in the satisfaction of others so far as it is their own work. But I maintain that in such a case an action of this kind, however proper, however amiable it may be, has nevertheless no true moral worth, but is on a level with other inclinations, *e.g.* the inclination to honour, which, if it is happily directed to that which is in fact of public utility and accordant with duty, and consequently honourable, deserves praise and encouragement, but not esteem. For the maxim lacks the moral import, namely, that such actions be done *from duty,* not from inclination. Put the case that the mind of that philanthropist were clouded by sorrow of his own, extinguishing all sympathy with the lot of others, and that while he still has the power to benefit others in distress, he is not touched by their trouble because he is absorbed with his own; and now suppose that he tears himself out of this dead insensibility, and performs the action without any inclination to it, but simply from duty, then first has his action its genuine moral worth. Further still; if nature has put little sympathy in the heart of this or that man; if he, supposed to be an upright man, is by temperament cold and indifferent to the sufferings of others, per-

4:398

haps because in respect of his own he is provided with the special gift of patience and fortitude, and supposes, or even requires, that others should have the same—and such a man would certainly not be the meanest product of nature—but if nature had not specially framed him for a philanthropist, would he not still find in himself a source from whence to give himself a far higher worth than that of a good-natured temperament could be? Unquestionably. It is just in this that the moral worth of the character is brought out which is incomparably the highest of all, namely, that he is beneficent, not 4:399 from inclination, but from duty.

To secure one's own happiness is a duty, at least indirectly; for discontent with one's condition, under a pressure of many anxieties and amidst unsatisfied wants, might easily become a great *temptation to transgression of duty.* But here again, without looking to duty, all men have already the strongest and most intimate inclination to happiness, because it is just in this idea that all inclinations are combined in one total. But the precept of happiness is often of such a sort that it greatly interferes with some inclinations, and yet a man cannot form any definite and certain conception of the sum of satisfaction of all of them which is called happiness. It is not then to be wondered at that a single inclination, definite both as to what it promises and as to the time within which it can be gratified, is often able to overcome such a fluctuating idea, and that a gouty patient, for instance, can choose to enjoy what he likes, and to suffer what he may, since, according to his calculation, on this occasion at least, he has [only] not sacrificed the enjoyment of the present moment to a possibly mistaken expectation of a happiness which is supposed to be found in health. But even in this case, if the general desire for happiness did not influence his will, and supposing that in his particular case health was not a necessary element in this calculation, there yet remains in this, as in all other cases, this law, namely, that he should promote his happiness not from inclination but from duty, and by this would his conduct first acquire true moral worth.

It is in this manner, undoubtedly, that we are to understand those passages of Scripture also in which we are commanded to love our neighbour, even our enemy. For love, as an affection, cannot be commanded, but beneficence for duty's sake may; even though we are not impelled to it by any inclination—nay, are even repelled by a natural and unconquerable aversion. This is *practical* love, and not *pathological*—a love which is seated in the will, and not in the propensions of sense—in principles of action and not of tender sympathy; and it is this love alone which can be commanded.

4:400 The second proposition is: That an action done from duty derives its moral worth, *not from the purpose* which is to be attained by it, but from the maxim by which it is determined, and therefore does not depend on the realization of the object of the action, but merely on the *principle of volition* by which the action has taken place, without regard to any object of desire. It is clear from what precedes that the purposes which we may have in view in our actions, or their effects regarded as ends and springs of the will, cannot give to actions any unconditional or moral worth. In what, then, can their worth lie, if it is not to consist in the will and in reference to its expected effect? It cannot lie anywhere but in the *principle of the will* without regard to the ends which can be attained by the action. For the will stands between its *a priori* principle, which is formal, and its *a posteriori* spring, which is material, as between two roads, and as it must be determined by something, it follows that it must be determined by the formal principle of volition when an action is done from duty, in which case every material principle has been withdrawn from it.

The third proposition, which is a consequence of the two preceding, I would express thus: *Duty is the necessity of acting from respect for the law.* I may have *inclination* for an object as the effect of my proposed action, but I cannot have *respect* for it, just for this reason, that it is an effect and not an energy of will. Similarly, I cannot have respect for inclination, whether my own or another's; I can at most, if my own, approve it; if another's, sometimes even love it; *i.e.* look on it as favourable to my own interest. It is only what is connected with my will as a principle, by no means as an effect—what does not subserve my inclination, but overpowers it, or at least in case of choice excludes it from its calculation—in other words, simply the law of itself, which can be an object of respect, and hence a command. Now an action done from duty must wholly exclude the influence of inclination, and with it every object of the will, so that nothing remains which can determine the will except objectively the *law*, and subjectively *pure respect* for this practical law, and consequently the maxim[1] that I should follow this law even to the thwarting of all my inclinations. 4:401

Thus the moral worth of an action does not lie in the effect expected from it, nor in any principle of action which requires to borrow its motive from this expected effect. For all these effects—agreeableness of one's condition, and even the promotion of the happiness of others—could have been also brought about by other causes, so that for this there would have been no need of the will of a rational being; whereas it is in this alone that the supreme and unconditional good can be found. The pre-eminent good which we call moral can therefore consist in nothing else than *the conception of law* in itself, *which certainly is only possible in a rational being*, in so far as this conception, and not the expected effect, determines the will. This is a good which is already present in the person who acts accordingly, and we have not to wait for it to appear first in the result.[2]

1 A *maxim* is the subjective principle of volition. The objective principle (*i.e.* that which would also serve subjectively as a practical principle to all rational beings if reason had full power over the faculty of desire) is the practical *law*.

2 It might be here objected to me that I take refuge behind the word *respect* in an obscure feeling, instead of giving a distinct solution of the question by a concept of the reason. But although respect is a feeling, it is not a feeling *received* through influence, but is *self-wrought* by a rational concept, and, therefore, is specifically distinct from all feelings of the former kind, which may be referred either to inclination or fear. What I recognise immediately as a law for me, I recognise with respect. This merely signifies the consciousness that my will is *subordinate* to a law, without the intervention of other influences on my sense. The immediate determination of the will by the law, and the consciousness of this is called *respect*, so that this is regarded as an *effect* of the law on the subject, and not as the *cause* of it. Respect is properly the conception of a worth which thwarts my self-love. Accordingly it is something which is considered neither as an object of inclination nor of fear, although it has something analogous to both. The *object* of respect is the *law* only, and that, the law which we impose on *ourselves*, and yet recognise as necessary in itself. As a law, we are subjected to it without consulting self-love; as imposed by us on ourselves, it is a result of our will. In the former aspect it has an analogy to fear, in the latter to inclination. Respect for a person is properly only respect for the law (of honesty, &c.), of which he gives us an example. Since we also look on

4:402   But what sort of law can that be, the conception of which must determine the will, even without paying any regard to the effect expected from it, in order that this will may be called good absolutely and without qualification? As I have deprived the will of every impulse which could arise to it from obedience to any law, there remains nothing but the universal conformity of its actions to law in general, which alone is to serve the will as a principle, *i.e.* I am never to act otherwise than so *that I could also will that my maxim should become a universal law.* Here now, it is the simple conformity to law in general, without assuming any particular law applicable to certain actions, that serves the will as its principle, and must so serve it, if duty is not to be a vain delusion and a chimerical notion. The common reason of men in its practical judgments perfectly coincides with this, and always has in view the principle here suggested. Let the question be, for example: May I when in distress make a promise with the intention not to keep it? I readily distinguish here between the two significations which the question may have: Whether it is prudent, or whether it is right, to make a false promise. The former may undoubtedly often be the case. I see clearly indeed that it is not enough to extricate myself from a present difficulty by means of this subterfuge, but it must be well considered whether there may not hereafter spring from this lie much greater inconvenience than that from which I now free myself, and as, with all my supposed *cunning*, the consequences cannot be so easily foreseen but that credit once lost may be much more injurious to me than any mischief which I seek to avoid at present, it should be considered whether it would not be more *prudent* to act herein according to a universal maxim, and to make it a habit to promise nothing except with the intention of keeping it. But it is soon clear to me that such a maxim will still only be based on the fear of consequences. Now it is a wholly different thing to be truthful from duty, and to be so from apprehension of injurious consequences. In the first case, the very no-

---

the improvement of our talents as a duty, we consider that we see in a person of talents, as it were, the *example of a law* (viz. to become like him in this by exercise), and this constitutes our respect. All so-called moral *interest* consists simply in *respect* for the law.

tion of the action already implies a law for me; in the second case, I must first look about elsewhere to see what results may be combined with it which would affect myself. For to deviate from the principle of duty is beyond all doubt wicked; but to be unfaithful to my maxim of prudence may often be very advantageous to me, although to abide by it is certainly safer. The shortest way, however, and an unerring one, to discover the answer to this question whether a lying promise is consistent with duty, is to ask myself, Should I be content that my maxim (to extricate myself from difficulty by a false promise) should hold good as a universal law, for myself as well as for others? and should I be able to say to myself, "Every one may make a deceitful promise when he finds himself in a difficulty from which he cannot otherwise extricate himself"? Then I presently become aware that while I can will the lie, I can by no means will that lying should be a universal law. For with such a law there would be no promises at all, since it would be in vain to allege my intention in regard to my future actions to those who would not believe this allegation, or if they over-hastily did so would pay me back in my own coin. Hence my maxim, as soon as it should be made a universal law, would necessarily destroy itself. 4:403

I do not, therefore, need any far-reaching penetration to discern what I have to do in order that my will may be morally good. Inexperienced in the course of the world, incapable of being prepared for all its contingencies, I only ask myself: Canst thou also will that thy maxim should be a universal law? If not, then it must be rejected, and that not because of a disadvantage accruing from it to myself or even to others, but because it cannot enter as a principle into a possible universal legislation, and reason extorts from me immediate respect for such legislation. I do not indeed as yet *discern* on what this respect is based (this the philosopher may inquire), but at least I understand this, that it is an estimation of the worth which far outweighs all worth of what is recommended by inclination, and that the necessity of acting from *pure* respect for the practical law is what constitutes duty, to which every other motive must give place, because it is the condition of a will being good *in itself,* and the worth of such a will is above everything.

Thus, then, without quitting the moral knowledge of common
4:404 human reason, we have arrived at its principle. And although, no
doubt, common men do not conceive it in such an abstract and universal form, yet they always have it really before their eyes, and use
it as the standard of their decision. Here it would be easy to show
how, with this compass in hand, men are well able to distinguish, in
every case that occurs, what is good, what bad, conformably to duty
or inconsistent with it, if, without in the least teaching them anything new, we only, like Socrates, direct their attention to the principle they themselves employ; and that therefore we do not need
science and philosophy to know what we should do to be honest
and good, yea, even wise and virtuous. Indeed we might well have
conjectured beforehand that the knowledge of what every man is
bound to do, and therefore also to know, would be within the reach
of every man, even the commonest. Here we cannot forbear admiration when we see how great an advantage the practical judgment
has over the theoretical in the common understanding of men. In
the latter, if common reason ventures to depart from the laws of
experience and from the perceptions of the senses it falls into mere
inconceivabilities and self-contradictions, at least into a chaos of
uncertainty, obscurity, and instability. But in the practical sphere it
is just when the common understanding excludes all sensible
springs from practical laws that its power of judgment begins to
show itself to advantage. It then becomes even subtle, whether it be
that it chicanes with its own conscience or with other claims respecting what is to be called right, or whether it desires for its own
instruction to determine honestly the worth of actions; and, in the
latter case, it may even have as good a hope of hitting the mark as
any philosopher whatever can promise himself. Nay, it is almost
more sure of doing so, because the philosopher cannot have any
other principle, while he may easily perplex his judgment by a
multitude of considerations foreign to the matter, and so turn aside
from the right way. Would it not therefore be wiser in moral concerns to acquiesce in the judgment of common reason, or at most
only to call in philosophy for the purpose of rendering the system
of morals more complete and intelligible, and its rules more convenient for use (especially for disputation), but not so as to draw off

the common understanding from its happy simplicity, or to bring it by means of philosophy into a new path of inquiry and instruction?

Innocence is indeed a glorious thing, only, on the other hand, it is very sad that it cannot well maintain itself, and is easily seduced. On this account even wisdom—which otherwise consists more in conduct than in knowledge—yet has need of science, not in order to learn from it, but to secure for its precepts admission and permanence. Against all the commands of duty which reason represents to man as so deserving of respect, he feels in himself a powerful counterpoise in his wants and inclinations, the entire satisfaction of which he sums up under the name of happiness. Now reason issues its commands unyieldingly, without promising anything to the inclinations, and, as it were, with disregard and contempt for these claims, which are so impetuous, and at the same time so plausible, and which will not allow themselves to be suppressed by any command. Hence there arises a natural *dialectic, i.e.* a disposition, to argue against these strict laws of duty and to question their validity, or at least their purity and strictness; and, if possible, to make them more accordant with our wishes and inclinations, that is to say, to corrupt them at their very source, and entirely to destroy their worth—a thing which even common practical reason cannot ultimately call good.

4:405

Thus is the *common reason of man* compelled to go out of its sphere, and to take a step into the field of a *practical philosophy,* not to satisfy any speculative want (which never occurs to it as long as it is content to be mere sound reason), but even on practical grounds, in order to attain in it information and clear instruction respecting the source of its principle, and the correct determination of it in opposition to the maxims which are based on wants and inclinations, so that it may escape from the perplexity of opposite claims, and not run the risk of losing all genuine moral principles through the equivocation into which it easily falls. Thus, when practical reason cultivates itself, there insensibly arises in it a dialectic which forces it to seek aid in philosophy, just as happens to it in its theoretic use; and in this case, therefore, as well as in the other, it will find rest nowhere but in a thorough critical examination of our reason.

Second Section.

TRANSITION FROM POPULAR MORAL PHILOSOPHY TO THE METAPHYSIC OF MORALS.

If we have hitherto drawn our notion of duty from the common use of our practical reason, it is by no means to be inferred that we have treated it as an empirical notion. On the contrary, if we attend to the experience of men's conduct, we meet frequent and, as we ourselves allow, just complaints that one cannot find a single certain example of the disposition to act from pure duty. Although many things are done in *conformity* with what *duty* prescribes, it is nevertheless always doubtful whether they are done strictly *from duty*, so as to have a moral worth. Hence there have, at all times, been philosophers who have altogether denied that this disposition actually exists at all in human actions, and have ascribed everything to a more or less refined self-love. Not that they have on that account questioned the soundness of the conception of morality; on the contrary, they spoke with sincere regret of the frailty and corruption of human nature, which though noble enough to take as its rule an idea so worthy of respect, is yet too weak to follow it, and employs reason, which ought to give it the law only for the purpose of providing for the interest of the inclinations, whether singly or at the best in the greatest possible harmony with one another.

In fact, it is absolutely impossible to make out by experience 4:407 with complete certainty a single case in which the maxim of an action, however right in itself, rested simply on moral grounds and on the conception of duty. Sometimes it happens that with the sharpest self-examination we can find nothing beside the moral principle of duty which could have been powerful enough to move us to this or that action and to so great a sacrifice; yet we cannot from this infer with certainty that it was not really some secret impulse of self-love, under the false appearance of duty, that was the actual determining cause of the will. We like then to flatter ourselves by falsely taking credit for a more noble motive; whereas in fact we can never, even by the strictest examination, get completely behind the secret springs of action; since when the question is of moral worth, it is not with the actions which we see that we are concerned, but with those inward principles of them which we do not see.

Moreover, we cannot better serve the wishes of those who ridicule all morality as a mere chimera of human imagination overstepping itself from vanity, than by conceding to them that notions of duty must be drawn only from experience (as from indolence, people are ready to think is also the case with all other notions); for this is to prepare for them a certain triumph. I am willing to admit out of love of humanity that even most of our actions are correct, but if we look closer at them we everywhere come upon the dear self which is always prominent, and it is this they have in view, and not the strict command of duty which would often require self-denial. Without being an enemy of virtue, a cool observer, one that does not mistake the wish for good, however lively, for its reality, may sometimes doubt whether true virtue is actually found anywhere in the world, and this especially as years increase and the judgment is partly made wiser by experience, and partly also more acute in observation. This being so, nothing can secure us from falling away altogether from our ideas of duty, or maintain in the soul a well-grounded respect for its law, but the clear conviction

that although there should never have been actions which really
4:408 sprang from such pure sources, yet whether this or that takes place
is not at all the question; but that reason of itself, independent on
all experience, ordains what ought to take place, that accordingly
actions of which perhaps the world has hitherto never given an example, the feasibility even of which might be very much doubted
by one who founds everything on experience, are nevertheless in-
flexibly commanded by reason; that, *ex. gr.* even though there might
never yet have been a sincere friend, yet not a whit the less is pure
sincerity in friendship required of every man, because, prior to all
experience, this duty is involved as duty in the idea of a reason determining the will by *a priori* principles.

When we add further that, unless we deny that the notion of
morality has any truth or reference to any possible object, we must
admit that its law must be valid, not merely for men, but for all *rational creatures generally,* not merely under certain contingent conditions or with exceptions, but *with absolute necessity,* then it is clear that
no experience could enable us to infer even the possibility of such
apodictic laws. For with what right could we bring into unbounded
respect as a universal precept for every rational nature that which
perhaps holds only under the contingent conditions of humanity?
Or how could laws of the determination of *our* will be regarded as
laws of the determination of the will of rational beings generally,
and for us only as such, if they were merely empirical, and did not
take their origin wholly *a priori* from pure but practical reason?

Nor could anything be more fatal to morality than that we
should wish to derive it from examples. For every example of it that
is set before me must be first itself tested by principles of morality,
whether it is worthy to serve as an original example, *i.e.* as a pattern,
but by no means can it authoritatively furnish the conception of
morality. Even the Holy One of the Gospels must first be compared with our ideal of moral perfection before we can recognise
Him as such; and so He says of Himself, "Why call ye Me (whom
you see) good; none is good (the model of good) but God only
(whom ye do not see)?" But whence have we the conception of God
as the supreme good? Simply from the *idea* of moral perfection,

which reason frames *a priori*, and connects inseparably with the no- 4:409
tion of a free-will. Imitation finds no place at all in morality, and
examples serve only for encouragement, *i.e.* they put beyond doubt
the feasibility of what the law commands, they make visible that
which the practical rule expresses more generally, but they can
never authorize us to set aside the true original which lies in reason,
and to guide ourselves by examples.

If then there is no genuine supreme principle of morality but
what must rest simply on pure reason, independent on all experience, I think it is not necessary even to put the question, whether it
is good to exhibit these concepts in their generality (*in abstracto*) as
they are established *a priori* along with the principles belonging to
them, if our knowledge is to be distinguished from the *vulgar,* and
to be called philosophical. In our times indeed this might perhaps
be necessary; for if we collected votes, whether pure rational
knowledge separated from everything empirical, that is to say,
metaphysic of morals, or whether popular practical philosophy is
to be preferred, it is easy to guess which side would preponderate.

This descending to popular notions is certainly very commend-
able, if the ascent to the principles of pure reason has first taken
place and been satisfactorily accomplished. This implies that we
first *found* Ethics on Metaphysics, and then, when it is firmly established, procure a *hearing* for it by giving it a popular character. But
it is quite absurd to try to be popular in the first inquiry, on which
the soundness of the principles depends. It is not only that this proceeding can never lay claim to the very rare merit of a true *philosophical popularity,* since there is no art in being intelligible if one
renounces all thoroughness of insight; but also it produces a dis-
gusting medley of compiled observations and half-reasoned principles. Shallow pates enjoy this because it can be used for every-day
chat, but the sagacious find in it only confusion, and being unsatisfied and unable to help themselves, they turn away their eyes, while
philosophers, who see quite well through this delusion, are little 4:410
listened to when they call men off for a time from this pretended
popularity, in order that they might be rightfully popular after they
have attained a definite insight.

We need only look at the attempts of moralists in that favourite fashion, and we shall find at one time the special constitution of human nature (including, however, the idea of a rational nature generally), at one time perfection, at another happiness, here moral sense, there fear of God, a little of this, and a little of that, in marvellous mixture without its occurring to them to ask whether the principles of morality are to be sought in the knowledge of human nature at all (which we can have only from experience); and, if this is not so, if these principles are to be found altogether *a priori* free from everything empirical, in pure rational concepts only, and nowhere else, not even in the smallest degree; then rather to adopt the method of making this a separate inquiry, as pure practical philosophy, or (if one may use a name so decried) as metaphysic of morals,[3] to bring it by itself to completeness, and to require the public, which wishes for popular treatment, to await the issue of this undertaking.

Such a metaphysic of morals, completely isolated, not mixed with any anthropology, theology, physics, or hyperphysics, and still less with occult qualities (which we might call hypophysical), is not only an indispensable substratum of all sound theoretical knowledge of duties, but is at the same time a desideratum of the highest importance to the actual fulfilment of their precepts. For the pure conception of duty, unmixed with any foreign addition of empirical attractions, and, in a word, the conception of the moral law, exercises on the human heart, by way of reason alone (which first becomes aware with this that it can of itself be practical), an influence so much more powerful than all other springs[4] which may be

4:411

3 Just as pure mathematics are distinguished from applied, pure logic from applied, so if we choose we may also distinguish pure philosophy of morals (metaphysic) from applied (viz. applied to human nature). By this designation we are also at once reminded that moral principles are not based on properties of human nature, but must subsist *a priori* of themselves, while from such principles practical rules must be capable of being deduced for every rational nature, and accordingly for that of man.

4 I have a letter from the late excellent Sulzer, in which he asks me what can be the reason that moral instruction, although containing much that is convincing for the reason, yet accomplishes so little? My answer was postponed in order that I might make it complete. But it is simply this, that the teachers themselves have not got their own notions clear, and when

derived from the field of experience, that in the consciousness of its worth, it despises the latter, and can by degrees become their master; whereas a mixed ethics, compounded partly of motives drawn from feelings and inclinations, and partly also of conceptions of reason, must make the mind waver between motives which cannot be brought under any principle, which lead to good only by mere accident, and very often also to evil.

From what has been said, it is clear that all moral conceptions have their seat and origin completely *a priori* in the reason, and that, moreover, in the commonest reason just as truly as in that which is in the highest degree speculative; that they cannot be obtained by abstraction from any empirical, and therefore merely contingent knowledge; that it is just this purity of their origin that makes them worthy to serve as our supreme practical principle, and that just in proportion as we add anything empirical, we detract from their genuine influence, and from the absolute value of actions; that it is not only of the greatest necessity, in a purely speculative point of view, but is also of the greatest practical importance to derive these notions and laws from pure reason, to present them pure and unmixed, and even to determine the compass of this practical or pure rational knowledge, *i.e.* to determine the whole faculty of pure practical reason; and, in doing so, we must not make its principles 4:412 dependent on the particular nature of human reason, though in speculative philosophy this may be permitted, or may even at times be necessary; but since moral laws ought to hold good for every rational creature, we must derive them from the general concept of a rational being. In this way, although for its *application* to man moral-

---

they endeavour to make up for this by raking up motives of moral goodness from every quarter, trying to make their physic right strong, they spoil it. For the commonest understanding shows that if we imagine, on the one hand, an act of honesty done with steadfast mind, apart from every view to advantage of any kind in this world or another, and even under the greatest temptations of necessity or allurement, and, on the other hand, a similar act which was affected, in however low a degree, by a foreign motive, the former leaves far behind and eclipses the second; it elevates the soul, and inspires the wish to be able to act in like manner oneself. Even moderately young children feel this impression, and one should never represent duties to them in any other light.

ity has need of anthropology, yet, in the first instance, we must treat it independently as pure philosophy, *i.e.* as metaphysic, complete in itself (a thing which in such distinct branches of science is easily done); knowing well that unless we are in possession of this, it would not only be vain to determine the moral element of duty in right actions for purposes of speculative criticism, but it would be impossible to base morals on their genuine principles, even for common practical purposes, especially of moral instruction, so as to produce pure moral dispositions, and to engraft them on men's minds to the promotion of the greatest possible good in the world.

But in order that in this study we may not merely advance by the natural steps from the common moral judgment (in this case very worthy of respect) to the philosophical, as has been already done, but also from a popular philosophy, which goes no further than it can reach by groping with the help of examples, to metaphysic (which does not allow itself to be checked by anything empirical, and as it must measure the whole extent of this kind of rational knowledge, goes as far as ideal conceptions, where even examples fail us), we must follow and clearly describe the practical faculty of reason, from the general rules of its determination to the point where the notion of duty springs from it.

Everything in nature works according to laws. Rational beings alone have the faculty of acting according *to the conception* of laws, that is according to principles, *i.e.* have a *will*. Since the deduction of actions from principles requires *reason*, the will is nothing but practical reason. If reason infallibly determines the will, then the actions of such a being which are recognised as objectively necessary are subjectively necessary also, *i.e.* the will is a faculty to choose *that only* which reason independent on inclination recognises as practically necessary, *i.e.* as good. But if reason of itself does not sufficiently determine the will, if the latter is subject also to subjective conditions (particular impulses) which do not always coincide with the objective conditions; in a word, if the will does not *in itself* completely accord with reason (which is actually the case with men), then the actions which objectively are recognised as necessary are subjectively contingent, and the determination of such a will according to objective laws is *obligation,* that is to say, the relation of the objective laws to a will that is not thoroughly good is conceived as the determination of the will of a rational being by principles of reason, but which the will from its nature does not of necessity follow.

The conception of an objective principle, in so far as it is obligatory for a will, is called a command (of reason), and the formula of the command is called an Imperative.

All imperatives are expressed by the word *ought* [or *shall*], and thereby indicate the relation of an objective law of reason to a will, which from its subjective constitution is not necessarily determined by it (an obligation). They say that something would be good to do or to forbear, but they say it to a will which does not always do a thing because it is conceived to be good to do it. That is practically *good,* however, which determines the will by means of the conceptions of reason, and consequently not from subjective causes, but objectively, that is on principles which are valid for every rational being as such. It is distinguished from the *pleasant,* as that which influences the will only by means of sensation from merely subjective causes, valid only for the sense of this or that one, and not as a principle of reason, which holds for every one.[5]

A perfectly good will would therefore be equally subject to ob-   4:414 jective laws (viz. laws of good), but could not be conceived as *obliged* thereby to act lawfully, because of itself from its subjective constitution it can only be determined by the conception of good. There-

5 The dependence of the desires on sensations is called inclination, and this accordingly always indicates a *want.* The dependence of a contingently determinable will on principles of reason is called an *interest.* This therefore is found only in the case of a dependent will, which does not always of itself conform to reason; in the Divine will we cannot conceive any interest. But the human will can also *take an interest* in a thing without therefore acting *from interest.* The former signifies the *practical* interest in the action, the latter the *pathological* in the object of the action. The former indicates only dependence of the will on principles of reason in themselves; the second, dependence on principles of reason for the sake of inclination, reason supplying only the practical rules how the requirement of the inclination may be satisfied. In the first case the action interests me; in the second the object of the action (because it is pleasant to me). We have seen in the first section that in an action done from duty we must look not to the interest in the object, but only to that in the action itself, and in its rational principle (viz. the law).

fore no imperatives hold for the Divine will, or in general for a *holy* will; *ought* is here out of place, because the volition is already of itself necessarily in unison with the law. Therefore imperatives are only formulæ to express the relation of objective laws of all volition to the subjective imperfection of the will of this or that rational being, *e.g.* the human will.

Now all *imperatives* command either *hypothetically* or *categorically.* The former represent the practical necessity of a possible action as means to something else that is willed (or at least which one might possibly will). The categorical imperative would be that which represented an action as necessary of itself without reference to another end, *i.e.* as objectively necessary.

Since every practical law represents a possible action as good, and on this account, for a subject who is practically determinable by reason, necessary, all imperatives are formulæ determining an action which is necessary according to the principle of a will good in some respects. If now the action is good only as a means *to something else*, then the imperative is *hypothetical;* if it is conceived as good *in itself* and consequently as being necessarily the principle of a will which of itself conforms to reason, then it is *categorical.*

Thus the imperative declares what action possible by me would be good, and presents the practical rule in relation to a will which does not forthwith perform an action simply because it is good, whether because the subject does not always know that it is good, or because, even if it know this, yet its maxims might be opposed to the objective principles of practical reason.

Accordingly the hypothetical imperative only says that the action is good for some purpose, *possible* or *actual.* In the first case it is a Problematical, in the second an Assertorial practical principle. The categorical imperative which declares an action to be objectively necessary in itself without reference to any purpose, *i.e.* without any other end, is valid as an Apodictic (practical) principle.

Whatever is possible only by the power of some rational being may also be conceived as a possible purpose of some will; and therefore the principles of action as regards the means necessary to attain some possible purpose are in fact infinitely numerous. All sciences have a practical part, consisting of problems expressing that some end is possible for us, and of imperatives directing how it may be attained. These may, therefore, be called in general imperatives of Skill. Here there is no question whether the end is rational and good, but only what one must do in order to attain it. The precepts for the physician to make his patient thoroughly healthy, and for a poisoner to ensure certain death; are of equal value in this respect, that each serves to effect its purpose perfectly. Since in early youth it cannot be known what ends are likely to occur to us in the course of life, parents seek to have their children taught a *great many things,* and provide for their *skill* in the use of means for all sorts of arbitrary ends, of none of which can they determine whether it may not perhaps hereafter be an object to their pupil, but which it is at all events *possible* that he might aim at; and this anxiety is so great that they commonly neglect to form and correct their judgment on the value of the things which may be chosen as ends.

There is *one* end, however, which may be assumed to be actually such to all rational beings (so far as imperatives apply to them, viz. as dependent beings), and therefore, one purpose which they not merely *may* have, but which we may with certainty assume that they all actually *have* by a natural necessity, and this is *happiness.* The hypothetical imperative which expresses the practical necessity of an action as means to the advancement of happiness is Assertorial. We are not to present it as necessary for an uncertain and merely possible purpose, but for a purpose which we may presuppose with certainty and *a priori* in every man, because it belongs to his being. Now skill in the choice of means to his own greatest well-being may be called *prudence,*[6] in the narrowest sense. And thus the imperative which refers to the choice of means to one's own 4:416

6 The word *prudence* is taken in two senses: in the one it may bear the name of knowledge of the world, in the other that of private prudence. The former is a man's ability to influence others so as to use them for his own purposes. The latter is the sagacity to combine all these purposes for his own lasting benefit. This latter is properly that to which the value even of the former is reduced, and when a man is prudent in the former sense, but not in the latter, we might better say of him that he is clever and cunning, but, on the whole, imprudent.

happiness, *i.e.* the precept of prudence, is still always *hypothetical*; the action is not commanded absolutely, but only as means to another purpose.

Finally, there is an imperative which commands a certain conduct immediately, without having as its condition any other purpose to be attained by it. This imperative is Categorical. It concerns not the matter of the action, or its intended result, but its form and the principle of which it is itself a result; and what is essentially good in it consists in the mental disposition, let the consequence be what it may. This imperative may be called that of Morality.

There is a marked distinction also between the volitions on these three sorts of principles in the *dissimilarity* of the obligation of the will. In order to mark this difference more clearly, I think they would be most suitably named in their order if we said they are either *rules* of skill, or *counsels* of prudence, or *commands* (*laws*) of morality. For it is *law* only that involves the conception of an *unconditional* and objective necessity, which is consequently universally valid; and commands are laws which must be obeyed, that is, must be followed, even in opposition to inclination. *Counsels*, indeed, involve necessity, but one which can only hold under a contingent subjective condition, viz. they depend on whether this or that man reckons this or that as part of his happiness; the categorical imperative, on the contrary, is not limited by any condition, and as being absolutely, although practically, necessary, may be quite properly called a command. We might also call the first kind of imperatives *technical* (belonging to art), the second *pragmatic*[7] (to welfare), the third *moral* (belonging to free conduct generally, that is, to morals).

4:417

Now arises the question, how are all these imperatives possible? This question does not seek to know how we can conceive the accomplishment of the action which the imperative ordains, but merely how we can conceive the obligation of the will which the

---

7 It seems to me that the proper signification of the word *pragmatic* may be most accurately defined in this way. For *sanctions* are called pragmatic which flow properly not from the law of the states as necessary enactments, but from *precaution* for the general welfare. A history is composed pragmatically when it teaches *prudence, i.e.* instructs the world how it can provide for its interests better, or at least as well, as the men of former time.

imperative expresses. No special explanation is needed to show how an imperative of skill is possible. Whoever wills the end, wills also (so far as reason decides his conduct) the means in his power which are indispensably necessary thereto. This proposition is, as regards the volition, analytical; for, in willing an object as my effect, there is already thought the causality of myself as an acting cause, that is to say, the use of the means; and the imperative educes from the conception of volition of an end the conception of actions necessary to this end. Synthetical propositions must no doubt be employed in defining the means to a proposed end; but they do not concern the principle, the act of the will, but the object and its realization. *Ex. gr.*, that in order to bisect a line on an unerring principle I must draw from its extremities two intersecting arcs; this no doubt is taught by mathematics only in synthetical propositions; but if I know that it is only by this process that the intended operation can be performed, then to say that if I fully will the operation, I also will the action required for it, is an analytical proposition; for it is one and the same thing to conceive something as an effect which I can produce in a certain way, and to conceive myself as acting in this way.

If it were only equally easy to give a definite conception of happiness, the imperatives of prudence would correspond exactly with those of skill, and would likewise be analytical. For in this case as in that, it could be said, whoever wills the end, wills also (according to the dictate of reason necessarily) the indispensable means thereto which are in his power. But, unfortunately, the notion of happiness is so indefinite that although every man wishes to attain it, yet he never can say definitely and consistently what it is that he really wishes and wills. The reason of this is that all the elements which belong to the notion of happiness are altogether empirical, *i.e.* they must be borrowed from experience, and nevertheless the idea of happiness requires an absolute whole, a maximum of welfare in my present and all future circumstances. Now it is impossible that the most clear-sighted, and at the same time most powerful being (supposed finite) should frame to himself a definite conception of what he really wills in this. Does he will riches, how much anxiety, envy,

4:418

and snares might he not thereby draw upon his shoulders? Does he will knowledge and discernment, perhaps it might prove to be only an eye so much the sharper to show him so much the more fearfully the evils that are now concealed from him, and that cannot be avoided, or to impose more wants on his desires, which already give him concern enough. Would he have long life, who guarantees to him that it would not be a long misery? would he at least have health? how often has uneasiness of the body restrained from excesses into which perfect health would have allowed one to fall? and so on. In short he is unable, on any principle, to determine with certainty what would make him truly happy; because to do so he would need to be omniscient. We cannot therefore act on any definite principles to secure happiness, but only on empirical counsels, *ex. gr.* of regimen, frugality, courtesy, reserve, &c., which experience teaches do, on the average, most promote well-being. Hence it follows that the imperatives of prudence do not, strictly speaking, command at all, that is, they cannot present actions objectively as practically *necessary;* that they are rather to be regarded as counsels (*consilia*) than precepts (*præcepta*) of reason, that the problem to determine certainly and universally what action would promote the happiness of a rational being is completely insoluble, and consequently no imperative respecting it is possible which should, in the strict sense, command to do what makes happy; because happiness is not an ideal of reason but of imagination, resting solely on empirical grounds, and it is vain to expect that these should define an action by which one could attain the totality of a series of consequences which is really endless. This imperative of prudence would however be an analytical proposition if we assume that the means to happiness could be certainly assigned; for it is distinguished from the imperative of skill only by this, that in the latter the end is merely possible, in the former it is given; as however both only ordain the means to that which we suppose to be willed as an end, it follows that the imperative which ordains the willing of the means to him who wills the end is in both cases analytical. Thus there is no difficulty in regard to the possibility of an imperative of this kind either.

4:419

On the other hand the question, how the imperative of *morality* is possible, is undoubtedly one, the only one, demanding a solution, as this is not at all hypothetical, and the objective necessity which it presents cannot rest on any hypothesis, as is the case with the hypothetical imperatives. Only here we must never leave out of consideration that we *cannot* make out *by any example*, in other words empirically, whether there is such an imperative at all; but it is rather to be feared that all those which seem to be categorical may yet be at bottom hypothetical. For instance, when the precept is: Thou shalt not promise deceitfully; and it is assumed that the necessity of this is not a mere counsel to avoid some other evil, so that it should mean: thou shalt not make a lying promise, lest if it become known thou shouldst destroy thy credit, but that an action of this kind must be regarded as evil in itself, so that the imperative of the prohibition is categorical; then we cannot show with certainty in any example that the will was determined merely by the law, without any other spring of action, although it may appear to be so. For it is always possible that fear of disgrace, perhaps also obscure dread of other dangers, may have a secret influence on the will. Who can prove by experience the non-existence of a cause when all that experience tells us is that we do not perceive it? But in such a case the so-called moral imperative, which as such appears to be categorical and unconditional, would in reality be only a pragmatic precept, drawing our attention to our own interests, and merely teaching us to take these into consideration.

We shall therefore have to investigate *a priori* the possibility of a categorical imperative, as we have not in this case the advantage of 4:420 its reality being given in experience, so that [the elucidation of] its possibility should be requisite only for its explanation, not for its establishment. In the meantime it may be discerned beforehand that the categorical imperative alone has the purport of a practical law: all the rest may indeed be called *principles* of the will but not laws, since whatever is only necessary for the attainment of some arbitrary purpose may be considered as in itself contingent, and we can at any time be free from the precept if we give up the purpose: on the contrary, the unconditional command leaves the will no liberty to choose the opposite; consequently it alone carries with it that necessity which we require in a law.

Secondly, in the case of this categorical imperative or law of morality, the difficulty (of discerning its possibility) is a very profound one. It is an *a priori* synthetical practical proposition;[8] and as there is so much difficulty in discerning the possibility of speculative propositions of this kind, it may readily be supposed that the difficulty will be no less with the practical.

In this problem we will first inquire whether the mere conception of a categorical imperative may not perhaps supply us also with the formula of it, containing the proposition which alone can be a categorical imperative; for even if we know the tenor of such an absolute command, yet how it is possible will require further special and laborious study, which we postpone to the last section.

When I conceive a hypothetical imperative in general I do not know beforehand what it will contain until I am given the condition. But when I conceive a categorical imperative I know at once what it contains. For as the imperative contains besides the law only 4:421 the necessity that the maxims[9] shall conform to this law, while the law contains no conditions restricting it, there remains nothing but the general statement that the maxim of the action should conform to a universal law, and it is this conformity alone that the imperative properly represents as necessary.

There is therefore but one categorical imperative, namely this: *Act only on that maxim whereby thou canst at the same time will that it should become a universal law.*

8 I connect the act with the will without presupposing any condition resulting from any inclination, but *a priori*, and therefore necessarily (though only objectively, *i.e.* assuming the idea of a reason possessing full power over all subjective motives). This is accordingly a practical proposition which does not deduce the willing of an action by mere analysis from another already presupposed (for we have not such a perfect will), but connects it immediately with the conception of the will of a rational being, as something not contained in it.

9 A MAXIM is a subjective principle of action, and must be distinguished from the *objective principle*, namely, practical law. The former contains the practical rule set by reason according to the conditions of the subject (often its ignorance or its inclinations), so that it is the principle on which the subject *acts;* but the law is the objective principle valid for every rational being, and is the principle on which it *ought to act* that is an imperative.

Now if all imperatives of duty can be deduced from this one imperative as from their principle, then, although it should remain undecided whether what is called duty is not merely a vain notion, yet at least we shall be able to show what we understand by it and what this notion means.

Since the universality of the law according to which effects are produced constitutes what is properly called *nature* in the most general sense (as to form), that is the existence of things so far as it is determined by general laws, the imperative of duty may be expressed thus: *Act as if the maxim of thy action were to become by thy will a Universal Law of Nature.*

We will now enumerate a few duties, adopting the usual division of them into duties to ourselves and to others, and into perfect and imperfect duties.[10]

1. A man reduced to despair by a series of misfortunes feels wearied of life, but is still so far in possession of his reason that he can ask himself whether it would not be contrary to his duty to himself to take his own life. Now he inquires whether the maxim of his action could become a universal law of nature. His maxim is: From self-love I adopt it as a principle to shorten my life when its longer duration is likely to bring more evil than satisfaction. It is asked then simply whether this principle founded on self-love can become a universal law of nature. Now we see at once that a system of nature of which it should be a law to destroy life by means of the very feeling whose special nature it is to impel to the improvement of life would contradict itself, and therefore could not exist as a system of nature; hence that maxim cannot possibly exist as a universal law of nature, and consequently would be wholly inconsistent with the supreme principle of all duty.

2. Another finds himself forced by necessity to borrow money.

4:422

10 It must be noted here that I reserve the division of duties for a future *metaphysic of morals;* so that I give it here only as an arbitrary one (in order to arrange my examples). For the rest, I understand by a perfect duty one that admits no exception in favour of inclination, and then I have not merely external, but also internal perfect duties. This is contrary to the use of the word adopted in the schools; but I do not intend to justify it here, as it is all one for my purpose whether it is admitted or not.

He knows that he will not be able to repay it, but sees also that nothing will be lent to him, unless he promises stoutly to repay it in a definite time. He desires to make this promise, but he has still so much conscience as to ask himself: Is it not unlawful and inconsistent with duty to get out of a difficulty in this way? Suppose however that he resolves to do so, then the maxim of his action would be expressed thus: When I think myself in want of money, I will borrow money and promise to repay it, although I know that I never can do so. Now this principle of self-love or of one's own advantage may perhaps be consistent with my whole future welfare; but the question now is, Is it right? I change then the suggestion of self-love into a universal law, and state the question thus: How would it be if my maxim were a universal law? Then I see at once that it could never hold as a universal law of nature, but would necessarily contradict itself. For supposing it to be a universal law that everyone when he thinks himself in a difficulty should be able to promise whatever he pleases, with the purpose of not keeping his promise, the promise itself would become impossible, as well as the end that one might have in view in it, since no one would consider that anything was promised to him, but would ridicule all such statements as vain pretences.

3. A third finds in himself a talent which with the help of some culture might make him a useful man in many respects. But he finds himself in comfortable circumstances, and prefers to indulge in pleasure rather than to take pains in enlarging and improving his happy natural capacities. He asks, however, whether his maxim of neglect of his natural gifts, besides agreeing with his inclination to indulgence, agrees also with what is called duty. He sees then that a system of nature could indeed subsist with such a universal law although men (like the South Sea islanders) should let their talents rust, and resolve to devote their lives merely to idleness, amusement, and propagation of their species—in a word, to enjoyment; but he cannot possibly *will* that this should be a universal law of nature, or be implanted in us as such by a natural instinct. For, as a rational being, he necessarily wills that his faculties be developed, since they serve him, and have been given him, for all sorts of possible purposes.

4. A fourth, who is in prosperity, while he sees that others have to contend with great wretchedness and that he could help them, thinks: What concern is it of mine? Let everyone be as happy as heaven pleases, or as he can make himself; I will take nothing from him nor even envy him, only I do not wish to contribute anything to his welfare or to his assistance in distress! Now no doubt if such a mode of thinking were a universal law, the human race might very well subsist, and doubtless even better than in a state in which everyone talks of sympathy and good-will, or even takes care occasionally to put it into practice, but on the other side, also cheats when he can, betrays the rights of men, or otherwise violates them. But although it is possible that a universal law of nature might exist in accordance with that maxim, it is impossible to *will* that such a principle should have the universal validity of a law of nature. For a will which resolved this would contradict itself, inasmuch as many cases might occur in which one would have need of the love and sympathy of others, and in which, by such a law of nature, sprung from his own will, he would deprive himself of all hope of the aid he desires.

These are a few of the many actual duties, or at least what we regard as such, which obviously fall into two classes on the one principle that we have laid down. We must be *able to will* that a maxim of 4:424 our action should be a universal law. This is the canon of the moral appreciation of the action generally. Some actions are of such a character that their maxim cannot without contradiction be even *conceived* as a universal law of nature, far from it being possible that we should *will* that it *should* be so. In others this intrinsic impossibility is not found, but still it is impossible to *will* that their maxim should be raised to the universality of a law of nature, since such a will would contradict itself. It is easily seen that the former violate strict or rigorous (inflexible) duty; the latter only laxer (meritorious) duty. Thus it has been completely shown by these examples how all duties depend as regards the nature of the obligation (not the object of the action) on the same principle.

If now we attend to ourselves on occasion of any transgression of duty, we shall find that we in fact do not will that our maxim should be a universal law, for that is impossible for us; on the contrary we will that the opposite should remain a universal law, only we assume the liberty of making an *exception* in our own favour or (just for this time only) in favour of our inclination. Consequently if we considered all cases from one and the same point of view, namely, that of reason, we should find a contradiction in our own will, namely, that a certain principle should be objectively necessary as a universal law, and yet subjectively should not be universal, but admit of exceptions. As however we at one moment regard our action from the point of view of a will wholly conformed to reason, and then again look at the same action from the point of view of a will affected by inclination, there is not really any contradiction, but an antagonism of inclination to the precept of reason, whereby the universality of the principle is changed into a mere generality, so that the practical principle of reason shall meet the maxim half way. Now, although this cannot be justified in our own impartial judgment, yet it proves that we do really recognise the validity of the categorical imperative and (with all respect for it) only allow ourselves a few exceptions, which we think unimportant and forced from us.

4:425 We have thus established at least this much, that if duty is a conception which is to have any import and real legislative authority for our actions, it can only be expressed in categorical, and not at all in hypothetical imperatives. We have also, which is of great importance, exhibited clearly and definitely for every practical application the content of the categorical imperative, which must contain the principle of all duty if there is such a thing at all. We have not yet, however, advanced so far as to prove *a priori* that there actually is such an imperative, that there is a practical law which commands absolutely of itself, and without any other impulse, and that the following of this law is duty.

With the view of attaining to this it is of extreme importance to remember that we must not allow ourselves to think of deducing the reality of this principle from the *particular attributes of human nature.* For duty is to be a practical, unconditional necessity of action; it must therefore hold for all rational beings (to whom an imperative can apply at all) and *for this reason only* be also a law for all human wills. On the contrary, whatever is deduced from the particular natural characteristics of humanity, from certain feelings and propensions, nay even, if possible, from any particular tendency proper to human reason, and which need not necessarily hold for the will of every rational being; this may indeed supply us with a maxim, but not with a law; with a subjective principle on which we may have a propension and inclination to act, but not with an objective principle on which we should be *enjoined* to act, even though all our propensions, inclinations, and natural dispositions were opposed to it. In fact the sublimity and intrinsic dignity of the command in duty are so much the more evident, the less the subjective impulses favour it and the more they oppose it, without being able in the slightest degree to weaken the obligation of the law or to diminish its validity.

Here then we see philosophy brought to a critical position, since it has to be firmly fixed, notwithstanding that it has nothing to support it either in heaven or earth. Here it must show its purity as absolute dictator of its own laws, not the herald of those which are whispered to it by an implanted sense or who knows what tutelary nature. Although these may be better than nothing, yet they can 4:426 never afford principles dictated by reason, which must have their source wholly *a priori* and thence their commanding authority, expecting everything from the supremacy of the law and the due respect for it, nothing from inclination, or else condemning the man to self-contempt and inward abhorrence.

Thus every empirical element is not only quite incapable of being an aid to the principle of morality, but is even highly prejudicial to the purity of morals, for the proper and inestimable worth of an absolutely good will consists just in this, that the principle of action is free from all influence of contingent grounds, which alone experience can furnish. We cannot too much or too often repeat our warning against this lax and even mean habit of thought which seeks for its principle amongst empirical motives and laws; for human reason in its weariness is glad to rest on this pillow, and in a dream of sweet illusions (in which, instead of Juno, it embraces a cloud) it substitutes for morality a bastard patched up from limbs of various derivation, which looks like anything one chooses to see in it; only not like virtue to one who has once beheld her in her true form.[11]

The question then is this: Is it a necessary law *for all rational beings* that they should always judge of their actions by maxims of which they can themselves will that they should serve as universal laws? If it is so, then it must be connected (altogether *a priori*) with the very conception of the will of a rational being generally. But in order to discover this connexion we must, however reluctantly, take a step into metaphysic, although into a domain of it which is distinct from speculative philosophy, namely, the metaphysic of morals. In a practical philosophy, where it is not the reasons of what *happens* that we have to ascertain, but the laws of what *ought to happen*, even although it never does, *i.e.* objective practical laws, there it is not necessary to inquire into the reasons why anything pleases or displeases, how the pleasure of mere sensation differs from taste, and whether the latter is distinct from a general satisfaction of reason; on what the feeling of pleasure or pain rests, and how from it desires and inclinations arise, and from these again maxims by the co-operation of reason: for all this belongs to an empirical psychology, which would constitute the second part of physics, if we regard physics as the *philosophy of nature*, so far as it is based on *empirical laws*. But here we are concerned with objective practical laws, and consequently with the relation of the will to itself so far as it is determined by reason alone, in which case whatever has reference to anything empirical is necessarily excluded; since if *reason of itself alone* determines the conduct (and it is the possibility of this that we are now investigating), it must necessarily do so *a priori*.

The will is conceived as a faculty of determining oneself to action *in accordance with the conception of certain laws*. And such a faculty can be found only in rational beings. Now that which serves the

4:427

---

11 To behold virtue in her proper form is nothing else but to contemplate morality stripped of all admixture of sensible things and of every spurious ornament of reward or self-love. How much she then eclipses everything else that appears charming to the affections, every one may readily perceive with the least exertion of his reason, if it be not wholly spoiled for abstraction.

will as the objective ground of its self-determination is the *end,* and if this is assigned by reason alone, it must hold for all rational beings. On the other hand, that which merely contains the ground of possibility of the action of which the effect is the end, this is called the *means.* The subjective ground of the desire is the *spring,* the objective ground of the volition is the *motive;* hence the distinction between subjective ends which rest on springs, and objective ends which depend on motives valid for every rational being. Practical principles are *formal* when they abstract from all subjective ends, 4:428 they are *material* when they assume these, and therefore particular springs of action. The ends which a rational being proposes to himself at pleasure as *effects* of his actions (material ends) are all only relative, for it is only their relation to the particular desires of the subject that gives them their worth, which therefore cannot furnish principles universal and necessary for all rational beings and for every volition, that is to say practical laws. Hence all these relative ends can give rise only to hypothetical imperatives.

Supposing, however, that there were something *whose existence* has *in itself* an absolute worth, something which, being *an end in itself,* could be a source of definite laws, then in this and this alone would lie the source of a possible categorical imperative, *i.e.* a practical law.

Now I say: man and generally any rational being *exists* as an end in himself, *not merely as a means* to be arbitrarily used by this or that will, but in all his actions, whether they concern himself or other rational beings, must be always regarded at the same time as an end. All objects of the inclinations have only a conditional worth, for if the inclinations and the wants founded on them did not exist, then their object would be without value. But the inclinations themselves being sources of want, are so far from having an absolute worth for which they should be desired, that on the contrary it must be the universal wish of every rational being to be wholly free from them. Thus the worth of any object which is *to be acquired* by our action is always conditional. Beings whose existence depends not on our will but on nature's, have nevertheless, if they are irrational beings, only a relative value as means, and are therefore called *things;*

rational beings, on the contrary, are called *persons*, because their very nature points them out as ends in themselves, that is as something which must not be used merely as means, and so far therefore restricts freedom of action (and is an object of respect). These, therefore, are not merely subjective ends whose existence has a worth *for us* as an effect of our action, but *objective ends*, that is things whose existence is an end in itself: an end moreover for which no other can be substituted, which they should subserve *merely* as means, for otherwise nothing whatever would possess *absolute worth*; but if all worth were conditioned and therefore contingent, then there would be no supreme practical principle of reason whatever.

If then there is a supreme practical principle or, in respect of the human will, a categorical imperative, it must be one which being drawn from the conception of that which is necessarily an end for every one because it is *an end in itself*, constitutes an *objective* principle of will, and can therefore serve as a universal practical law. The foundation of this principle is: *rational nature exists as an end in itself.*
4:429 Man necessarily conceives his own existence as being so: so far then this is a *subjective* principle of human actions. But every other rational being regards its existence similarly, just on the same rational principle that holds for me:[12] so that it is at the same time an objective principle, from which as a supreme practical law all laws of the will must be capable of being deduced. Accordingly the practical imperative will be as follows: *So act as to treat humanity, whether in thine own person or in that of any other, in every case as an end withal, never as means only.* We will now inquire whether this can be practically carried out.

To abide by the previous examples:

Firstly, under the head of necessary duty to oneself: He who contemplates suicide should ask himself whether his action can be consistent with the idea of humanity *as an end in itself.* If he destroys himself in order to escape from painful circumstances, he uses a person merely as *a mean* to maintain a tolerable condition up to the

---

12 This proposition is here stated as a postulate. The grounds of it will be found in the concluding section.

end of life. But a man is not a thing, that is to say, something which 4:430
can be used merely as means, but must in all his actions be always
considered as an end in himself. I cannot, therefore, dispose in any
way of a man in my own person so as to mutilate him, to damage or
kill him. (It belongs to ethics proper to define this principle more
precisely so as to avoid all misunderstanding, *e.g.* as to the amputa-
tion of the limbs in order to preserve myself; as to exposing my life
to danger with a view to preserve it, &c. This question is therefore
omitted here.)

Secondly, as regards necessary duties, or those of strict obligation,
towards others; he who is thinking of making a lying promise to
others will see at once that he would be using another man *merely as
a mean,* without the latter containing at the same time the end in
himself. For he whom I propose by such a promise to use for my
own purposes cannot possibly assent to my mode of acting towards
him, and therefore cannot himself contain the end of this action.
This violation of the principle of humanity in other men is more
obvious if we take in examples of attacks on the freedom and property of others. For then it is clear that he who transgresses the
rights of men, intends to use the person of others merely as means,
without considering that as rational beings they ought always to be
esteemed also as ends, that is, as beings who must be capable of
containing in themselves the end of the very same action.[13]

Thirdly, as regards contingent (meritorious) duties to oneself; it is
not enough that the action does not violate humanity in our own
person as an end in itself, it must also *harmonise with* it. Now there
are in humanity capacities of greater perfection, which belong to
the end that nature has in view in regard to humanity in ourselves
as the subject: to neglect these might perhaps be consistent with the

---

13 Let it not be thought that the common: *quod tibi non vis fieri, &c.,* could serve here as
the rule or principle. For it is only a deduction from the former, though with several limitations; it cannot be a universal law, for it does not contain the principle of duties to oneself,
nor of the duties of benevolence to others (for many a one would gladly consent that others
should not benefit him, provided only that he might be excused from showing benevolence
to them), nor finally that of duties of strict obligation to one another, for on this principle the
criminal might argue against the judge who punishes him, and so on.

maintenance of humanity as an end in itself, but not with the *advancement* of this end.

Fourthly, as regards meritorious duties towards others: the natural end which all men have is their own happiness. Now humanity might indeed subsist, although no one should contribute anything to the happiness of others, provided he did not intentionally withdraw anything from it; but after all this would only harmonise negatively not positively with *humanity as an end in itself,* if every one does not also endeavour, as far as in him lies, to forward the ends of others. For the ends of any subject which is an end in himself, ought as far as possible to be *my* ends also, if that conception is to have its *full* effect with me.

This principle, that humanity and generally every rational nature is *an end in itself* (which is the supreme limiting condition of every man's freedom of action), is not borrowed from experience, *firstly,* because it is universal, applying as it does to all rational beings whatever, and experience is not capable of determining anything about them; *secondly,* because it does not present humanity as an end to men (subjectively), that is as an object which men do of themselves actually adopt as an end; but as an objective end, which must as a law constitute the supreme limiting condition of all our subjective ends, let them be what we will; it must therefore spring from pure reason. In fact the objective principle of all practical legislation lies (according to the first principle) in *the rule* and its form of universality which makes it capable of being a law (say, *e.g.,* a law of nature); but the *subjective* principle is in the *end;* now by the second principle the subject of all ends is each rational being, inasmuch as it is an end in itself. Hence follows the third practical principle of the will, which is the ultimate condition of its harmony with the universal practical reason, viz.: the idea of *the will of every rational being as a universally legislative will.*

On this principle all maxims are rejected which are inconsistent with the will being itself universal legislator. Thus the will is not subject simply to the law, but so subject that it must be regarded *as itself giving the law,* and on this ground only, subject to the law (of which it can regard itself as the author).

4:431

In the previous imperatives, namely, that based on the conception of the conformity of actions to general laws, as in a *physical system of nature*, and that based on the universal *prerogative* of rational beings as *ends* in themselves—these imperatives just because they were conceived as categorical, excluded from any share in their authority all admixture of any interest as a spring of action; they were however only *assumed* to be categorical, because such an assumption was necessary to explain the conception of duty. But we could not prove independently that there are practical propositions which command categorically, nor can it be proved in this section; one thing however could be done, namely, to indicate in the imperative itself by some determinate expression, that in the case of volition from duty all interest is renounced, which is the specific criterion of categorical as distinguished from hypothetical imperatives. This is done in the present (third) formula of the principle, namely, in the idea of the will of every rational being as a *universally legislating will*. 4:432

For although a will *which is subject to laws* may be attached to this law by means of an interest, yet a will which is itself a supreme lawgiver so far as it is such cannot possibly depend on any interest, since a will so dependent would itself still need another law restricting the interest of its self-love by the condition that it should be valid as universal law.

Thus the *principle* that every human will is *a will which in all its maxims gives universal laws*,[14] provided it be otherwise justified, would be very *well adapted* to be the categorical imperative, in this respect, namely, that just because of the idea of universal legislation it is *not based on any interest*, and therefore it alone among all possible imperatives can be *unconditional*. Or still better, converting the proposition, if there is a categorical imperative (*i.e.* a law for the will of every rational being), it can only command that everything be done from maxims of one's will regarded as a will which could at the same time will that it should itself give universal laws, for in

14 I may be excused from adducing examples to elucidate this principle, as those which have already been used to elucidate the categorical imperative and its formula would all serve for the like purpose here.

190 · Basic Writings of Kant

that case only the practical principle and the imperative which it obeys are unconditional, since they cannot be based on any interest.

Looking back now on all previous attempts to discover the principle of morality, we need not wonder why they all failed. It was seen that man was bound to laws by duty, but it was not observed that the laws to which he is subject are *only those of his own giving*, though at the same time they are *universal*, and that he is only bound to act in conformity with his own will; a will, however, which is designed by nature to give universal laws. For when one has conceived man only as subject to a law (no matter what), then this law required some interest, either by way of attraction or constraint, since it did not originate as a law from *his own* will, but this will was according to a law obliged by *something else* to act in a certain manner. Now by this necessary consequence all the labour spent in finding a supreme principle of *duty* was irrevocably lost. For men never elicited duty, but only a necessity of acting from a certain interest. Whether this interest was private or otherwise, in any case the imperative must be conditional, and could not by any means be capable of being a moral command. I will therefore call this the principle of *Autonomy* of the will, in contrast with every other which I accordingly reckon as *Heteronomy*.

The conception of every rational being as one which must consider itself as giving in all the maxims of its will universal laws, so as to judge itself and its actions from this point of view—this conception leads to another which depends on it and is very fruitful, namely, that of *a kingdom of ends*.

By a *kingdom* I understand the union of different rational beings in a system by common laws. Now since it is by laws that ends are determined as regards their universal validity, hence, if we abstract from the personal differences of rational beings, and likewise from all the content of their private ends, we shall be able to conceive all ends combined in a systematic whole (including both rational beings as ends in themselves, and also the special ends which each may propose to himself), that is to say, we can conceive a kingdom of ends, which on the preceding principles is possible.

For all rational beings come under the *law* that each of them must treat itself and all others *never merely as means*, but in every case *at the same time as ends in themselves.* Hence results a systematic union of rational beings by common objective laws, *i.e.* a kingdom which may be called a kingdom of ends, since what these laws have in view is just the relation of these beings to one another as ends and means. It is certainly only an ideal.

A rational being belongs as a *member* to the kingdom of ends 4:434 when, although giving universal laws in it, he is also himself subject to these laws. He belongs to it *as sovereign* when, while giving laws, he is not subject to the will of any other.

A rational being must always regard himself as giving laws either as member or as sovereign in a kingdom of ends which is rendered possible by the freedom of will. He cannot, however, maintain the latter position merely by the maxims of his will, but only in case he is a completely independent being without wants and with unrestricted power adequate to his will.

Morality consists then in the reference of all action to the legislation which alone can render a kingdom of ends possible. This legislation must be capable of existing in every rational being, and of emanating from his will, so that the principle of this will is, never to act on any maxim which could not without contradiction be also a universal law, and accordingly always so to act *that the will could at the same time regard itself as giving in its maxims universal laws.* If now the maxims of rational beings are not by their own nature coincident with this objective principle, then the necessity of acting on it is called practical necessitation, *i.e. duty.* Duty does not apply to the sovereign in the kingdom of ends, but it does to every member of it and to all in the same degree.

The practical necessity of acting on this principle, *i.e.* duty, does not rest at all on feelings, impulses, or inclinations, but solely on the relation of rational beings to one another, a relation in which the will of a rational being must always be regarded as *legislative,* since otherwise it could not be conceived *as an end in itself.* Reason then refers every maxim of the will, regarding it as legislating universally, to every other will and also to every action towards oneself; and this not on account of any other practical motive or any future advantage, but from the idea of the *dignity* of a rational being, obeying no law but that which he himself also gives.

In the kingdom of ends everything has either Value or Dignity. Whatever has a value can be replaced by something else which is *equivalent;* whatever, on the other hand, is above all value, and therefore admits of no equivalent, has a dignity.

4:435 Whatever has reference to the general inclinations and wants of mankind has a *market value;* whatever, without presupposing a want, corresponds to a certain taste, that is to a satisfaction in the mere purposeless play of our faculties, has a *fancy value;* but that which constitutes the condition under which alone anything can be an end in itself, this has not merely a relative worth, *i.e.* value, but an intrinsic worth, that is *dignity.*

Now morality is the condition under which alone a rational being can be an end in himself, since by this alone is it possible that he should be a legislating member in the kingdom of ends. Thus morality, and humanity as capable of it, is that which alone has dignity. Skill and diligence in labour have a market value; wit, lively imagination, and humour, have fancy value; on the other hand, fidelity to promises, benevolence from principle (not from instinct), have an intrinsic worth. Neither nature nor art contains anything which in default of these it could put in their place, for their worth consists not in the effects which spring from them, not in the use and advantage which they secure, but in the disposition of mind, that is, the maxims of the will which are ready to manifest themselves in such actions, even though they should not have the desired effect. These actions also need no recommendation from any subjective taste or sentiment, that they may be looked on with immediate favour and satisfaction: they need no immediate propension or feeling for them; they exhibit the will that performs them as an object of an immediate respect, and nothing but reason is required to *impose* them on the will; not to *flatter* it into them, which, in the case of duties, would be a contradiction. This estimation therefore shows that the worth of such a disposition is dignity, and places it infinitely above all value, with which it cannot for a moment be brought into comparison or competition without as it were violating its sanctity.

What then is it which justifies virtue or the morally good disposition, in making such lofty claims? It is nothing less than the privilege it secures to the rational being of participating in the giving of universal laws, by which it qualifies him to be a member of a possible kingdom of ends, a privilege to which he was already destined by his own nature as being an end in himself, and on that account legislating in the kingdom of ends; free as regards all laws of physical nature, and obeying those only which he himself gives, and by which his maxims can belong to a system of universal law, to which at the same time he submits himself. For nothing has any worth except what the law assigns it. Now the legislation itself which assigns the worth of everything, must for that very reason possess dignity, that is an unconditional incomparable worth, and the word *respect* alone supplies a becoming expression for the esteem which a rational being must have for it. *Autonomy* then is the basis of the dignity of human and of every rational nature.

4:436

The three modes of presenting the principle of morality that have been adduced are at bottom only so many formulæ of the very same law, and each of itself involves the other two. There is, however, a difference in them, but it is rather subjectively than objectively practical, intended namely to bring an idea of the reason nearer to intuition (by means of a certain analogy), and thereby nearer to feeling. All maxims, in fact, have—

1. A *form*, consisting in universality; and in this view the formula of the moral imperative is expressed thus, that the maxims must be so chosen as if they were to serve as universal laws of nature.

2. A *matter*, namely, an end, and here the formula says that the rational being, as it is an end by its own nature and therefore an end in itself, must in every maxim serve as the condition limiting all merely relative and arbitrary ends.

3. A *complete characterisation* of all maxims by means of that formula, namely, that all maxims ought by their own legislation to harmonise with a possible kingdom of ends as with a kingdom of nature.[15] There is a progress here in the order of the categories of

15 Teleology considers nature as a kingdom of ends; Ethics regards a possible kingdom of ends as a kingdom of nature. In the first case, the kingdom of ends is a theoretical idea, adopted to explain what actually is. In the latter it is a practical idea, adopted to bring about that which is not yet, but which can be realised by our conduct, namely, if it conforms to this idea.

unity of the form of the will (its universality), *plurality* of the matter (the objects, *i.e.* the ends), and *totality* of the system of these. In 4:437 forming our moral *judgment* of actions it is better to proceed always on the strict method, and start from the general formula of the categorical imperative: *Act according to a maxim which can at the same time make itself a universal law.* If, however, we wish to gain an *entrance* for the moral law, it is very useful to bring one and the same action under the three specified conceptions, and thereby as far as possible to bring it nearer to intuition.

We can now end where we started at the beginning, namely, with the conception of a will unconditionally good. *That will* is *absolutely good* which cannot be evil, in other words, whose maxim, if made a universal law, could never contradict itself. This principle then is its supreme law: Act always on such a maxim as thou canst at the same time will to be a universal law; this is the sole condition under which a will can never contradict itself; and such an imperative is categorical. Since the validity of the will as a universal law for possible actions is analogous to the universal connexion of the existence of things by general laws, which is the formal notion of nature in general, the categorical imperative can also be expressed thus: *Act on maxims which can at the same time have for their object themselves as universal laws of nature.* Such then is the formula of an absolutely good will.

Rational nature is distinguished from the rest of nature by this, that it sets before itself an end. This end would be the matter of every good will. But since in the idea of a will that is absolutely good without being limited by any condition (of attaining this or that end) we must abstract wholly from every end *to be effected* (since this would make every will only relatively good), it follows that in this case the end must be conceived, not as an end to be effected, but as an *independently* existing end. Consequently it is conceived only negatively, *i.e.* as that which we must never act against, and which, therefore, must never be regarded merely as means, but must in every volition be esteemed as an end likewise. Now this end can be nothing but the subject of all possible ends, since this is also the subject of a possible absolutely good will; for such a will cannot without contradiction be postponed to any other object. The principle: So act in regard to every rational being (thyself and others), that he may always have place in thy maxim as an end in himself, is accordingly essentially identical with this other: Act 4:438 upon a maxim which, at the same time, involves its own universal validity for every rational being. For that in using means for every end I should limit my maxim by the condition of its holding good as a law for every subject, this comes to the same thing as that the fundamental principle of all maxims of action must be that the subject of all ends, *i.e.* the rational being himself, be never employed merely as means, but as the supreme condition restricting the use of all means, that is in every case as an end likewise.

It follows incontestably that, to whatever laws any rational being may be subject, he being an end in himself must be able to regard himself as also legislating universally in respect of these same laws, since it is just this fitness of his maxims for universal legislation that distinguishes him as an end in himself; also it follows that this implies his dignity (prerogative) above all mere physical beings, that he must always take his maxims from the point of view which regards himself, and likewise every other rational being, as lawgiving beings (on which account they are called persons). In this way a world of rational beings *(mundus intelligibilis)* is possible as a kingdom of ends, and this by virtue of the legislation proper to all persons as members. Therefore every rational being must so act as if he were by his maxims in every case a legislating member in the universal kingdom of ends. The formal principle of these maxims is: So act as if thy maxim were to serve likewise as the universal law (of all rational beings). A kingdom of ends is thus only possible on the analogy of a kingdom of nature, the former however only by maxims, that is self-imposed rules, the latter only by the laws of efficient causes acting under necessitation from without. Nevertheless, although the system of nature is looked upon as a machine, yet so far as it has reference to rational beings as its ends, it is given on this account the name of a kingdom of nature. Now such a kingdom of ends would be actually realised by means of maxims conforming to the canon which the categorical imperative prescribes to all rational beings, *if they were universally followed*. But although a rational being, even if he punctually follows this maxim himself, cannot reckon upon all others being therefore true to the same, nor expect that the kingdom of nature and its orderly arrangements shall be in harmony with him as a fitting member, so as to form a

4:439 kingdom of ends to which he himself contributes, that is to say, that it shall favour his expectation of happiness, still that law: Act according to the maxims of a member of a merely possible kingdom of ends legislating in it universally, remains in its full force, inasmuch as it commands categorically. And it is just in this that the paradox lies; that the mere dignity of man as a rational creature, without any other end or advantage to be attained thereby, in other words, respect for a mere idea, should yet serve as an inflexible precept of the will, and that it is precisely in this independence of the maxim on all such springs of action that its sublimity consists; and it is this that makes every rational subject worthy to be a legislative member in the kingdom of ends: for otherwise he would have to be conceived only as subject to the physical law of his wants. And although we should suppose the kingdom of nature and the kingdom of ends to be united under one sovereign, so that the latter kingdom thereby ceased to be a mere idea and acquired true reality, then it would no doubt gain the accession of a strong spring, but by no means any increase of its intrinsic worth. For this sole absolute lawgiver must, notwithstanding this, be always conceived as estimating the worth of rational beings only by their disinterested behaviour, as prescribed to themselves from that idea [the dignity of man] alone. The essence of things is not altered by their external relations, and that which abstracting from these, alone constitutes the absolute worth of man, is also that by which he must be judged, whoever the judge may be, and even by the Supreme Being. *Morality* then is the relation of actions to the autonomy of the will, that is, to the potential universal legislation by its maxims. An action that is consistent with the autonomy of the will is *permitted;* one that does not agree therewith is *forbidden*. A will whose maxims necessarily coincide with the laws of autonomy is a *holy* will, good absolutely. The dependence of a will not absolutely good on the principle of autonomy (moral necessitation) is obligation. This then cannot be applied to a holy being. The objective necessity of actions from obligation is called *duty*.

From what has just been said, it is easy to see how it happens that although the conception of duty implies subjection to the law, we 4:440 yet ascribe a certain *dignity* and sublimity to the person who fulfils all his duties. There is not, indeed, any sublimity in him, so far as he is *subject* to the moral law; but inasmuch as in regard to that very law he is likewise a *legislator,* and on that account alone subject to it, he has sublimity. We have also shown above that neither fear nor inclination, but simply respect for the law, is the spring which can give actions a moral worth. Our own will, so far as we suppose it to act only under the condition that its maxims are potentially universal laws, this ideal will which is possible to us is the proper object of respect, and the dignity of humanity consists just in this capacity of being universally legislative, though with the condition that it is itself subject to this same legislation.

The Autonomy of the Will as the Supreme Principle of Morality.

Autonomy of the will is that property of it by which it is a law to itself (independently on any property of the objects of volition). The principle of autonomy then is: Always so to choose that the same volition shall comprehend the maxims of our choice as a universal law. We cannot prove that this practical rule is an imperative, *i.e.* that the will of every rational being is necessarily bound to it as a condition, by a mere analysis of the conceptions which occur in it, since it is a synthetical proposition; we must advance beyond the cognition of the objects to a critical examination of the subject, that is of the pure practical reason, for this synthetic proposition which commands apodictically must be capable of being cognised wholly *a priori*. This matter, however, does not belong to the present section. But that the principle of autonomy in question is the sole principle of morals can be readily shown by mere analysis of the conceptions of morality. For by this analysis we find that its principle must be a categorical imperative, and that what this commands is neither more nor less than this very autonomy.

4:441

Heteronomy of the Will as the Source of all spurious Principles of Morality.

If the will seeks the law which is to determine it *anywhere else* than in the fitness of its maxims to be universal laws of its own dictation, consequently if it goes out of itself and seeks this law in the character of any of its objects, there always results *heteronomy*. The will in that case does not give itself the law, but it is given by the object through its relation to the will. This relation whether it rests on inclination or on conceptions of reason only admits of hypothetical imperatives: I ought to do something *because I wish for something else*. On the contrary, the moral, and therefore categorical, imperative says: I ought to do so and so, even though I should not wish for anything else. *Ex. gr.*, the former says: I ought not to lie if I would retain my reputation; the latter says: I ought not to lie although it should not bring me the least discredit. The latter therefore must so far abstract from all objects that they shall have no *influence* on the will, in order that practical reason (will) may not be restricted to administering an interest not belonging to it, but may simply show its own commanding authority as the supreme legislation. Thus, *ex. gr.*, I ought to endeavour to promote the happiness of others, not as if its realization involved any concern of mine (whether by immediate inclination or by any satisfaction indirectly gained through reason), but simply because a maxim which excludes it cannot be comprehended as a universal law in one and the same volition.

CLASSIFICATION

Of all Principles of Morality which can be founded on the Conception of Heteronomy.

Here as elsewhere human reason in its pure use, so long as it was not critically examined, has first tried all possible wrong ways before it succeeded in finding the one true way.

All principles which can be taken from this point of view are either *empirical* or *rational*. The *former*, drawn from the principle of

4:442

happiness, are built on physical or moral feelings; the *latter*, drawn from the principle of *perfection*, are built either on the rational conception of perfection as a possible effect, or on that of an independent perfection (the will of God) as the determining cause of our will.

Empirical principles are wholly incapable of serving as a foundation for moral laws. For the universality with which these should hold for all rational beings without distinction, the unconditional practical necessity which is thereby imposed on them is lost when their foundation is taken from the *particular constitution of human nature*, or the accidental circumstances in which it is placed. The principle of *private happiness*, however, is the most objectionable, not merely because it is false, and experience contradicts the supposition that prosperity is always proportioned to good conduct, nor yet merely because it contributes nothing to the establishment of morality—since it is quite a different thing to make a prosperous man and a good man, or to make one prudent and sharp-sighted for his own interests, and to make him virtuous—but because the springs it provides for morality are such as rather undermine it and destroy its sublimity, since they put the motives to virtue and to vice in the same class, and only teach us to make a better calculation, the specific difference between virtue and vice being entirely extinguished. On the other hand, as to moral feeling, this supposed special sense,[16] the appeal to it is indeed superficial when those who cannot *think* believe that *feeling* will help them out, even in what concerns general laws: and besides, feelings which naturally differ infinitely in degree cannot furnish a uniform standard of good and evil, nor has any one a right to form judgments for others by his own feelings: nevertheless this moral feeling is nearer to morality and its dignity in this respect, that it pays virtue the honour of ascribing to her *immediately* the satisfaction and esteem we have for

16 I class the principle of moral feeling under that of happiness, because every empirical interest promises to contribute to our well-being by the agreeableness that a thing affords, whether it be immediately and without a view to profit, or whether profit be regarded. We must likewise, with Hutcheson, class the principle of sympathy with the happiness of others under his assumed moral sense.

her, and does not, as it were, tell her to her face that we are not at-
4:443 tached to her by her beauty but by profit.

Amongst the *rational* principles of morality, the ontological conception of *perfection*, notwithstanding its defects, is better than the
theological conception which derives morality from a Divine absolutely perfect will. The former is, no doubt, empty and indefinite,
and consequently useless for finding in the boundless field of possible reality the greatest amount suitable for us; moreover, in attempting to distinguish specifically the reality of which we are now
speaking from every other, it inevitably tends to turn in a circle,
and cannot avoid tacitly presupposing the morality which it is to
explain; it is nevertheless preferable to the theological view, first,
because we have no intuition of the Divine perfection, and can
only deduce it from our own conceptions, the most important of
which is that of morality, and our explanation would thus be involved in a gross circle; and, in the next place, if we avoid this, the
only notion of the Divine will remaining to us is a conception
made up of the attributes of desire of glory and dominion, combined with the awful conceptions of might and vengeance, and any
system of morals erected on this foundation would be directly opposed to morality.

However, if I had to choose between the notion of the moral
sense and that of perfection in general (two systems which at least
do not weaken morality, although they are totally incapable of
serving as its foundation), then I should decide for the latter, because it at least withdraws the decision of the question from the
sensibility and brings it to the court of pure reason; and although
even here it decides nothing, it at all events preserves the indefinite
idea (of a will good in itself) free from corruption, until it shall be
more precisely defined.

For the rest I think I may be excused here from a detailed refutation of all these doctrines; that would only be superfluous labour,
since it is so easy, and is probably so well seen even by those whose
office requires them to decide for one of these theories (because
their hearers would not tolerate suspension of judgment). But what
interests us more here is to know that the prime foundation of

morality laid down by all these principles is nothing but heteronomy of the will, and for this reason they must necessarily miss their aim.

In every case where an object of the will has to be supposed, in order that the rule may be prescribed which is to determine the will, there the rule is simply heteronomy; the imperative is conditional, namely, *if* or *because* one wishes for this object, one should act so and so: hence it can never command morally, that is categorically. Whether the object determines the will by means of inclination, as in the principle of private happiness, or by means of reason directed to objects of our possible volition generally, as in the principle of perfection, in either case the will never determines itself *immediately* by the conception of the action, but only by the influence which the foreseen effect of the action has on the will; *I ought to do something, on this account, because I wish for something else*; and here there must be yet another law assumed in me as its subject, by which I necessarily will this other thing, and this law again requires an imperative to restrict this maxim. For the influence which the conception of an object within the reach of our faculties can exercise on the will of the subject in consequence of its natural properties, depends on the nature of the subject, either the sensibility (inclination and taste), or the understanding and reason, the employment of which is by the peculiar constitution of their nature attended with satisfaction. It follows that the law would be, properly speaking, given by nature, and as such, it must be known and proved by experience, and would consequently be contingent, and therefore incapable of being an apodictic practical rule, such as the moral rule must be. Not only so, but it is *inevitably only heteronomy;* the will does not give itself the law, but it is given by a foreign impulse by means of a particular natural constitution of the subject adapted to receive it. An absolutely good will then, the principle of which must be a categorical imperative, will be indeterminate as regards all objects, and will contain merely the *form of volition* generally, and that as autonomy, that is to say, the capability of the maxims of every good will to make themselves a universal law, is itself the only law which the will of every rational being imposes on

4:444

itself, without needing to assume any spring or interest as a foundation.

How such a synthetical practical a priori *proposition is possible* and why it is necessary, is a problem whose solution does not lie within the bounds of the metaphysic of morals; and we have not here affirmed its truth, much less professed to have a proof of it in our power. We simply showed by the development of the universally received notion of morality that an autonomy of the will is inevitably connected with it, or rather is its foundation. Whoever then holds morality to be anything real, and not a chimerical idea without any truth, must likewise admit the principle of it that is here assigned. This section then, like the first, was merely analytical. Now to prove that morality is no creation of the brain, which it cannot be if the categorical imperative and with it the autonomy of the will is true, and as an *a priori* principle absolutely necessary, this supposes the *possibility of a synthetic use of pure practical reason*, which however we cannot venture on without first giving a critical examination of this faculty of reason. In the concluding section we shall give the principal outlines of this critical examination as far as is sufficient for our purpose.

THIRD SECTION.

TRANSITION FROM THE METAPHYSIC OF MORALS TO THE CRITIQUE OF PURE PRACTICAL REASON.

The Concept of Freedom is the Key that explains the Autonomy of the Will.

The *will* is a kind of causality belonging to living beings in so far as they are rational, and *freedom* would be this property of such causality that it can be efficient, independently on foreign causes *determining* it; just as *physical necessity* is the property that the causality of all irrational beings has of being determined to activity by the influence of foreign causes.

The preceding definition of freedom is *negative,* and therefore unfruitful for the discovery of its essence; but it leads to a *positive* conception which is so much the more full and fruitful. Since the conception of causality involves that of laws, according to which, by something that we call cause, something else, namely, the effect, must be laid down hence, although freedom is not a property of the will depending on physical laws, yet it is not for that reason lawless; on the contrary it must be a causality acting according to immutable laws, but of a peculiar kind; otherwise a free will would be an absurdity. Physical necessity is a heteronomy of the efficient causes, for every effect is possible only according to this law, that something else determines the efficient cause to exert its causality. What else then can freedom of the will be but autonomy, that is the property of the will to be a law to itself? But the proposition: The will is in every action a law to itself, only expresses the principle, to act on no other maxim than that which can also have as an object itself as a universal law. Now this is precisely the formula of the categorical imperative and is the principle of morality, so that a free will and a will subject to moral laws are one and the same.

On the hypothesis then of freedom of the will, morality together with its principle follows from it by mere analysis of the conception. However the latter is still a synthetic proposition; viz., an absolutely good will is that whose maxim can always include itself regarded as a universal law; for this property of its maxim can never be discovered by analysing the conception of an absolutely good will. Now such synthetic propositions are only possible in this way: that the two cognitions are connected together by their union with a third in which they are both to be found. The *positive* concept of freedom furnishes this third cognition, which cannot, as with physical causes, be the nature of the sensible world (in the concept of which we find conjoined the concept of something in relation as cause to *something else* as effect). We cannot now at once show what this third is to which freedom points us, and of which we have an idea *a priori,* nor can we make intelligible how the concept of freedom is shown to be legitimate from principles of pure practical reason, and with it the possibility of a categorical imperative; but some further preparation is required.

FREEDOM

Must be presupposed as a Property of the Will of all Rational Beings.

It is not enough to predicate freedom of our own will, from whatever reason, if we have not sufficient grounds for predicating the same of all rational beings. For as morality serves as a law for us only because we are *rational beings,* it must also hold for all rational beings; and as it must be deduced simply from the property of freedom, it must be shown that freedom also is a property of all rational beings. It is not enough then to prove it from certain supposed experiences of human nature (which indeed is quite impossible, and it can only be shown *a priori*), but we must show that it belongs to the activity of all rational beings endowed with a will. Now I say every being that cannot act except *under the idea of freedom* is just for that reason in a practical point of view really free, that is to say, all laws which are inseparably connected with freedom have the same force for him as if his will had been shown to be free in itself by a proof theoretically conclusive.[17] Now I affirm that we must attribute to every rational being which has a will that it has also the idea of freedom and acts entirely under this idea. For in such a being we conceive a reason that is practical, that is, has causality in reference to its objects. Now we cannot possibly conceive a reason consciously receiving a bias from any other quarter with respect to its judgments, for then the subject would ascribe the determination of its judgment not to its own reason, but to an impulse. It must regard itself as the author of its principles independent on foreign influences. Consequently as practical reason or as the will of a rational being it must regard itself as free, that is to say, the will of such a being cannot be a will of its own except under the idea of freedom. This idea must therefore in a practical point of view be ascribed to every rational being.

OF THE INTEREST ATTACHING TO THE IDEAS OF MORALITY

We have finally reduced the definite conception of morality to the idea of freedom. This latter, however, we could not prove to be ac-

4:448

---

17 I adopt this method of assuming freedom merely *as an idea* which rational beings suppose in their actions, in order to avoid the necessity of proving it in its theoretical aspect also. The former is sufficient for my purpose; for even though the speculative proof should not be made out, yet a being that cannot act except with the idea of freedom is bound by the same laws that would oblige a being who was actually free. Thus we can escape here from the onus which presses on the theory.

4:449 tually a property of ourselves or of human nature; only we saw that it must be presupposed if we would conceive a being as rational and conscious of its causality in respect of its actions, *i.e.* as endowed with a will; and so we find that on just the same grounds we must ascribe to every being endowed with reason and will this attribute of determining itself to action under the idea of its freedom.

Now it resulted also from the presupposition of this idea that we became aware of a law that the subjective principles of action, *i.e.* maxims, must always be so assumed that they can also hold as objective, that is, universal principles, and so serve as universal laws of our own dictation. But why then should I subject myself to this principle and that simply as a rational being, thus also subjecting to it all other beings endowed with reason? I will allow that no interest *urges* me to this, for that would not give a categorical imperative, but I must *take* an interest in it and discern how this comes to pass; for this "I ought" is properly an "I would," valid for every rational being, provided only that reason determined his actions without any hindrance. But for beings that are in addition affected as we are by springs of a different kind, namely, sensibility, and in whose case that is not always done which reason alone would do for these that necessity is expressed only as an "ought," and the subjective necessity is different from the objective.

It seems then as if the moral law, that is, the principle of autonomy of the will, were properly speaking only presupposed in the idea of freedom, and as if we could not prove its reality and objective necessity independently. In that case we should still have gained something considerable by at least determining the true principle more exactly than had previously been done; but as regards its validity and the practical necessity of subjecting oneself to it, we should not have advanced a step. For if we were asked why the universal validity of our maxim as a law must be the condition restricting our actions, and on what we ground the worth which we assign to this manner of acting—a worth so great that there cannot be any higher interest; and if we were asked further how it happens that it is by this alone a man believes he feels his own personal

worth, in comparison with which that of an agreeable or disagree- 4:450
able condition is to be regarded as nothing, to these questions we
could give no satisfactory answer.

We find indeed sometimes that we can take an interest in a personal quality which does not involve any interest of external condition, provided this quality makes us capable of participating in
the condition in case reason were to effect the allotment; that is to
say, the mere being worthy of happiness can interest of itself even
without the motive of participating in this happiness. This judgment, however, is in fact only the effect of the importance of the
moral law which we before presupposed (when by the idea of freedom we detach ourselves from every empirical interest); but that
we ought to detach ourselves from these interests, *i.e.* to consider
ourselves as free in action and yet as subject to certain laws, so as to
find a worth simply in our own person which can compensate us for
the loss of everything that gives worth to our condition; this we are
not yet able to discern in this way, nor do we see how it is possible
so to act—in other words, *whence the moral law derives its obligation.*

It must be freely admitted that there is a sort of circle here from
which it seems impossible to escape. In the order of efficient causes
we assume ourselves free, in order that in the order of ends we may
conceive ourselves as subject to moral laws: and we afterwards conceive ourselves as subject to these laws, because we have attributed
to ourselves freedom of will: for freedom and self-legislation of
will are both autonomy, and therefore are reciprocal conceptions,
and for this very reason one must not be used to explain the other
or give the reason of it, but at most only for logical purposes to reduce apparently different notions of the same object to one single
concept (as we reduce different fractions of the same value to the
lowest terms).

One resource remains to us, namely, to inquire whether we do
not occupy different points of view when by means of freedom we
think ourselves as causes efficient *a priori,* and when we form our
conception of ourselves from our actions as effects which we see
before our eyes.

It is a remark which needs no subtle reflection to make, but

4:451 which we may assume that even the commonest understanding can make, although it be after its fashion by an obscure discernment of judgment which it calls feeling, that all the "ideas" that come to us involuntarily (as those of the senses) do not enable us to know objects otherwise than as they affect us; so that what they may be in themselves remains unknown to us, and consequently that as regards "ideas" of this kind even with the closest attention and clearness that the understanding can apply to them, we can by them only attain to the knowledge of *appearances,* never to that of *things in themselves.* As soon as this distinction has once been made (perhaps merely in consequence of the difference observed between the ideas given us from without, and in which we are passive, and those that we produce simply from ourselves, and in which we show our own activity), then it follows of itself that we must admit and assume behind the appearance something else that is not an appearance, namely, the things in themselves; although we must admit that as they can never be known to us except as they affect us, we can come no nearer to them, nor can we ever know what they are in themselves. This must furnish a distinction, however crude, between a *world of sense* and the *world of understanding,* of which the former may be different according to the difference of the sensuous impressions in various observers, while the second which is its basis always remains the same. Even as to himself, a man cannot pretend to know what he is in himself from the knowledge he has by internal sensation. For as he does not as it were create himself, and does not come by the conception of himself *a priori* but empirically, it naturally follows that he can obtain his knowledge even of himself only by the inner sense, and consequently only through the appearances of his nature and the way in which his consciousness is affected. At the same time beyond these characteristics of his own subject, made up of mere appearances, he must necessarily suppose something else as their basis, namely, his *ego,* whatever its characteristics in itself may be. Thus in respect to mere perception and receptivity of sensations he must reckon himself as belonging to the *world of sense,* but in respect of whatever there may be of pure activity in him (that which reaches consciousness immediately and

not through affecting the senses) he must reckon himself as belonging to the *intellectual world*, of which however he has no further
knowledge. To such a conclusion the reflecting man must come
with respect to all the things which can be presented to him: it is
probably to be met with even in persons of the commonest under- 4:452
standing, who, as is well known, are very much inclined to suppose
behind the objects of the senses something else invisible and acting
of itself. They spoil it however by presently sensualizing this invisible again; that is to say, wanting to make it an object of intuition, so
that they do not become a whit the wiser.

Now man really finds in himself a faculty by which he distinguishes himself from everything else, even from himself as affected
by objects, and that is *Reason*. This being pure spontaneity is even
elevated above the *understanding*. For although the latter is a spontaneity and does not, like sense, merely contain intuitions that arise
when we are affected by things (and are therefore passive), yet it
cannot produce from its activity any other conceptions than those
which merely serve *to bring the intuitions of sense under rules*, and
thereby to unite them in one consciousness, and without this use of
the sensibility it could not think at all; whereas, on the contrary,
Reason shows so pure a spontaneity in the case of what I call Ideas
[Ideal Conceptions] that it thereby far transcends everything that
the sensibility can give it, and exhibits its most important function
in distinguishing the world of sense from that of understanding,
and thereby prescribing the limits of the understanding itself.

For this reason a rational being must regard himself *qua* intelligence (not from the side of his lower faculties) as belonging not to
the world of sense, but to that of understanding; hence he has two
points of view from which he can regard himself, and recognize
laws of the exercise of his faculties, and consequently of all his actions: *first*, so far as he belongs to the world of sense, he finds himself subject to laws of nature (heteronomy); *secondly*, as belonging to
the intelligible world, under laws which being independent on nature have their foundation not in experience but in reason alone.

As a rational being, and consequently belonging to the intelligible world, man can never conceive the causality of his own will

otherwise than on condition of the idea of freedom, for independence on the determining causes of the sensible world (an independence which Reason must always ascribe to itself) is freedom. Now the idea of freedom is inseparably connected with the conception of *autonomy*, and this again with the universal principle of morality which is ideally the foundation of all actions of *rational* beings, just as the law of nature is of all phenomena.

4:453

Now the suspicion is removed which we raised above, that there was a latent circle involved in our reasoning from freedom to autonomy, and from this to the moral law, viz.: that we laid down the idea of freedom because of the moral law only that we might afterwards in turn infer the latter from freedom, and that consequently we could assign no reason at all for this law, but could only [present] it as a *petitio principii* which well disposed minds would gladly concede to us, but which we could never put forward as a provable proposition. For now we see that when we conceive ourselves as free we transfer ourselves into the world of understanding as members of it, and recognise the autonomy of the will with its consequence, morality; whereas, if we conceive ourselves as under obligation we consider ourselves as belonging to the world of sense, and at the same time to the world of understanding.

How is a Categorical Imperative Possible?

Every rational being reckons himself *qua* intelligence as belonging to the world of understanding, and it is simply as an efficient cause belonging to that world that he calls his causality a *will*. On the other side he is also conscious of himself as a part of the world of sense in which his actions which are mere appearances [phenomena] of that causality are displayed; we cannot however discern how they are possible from this causality which we do not know; but instead of that, these actions as belonging to the sensible world must be viewed as determined by other phenomena, namely, desires and inclinations. If therefore I were only a member of the world of understanding, then all my actions would perfectly conform to the principle of autonomy of the pure will; if I were only a

part of the world of sense they would necessarily be assumed to conform wholly to the natural law of desires and inclinations, in other words, to the heteronomy of nature. (The former would rest on morality as the supreme principle, the latter on happiness.) Since however *the world of understanding contains the foundation of the world of sense, and consequently of its laws also*, and accordingly gives the law to my will (which belongs wholly to the world of understanding) directly, and must be conceived as doing so, it follows   4:454
that, although on the one side I must regard myself as a being belonging to the world of sense, yet on the other side I must recognise myself as subject as an intelligence to the law of the world of understanding, *i.e.*, to reason, which contains this law in the idea of freedom, and therefore as subject to the autonomy of the will: consequently I must regard the laws of the world of understanding as imperatives for me, and the actions which conform to them as duties.

And thus what makes categorical imperatives possible is this, that the idea of freedom makes me a member of an intelligible world, in consequence of which if I were nothing else all my actions *would* always conform to the autonomy of the will; but as I at the same time intuit myself as a member of the world of sense, they *ought* so to conform, and this *categorical* "ought" implies a synthetic *a priori* proposition, inasmuch as besides my will as affected by sensible desires there is added further the idea of the same will but as belonging to the world of the understanding, pure and practical of itself, which contains the supreme condition according to Reason of the former will; precisely as to the intuitions of sense there are added concepts of the understanding which of themselves signify nothing but regular form in general, and in this way synthetic *a priori* propositions become possible, on which all knowledge of physical nature rests.

The practical use of common human reason confirms this reasoning. There is no one, not even the most consummate villain, provided only that he is otherwise accustomed to the use of reason, who, when we set before him examples of honesty of purpose, of steadfastness in following good maxims, of sympathy and general benevolence (even combined with great sacrifices of advantages and comfort), does not wish that he might also possess these qualities. Only on account of his inclinations and impulses he cannot attain this in himself, but at the same time he wishes to be free from such inclinations which are bundensome to himself. He proves by this that he transfers himself in thought with a will free from the impulses of the sensibility into an order of things wholly different from that of his desires in the field of the sensibility; since he cannot expect to obtain by that wish any gratification of his desires, nor any position which would satisfy any of his actual or supposable inclinations (for this would destroy the pre-eminence of the very idea which wrests that wish from him): he can only expect a greater intrinsic worth of his own person. This better person, however, he imagines himself to be when he transfers himself to the point of 4:455 view of a member of the world of the understanding, to which he is involuntarily forced by the idea of freedom, *i.e.*, of independence on *determining* causes of the world of sense; and from this point of view he is conscious of a good will, which by his own confession constitutes the law for the bad will that he possesses as a member of the world of sense—a law whose authority he recognises while transgressing it. What he morally "ought" is then what he necessarily "would" as a member of the world of the understanding, and is conceived by him as an "ought" only inasmuch as he likewise considers himself as a member of the world of sense.

On the Extreme Limits of all Practical Philosophy.

All men attribute to themselves freedom of will. Hence come all judgments upon actions as being such as *ought to have been done*, although they *have not been* done. However this freedom is not a conception of experience, nor can it be so, since it still remains, even though experience shows the contrary of what on supposition of freedom are conceived as its necessary consequences. On the other side it is equally necessary that everything that takes place should be fixedly determined according to laws of nature. This necessity of nature is likewise not an empirical conception, just for this reason, that it involves the motion of necessity and consequently of *a priori* cognition. But this conception of a system of nature is confirmed by experience, and it must even be inevitably presupposed if experience itself is to be possible, that is, a connected knowledge of the objects of sense resting on general laws. Therefore freedom is only an Idea of Reason, and its objective reality in itself is doubtful, while nature is a *concept* of the *understanding* which proves, and must necessarily prove, its reality in examples of experience.

There arises from this a dialectic of Reason, since the freedom attributed to the will appears to contradict the necessity of nature, and placed between these two ways Reason for *speculative purposes* finds the road of physical necessity much more beaten and more appropriate than that of freedom; yet for *practical purposes* the narrow footpath of freedom is the only one on which it is possible to make use of reason in our conduct; hence it is just as impossible for the subtlest philosophy as for the commonest reason of men to argue away freedom. Philosophy must then assume that no real contradiction will be found between freedom and physical necessity of the same human actions, for it cannot give up the conception of nature any more than that of freedom. 4:456

Nevertheless, even though we should never be able to comprehend how freedom is possible, we must at least remove this apparent contradiction in a convincing manner. For if the thought of freedom contradicts either itself or nature, which is equally necessary, it must in competition with physical necessity be entirely given up. 4:457

It would, however, be impossible to escape this contradiction if the thinking subject, which seems to itself free, conceived itself *in the same sense* or in *the very same relation* when it calls itself free as when in respect of the same action it assumes itself to be subject to the law of nature. Hence it is an indispensable problem of speculative philosophy to show that its illusion respecting the contradiction rests on this, that we think of man in a different sense and relation when we call him free, and when we regard him as subject to the laws of nature as being part and parcel of nature. It must therefore show that not only *can* both these very well co-exist, but that both must be thought *as necessarily united* in the same subject, since otherwise no reason could be given why we should burden reason with an idea which, though it may possibly *without contradiction* be reconciled with another that is sufficiently established, yet entangles us in a perplexity which sorely embarrasses Reason in its theoretic employment. This duty, however, belongs only to specu- lative philosophy, in order that it may clear the way for practical philosophy. The philosopher then has no option whether he will remove the apparent contradiction or leave it untouched; for in the latter case the theory respecting this would be *bonum vacans* into the possession of which the fatalist would have a right to enter, and chase all morality out of its supposed domain as occupying it with- out title.

We cannot, however, as yet say that we are touching the bounds of practical philosophy. For the settlement of that controversy does not belong to it; it only demands from speculative reason that it should put an end to the discord in which it entangles itself in the- oretical questions, so that practical reason may have rest and secu- rity from external attacks which might make the ground debatable on which it desires to build.

The claims to freedom of will made even by common reason are founded on the consciousness and the admitted supposition that reason is independent on merely subjectively determined causes which together constitute what belongs to sensation only, and which consequently come under the general designation of sensi- bility. Man considering himself in this way as an intelligence, places himself thereby in a different order of things and in a rela- tion to determining grounds of a wholly different kind when on the one hand he thinks of himself as an intelligence endowed with a will, and consequently with causality, and when on the other he perceives himself as a phenomenon in the world of sense (as he re- ally is also), and affirms that his causality is subject to external de- termination according to laws of nature. Now he soon becomes aware that both can hold good, nay, must hold good at the same time. For there is not the smallest contradiction in saying that a *thing in appearance* (belonging to the world of sense) is subject to certain laws, on which the very same *as a thing* or being *in itself* is independent; and that he must conceive and think of himself in this two-fold way, rests as to the first on the consciousness of himself as an object affected through the senses, and as to the second on the consciousness of himself as an intelligence, *i.e.* as independent on sensible impressions in the employment of his reason (in other words as belonging to the world of understanding).

Hence it comes to pass that man claims the possession of a will which takes no account of anything that comes under the head of desires and inclinations, and on the contrary conceives actions as possible to him, nay, even as necessary, which can only be done by disregarding all desires and sensible inclinations. The causality of such actions lies in him as an intelligence and in the laws of effects and actions [which depend] on the principles of an intelligible world, of which indeed he knows nothing more than that in it pure reason alone independent on sensibility gives the law; moreover since it is only in that world, as an intelligence, that he is his proper self (being as man only the appearance of himself) those laws apply to him directly and categorically, so that the incitements of inclinations and appetites (in other words the whole nature of the world of sense) cannot impair the laws of his volition as an intelligence. Nay, he does not even hold himself responsible for the former or ascribe them to his proper self, *i.e.* his will: he only ascribes to his will any indulgence which he might yield them if he allowed them to influence his maxims to the prejudice of the rational laws of the will. 4:458

When practical Reason *thinks* itself into a world of understanding it does not thereby transcend its own limits, as it would if it tried to enter it by *intuition* or *sensation*. The former is only a negative thought in respect of the world of sense, which does not give any laws to reason in determining the will, and is positive only in this single point that this freedom as a negative characteristic is at the same time conjoined with a (positive) faculty and even with a causality of reason, which we designate a will, namely, a faculty of so acting that the principle of the actions shall conform to the essential character of a rational motive, *i.e.* the condition that the maxim have universal validity as a law. But were it to borrow an *object of will*, that is, a motive, from the world of understanding, then it would overstep its bounds and pretend to be acquainted with something of which it knows nothing. The conception of a world of the understanding is then only a *point of view* which Reason finds itself compelled to take outside the appearances in order to *conceive itself as practical*, which would not be possible if the influences of the sensibility had a determining power on man, but which is necessary unless he is to be denied the consciousness of himself as an intelligence, and consequently as a rational cause, energizing by reason, that is, operating freely. This thought certainly involves the idea of an order and a system of laws different from that of the mechanism of nature which belongs to the sensible world, and it makes the conception of an intelligible world necessary (that is to say, the whole system of rational beings as things in themselves). But it does not in the least authorize us to think of it further than as to its *formal* condition only, that is, the universality of the maxims of the will as laws, and consequently the autonomy of the latter, which alone is consistent with its freedom; whereas, on the contrary, all laws that refer to a definite object give heteronomy, which only belongs to laws of nature, and can only apply to the sensible world.

4:459   But Reason would overstep all its bounds if it undertook to *explain how* pure reason can be practical, which would be exactly the same problem as to explain *how freedom is possible*.

For we can explain nothing but that which we can reduce to laws, the object of which can be given in some possible experience. But freedom is a mere Idea, the objective reality of which can in no wise be shown according to laws of nature, and consequently not in any possible experience; and for this reason it can never be comprehended or understood, because we cannot support it by any sort of example or analogy. It holds good only as a necessary hypothesis of reason in a being that believes itself conscious of a will, that is, of a faculty distinct from mere desire (namely a faculty of determining itself to action as an intelligence, in other words, by laws of reason independently on natural instincts). Now where determination according to laws of nature ceases, there all *explanation* ceases also, and nothing remains but *defence*, *i.e.* the removal of the objections of those who pretend to have seen deeper into the nature of things, and thereupon boldly declare freedom impossible. We can only point out to them that the supposed contradiction that they have discovered in it arises only from this, that in order to be able to apply the law of nature to human actions, they must necessarily consider man as an appearance: then when we demand of them that they should also think of him *qua* intelligence as a thing in itself, they still persist in considering him in this respect also as an appearance. In this view it would no doubt be a contradiction to suppose the causality of the same subject (that is, his will) to be withdrawn from all the natural laws of the sensible world. But this contradiction disappears, if they would only bethink themselves and admit, as is reasonable, that behind the appearances there must also lie at their root (although hidden) the things in themselves, and that we cannot expect the laws of these to be the same as those that govern their appearances.

The subjective impossibility of explaining the freedom of the will is identical with the impossibility of discovering and explaining an interest[18] which man can take in the moral law. Nevertheless he does actually take an interest in it, the basis of which in us we call the moral feeling, which some have falsely assigned as the standard of our moral judgment, whereas it must rather be viewed as the *subjective* effect that the law exercises on the will, the objective principle of which is furnished by Reason alone. 4:460

In order indeed that a rational being who is also affected through

---

18 Interest is that by which reason becomes practical, *i.e.* a cause determining the will. Hence we say of rational beings only that they take an interest in a thing; irrational beings only feel sensual appetites. Reason takes a direct interest in action then only when the universal validity of its maxims is alone sufficient to determine the will. Such an interest alone is pure. But if it can determine the will only by means of another object of desire or on the suggestion of a particular feeling of the subject, then Reason takes only an indirect interest in the action, and as Reason by itself without experience cannot discover either objects of the will or a special feeling actuating it, this latter interest would only be empirical, and not a pure rational interest. The logical interest of Reason (namely, to extend its insight) is never direct, but presupposes purposes for which reason is employed.

the senses should will what Reason alone directs such beings that they ought to will, it is no doubt requisite that reason should have a power *to infuse a feeling of pleasure* or satisfaction in the fulfilment of duty, that is to say, that it should have a causality by which it determines the sensibility according to its own principles. But it is quite impossible to discern, *i.e.* to make it intelligible *a priori,* how a mere thought, which itself contains nothing sensible, can itself produce a sensation of pleasure or pain; for this is a particular kind of causality of which as of every other causality we can determine nothing whatever *a priori;* we must only consult experience about it. But as this cannot supply us with any relation of cause and effect except between two objects of experience, whereas in this case, although indeed the effect produced lies within experience, yet the cause is supposed to be pure reason acting through mere ideas which offer no object to experience, it follows that for us men it is quite impossible to explain how and why the *universality of the maxim as a law,* that is, morality, interests. This only is certain, that it is not *because it interests* us that it has validity for us (for that would be heteronomy and dependence of practical reason on sensibility, namely, on a feeling as its principle, in which case it could never give moral laws), but that it interests us because it is valid for us as men, inasmuch as it had its source in our will as intelligences, in other words in our proper self, *and what belongs to mere appearance is necessarily subordinated by reason to the nature of the thing in itself.*

4:461

The question then: How a categorical imperative is possible can be answered to this extent that we can assign the only hypothesis on which it is possible, namely, the idea of freedom; and we can also discern the necessity of this hypothesis, and this is sufficient for the *practical exercise* of reason, that is, for the conviction of the *validity of this imperative,* and hence of the moral law; but how this hypothesis itself is possible can never be discerned by any human reason. On the hypothesis, however, that the will of an intelligence is free, its *autonomy,* as the essential formal condition of its determination, is a necessary consequence. Moreover, this freedom of will is not merely quite *possible* as a hypothesis (not involving any contradiction to the principle of physical necessity in the connexion of the phenomena of the sensible world) as speculative philosophy can show: but further, a rational being who is conscious of a causality through reason, that is to say, of a will (distinct from desires), must *of necessity* make it practically, that is, in idea, the condition of all his voluntary actions. But to explain how pure reason can be of itself practical without the aid of any spring of action that could be derived from any other source, *i.e.* how the mere principle of the *universal validity of all its maxims as laws* (which would certainly be the form of a pure practical reason) can of itself supply a spring, without any matter (object) of the will in which one could antecedently take any interest; and how it can produce an interest which would be called purely *moral;* or in other words, *how pure reason can be practical*—to explain this is beyond the power of human reason, and all the labour and pains of seeking an explanation of it are lost.

It is just the same as if I sought to find out how freedom itself is possible as the causality of a will. For then I quit the ground of 4:462 philosophical explanation, and I have no other to go upon. I might indeed revel in the world of intelligences which still remains to me, but although I have an *idea* of it which is well founded, yet I have not the least *knowledge* of it, nor can I ever attain to such knowledge with all the efforts of my natural faculty of reason. It signifies only a something that remains over when I have eliminated everything belonging to the world of sense from the actuating principles of my will, serving merely to keep in bounds the principle of motives taken from the field of sensibility; fixing its limits and showing that it does not contain all in all within itself, but that there is more beyond it; but this something more I know no further. Of pure reason which frames this ideal, there remains after the abstraction of all matter, *i.e.* knowledge of objects, nothing but the form, namely, the practical law of the universality of the maxims, and in conformity with this the conception of reason in reference to a pure world of understanding as a possible efficient cause, that is a cause determining the will. There must here be a total absence of springs; unless this idea of an intelligible world is itself the spring, or that in which reason primarily takes an interest; but to make this intelligible is precisely the problem that we cannot solve.

Here now is the extreme limit of all moral inquiry, and it is of great importance to determine it even on this account, in order that reason may not on the one hand, to the prejudice of morals, seek about in the world of sense for the supreme motive and an interest comprehensible but empirical; and on the other hand, that it may not impotently flap its wings without being able to move in the (for it) empty space of transcendent concepts which we call the intelligible world, and so lose itself amidst chimeras. For the rest, the idea of a pure world of understanding as a system of all intelligences, and to which we ourselves as rational beings belong (although we are likewise on the other side members of the sensible world), this remains always a useful and legitimate idea for the purposes of rational belief, although all knowledge stops at its threshold, useful, namely, to produce in us a lively interest in the moral law by means 4:463 of the noble ideal of a universal kingdom of *ends in themselves* (rational beings), to which we can belong as members then only when we carefully conduct ourselves according to the maxims of freedom as if they were laws of nature.

Concluding Remark.

The speculative employment of reason *with respect to nature* leads to the absolute necessity of some supreme cause of *the world:* the practical employment of reason *with a view to freedom* leads also to absolute necessity, but only *of the laws of the actions* of a rational being as such. Now it is an essential *principle* of reason, however employed, to push its knowledge to a consciousness of its *necessity* (without which it would not be rational knowledge). It is however an equally essential *restriction* of the same reason that it can neither discern the *necessity* of what is or what happens, nor of what ought to happen, unless a condition is supposed on which it is or happens or ought to happen. In this way, however, by the constant inquiry for the condition, the satisfaction of reason is only further and further postponed. Hence it unceasingly seeks the unconditionally necessary, and finds itself forced to assume it, although without any means of making it comprehensible to itself, happy enough if only it can discover a conception which agrees with this assumption. It is therefore no fault in our deduction of the supreme principle of morality, but an objection that should be made to human reason in general, that it cannot enable us to conceive the absolute necessity of an unconditional practical law (such as the categorical imperative must be). It cannot be blamed for refusing to explain this necessity by a condition, that is to say, by means of some interest assumed as a basis, since the law would then cease to be a moral law, *i.e.* a supreme law of freedom. And thus while we do not comprehend the practical unconditional necessity of the moral imperative, we yet comprehend its *incomprehensibility*, and this is all that can be fairly demanded of a philosophy which strives to carry its principles up to the very limit of human reason.

SELECTIONS FROM

CRITIQUE OF
PRACTICAL REASON

[1788]

Translated by Thomas K. Abbott

revenged, and yet he may see that this is not a practical law, but only his own maxim; that, on the contrary, regarded as being in one and the same maxim a rule for the will of every rational being, it must contradict itself. In natural philosophy the principles of what happens (*e.g.* the principle of equality of action and reaction in the communication of motion) are at the same time laws of nature; for the use of reason there is theoretical, and determined by the nature of the object. In practical philosophy, *i.e.* that which has to do only with the grounds of determination of the will, the principles which a man makes for himself are not laws by which one is inevitably bound; because reason in practical matters has to do with the subject, namely, with the faculty of desire, the special character of which may occasion variety in the rule. The practical rule is always a product of reason, because it prescribes action as a means to the effect. But in the case of a being with whom reason does not of itself determine the will, this rule is an *imperative, i.e.* a rule characterised by "shall," which expresses the objective necessitation of the action, and signifies that if reason completely determined the will, the action would inevitably take place according to this rule. Imperatives, therefore, are objectively valid, and are quite distinct from maxims, which are subjective principles. The former either determine the conditions of the causality of the rational being as an efficient cause, *i.e.* merely in reference to the effect and the means of attaining it; or they determine the will only, whether it is adequate to the effect or not. The former would be hypothetical imperatives, and contain mere precepts of skill; the latter, on the contrary, would be categorical, and would alone be practical laws. Thus maxims are *principles*, but not *imperatives*. Imperatives themselves, however, when they are conditional (*i.e.* do not determine the will simply as will, but only in respect to a desired effect, that is, when they are hypothetical imperatives), are practical *precepts* but not *laws*. Laws must be sufficient to determine the will as will, even before I ask whether I have power sufficient for a desired effect, or the means necessary to produce it; hence they are categorical: otherwise they are not laws at all, because the necessity is wanting, which, if it is to be practical, must be independent on conditions which are pathological, and are therefore only contingently connected with the will. Tell a man, for example, that he must be industrious and thrifty in youth, in order that he may not want in old age; this is a correct and important practical precept of the will. But it is easy to see that in this case the will is directed to something *else* which it is presupposed that it desires; and as to this desire, we must leave it to the actor himself whether he looks forward to other resources than those of his own acquisition, or does not expect to be old, or thinks that in case of future necessity he will be able to make shift with little. Reason, from which alone can spring a rule involving necessity, does, indeed, give necessity to this precept (else it would not be an imperative), but this is a necessity dependent on subjective conditions, and cannot be supposed in the same degree in all subjects. But that reason may give laws it is necessary that it should only need to presuppose *itself*, because rules are objectively and universally valid only when they hold without any contingent subjective conditions, which distinguish one rational being from another. Now tell a man that he should never make a deceitful promise, this is a rule which only concerns his will, whether the purposes he may have can be attained thereby or not; it is the volition only which is to be determined *a priori* by that rule. If now it is found that this rule is practically right, then it is a law, because it is a categorical imperative. Thus, practical laws refer to the will only, without considering what is attained by its causality, and we may disregard this latter (as belonging to the world of sense) in order to have them quite pure. 5:21

§ II.—THEOREM I.

All practical principles which presuppose an object (matter) of the faculty of desire as the ground of determination of the will are empirical, and can furnish no practical laws.

By the matter of the faculty of desire I mean an object the realization of which is desired. Now, if the desire for this object *precedes* the practical rule, and is the condition of our making it a principle, then I say (*in the first place*) this principle is in that case wholly empirical, for then what determines the choice is the idea of an object, and that relation of this idea to the subject by which its faculty of desire is determined to its realization. Such a relation to the subject is called the *pleasure* in the realization of an object. This, then, must be presupposed as a condition of the possibility of determination of the will. But it is impossible to know *a priori* of any idea of an object whether it will be connected with *pleasure* or *pain*, or be indifferent. In such cases, therefore, the determining principle of the choice must be empirical, and, therefore, also the practical material principle which presupposes it as a condition.

In the second place, since susceptibility to a pleasure or pain can be known only empirically, and cannot hold in the same degree for all rational beings, a principle which is based on this subjective condition may serve indeed as a *maxim* for the subject which possesses this susceptibility, but not as a *law* even to him (because it is wanting in objective necessity, which must be recognized *a priori*); it follows, therefore, that such a principle can never furnish a practical law.

5:22

§ III.—THEOREM II.

All material practical principles as such are of one and the same kind, and come under the general principle of self-love or private happiness.

Pleasure arising from the idea of the existence of a thing, in so far as it is to determine the desire of this thing, is founded on the *susceptibility* of the subject, since it *depends* on the presence of an object; hence it belongs to sense (feeling), and not to understanding, which expresses a relation of the idea *to an object* according to concepts, not to the subject according to feelings. It is then practical only in so far as the faculty of desire is determined by the sensation of agreeableness which the subject expects from the actual existence of the object. Now, a rational being's consciousness of the pleasantness of life uninterruptedly accompanying his whole existence is happiness, and the principle which makes this the supreme ground of determination of the will is the principle of self-love. All material principles, then, which place the determining ground of the will in the pleasure or pain to be received from the existence of any object are all of the same kind, inasmuch as they all belong to the principle of self-love or private happiness.

Corollary.

All *material* practical rules place the determining principle of the will in the *lower desires*, and if there were no *purely formal* laws of the will adequate to determine it, then we could not admit *any higher desire* at all.

Remark I.

It is surprising that men, otherwise acute, can think it possible to distinguish between *higher* and *lower desires*, according as the ideas which are connected with the feeling of pleasure have their origin in the *senses* or in the *understanding*; for when we inquire what are the determining grounds of desire, and place them in some expected pleasantness, it is of no consequence whence the *idea* of this pleasing object is derived, but only how much it *pleases*. Whether an idea has its seat and source in the understanding or not, if it can only determine the choice by presupposing a feeling of pleasure in the subject, it follows that its capability of determining the choice depends altogether on the nature of the inner sense, namely, that this can be agreeably affected by it. However dissimilar ideas of objects may be, though they be ideas of the understanding, or even of the reason in contrast to ideas of sense, yet the feeling of pleasure, by means of which they constitute the determining principle of the will (the expected satisfaction which impels the activity to the production of the object), is of one and the same kind, not only inasmuch as it can be only known empirically, but also inasmuch as it affects one and the same vital force which manifests itself in the faculty of desire, and in this respect can only differ in degree from every other ground of determination. Otherwise, how could we compare in respect of *magnitude* two principles of determination, the ideas of which depend upon different faculties, so as to prefer that which affects the faculty of desire in the highest degree. The same man may return unread an instructive book which he cannot again obtain, in order not to miss a hunt; he may depart in the midst of a fine speech, in order not to be late for dinner; he may leave a rational conversation, such as he otherwise values highly, to take his place at the gaming-table; he may even repulse a poor man whom he at other times takes pleasure in benefiting, because he has only just enough money in his pocket to pay for his admission to the theatre. If the determination of his will rests on the feeling of the agreeableness or disagreeableness that he expects from any cause, it is all the same to him by what sort of ideas he will be affected. The only thing that concerns him, in order to decide his choice, is, how great, how long continued, how easily obtained, and how often repeated, this agreeableness is. Just as to the man who wants money to spend, it is all the same whether the gold was dug out of the mountain or washed out of the sand, provided it is everywhere accepted at the same value; so the man who cares only for the enjoyment of life does not ask whether the ideas are of the understanding or the senses, but only *how much* and *how great pleasure* they will give for the longest time. It is only those that would gladly deny to pure reason the power of determining the will, without the presupposition of any feeling, who could deviate so far from their own exposition as to describe as quite heterogeneous what they have themselves previously brought under one and the same principle. Thus, for example, it is observed that we can find pleasure in the mere *exercise of power*, in the consciousness of our strength of mind in overcoming obstacles which are opposed to our designs, in the culture of our mental talents, etc.; and we justly call these more refined pleasures and enjoyments, because they are more in our power than others; they do not wear out, but rather increase the capacity for further enjoyment of them, and while they delight they at the same time cultivate. But to say on this account that they determine the will in a different way, and not through sense, whereas the possibility of the pleasure presupposes a feeling for it implanted in us, which is the first condition of this satisfaction; this is just as when ignorant persons that like to dabble in metaphysics imagine matter so subtle, so super-subtle, that they almost make themselves giddy with it, and then think that in this way they have conceived it as a *spiritual* and yet extended being. If with *Epicurus* we make virtue determine the will only by means of the pleasure it promises, we cannot afterwards blame him for holding that this pleasure is of the same kind as those of the coarsest senses. For we have no reason whatever to charge him with holding that the ideas by which this feeling is excited in us belong merely to the bodily senses. As far as can be conjectured, he sought the source of many of them in the use of the higher cognitive faculty; but this did not prevent him, and could not prevent him, from holding on the principle above stated, that the pleasure itself which those intellectual ideas give us, and by which alone they can determine the will, is just of the same kind. *Consistency* is the highest obligation of a philosopher, and yet the most rarely found. The ancient Greek schools give us more examples of it than we find in our *syncretistic* age, in which a certain shallow and dishonest *system of compromise* of contradictory principles is devised, because it commends itself better to a public which is content to know something of everything and nothing thoroughly, so as to please every party.

The principle of private happiness, however much understanding and reason may be used in it, cannot contain any other determining principles for the will than those which belong to the *lower* desires; and either there are no [higher] desires at all, or *pure* reason must of itself alone be practical: that is, it must be able to determine the will by the mere form of the practical rule without supposing any feeling, and consequently without any idea of the pleasant or unpleasant, which is the matter of the desire, and which is always an empirical condition of the principles. Then only, when reason of itself determines the will (not as the servant of the inclination), it is really a *higher* desire to which that which is pathologically determined is subordinate, and is really, and even specifically, distinct from the latter, so that even the slightest admixture of the motives of the latter impairs its strength and superiority; just as in a mathematical demonstration the least empirical condition would degrade and destroy its force and value. Reason, with its practical law, determines the will immediately, not by means of an intervening feeling of pleasure or pain, not even of pleasure in the law itself, and it is only because it can, as pure reason, be practical, that it is possible for it to be *legislative*.

5:25

Remark II.

To be happy is necessarily the wish of every finite rational being, and this, therefore, is inevitably a determining principle of its faculty of desire. For we are not in possession originally of satisfaction with our whole existence—a bliss which would imply a consciousness of our own independent self-sufficiency—this is a problem imposed upon us by our own finite nature, because we have wants, and these wants regard the matter of our desires, that is, something that is relative to a subjective feeling of pleasure or pain, which determines what we need in order to be satisfied with our condition. But just because this material principle of determination can only be empirically known by the subject, it is impossible to regard this problem as a law; for a law being objective must contain the *very same principle of determination* of the will in all cases and for all rational beings. For, although the notion of happiness is *in every case* the foundation of the practical relation of the *objects* to the desires, yet it is only a general name for the subjective determining principles, and determines nothing specifically; whereas this is what alone we are concerned with in this practical problem, which cannot be solved at all without such specific determination. For it is every man's own special feeling of pleasure and pain that decides in what he is to place his happiness, and even in the same subject this will vary with the difference of his wants according as this feeling changes, and thus a law which is *subjectively necessary* (as a law of nature) is *objectively* a very contingent practical principle, which can and must be very different in different subjects, and therefore can never furnish a law; since, in the desire for happiness it is not the form of conformity to law that is decisive, but simply the matter, namely, whether I am to expect pleasure in following the law, and how much. Principles of self-love may, indeed, contain universal precepts of skill (how to find means to accomplish one's purposes), 5:26 but in that case they are merely theoretical principles;[1] as, for ex-

---

1 Propositions which in mathematics or physics are called *practical* ought properly to be called *technical*. For they have nothing to do with the determination of the will; they only point out how a certain effect is to be produced, and are therefore just as theoretical as any

ample, how he who would like to eat bread should contrive a mill; but practical precepts founded on them can never be universal, for the determining principle of the desire is based on the feeling of pleasure and pain, which can never be supposed to be universally directed to the same objects.

Even supposing, however, that all finite rational beings were thoroughly agreed as to what were the objects of their feelings of pleasure and pain, and also as to the means which they must employ to attain the one and avoid the other; still, they could *by no means* set up the *principle of self-love* as a *practical law,* for this unanimity itself would be only contingent. The principle of determination would still be only subjectively valid and merely empirical, and would not possess the necessity which is conceived in every law, namely, an objective necessity arising from *a priori* grounds; unless, indeed, we hold this necessity to be not at all practical, but merely physical, viz. that our action is as inevitably determined by our inclination, as yawning when we see others yawn. It would be better to maintain that there are no practical laws at all, but only *counsels* for the service of our desires, than to raise merely subjective principles to the rank of practical laws, which have objective necessity, and not merely subjective, and which must be known by reason *a priori*, not by experience (however empirically universal this may be). Even the rules of corresponding phenomena are only called laws of nature (*e.g.* the mechanical laws), when we either know them really *a priori,* or (as in the case of chemical laws) suppose that they would be known *a priori* from objective grounds if our insight reached further. But in the case of merely subjective practical principles, it is expressly made a condition that they rest not on objective but on subjective conditions of choice, and hence that they must always be represented as mere maxims; never as practical laws. This second remark seems at first sight to be mere verbal refinement, but it defines the terms of the most important distinction which can come into consideration in practical investigations.

---

propositions which express the connexion of a cause with an effect. Now whoever chooses the effect must also choose the cause.

5:27

§ IV.—THEOREM III.

A rational being cannot regard his maxims as practical universal laws, unless he conceives them as principles which determine the will, not by their matter, but by their form only.

By the matter of a practical principle I mean the object of the will. This object is either the determining ground of the will or it is not. In the former case the rule of the will is subjected to an empirical condition (viz. the relation of the determining idea to the feeling of pleasure and pain), consequently it cannot be a practical law. Now, when we abstract from a law all matter, *i.e.* every object of the will (as a determining principle), nothing is left but the mere *form* of a universal legislation. Therefore, either a rational being cannot conceive his subjective practical principles, that is, his maxims, as being at the same time universal laws, or he must suppose that their mere form, by which they are fitted for universal legislation, is alone what makes them practical laws.

Remark.

The commonest understanding can distinguish without instruction what form of maxim is adapted for universal legislation, and what is not. Suppose, for example, that I have made it my maxim to increase my fortune by every safe means. Now, I have a deposit in my hands, the owner of which is dead and has left no writing about it. This is just the case for my maxim. I desire then to know whether that maxim can also hold good as a universal practical law. I apply it, therefore, to the present case, and ask whether it could take the form of a law, and consequently whether I can by my maxim at the same time give such a law as this, that everyone may deny a deposit of which no one can produce a proof. I at once become aware that such a principle, viewed as a law, would annihilate itself, because the result would be that there would be no deposits. A practical law which I recognize as such must be qualified for universal legislation; this is an identical proposition, and therefore self-evident. Now, if I say that my will is subject to a practical law, I cannot adduce my inclination (*e.g.* in the present case my avarice) as a princi-

ple of determination fitted to be a universal practical law; for this is 5:28
so far from being fitted for a universal legislation that, if put in the
form of a universal law, it would destroy itself.

It is, therefore, surprising that intelligent men could have
thought of calling the desire of happiness a universal *practical law*
on the ground that the desire is universal, and, therefore, also the
maxim by which everyone makes this desire determine his will. For
whereas in other cases a universal law of nature makes everything
harmonious; here, on the contrary, if we attribute to the maxim the
universality of a law, the extreme opposite of harmony will follow,
the greatest opposition, and the complete destruction of the maxim
itself, and its purpose. For, in that case, the will of all has not one
and the same object, but everyone has his own (his private welfare),
which may accidentally accord with the purposes of others which
are equally selfish, but it is far from sufficing for a law; because the
occasional exceptions which one is permitted to make are endless,
and cannot be definitely embraced in one universal rule. In this
manner, then, results a harmony like that which a certain satirical
poem depicts as existing between a married couple bent on going
to ruin, "O, marvellous harmony, what he wishes, she wishes also";
or like what is said of the pledge of Francis I. to the emperor
Charles V., "What my brother Charles wishes that I wish also" (viz.
Milan). Empirical principles of determination are not fit for any
universal external legislation, but just as little for internal; for each
man makes his own subject the foundation of his inclination, and in
the same subject sometimes one inclination, sometimes another,
has the preponderance. To discover a law which would govern
them all under this condition, namely, bringing them all into harmony, is quite impossible.

§ V.—PROBLEM I.

Supposing that the mere legislative form of maxims is alone the
sufficient determining principle of a will, to find the nature of the
will which can be determined by it alone.

Since the bare form of the law can only be conceived by reason,
and is, therefore, not an object of the senses, and consequently does

not belong to the class of phenomena, it follows that the idea of it, which determines the will, is distinct from all the principles that 5:29 determine events in nature according to the law of causality, because in their case the determining principles must themselves be phenomena. Now, if no other determining principle can serve as a law for the will except that universal legislative form, such a will must be conceived as quite independent on the natural law of phenomena in their mutual relation, namely, the law of causality; such independence is called *freedom* in the strictest, that is in the transcendental sense; consequently, a will which can have its law in nothing but the mere legislative form of the maxim is a free will.

§ VI.—PROBLEM II.

Supposing that a will is free, to find the law which alone is competent to determine it necessarily.

Since the matter of the practical law, *i.e.* an object of the maxim, can never be given otherwise than empirically, and the free will is independent on empirical conditions (that is, conditions belonging to the world of sense) and yet is determinable, consequently a free will must find its principle of determination in the law, and yet independently of the matter of the law. But, besides the matter of the law, nothing is contained in it except the legislative form. It is the legislative form, then, contained in the maxim, which can alone constitute a principle of determination of the [free] will.

Remark.

Thus freedom and an unconditional practical law reciprocally imply each other. Now I do not ask here whether they are in fact distinct, or whether an unconditioned law is not rather merely the consciousness of a pure practical reason, and the latter identical with the positive concept of freedom; I only ask, whence *begins* our *knowledge* of the unconditionally practical, whether it is from freedom or from the practical law? Now it cannot begin from freedom, for of this we cannot be immediately conscious, since the first concept of it is negative; nor can we infer it from experience, for experience gives us the knowledge only of the law of phenomena, and hence of the mechanism of nature, the direct opposite of freedom. It is therefore the moral law, of which we become directly conscious (as soon as we trace for ourselves maxims of the will), that *first* presents itself to us, and leads directly to the concept of freedom, inasmuch as reason presents it as a principle of determination not to be outweighed by any sensible conditions, nay, wholly independent of them. But how is the consciousness of that moral law possible? We can become conscious of pure practical laws just as we are conscious of pure theoretical principles, by attending to the necessity with which reason prescribes them, and to the elimination of all empirical conditions, which it directs. The concept of a pure will arises out of the former, as that of a pure understanding arises out of the latter. That this is the true subordination of our concepts, and that it is morality that first discovers to us the notion of freedom, hence that it is *practical reason* which, with this concept, first proposes to speculative reason the most insoluble problem, thereby placing it in the greatest perplexity, is evident from the following consideration:—Since nothing in phenomena can be explained by the concept of freedom, but the mechanism of nature must constitute the only clue; moreover, when pure reason tries to ascend in the series of causes to the unconditioned, it falls into an antinomy which is entangled in incomprehensibilities on the one side as much as the other; whilst the latter (namely, mechanism) is at least useful in the explanation of phenomena, therefore no one would ever have been so rash as to introduce freedom into science, had not the moral law, and with it practical reason, come in and forced this notion upon us. Experience, however, confirms this order of notions. Suppose some one asserts of his lustful appetite that, when the desired object and the opportunity are present, it is quite irresistible. [Ask him]—if a gallows were erected before the house where he finds this opportunity, in order that he should be hanged thereon immediately after the gratification of his lust, whether he could not then control his passion; we need not be long in doubt what he would reply. Ask him, however—if his sovereign ordered him, on pain of the same immediate execution, to bear false witness against an honourable man, whom the prince might wish to destroy under a plausible pretext, would he consider it pos-

5:30

sible in that case to overcome his love of life, however great it may be. He would perhaps not venture to affirm whether he would do so or not, but he must unhesitatingly admit that it is possible to do so. He judges, therefore, that he can do a certain thing because he is conscious that he ought, and he recognizes that he is free, a fact which but for the moral law he would never have known.

§ VII.—FUNDAMENTAL LAW OF THE PURE PRACTICAL REASON.

Act so that the maxim of thy will can always at the same time hold good as a principle of universal legislation.

Remark.

5:31

Pure geometry has postulates which are practical propositions, but contain nothing further than the assumption that we *can* do something if it is required that we *should* do it, and these are the only geometrical propositions that concern actual existence. They are, then, practical rules under a problematical condition of the will; but here the rule says:—We absolutely must proceed in a certain manner. The practical rule is, therefore, unconditional, and hence it is conceived *a priori* as a categorically practical proposition by which the will is objectively determined absolutely and immediately (by the practical rule itself, which thus is in this case a law); for *pure reason practical of itself* is here directly legislative. The will is thought as independent on empirical conditions, and, therefore, as pure will determined by *the mere form of the law*, and this principle of determination is regarded as the supreme condition of all maxims. The thing is strange enough, and has no parallel in all the rest of our practical knowledge. For the *a priori* thought of a possible universal legislation which is therefore merely problematical, is unconditionally commanded as a law without borrowing anything from experience or from any external will. This, however, is not a precept to do something by which some desired effect can be attained (for then the will would depend on physical conditions), but a rule that determines the will *a priori* only so far as regards the forms of its maxims; and thus it is at least not impossible to conceive that a law, which only applies to the *subjective* form of princi-ples, yet serves as a principle of determination by means of the *ob-jective* form of law in general. We may call the consciousness of this fundamental law a fact of reason, because we cannot reason it out from antecedent data of reason, *e.g.* the consciousness of freedom (for this is not antecedently given), but it forces itself on us as a syn-thetic *a priori* proposition, which is not based on any intuition, ei-ther pure or empirical. It would, indeed, be analytical if the freedom of the will were presupposed, but to presuppose freedom as a positive *concept* would require an intellectual intuition, which cannot here be assumed; however, when we regard this law as *given*, it must be observed, in order not to fall into any misconception that it is not an empirical fact, but the sole fact of the pure reason, which thereby announces itself as originally legislative (*sic volo, sic jubeo*).

Corollary.

Pure reason is practical of itself alone, and gives (to man) a univer-sal law which we call the *Moral Law.*

Remark.

5:32

The fact just mentioned is undeniable. It is only necessary to analyse the judgment that men pass on the lawfulness of their ac-tions, in order to find that, whatever inclination may say to the con-trary, reason, incorruptible and self-constrained, always confronts the maxim of the will in any action with the pure will, that is, with itself, considering itself as *a priori* practical. Now this principle of morality, just on account of the universality of the legislation which makes it the formal supreme determining principle of the will, without regard to any subjective differences, is declared by the reason to be a law for all rational beings, in so far as they have a will, that is, a power to determine their causality by the conception of rules; and, therefore, so far as they are capable of acting according to principles, and consequently also according to practical *a priori* principles (for these alone have the necessity that reason requires in a principle). It is, therefore, not limited to men only, but applies to all finite beings that possess reason and will, nay, it even includes

240 of Basic Writings of Kant

the Infinite Being as the supreme intelligence. In the former case, however, the law has the form of an imperative, because in them, as rational beings, we can suppose a *pure* will, but being creatures affected with wants and physical motives, not a *holy* will, that is, one which would be incapable of any maxim conflicting with the moral law. In their case, therefore, the moral law is an *imperative*, which commands categorically, because the law is unconditioned; the relation of such a will to this law is *dependence* under the name of *obligation*, which implies a *constraint* to an action, though only by reason and its objective law; and this action is called *duty*, because an elective will, subject to pathological affections (though not determined by them, and therefore still free), implies a wish that arises from *subjective* causes, and therefore may often be opposed to the pure objective determining principle; whence it requires the moral constraint of a resistance of the practical reason, which may be called an internal, but intellectual compulsion. In the supreme intelligence the elective will is rightly conceived as incapable of any maxim which could not at the same time be objectively a law; and the notion of *holiness*, which on that account belongs to it, places it, not indeed above all practical laws, but above all practically restrictive laws, and consequently above obligation and duty. This holiness of will is, however, a practical idea, which must necessarily serve as a type to which finite rational beings can only approximate indefinitely, and which the pure moral law, which is itself on this account called holy, constantly and rightly holds before their eyes. The utmost that finite practical reason can effect is 5:33 to be certain of this indefinite progress of one's maxims, and of their steady disposition to advance. This is virtue, and virtue, at least as a naturally acquired faculty, can never be perfect, because assurance in such a case never becomes apodictic certainty, and when it only amounts to persuasion is very dangerous.

§ VIII.—THEOREM IV.

The *autonomy* of the will is the sole principle of all moral laws, and of all duties which conform to them; on the other hand, *heteronomy* of the elective will not only cannot be the basis of any obligation, but is, on the contrary, opposed to the principle thereof, and to the morality of the will.

In fact the sole principle of morality consists in the independence on all matter of the law (namely, a desired object), and in the determination of the elective will by the mere universal legislative form of which its maxim must be capable. Now this *independence* is *freedom* in the *negative* sense, and this *self-legislation* of the pure, and, therefore, practical reason, is freedom in the *positive* sense. Thus the moral law expresses nothing else than the *autonomy* of the pure practical reason; that is, freedom; and this is itself the formal condition of all maxims, and on this condition only can they agree with the supreme practical law. If therefore the matter of the volition, which can be nothing else than the object of a desire that is connected with the law, enters into the practical law, *as the condition of its possibility*, there results heteronomy of the elective will, namely, dependence on the physical law that we should follow some impulse or inclination. In that case the will does not give itself the law, but only the precept how rationally to follow pathological law; and the maxim which, in such a case, never contains the universally legislative form, not only produces no obligation, but is itself opposed to the principle of a pure practical reason, and, therefore, also to the moral disposition, even though the resulting action may be comformable to the law.

Remark I.

5:34

Hence a practical precept, which contains a material (and therefore empirical) condition, must never be reckoned a practical law. For the law of the pure will, which is free, brings the will into a sphere quite different from the empirical; and as the necessity involved in the law is not a physical necessity, it can only consist in the formal conditions of the possibility of a law in general. All the matter of practical rules rests on subjective conditions, which give them only a conditional universality (in case I *desire* this or that, what I must do in order to obtain it), and they all turn on the principle of *private happiness*. Now, it is indeed undeniable that every volition must have an object, and therefore a matter; but it does not follow that this is the determining principle, and the condition of the maxim; for, if it is so, then this cannot be exhibited in a universally legislative form, since in that case the expectation of the existence of the object would be the determining cause of the choice, and the volition must presuppose the dependence of the faculty of desire on the existence of something; but this dependence can only be sought in empirical conditions, and therefore can never furnish a foundation for a necessary and universal rule. Thus, the happiness of others may be the object of the will of a rational being. But if it were the determining principle of the maxim, we must assume that we find not only a rational satisfaction in the welfare of others, but also a want such as the sympathetic disposition in some men occasions. But I cannot assume the existence of this want in every rational being (not at all in God). The matter then of the maxim may remain, but it must not be the condition of it, else the maxim could not be fit for a law. Hence, the mere form of law, which limits the matter, must also be a reason for adding this matter to the will, not for presupposing it. For example, let the matter be my own happiness. This (rule), if I attribute it to everyone (as, in fact, I may, in the case of every finite being), can become an *objective* practical law only if I include the happiness of others. Therefore, the law that we should promote the happiness of others does not arise from the assumption that this is an object of everyone's choice, but merely from this, that the form of universality which reason requires as the condition of giving to a maxim of self-love the objective validity of a law, is the principle that determines the will. Therefore it was not the object (the happiness of others) that determined the pure will, but it was the form of law only, by which I restricted my maxim, founded on inclination, so as to give it the universality of a law, and thus to adapt it to the practical reason; and it is this restriction alone, and not the addition of an external spring, that can give rise to the notion of the *obligation* to extend the maxim of my self-love to the happiness of others.

5:35

Remark II.

The direct opposite of the principle of morality is, when the principle of *private* happiness is made the determining principle of the will, and with this is to be reckoned, as I have shown above, everything that places the determining principle which is to serve as a law anywhere but in the legislative form of the maxim. This contradiction, however, is not merely logical, like that which would arise between rules empirically conditioned, if they were raised to the rank of necessary principles of cognition, but is practical, and would ruin morality altogether were not the voice of reason in reference to the will so clear, so irrepressible, so distinctly audible even, to the commonest men. It can only, indeed, be maintained in the perplexing speculations of the schools, which are bold enough to shut their ears against that heavenly voice, in order to support a theory that costs no trouble.

Suppose that an acquaintance whom you otherwise liked were to attempt to justify himself to you for having borne false witness, first by alleging the, in his view, sacred duty of consulting his own happiness; then by enumerating the advantages which he had gained thereby, pointing out the prudence he had shown in securing himself against detection, even by yourself, to whom he now reveals the secret, only in order that he may be able to deny it at any time; and suppose he were then to affirm, in all seriousness, that he has fulfilled a true human duty; you would either laugh in his face, or shrink back from him with disgust; and yet, if a man has regulated his principles of action solely with a view to his own advantage, you would have nothing whatever to object against this mode of proceeding. Or suppose some one recommends you a man as steward, as a man to whom you can blindly trust all your affairs; and, in order to inspire you with confidence, extols him as a prudent man who thoroughly understands his own interest, and is so indefatigably active that he lets slip no opportunity of advancing it; lastly, lest you should be afraid of finding a vulgar selfishness in him, praises the good taste with which he lives; not seeking his pleasure in money-making, or in coarse wantonness, but in the enlargement of his knowledge, in instructive intercourse with a select circle, and even in relieving the needy; while as to the means (which, of course, derive all their value from the end) he is not particular, and is ready to use other people's money for the purpose as if it were his own, provided only he knows that he can do so safely, 6:26

and without discovery; you would either believe that the recommender was mocking you, or that he had lost his senses. So sharply and clearly marked are the boundaries of morality and self-love that even the commonest eye cannot fail to distinguish whether a thing belongs to the one or the other. The few remarks that follow may appear superfluous where the truth is so plain, but at least they may serve to give a little more distinctness to the judgment of common sense.

The principle of happiness may, indeed, furnish maxims, but never such as would be competent to be laws of the will, even if *universal* happiness were made the object. For since the knowledge of this rests on mere empirical data, since every man's judgment on it depends very much on his particular point of view, which is itself moreover very variable, it can supply only *general* rules, not *universal;* that is, it can give rules which on the average will most frequently fit, but not rules which must hold good always and necessarily; hence, no practical *laws* can be founded on it. Just because in this case an object of choice is the foundation of the rule, and must therefore precede it; the rule can refer to nothing but what is [felt], and therefore it refers to experience and is founded on it, and then the variety of judgment must be endless. This principle, therefore, does not prescribe the same practical rules to all rational beings, although the rules are all included under a common title, namely, that of happiness. The moral law, however, is conceived as objectively necessary, only because it holds for everyone that has reason and will.

The maxim of self-love (prudence) only *advises;* the law of morality *commands.* Now there is a great difference between that which we are *advised* to do and that to which we are *obliged.*

The commonest intelligence can easily and without hesitation see what, on the principle of autonomy of the will, requires to be done; but on supposition of heteronomy of the will, it is hard and requires knowledge of the world to see what is to be done. That is to say, what *duty* is, is plain of itself to everyone; but what is to bring true durable advantage, such as will extend to the whole of one's existence, is always veiled in impenetrable obscurity; and much prudence is required to adapt the practical rule founded on it to the ends of life, even tolerably, by making proper exceptions. But the moral law commands the most punctual obedience from everyone; it must, therefore, not be so difficult to judge what it requires to be done, that the commonest unpractised understanding, even without worldly prudence, should fail to apply it rightly.

It is always in everyone's power to satisfy the categorical command of morality; whereas it is but seldom possible, and by no means so to everyone, to satisfy the empirically conditioned precept of happiness, even with regard to a single purpose. The reason is, that in the former case there is question only of the maxim, which must be genuine and pure; but in the latter case there is question also of one's capacity and physical power to realise a desired object. A command that everyone should try to make himself happy would be foolish, for one never commands anyone to do what he of himself infallibly wishes to do. We must only command the means, or rather supply them, since he cannot do everything that he wishes. But to command morality under the name of duty is quite rational; for, in the first place, not everyone is willing to obey its precepts if they oppose his inclinations; and as to the means of obeying this law, these need not in this case be taught, for in this respect whatever he wishes to do he can do.

6:37

He who has *lost* at play may be *vexed* at himself and his folly, but if he is conscious of having *cheated* at play (although he has gained thereby), he must *despise* himself as soon as he compares himself with the moral law. This must, therefore, be something different from the principle of private happiness. For a man must have a different criterion when he is compelled to say to himself: I am a *worthless* fellow, though I have filled my purse; and when he approves himself, and says: I am a *prudent* man, for I have enriched my treasure.

Finally, there is something further in the idea of our practical reason, which accompanies the transgression of a moral law— namely, its *ill desert*. Now the notion of punishment, as such, cannot be united with that of becoming a partaker of happiness; for although he who inflicts the punishment may at the same time have the benevolent purpose of directing this punishment to this end,

246 · Basic Writings of Kant

yet it must first be justified in itself as punishment, *i.e.* as mere harm, so that if it stopped there, and the person punished could get no glimpse of kindness hidden behind this harshness, he must yet admit that justice was done him, and that his reward was perfectly suitable to his conduct. In every punishment, as such, there must first be justice, and this constitutes the essence of the notion. Benevolence may, indeed, be united with it, but the man who has deserved punishment has not the least reason to reckon upon this. Punishment, then, is a physical evil, which, though it be not connected with moral evil as a *natural* consequence, ought to be connected with it as a consequence by the principles of a moral legislation. Now, if every crime, even without regarding the physical consequence with respect to the actor, is in itself punishable, that is, forfeits happiness (at least partially), it is obviously absurd to say that the crime consisted just in this, that he has drawn punishment on himself, thereby injuring his private happiness (which, on the principle of self-love, must be the proper notion of all crime). According to this view the punishment would be the reason for calling anything a crime, and justice would, on the contrary, consist in omitting all punishment, and even preventing that which naturally follows; for, if this were done, there would no longer be any evil in the action, since the harm which otherwise followed it, and on account of which alone the action was called evil, would now be prevented. To look, however, on all rewards and punishments as merely the machinery in the hand of a higher power, which is to serve only to set rational creatures striving after their final end (happiness), this is to reduce the will to a mechanism destructive of freedom; this is so evident that it need not detain us.

More refined, though equally false, is the theory of those who suppose a certain special moral sense, which sense and not reason determines the moral law, and in consequence of which the consciousness of virtue is supposed to be directly connected with contentment and pleasure; that of vice, with mental dissatisfaction and pain; thus reducing the whole to the desire of private happiness. Without repeating what has been said above, I will here only remark the fallacy they fall into. In order to imagine the vicious man

as tormented with mental dissatisfaction by the consciousness of
his transgressions, they must first represent him as in the main basis
of his character, at least in some degree, morally good; just as he
who is pleased with the consciousness of right conduct must be
conceived as already virtuous. The notion of morality and duty
must, therefore, have preceded any regard to this satisfaction, and
cannot be derived from it. A man must first appreciate the importance of what we call duty, the authority of the moral law, and the
immediate dignity which the following of it gives to the person in
his own eyes, in order to feel that satisfaction in the consciousness
of his conformity to it, and the bitter remorse that accompanies the
consciousness of its transgression. It is, therefore, impossible to feel
this satisfaction or dissatisfaction prior to the knowledge of obligation, or to make it the basis of the latter. A man must be at least half
honest in order even to be able to form a conception of these feelings. I do not deny that as the human will is, by virtue of liberty capable of being immediately determined by the moral law, so
frequent practice in accordance with this principle of determination can, at last, produce subjectively a feeling of satisfaction; on
the contrary, it is a duty to establish and to cultivate this, which
alone deserves to be called properly the moral feeling; but the notion of duty cannot be derived from it, else we should have to suppose a feeling for the law as such, and thus make that an object of
sensation which can only be thought by the reason; and this, if it is 5:39
not to be a flat contradiction, would destroy all notion of duty, and
put in its place a mere mechanical play of refined inclinations
sometimes contending with the coarser.

If now we compare our *formal* supreme principle of pure practical reason (that of autonomy of the will) with all previous *material*
principles or morality, we can exhibit them all in a table in which
all possible cases are exhausted, except the one formal principle;
and thus we can show visibly that it is vain to look for any other
principle than that now proposed. In fact all possible principles of
determination of the will are either merely *subjective,* and therefore
empirical, or are also *objective* and rational; and both are either *external* or *internal.*

5:40

Practical Material Principles of Determination taken as the
Foundation of Morality, are:—

SUBJECTIVE.		OBJECTIVE.	
EXTERNAL.	INTERNAL.	INTERNAL.	EXTERNAL.
Education.	Physical feeling.	Perfection.	Will of God.
(*Montaigne*).	(*Epicurus*).	(*Wolf* and	(*Crusius* and other
The civil	Moral feeling.	the *Stoics*).	*theological*
Constitution	(*Hutcheson*).		Moralists).
(*Mandeville*).			

5:41   Those at the left hand are all empirical, and evidently incapable of furnishing the universal principle of morality; but those on the right hand are based on reason (for perfection as a quality of things, and the highest perfection conceived as *substance*, that is, God, can only be thought by means of rational concepts). But the former notion, namely, that of *perfection*, may either be taken in a *theoretic* signification, and then it means nothing but the completeness of each thing in its own kind (transcendental), or that of a thing, merely as a thing (metaphysical); and with that we are not concerned here. But the notion of perfection in a *practical* sense is the fitness or sufficiency of a thing for all sorts of purposes. This perfection, as a *quality* of man, and consequently internal, is nothing but *talent*, and, what strengthens or completes this, *skill*. Supreme perfection conceived as *substance*, that is God, and consequently external (considered practically), is the sufficiency of this being for all ends. Ends then must first be given, relatively to which only can the notion of *perfection* (whether internal in ourselves or external in God) be the determining principle of the will. But an end—being an *object* which must precede the determination of the will by a practical rule, and contain the ground of the possibility of this determination, and therefore contain also the matter of the will, taken as its determining principle—such an end is always empirical, and, therefore, may serve for the *Epicurean* principle of the happiness theory, but not for the pure rational principle of morality and duty. Thus, talents and the improvement of them, because they contribute to the advantages of life; or the will of God, if agreement with it be taken as the object of the will, without any antecedent independent practical principle, can be motives only by reason of the *happiness* expected therefrom. Hence it follows, *first,* that all the principles here stated are *material; secondly,* that they include all possible material principles; and, finally, the conclusion, that since material principles are quite incapable of furnishing the supreme moral law (as has been shown), the *formal practical principle* of the pure reason (according to which the mere form of a universal legislation must constitute the supreme and immediate determining principle of the will) is the *only* one *possible* which is adequate to furnish categorical imperatives; that is, practical laws (which make actions a duty); and in general to serve as the principle of morality, both in criticising conduct and also in its application to the human will to determine it.

Table of the Categories of Freedom relatively to the Notions of Good and Evil. 5:66

I.—QUANTITY.

Subjective, according to maxims (*practical opinions* of the individual).
Objective, according to principles (*precepts*).
A priori both objective and subjective principles of freedom (*laws*).

II.—QUALITY.

Practical rules of *action (præceptivæ).*
Practical rules of *omission (prohibitivæ).*
Practical rules of *exceptions (exceptivæ).*

III.—RELATION.

To *personality.*
To the *condition* of the person.
Reciprocal, of one person to the condition of the others.

IV.—MODALITY.

The *permitted* and the *forbidden.*
Duty and the *contrary to duty.*
Perfect and *imperfect duty.*

It will at once be observed that in this table freedom is considered as a sort of causality not subject to empirical principles of determination, in regard to actions possible by it, which are phenomena in the world of sense, and that consequently it is referred to the categories which concern its physical possibility, whilst yet each category is taken so universally that the determining principle of that causality can be placed outside the world of sense in freedom as a property of a being in the world of intelligence; and finally the categories of modality introduce the transition from practical principles generally to those of morality, but only *problematically*. These can be established *dogmatically* only by the moral law.

I add nothing further here in explanation of the present table, since it is intelligible enough of itself. A division of this kind based on principles is very useful in any science, both for the sake of thoroughness and intelligibility. Thus, for instance, we know from the preceding table and its first number what we must begin from in practical inquiries, namely, from the maxims which everyone founds on his own inclinations; the precepts which hold for a species of rational beings so far as they agree in certain inclinations; and finally the law which holds for all without regard to their inclinations, &c. In this way we survey the whole plan of what has to be done, every question of practical philosophy that has to be answered, and also the order that is to be followed.

Of the Typic of the Pure Practical Judgment.

It is the notions of good and evil that first determine an object of the will. They themselves, however, are subject to a practical rule of reason, which, if it is pure reason, determines the will *a priori* relatively to its object. Now, whether an action which is possible to us in the world of sense, comes under the rule or not, is a question to be decided by the practical Judgment, by which what is said in the rule universally (*in abstracto*) is applied to an action *in concreto*. But since a practical rule of pure reason *in the first place* as *practical* concerns the existence of an object, and in *the second place* as a *practical rule* of pure reason, implies necessity as regards the existence of the action, and therefore is a practical law, not a physical law depending on empirical principles of determination, but a law of freedom by which the will is to be determined independently on anything empirical (merely by the conception of a law and its form), whereas all instances that can occur of possible actions can only be empirical, that is, belong to the experience of physical nature; hence, it seems absurd to expect to find in the world of sense a case which, while as such it depends only on the law of nature, yet admits of the application to it of a law of freedom, and to which we can apply the supersensible idea of the morally good which is to be exhibited in it *in concreto.* Thus, the Judgment of the pure practical reason is subject to the same difficulties as that of the pure theoretical reason. The latter, however, had means at hand of escaping from these difficulties, because, in regard to the theoretical employment, intuitions were required to which pure concepts of the understanding could be applied, and such intuitions (though only of objects of the senses) can be given *a priori,* and therefore, as far as regards the union of the manifold in them, conforming to the pure *a priori* concepts of the understanding as *schemata.* On the other hand, the morally good is something whose object is supersensible; for which, therefore, nothing corresponding can be found in any sensible intuition. Judgment depending on laws of pure practical reason seems, therefore, to be subject to special difficulties arising from this, that a law of freedom is to be applied to actions, which are events taking place in the world of sense, and which, so far, belong to physical nature.

But here again is opened a favourable prospect for the pure practical Judgment. When I subsume under a *pure practical law* an action possible to me in the world of sense, I am not concerned with the possibility of the *action* as an event in the world of sense. This is a matter that belongs to the decision of reason in its theoretic use according to the law of causality, which is a pure concept of the understanding, for which reason has a *schema* in the sensible intuition. Physical causality, or the condition under which it takes place, belongs to the physical concepts, the schema of which is sketched by transcendental imagination. Here, however, we have to do, not with the schema of a case that occurs according to laws, but with the schema of a law itself (if the word is allowable here), since the fact that the will (not the action relatively to its effect) is deter-

5:69 mined by the law alone without any other principle, connects the notion of causality with quite different conditions from those which constitute physical connexion.

The physical law being a law to which the objects of sensible intuition, as such, are subject, must have a schema corresponding to it—that is, a general procedure of the imagination (by which it exhibits *a priori* to the senses the pure concept of the understanding which the law determines). But the law of freedom (that is, of a causality not subject to sensible conditions), and consequently the concept of the unconditionally good, cannot have any intuition, nor consequently any schema supplied to it for the purpose of its application *in concreto.* Consequently the moral law has no faculty but the understanding to aid its application to physical objects (not the imagination); and the understanding for the purposes of the Judgment can provide for an idea of the reason, not a *schema* of the sensibility, but a law, though only as to its form as law; such a law, however, as can be exhibited *in concreto* in objects of the senses, and therefore a law of nature. We can therefore call this law the *Type* of the moral law.

The rule of the Judgment according to laws of pure practical reason is this: ask yourself whether, if the action you propose were to take place by a law of the system of nature of which you were yourself a part, you could regard it as possible by your own will. Everyone does, in fact, decide by this rule whether actions are morally good or evil. Thus, people say: If *everyone* permitted himself to deceive, when he thought it to his advantage; or thought himself justified in shortening his life as soon as he was thoroughly weary of it; or looked with perfect indifference on the necessity of others; and if you belonged to such an order of things, would you do so with the assent of your own will? Now everyone knows well that if he secretly allows himself to deceive, it does not follow that everyone else does so; or if, unobserved, he is destitute of compassion, others would not necessarily be so to him; hence, this comparison of the maxim of his actions with a universal law of nature is not the determining principle of his will. Such a law is, nevertheless, a *type* of the estimation of the maxim on moral principles. If the maxim of the action is not such as to stand the test of the form 5:70 of a universal law of nature, then it is morally impossible. This is the judgment even of common sense; for its ordinary judgments, even those of experience, are always based on the law of nature. It has it therefore always at hand, only that in cases where *causality from freedom* is to be criticised, it makes that *law of nature* only the type of a *law of freedom*, because without something which it could use as an example in a case of experience, it could not give the law of a pure practical reason its proper use in practice.

It is therefore allowable to use the *system of the world of sense* as the *type* of a *supersensible system of things*, provided I do not transfer to the latter the intuitions, and what depends on them, but merely apply to it the *form* of *law* in general (the notion of which occurs even in the [commonest] use of reason, but cannot be definitely known *a priori* for any other purpose than the pure practical use of reason); for laws, as such, are so far identical, no matter from what they derive their determining principles.

Further, since of all the supersensible absolutely nothing [is known] except freedom (through the moral law), and this only so far as it is inseparably implied in that law, and moreover all supersensible objects to which reason might lead us, following the guidance of that law, have still no reality for us, except for the purpose of that law, and for the use of mere practical reason; and as Reason is authorized and even compelled to use physical nature (in its pure form as an object of the understanding) as the type of the Judgment; hence, the present remark will serve to guard against reckoning amongst concepts themselves that which belongs only to the *typic* of concepts. This, namely, as a typic of the Judgment, guards against the *empiricism* of practical reason, which founds the practical notions of good and evil merely on experienced consequences (so called happiness). No doubt happiness and the infinite advantages which would result from a will determined by self-love, if this will at the same time erected itself into a universal law of nature, may certainly serve as a perfectly suitable type for the morally Good, but it is not identical with it. The same typic guards also against the *mysticism* of practical reason, which turns what served

5:71 only as a *symbol* into a *schema,* that is, proposes to provide for the moral concepts actual intuitions, which, however, are not sensible (intuitions of an invisible Kingdom of God), and thus plunges into the transcendent. What is befitting the use of the moral concepts is only the *rationalism* of the Judgment, which takes from the sensible system of nature only what pure reason can also conceive of itself, that is, conformity to law, and transfers into the supersensible nothing but what can conversely be actually exhibited by actions in the world of sense according to the formal rule of a law of nature. However, the caution against *empiricism* of practical reason is much more important; for *mysticism* is quite reconcilable with the purity and sublimity of the moral law, and, besides, it is not very natural or agreeable to common habits of thought to strain one's imagination to supersensible intuitions; and hence the danger on this side is not so general. Empiricism, on the contrary, cuts up at the roots the morality of intentions (in which, and not in actions only, consists the high worth that men can and ought to give to themselves), and substitutes for duty something quite different, namely, an empirical interest, with which the inclinations generally are secretly leagued; and empiricism, moreover, being on this account allied with all the inclinations which (no matter what fashion they put on) degrade humanity when they are raised to the dignity of a supreme practical principle; and as these nevertheless are so favourable to everyone's feelings, it is for that reason much more dangerous than mysticism, which can never constitute a lasting condition of any great number of persons.

CHAPTER III.

OF THE MOTIVES OF PURE PRACTICAL REASON.

What is essential in the moral worth of actions is *that the moral law should directly determine the will.* If the determination of the will takes place in conformity indeed to the moral law, but only by means of a feeling, no matter of what kind, which has to be presupposed in order that the law may be sufficient to determine the will, and therefore not *for the sake of the law,* then the action will possess *legality* but not *morality.* Now, if we understand by *motive* [or *spring*] (*elater animi*) the subjective ground of determination of the will of a being whose Reason does not necessarily conform to the objective law, by virtue of its own nature, then it will follow, first, that no motives can be attributed to the Divine will, and that the motives of the human will (as well as that of every created rational being) can never be anything else than the moral law, and consequently that the objective principle of determination must always and alone be also the subjectively sufficient determining principle of the action, if this is not merely to fulfil the *letter* of the law, without containing its *spirit.*[2]

Since, then, for the purpose of giving the moral law influence over the will, we must not seek for any other motives that might enable us to dispense with the motive of the law itself, because that would produce mere hypocrisy, without consistency; and it is even *dangerous* to allow other motives (for instance, that of interest) even to co-operate *along with* the moral law; hence nothing is left us but to determine carefully in what way the moral law becomes a motive, and what effect this has upon the faculty of desire. For as to the question how a law can be directly and of itself a determining principle of the will (which is the essence of morality), this is, for human reason, an insoluble problem and identical with the question: how a free will is possible. Therefore what we have to show *a priori* is, not why the moral law in itself supplies a motive, but what effect it, as such, produces (or, more correctly speaking, must produce) on the mind.

The essential point in every determination of the will by the moral law is that being a free will it is determined simply by the moral law, not only without the co-operation of sensible impulses, but even to the rejection of all such, and to the checking of all inclinations so far as they might be opposed to that law. So far, then,

5:72

5:73

---

2 We may say of every action that conforms to the law, but is not done for the sake of the law, that it is morally good in the *letter,* not in the *spirit* (the intention).

the effect of the moral law as a motive is only negative, and this motive can be known *a priori* to be such. For all inclination and every sensible impulse is founded on feeling, and the negative effect produced on feeling (by the check on the inclinations) is itself feeling; consequently, we can see *a priori* that the moral law, as a determining principle of the will, must by thwarting all our inclinations produce a feeling which may be called pain; and in this we have the first, perhaps the only instance, in which we are able from *a priori* considerations to determine the relation of a cognition (in this case of pure practical reason) to the feeling of pleasure or displeasure. All the inclinations together (which can be reduced to a tolerable system, in which case their satisfaction is called happiness) constitute *self-regard* (*solipsismus*). This is either the *self-love* that consists in an excessive *fondness* for oneself (*philautia*), or satisfaction with oneself (*arrogantia*). The former is called particularly *selfishness;* the latter *self-conceit.* Pure practical reason only *checks* selfishness, looking on it as natural and active in us even prior to the moral law, so far as to limit it to the condition of agreement with this law, and then it is called *rational self-love.* But self-conceit Reason *strikes down* altogether, since all claims to self-esteem which precede agreement with the moral law are vain and unjustifiable, for the certainty of a state of mind that coincides with this law is the first condition of personal worth (as we shall presently show more clearly), and prior to this conformity any pretension to worth is false and unlawful. Now the propensity to self-esteem is one of the inclinations which the moral law checks, inasmuch as that esteem rests only on morality. Therefore the moral law breaks down self-conceit. But as this law is something positive in itself, namely, the form of an intellectual causality, that is, of freedom, it must be an object of respect; for by opposing the subjective antagonism of the inclinations it *weakens* self-conceit; and since it even *breaks down*, that is, humiliates this conceit, it is an object of the highest respect, and consequently is the foundation of a positive feeling which is not of empirical origin, but is known *a priori.* Therefore respect for the moral law is a feeling which is produced by an intellectual cause, and this feeling is the only one that we know quite *a priori,* and the necessity of which we can perceive.

In the preceding chapter we have seen that everything that presents itself as an object of the will prior to the moral law is by that law itself, which is the supreme condition of practical reason, excluded from the determining principles of the will which we have called the unconditionally good; and that the mere practical form which consists in the adaptation of the maxims to universal legislation first determines what is good in itself and absolutely, and is the basis of the maxims of a pure will, which alone is good in every respect. However, we find that our nature as sensible beings is such that the matter of desire (objects of inclination, whether of hope or fear) first presents itself to us; and our pathologically affected self, although it is in its maxims quite unfit for universal legislation; yet, just as if it constituted our entire self, strives to put its pretensions forward first, and to have them acknowledged as the first and original. This propensity to make ourselves in the subjective determining principles of our choice serve as the objective determining principle of the will generally may be called *self-love;* and if this pretends to be legislative as an unconditional practical principle it may be called *self-conceit.* Now the moral law, which alone is truly objective (namely, in every respect), entirely excludes the influence of self-love on the supreme practical principle, and indefinitely checks the self-conceit that prescribes the subjective conditions of the former as laws. Now whatever checks our self-conceit in our own judgment humiliates; therefore the moral law inevitably humbles every man when he compares with it the physical propensities of his nature. That, the idea of which as a *determining principle of our will* humbles us in our self-consciousness, awakes *respect* for itself, so far as it is itself positive, and a determining principle. Therefore the moral law is even subjectively a cause of respect. Now since everything that enters into self-love belongs to inclination, and all inclination rests on feelings, and consequently whatever checks all the feelings together in self-love has necessarily, by this very circumstance, an influence on feeling; hence we comprehend how it is possible to perceive *a priori* that the moral law can produce an effect on feeling, in that it excludes the inclinations and the propensity to make them the supreme practical condition, *i.e.* self-love, from all participation in the supreme legislation. This effect is on

one side merely *negative*, but on the other side, relatively to the re-
5:75 stricting principle of pure practical reason, it is *positive*. No special
kind of feeling need be assumed for this under the name of a practical or moral feeling as antecedent to the moral law, and serving as
its foundation.

The negative effect on feeling (unpleasantness) is *pathological*,
like every influence on feeling, and like every feeling generally. But
as an effect of the consciousness of the moral law, and consequently in relation to a supersensible cause, namely, the subject of
pure practical reason which is the supreme lawgiver, this feeling of
a rational being affected by inclinations is called humiliation (intellectual self-depreciation); but with reference to the positive source
of this humiliation, the law, it is respect for it. There is indeed no
feeling for this law; but inasmuch as it removes the resistance out of
the way, this removal of an obstacle is, in the judgment of reason
esteemed equivalent to a positive help to its causality. Therefore
this feeling may also be called a feeling of respect for the moral law,
and for both reasons together *a moral feeling*.

While the moral law, therefore, is a formal determining principle of action by practical pure reason, and is moreover a material
though only objective determining principle of the objects of action as called good and evil, it is also a subjective determining principle, that is, a motive to this action, inasmuch as it has influence on
the morality of the subject, and produces a feeling conducive to the
influence of the law on the will. There is here in the subject no *antecedent* feeling tending to morality. For this is impossible, since
every feeling is sensible, and the motive of moral intention must be
free from all sensible conditions. On the contrary, while the sensible feeling which is at the bottom of all our inclinations is the condition of that impression which we call respect, the cause that
determines it lies in the pure practical reason; and this impression
therefore, on account of its origin, must be called, not a pathological, but a *practical effect*. For by the fact that the conception of the
moral law deprives self-love of its influence, and self-conceit of its
5:76 allusion, it lessons the obstacle to pure practical reason, and produces the conception of the superiority of its objective law to the

impulses of the sensibility; and thus, by removing the counterpoise, it gives relatively greater weight to the law in the judgment of reason (in the case of a will affected by the aforesaid impulses). Thus the respect for the law is not a motive to morality, but is morality itself subjectively considered as a motive, inasmuch as pure practical reason, by rejecting all the rival pretensions of self-love, gives authority to the law which now alone has influence. Now it is to be observed that as respect is an effect on feeling, and therefore on the sensibility, of a rational being, it presupposes this sensibility, and therefore also the finiteness of such beings on whom the moral law imposes respect; and that respect for the *law* cannot be attributed to a supreme being, or to any being free from all sensibility, and in whom, therefore, this sensibility cannot be an obstacle to practical reason.

This feeling [sentiment] (which we call the moral feeling) is therefore produced simply by reason. It does not serve for the estimation of actions nor for the foundation of the objective moral law itself, but merely as a motive to make this of itself a maxim. But what name could we more suitably apply to this singular feeling which cannot be compared to any pathological feeling? It is of such a peculiar kind that it seems to be at the disposal of reason only, and that pure practical reason.

Respect applies always to persons only—not to things. The latter may arouse inclination, and if they are animals (*e.g.* horses, dogs, &c.), even *love* or *fear,* like the sea, a volcano, a beast of prey; but never *respect.* Something that comes nearer to this feeling is *admiration,* and this, as an affection, astonishment, can apply to things also, *e.g.* lofty mountains, the magnitude, number, and distance of the heavenly bodies, the strength and swiftness of many animals, &c. But all this is not respect. A man also may be an object to me of love, fear, or admiration, even to astonishment, and yet not be an object of respect. His jocose humour, his courage and strength, his power from the rank he has amongst others, may inspire me with sentiments of this kind, but still inner respect for him is wanting. *Fontenelle* says, "I bow before a great man, but my mind does not bow." I would add, before an humble, plain man, in whom I per-

5:77 ceive uprightness of character in a higher degree than I am conscious of in myself, *my mind bows* whether I choose it or not, and though I bear my head never so high that he may not forget my superior rank. Why is this? Because his example exhibits to me a law that humbles my self-conceit when I compare it with my conduct: a law, the *practicability* of obedience to which I see proved by fact before my eyes. Now, I may even be conscious of a like degree of uprightness, and yet the respect remains. For since in man all good is defective, the law made visible by an example still humbles my pride, my standard being furnished by a man whose imperfections, whatever they may be, are not known to me as my own are, and who therefore appears to me in a more favourable light. *Respect* is a *tribute* which we cannot refuse to merit, whether we will or not; we may indeed outwardly withhold it, but we cannot help feeling it inwardly.

Respect is so *far from being* a feeling of pleasure that we only reluctantly give way to it as regards a man. We try to find out something that may lighten the burden of it, some fault to compensate us for the humiliation which such an example causes. Even the dead are not always secure from this criticism, especially if their example appears inimitable. Even the moral law itself in its *solemn majesty* is exposed to this endeavour to save oneself from yielding it respect. Can it be thought that it is for any other reason that we are so ready to reduce it to the level of our familiar inclination, or that it is for any other reason that we all take such trouble to make it out to be the chosen precept of our own interest well understood, but that we want to be free from the deterrent respect which shows us our own unworthiness with such severity? Nevertheless, on the other hand, so *little* is there *pain* in it that if once one has laid aside self-conceit and allowed practical influence to that respect, he can never be satisfied with contemplating the majesty of this law, and the soul believes itself elevated in proportion as it sees the holy law elevated 5:78 above it and its frail nature. No doubt great talents and activity proportioned to them may also occasion respect or an analogous feeling. It is very proper to yield it to them, and then it appears as if this sentiment were the same thing as admiration. But if we look closer we shall observe that it is always uncertain how much of the ability is due to native talent, and how much to diligence in cultivating it. Reason represents it to us as probably the fruit of cultivation, and therefore as meritorious, and this notably reduces our self-conceit, and either casts a reproach on us or urges us to follow such an example in the way that is suitable to us. This respect then which we show to such a person (properly speaking, to the law that his example exhibits) is not mere admiration; and this is confirmed also by the fact, that when the common run of admirers think they have learned from any source the badness of such a man's character (for instance Voltaire's) they give up all respect for him; whereas the true scholar still feels it at least with regard to his talents, because he is himself engaged in a business and a vocation which make imitation of such a man in some degree a law.

Respect for the moral law is therefore the only and the undoubted moral motive, and this feeling is directed to no object, except on the ground of this law. The moral law first determines the will objectively and directly in the judgment of reason; and freedom, whose causality can be determined only by the law, consists just in this, that it restricts all inclinations, and consequently self-esteem, by the condition of obedience to its pure law. This restriction now has an effect on feeling, and produces the impression of displeasure which can be known *a priori* from the moral law. Since it is so far only a *negative* effect which, arising from the influence of pure practical reason, checks the activity of the subject, so far as it is determined by inclinations, and hence checks the opinion of his personal worth (which, in the absence of agreement with the moral law, is reduced to nothing); hence, the effect of this law on feeling is merely humiliation. We can, therefore, perceive this *a priori*, but cannot know by it the force of the pure practical law as a motive, 5:79 but only the resistance to motives of the sensibility. But since the same law is objectively, that is, in the conception of pure reason, an immediate principle of determination of the will, and consequently this humiliation takes place only relatively to the purity of the law; hence, the lowering of the pretensions of moral self-esteem, that is, humiliation on the sensible side, is an elevation of the moral, *i.e.* practical, esteem for the law itself on the intellectual side; in a word, it is respect for the law, and therefore, as its cause is intellectual, a positive feeling which can be known *a priori*. For whatever diminishes the obstacles to an activity, furthers this activity itself. Now the recognition of the moral law is the consciousness of an activity of practical reason from objective principles, which only fails to reveal its effect in actions because subjective (pathological) causes hinder it. Respect for the moral law then must be regarded as a positive, though indirect effect of it on feeling, inasmuch as this respect weakens the impeding influence of inclinations by humiliating self-esteem; and hence also as a subjective principle of activity, that is, as a *motive* to obedience to the law, and as a principle of the maxims of a life conformable to it. From the notion of a motive arises that of an *interest*, which can never be attributed to any being unless it possesses reason, and which signifies a *motive* of the will in so far as it is conceived by the reason. Since in a morally good will the law itself must be the motive, the *moral interest* is a pure interest of practical reason alone, independent on sense. On the notion of an interest is based that of a *maxim*. This, therefore, is morally good only in case it rests simply on the interest taken in obedience to the law. All three notions, however, that of a *motive*, of an *interest*, and of a *maxim*, can be applied only to finite beings. For they all suppose a limitation of the nature of the being, in that the subjective character of his choice does not of itself agree with the objective law of a practical reason; they suppose that the being requires to be impelled to action by something, because an internal obstacle opposes itself. Therefore they cannot be applied to the Divine will.

There is something so singular in the unbounded esteem for the pure moral law, apart from all advantage, as it is presented for our obedience by practical reason, the voice of which makes even the boldest sinner tremble, and compels him to hide himself from it, that we cannot wonder if we find this influence of a mere intellectual idea on the feelings quite incomprehensible to speculative reason, and have to be satisfied with seeing so much of this *a priori*, that such a feeling is inseparably connected with the conception of the moral law in every finite rational being. If this feeling of respect were pathological, and therefore were a feeling of pleasure based on the inner *sense*, it would be in vain to try to discover a connexion of it with any idea *a priori*. But [it] is a feeling that applies merely to what is practical, and depends on the conception of a law, simply as to its form, not on account of any object, and therefore cannot be reckoned either as pleasure or pain, and yet produces an *interest* in obedience to the law, which we call the *moral interest*, just as the capacity of taking such an interest in the law (or respect for the moral law itself) is properly the *moral feeling* [or *sentiment*].

The consciousness of a *free* submission of the will to the law, yet combined with an inevitable constraint put upon all inclinations, though only by our own reason, is respect for the law. The law that demands this respect and inspires it is clearly no other than the moral (for no other precludes all inclinations from exercising any direct influence on the will). An action which is objectively practical according to this law, to the exclusion of every determining principle of inclination, is *duty*, and this by reason of that exclusion includes in its concept practical *obligation*, that is, a determination to actions, however *reluctantly* they may be done. The feeling that arises from the consciousness of this obligation is not pathological, as would be a feeling produced by an object of the senses, but practical only, that is, it is made possible by a preceding (objective) determination of the will and a causality of the reason. As *submission* to the law, therefore, that is, as a command (announcing constraint for the sensibly affected subject), it contains in it no pleasure, but on the contrary, so far, pain in the action. On the other hand, however, as this constraint is exercised merely by the legislation of our *own* reason, it also contains something *elevating*, and this subjective effect on feeling, inasmuch as pure practical reason is the sole cause of it, may be called in this respect *self-approbation*, since we recognize ourselves as determined thereto solely by the law without any interest, and are now conscious of a quite different interest subjectively produced thereby, and which is purely practical and *free*; and our taking this interest in an action of duty is not suggested by any inclination, but is commanded and actually brought about by reason through the practical law; whence this feeling obtains a special name, that of respect.

5:81

The notion of duty, therefore, requires in the action, *objectively*,

agreement with the law, and, subjectively in its maxim, that respect
for the law shall be the sole mode in which the will is determined
thereby. And on this rests the distinction between the consciousness of having acted *according to duty* and *from duty*, that is, from
respect for the law. The former (*legality*) is possible even if inclinations have been the determining principles of the will; but the latter (*morality*), moral worth, can be placed only in this, that the
action is done from duty, that is, simply for the sake of the law.[3]

It is of the greatest importance to attend with the utmost exact-
ness in all moral judgments to the subjective principle of all maxims, that all the morality of actions may be placed in the necessity
of acting *from duty* and from respect for the law, not from love and
inclination for that which the actions are to produce. For men and
all created rational beings moral necessity is constraint, that is obligation, and every action based on it is to be conceived as a duty,
not as a proceeding previously pleasing, or likely to be pleasing to
us of our own accord. As if indeed we could ever bring it about that
without respect for the law, which implies fear, or at least apprehension of transgression, we of ourselves, like the independent
Deity, could ever come into possession of *holiness* of will by the coincidence of our will with the pure moral law becoming as it were
part of our nature, never to be shaken (in which case the law would
cease to be a command for us, as we could never be tempted to be
untrue to it).

The moral law is in fact for the will of a perfect being a law of
holiness, but for the will of every finite rational being a law of *duty*,
of moral constraint, and of the determination of its actions by *respect* for this law and reverence for its duty. No other subjective
principle must be assumed as a motive, else while the action might
chance to be such as the law prescribes, yet as it does not proceed

5:82

3 If we examine accurately the notion of respect for persons as it has been already laid
down, we shall perceive that it always rests on the consciousness of a duty which an example
shows us, and that respect therefore can never have any but a moral ground, and that it is
very good and even, in a psychological point of view, very useful for the knowledge of
mankind, that whenever we use this expression we should attend to this secret and marvellous, yet often recurring, regard which men in their judgment pay to the moral law.

from duty, the intention, which is the thing properly in question in this legislation, is not moral.

It is a very beautiful thing to do good to men from love to them and from sympathetic good will, or to be just from love of order; but this is not yet the true moral maxim of our conduct which is suitable to our position amongst rational beings as *men,* when we pretend with fanciful pride to set ourselves above the thought of duty, like volunteers, and, as if we were independent on the command, to want to do of our own good pleasure what we think we need no command to do. We stand under a *discipline* of reason, and in all our maxims must not forget our subjection to it, nor withdraw anything therefrom, or by an egotistic presumption diminish aught of the authority of the law (although our own reason gives it) so as to set the determining principle of our will, even though the law be conformed to, anywhere else but in the law itself and in respect for this law. Duty and obligation are the only names that we must give to our relation to the moral law. We are indeed legislative members of a moral kingdom rendered possible by freedom, and presented to us by reason as an object of respect; but yet we are subjects in it, not the sovereign, and to mistake our inferior position as creatures and presumptuously to reject the authority of the moral law is already to revolt from it in spirit, even though the letter of it is fulfilled.

With this agrees very well the possibility of such a command as: 5:83
Love God above everything, and thy neighbour as thyself.[4] For as a command it requires respect for a law which *commands* love and does not leave it to our own arbitrary choice to make this our principle. Love to God, however, considered as an inclination (pathological love), is impossible, for He is not an object of the senses. The same affection towards men is possible no doubt, but cannot be commanded, for it is not in the power of any man to love anyone at command; therefore it is only *practical love* that is meant in that pith of all laws. To

---

4 This law is in striking contrast with the principle of private happiness which some make the supreme principle of morality. This would be expressed thus: *Love thyself above everything, and God and thy neighbour for thine own sake.*

love God means, in this sense, to like to do His commandments; to love one's neighbour means to like to practise all duties towards him. But the command that makes this a rule cannot command us to *have* this disposition in actions conformed to duty, but only to *endeavour* after it. For a command to like to do a thing is in itself contradictory, because if we already know of ourselves what we are bound to do, and if further we are conscious of liking to do it, a command would be quite needless; and if we do it not willingly, but only out of respect for the law, a command that makes this respect the motive of our maxim would directly counteract the disposition commanded. That law of all laws, therefore, like all the moral precepts of the Gospel, exhibits the moral disposition in all its perfection, in which, viewed as an Ideal of holiness, it is not attainable by any creature, but yet is the pattern which we should strive to approach, and in an uninterrupted but infinite progress become like to. In fact, if a rational creature could ever reach this point, that he thoroughly *likes* to do all moral laws, this would mean that there does not exist in him even the possibility of a desire that would tempt him to deviate from them; for to overcome such a desire always costs the subject some sacrifice, and therefore requires self-compulsion, that is, inward constraint to something that one does not quite like to do; and no creature can ever reach this stage of moral disposition. For, being a creature, and therefore always dependent with respect to what he requires for complete satisfaction, he can never be quite free from desires and inclinations, and as these rest on physical causes, they can never of themselves coincide with the moral law, the sources of which are quite different; and therefore they make it necessary to found the mental disposition of one's maxims on moral obligation, not on ready inclination, but on respect, which *demands* obedience to the law, even though one may not like it; not on love, which apprehends no inward reluctance of the will towards the law. Nevertheless, this latter, namely, love to the law (which would then cease to be a *command*, and then morality, which would have passed subjectively into holiness, would cease to be *virtue*), must be the constant though unattainable goal of his endeavours. For in the case of what we highly esteem, but yet (on account of the consciousness of our weakness) dread, the increased facility of satisfying it changes the most reverential awe into inclination, and respect into love: at least this would be the perfection of a disposition devoted to the law, if it were possible for a creature to attain it.

This reflection is intended not so much to clear up the evangelical command just cited, in order to prevent *religious fanaticism* in regard to love of God, but to define accurately the moral disposition with regard directly to our duties towards men, and to check, or if possible prevent, a *merely moral fanaticism* which infects many persons. The stage of morality on which man (and, as far as we can see, every rational creature) stands is respect for the moral law. The disposition that he ought to have in obeying this is to obey it from duty, not from spontaneous inclination, or from an endeavour taken up from liking and unbidden; and this proper moral condition in which he can always be is *virtue*, that is, moral disposition *militant*, and not *holiness* in the fancied *possession* of a perfect *purity* of the disposition of the will. It is nothing but moral fanaticism and exaggerated self-conceit that is infused into the mind by exhortation to actions as noble, sublime, and magnanimous, by which men are led into the delusion that it is not duty, that is, respect for the law, whose yoke (an easy yoke, indeed, because reason itself imposes it on us) they *must* bear, whether they like it or not, that constitutes the determining principle of their actions, and which always humbles them while they *obey* it; fancying that those actions are expected from them, not from duty, but as pure merit. For not only would they, in imitating such deeds from such a principle not have fulfilled the spirit of the law in the least, which consists not in the legality of the action (without regard to principle), but in the subjection of the mind to the law; not only do they make the motives *pathological* (seated in sympathy or self-love), not moral (in the law), but they produce in this way a vain high-flying fantastic way of thinking, flattering themselves with a spontaneous goodness of heart that needs neither spur nor bridle, for which no command is needed, and thereby forgetting their obligation, which they ought to think of rather than merit. Indeed actions of others which are

5:85

done with great sacrifice, and merely for the sake of duty, may be praised as *noble* and *sublime*, but only so far as there are traces which suggest that they were done wholly out of respect for duty and not from excited feelings. If these, however, are set before anyone as examples to be imitated, respect for duty (which is the only true moral feeling) must be employed as the motive—this severe holy precept which never allows our vain self-love to dally with pathological impulses (however analogous they may be to morality) and to take a pride in *meritorious* worth. Now if we search we shall find for all actions that are worthy of praise a law of duty which *commands*, and does not leave us to choose what may be agreeable to our inclinations. This is the only way of representing things that can give a moral training to the soul, because it alone is capable of solid and accurately defined principles.

If *fanaticism* in its most general sense is a deliberate overstepping of the limits of human reason, then *moral fanaticism* is such an overstepping of the bounds that practical pure reason sets to mankind, in that it forbids us to place the subjective determining principle of correct actions, that is, their moral *motive*, in anything but the law itself, or to place the disposition which is thereby brought into the maxims in anything but respect for this law, and hence commands us to take as the supreme *vital principle* of all morality in men the thought of duty, which strikes down all *arrogance* as well as vain *self-love*.

If this is so, it is not only writers of romance or sentimental educators (although they may be zealous opponents of sentimentalism), but sometimes even philosophers; nay, even the severest of all, the Stoics, that have brought in *moral fanaticism* instead of a sober but wise moral discipline, although the fanaticism of the latter was more heroic, that of the former of an insipid, effeminate character; and we may, without hypocrisy, say of the moral teaching of the Gospel, that it first, by the purity of its moral principle, and at the same time by its suitability to the limitations of finite beings, brought all the good conduct of men under the discipline of a duty plainly set before their eyes, which does not permit them to indulge in dreams of imaginary moral perfections; and that it also set the bounds of humility (that is, self-knowledge) to self-conceit as well as to self-love, both which are ready to mistake their limits.

Duty! Thou sublime and mighty name that dost embrace nothing charming or insinuating, but requirest submission, and yet seekest not to move the will by threatening aught that would arouse natural aversion or terror, but merely holdest forth a law which of itself finds entrance into the mind, and yet gains reluctant reverence (though not always obedience), a law before which all inclinations are dumb, even though they secretly counter-work it; what origin is there worthy of thee, and where is to be found the root of thy noble descent which proudly rejects all kindred with the inclinations; a root to be derived from which is the indispensable condition of the only worth which men can give themselves?

It can be nothing less than a power which elevates man above himself (as a part of the world of sense), a power which connects him with an order of things that only the understanding can conceive, with a world which at the same time commands the whole sensible world, and with it the empirically determinable existence of man in time, as well as the sum total of all ends (which totality alone suits such unconditional practical laws as the moral). This power is nothing but *personality,* that is, freedom and independence on the mechanism of nature, yet, regarded also as a faculty of a being which is subject to special laws, namely, pure practical laws given by its own reason; so that the person as belonging to the sensible world is subject to his own personality as belonging to the intelligible [supersensible] world. It is then not to be wondered at that man, as belonging to both worlds, must regard his own nature in reference to its second and highest characteristic only with reverence, and its laws with the highest respect. 5:87

On this origin are founded many expressions which designate the worth of objects according to moral ideas. The moral law is *holy* (inviolable). Man is indeed unholy enough, but he must regard *humanity* in his own person as holy. In all creation every thing one chooses, and over which one has any power, may be used *merely as means;* man alone, and with him every rational creature, is an *end in himself.* By virtue of the autonomy of his freedom he is the subject of the moral law, which is holy. Just for this reason every will, even every person's own individual will, in relation to itself, is restricted to the condition of agreement with the *autonomy* of the rational being, that is to say, that it is not to be subject to any purpose which cannot accord with a law which might arise from the will of the passive subject himself; the latter is, therefore, never to be employed merely as means, but as itself also, concurrently, an end. We justly attribute this condition even to the Divine will, with regard to the rational beings in the world, which are His creatures, since it rests on their *personality*, by which alone they are ends in themselves.

This respect-inspiring idea of personality which sets before our eyes the sublimity of our nature (in its higher aspect), while at the same time it shows us the want of accord of our conduct with it, and thereby strikes down self-conceit, is even natural to the commonest reason, and easily observed. Has not every even moderately honourable man sometimes found that, where by an otherwise inoffensive lie he might either have withdrawn himself from an unpleasant business, or even have procured some advantages for a loved and well-deserving friend, he has avoided it solely lest he should despise himself secretly in his own eyes? When an upright man is in the greatest distress, which he might have avoided if he could only have disregarded duty, is he not sustained by the consciousness that he has maintained humanity in its proper dignity in his own person and honoured it, that he has no reason to be ashamed of himself in his own sight, or to dread the inward glance of self-examination? This consolation is not happiness, it is not even the smallest part of it, for no one would wish to have occasion for it, or would, perhaps, even desire a life in such circumstances. But he lives, and he cannot endure that he should be in his own eyes unworthy of life. This inward peace is therefore merely negative as regards what can make life pleasant; it is, in fact, only escaping the danger of sinking in personal worth, after everything else that is valuable has been lost. It is the effect of a respect for something quite different from life, something in comparison and contrast with which life with all its enjoyment has no value. He still lives only because it is his duty, not because he finds anything pleasant in life.

Such is the nature of the true motive of pure practical reason; it is no other than the pure moral law itself, inasmuch as it makes us conscious of the sublimity of our own supersensible existence, and subjectively produces respect for their higher nature in men who are also conscious of their sensible existence and of the consequent dependence of their pathologically very susceptible nature. Now with this motive may be combined so many charms and satisfactions of life, that even on this account alone the most prudent choice of a rational *Epicurean* reflecting on the greatest advantage of life would declare itself on the side of moral conduct, and it may even be advisable to join this prospect of a cheerful enjoyment of life with that supreme motive which is already sufficient of itself; but only as a counterpoise to the attractions which vice does not fail to exhibit on the opposite side, and not so as, even in the smallest degree, to place in this the proper moving power when duty is in question. For that would be just the same as to wish to taint the purity of the moral disposition in its source. The majesty of duty 5:89 has nothing to do with enjoyment of life; it has its special law and its special tribunal, and though the two should be never so well shaken together to be given well mixed, like medicine, to the sick soul, yet they will soon separate of themselves, and if they do not the former will not act; and although physical life might gain somewhat in force, the moral life would fade away irrecoverably.

SELECTIONS FROM

CRITIQUE OF

JUDGMENT

[1793]

Translated by James C. Meredith

PART I

CRITIQUE OF ÆSTHETIC JUDGMENT
INTRODUCTION

I.

Division of Philosophy.

Philosophy contains the principles for rational knowledge that concepts afford us of things but not as Logic does, which contains merely the principles of the form of thought in general, irrespective of objects. Hence the usual course of dividing philosophy into the *theoretical* and the *practical* is perfectly sound. But then the concepts, which assign their object to the principles of this rational knowledge, must be different and specific because otherwise they fail to justify a classification. A classification always presupposes that the principles belonging to the rational knowledge of the several parts of a science are antithetical.

Now there are only two kinds of concepts and these yield a corresponding number of distinct principles for the possibility of their objects. These are the concepts of *nature* and the concepts of *freedom*. By the first, *theoretical* knowledge based on *a priori* principles becomes possible. However, in respect of such knowledge, the concept of freedom involves, by its very concept, no more than a negative principle, that of simple antithesis, while for determining the will it establishes principles which enlarge the scope of its activity and which are called *practical* on that account. Hence philosophy is properly divided into two parts, quite distinct in their principles; a theoretical part, as *Philosophy of Nature* and a practical part, as *Philosophy of Morals*, and this last is what is called practical legislation for the reason based upon the concept of freedom. However, up till now these expressions have been grossly misused in dividing the different principles, and through them, philosophy. For, what is practical according to concepts of nature has been taken as identical with what is practical according to the concept of freedom, with the result that a division has been made under these headings of theoretical and practical by means of which there has actually been no division at all, since both parts might have similar principles.

5:172

The will as a faculty of desire is one of the many natural causes in the world; it is the cause that acts according to concepts. Whatever is imagined as possible or necessary through the efficacy of will is called practically possible or necessary. This is done in order to distinguish its possibility or necessity from the physical possibility or necessity of an effect where the cause is not determined by concepts, but rather as with lifeless matter by mechanism, and as with animals by instinct. [In treating the matter thus] the question is left open whether the concept which provides the rule for the causality of the will is a concept of nature, or of freedom.

The latter distinction, however, is essential. If the concept determining the causality is a concept of nature, then the principles are *practical* in a *technical* sense, but if it is a concept of freedom, then they are *practical* in a *moral* sense. Now, in the division of a science of reason, everything turns on the difference between objects requiring different principles for their understanding. Hence technical principles belong to theoretical philosophy, as a science of nature, whereas moral principles alone form the second part, practical philosophy, as a science of morals or ethics.

All technical practical rules, those of art and skill in general or those of prudence as a skill exercising an influence over men and their wills, must, so far as their principles rest upon concepts, be considered only as corollaries of theoretical philosophy. They only concern the possibility of things according to concepts of nature and this includes not only the means discoverable in nature for the purpose, but even the will itself as a faculty of desire and hence as a natural faculty, so far as the will may be determined by natural motives according to these rules. Nevertheless these practical rules are not called laws like physical laws but only precepts. This is due to the fact that the will is not merely placed under the concept of nature, but is also placed under the concept of freedom. When related to freedom the principles of the will are called laws, and these principles, with the addition of what follows from them, alone constitute the second or practical part of philosophy.

The solution of the problems of pure geometry is not allocated 5:173 to a special part of that science, nor does the art of land surveying merit the name of a practical geometry, in distinction to pure geometry, as a second part of the general science of geometry. With as little or perhaps even less right can the mechanical or chemical art of experimentation or of observation be ranked as a practical part of the science of nature. Finally, neither can domestic, agricultural, nor political economy, the art of social intercourse, the principles of dietetics, nor even general instruction for attaining happiness, nor yet the restraining of the passions or the affections for this purpose be denominated as such. None of these may be counted as parts of practical philosophy; even less can they be constituted as the second part of philosophy in general. For all of them contain nothing more than rules of skill which are only practical in a technical sense, as a skill is directed to producing an effect possible according to natural causes and effects . . . .

III.

5:176

The Critique of Judgment as a Means of Linking the Two Parts of Philosophy Into a Whole.

Properly speaking the Critique, which deals with what our cognitive faculties are *a priori* capable of yielding, has no field in regard to objects; for it is not a doctrine, but merely investigates whether and how a doctrine may be possible, considering our [mental] faculties. The field of such a critique extends to all the pretensions of our faculties with a view to confining them within their legitimate bounds. But what cannot be included in the division of philosophy may yet be admitted as a principal part into the general critique of our faculty for pure knowledge if it contains principles which are not in themselves adapted for either theoretical or practical use.

The concepts of nature which contain the grounds for all theoretical knowledge *a priori* rest, as we saw, upon the law-giving authority of the intellect. The concept of freedom, which contains the grounds for all practical precepts *a priori* that are not conditioned by the senses, rests upon the authority of reason. Therefore both faculties have their own proper jurisdiction over their content 5:177 and since there is no higher (*a priori*) jurisdiction over their content, the division of philosophy into theoretical and practical parts is justified.

But in our group of higher thinking faculties there is yet a link between intellect and reason. This link is the *power of judgment* and by analogy we may reasonably surmise that it also contains, if not a special law-giving authority, at least its own principle for discovering laws, even if this principle is merely subjective *a priori*. This principle, even though it has no field of objects appropriate for its realm, may still have some territory of a certain character, for which this principle alone may be valid.

But judging by analogy there is yet a further ground, in addition to the above considerations, upon which judgment may be linked with another order of our powers of imagination. This reason appears to be of even greater importance than the kinship of judgment with the family of cognitive faculties. For all spiritual faculties or capacities may be reduced to three which cannot be 5:178 further deduced from a common ground: the *faculty of knowledge, the feeling of pleasure* or *displeasure* and the *faculty of desire*. . . . Between the faculties of knowledge and desire [discussed elsewhere] stands the feeling of pleasure, just as judgment stands between intellect and reason. Hence we may at least provisionally assume that judgment likewise contains an *a priori* principle of its own and, since pleasure or displeasure is necessarily connected with desire, that 5:179 judgment will effect a transition from the faculty of pure knowledge, i.e., from the realm of concepts of nature, to the faculty of the concept of freedom, just as in its logical employment judgment makes possible the transition from intellect to reason.

Despite the fact that philosophy may be divided only into two principal parts, theoretical and practical, and despite also that all we may have to say of the proper principles of judgment may have to be assigned to its theoretical part, i.e., to rational knowledge according to concepts of nature, nevertheless the critique of pure reason, which must figure this all out to determine what is possible before such a system can be constructed, consists of three parts: the critiques of pure intellect, of pure judgment, and of pure reason [proper], which faculties are called pure because they are lawgiving *a priori*.

IV.

Judgment as a Faculty by which Laws are Prescribed.
A Priori

In general, judgment is the faculty for thinking of the particular as contained under the general. If the general, i.e., the rule, principle, or law, is given, then the judgment which subsumes the particular under it *is determining*. This is so even where such a judgment is transcendental and as such indicates *a priori* the conditions according to which alone anything can be subsumed under that general [rule or principle]. If only the particular is given and the universal has to be found for it then the judgment is merely *reflecting*.

The determining judgment, which is subject to general transcendental laws furnished by the intellect, merely subsumes; the law is prescribed for it *a priori* and such a judgment has no need to devise a law for its own guidance for subordinating the particular in nature to the general. There are such manifold forms of nature; there are many modifications of the general transcendental concepts of nature that are left undetermined by the laws furnished by pure intellect *a priori* because these laws only concern the general possibility of nature as an object of the senses. Hence there must 5:180 also be laws on behalf [of the judgment which subsumes the forms under the general concepts of nature]. These laws, being empirical, may be fortuitous as far as *our* intellectual understanding goes, but if they are still to be called laws as the concept of nature requires, they must be regarded as necessary and flowing from a principle of the unity of the manifold, unknown though it may be to us. Therefore the reflecting judgment, obliged to ascend from the particular in nature to the general, stands in need of a principle. The reflecting judgment cannot borrow this principle from experience because it must establish the unity of all empirical principles under higher though likewise empirical principles, and therefore establish the possibility of the systematic subordination of the lower under the higher. The reflecting judgment can give such a transcendental principle as a law only to itself. As long as it derives this law elsewhere, it will remain a determining judgment. Nor can reflecting judgment prescribe such a principle to nature; for reflecting on the laws of nature adjusts itself [the reflection] to nature, and not nature to the conditions according to which we strive to obtain a concept of it—a concept that is quite fortuitous in respect to nature itself.

The principle [needed by the reflecting judgment] can only be this: since general laws of nature have their foundation in our intellect which prescribes them to nature, though only according to the general concept of it as nature, particular empirical laws must be considered in regard to what is left undetermined in them by these general laws. [They must be considered] as though there were a unity such as they would have if an intellect had supplied them for the benefit of our thinking faculties so as to render possible a system of experience according to particular natural laws. This is not to be taken as implying that such an intellect must be assumed as actually existing, for it is the reflecting judgment only that employs this idea as a principle for the purpose of reflecting and not for ascertaining anything. This faculty [reflecting judgment] thereby gives a law to itself alone and not to nature.

The concept of an object so far as it contains at the same time the grounds for the actual existence of this object is called its *end* [or objective or purpose]. The conformance of an object with that quality, which is only possible according to ends, or objectives or purposes, is called the appropriateness of the form [of the object].

Accordingly the principle of judgment regarding the form of the things of nature under empirical laws generally is the *fitness of nature* in its manifoldness and variety. In other words; by this concept nature is imagined as though an intellect contained the grounds for the unity of its manifold though empirical laws. 5:181

Therefore the fitness of nature is a particular *a priori* concept having its origin solely in the reflecting judgment. For we cannot ascribe to the products of nature themselves anything like a reference to their purposes. We can only make use of this concept for reflecting upon them in respect to the nexus of phenomena in nature which is given according to empirical laws. Furthermore, this concept is quite different from practical fitness [appropriateness] in human art or even morals, though it is doubtless based on this analogy.

V.

The Principle of the Formal Appropriateness of Nature [for its ends] is a Transcendental Principle of Judgment.

A transcendental principle is one through which we represent to ourselves *a priori* the only universal condition under which things can generally become objects of our knowledge. On the other hand, a principle is called metaphysical when it represents *a priori* the only condition under which objects, whose concept must be given empirically, may become further determined *a priori*. Thus the principle of the knowledge of bodies as substances, and as changeable substances, is transcendental when it states that the changing must have a cause; but the principle is metaphysical when it asserts that the changing must have an *external* cause. In the first case bodies need only be thought of in terms of ontological predicates (pure intellectual concepts), i.e., as substance, for the proposition is to be understood *a priori*. In the second case, the empirical concept of a body, as a movable thing in space, must be introduced to support the proposition; although once this is done it may be seen quite *a priori* that the latter predicate, movement only by means of an external cause, applies to a body. In this last way, as I shall show presently, the principle of the appropriateness (fitness) of nature in the multiplicity of its empirical laws is a transcendental principle.

5:182 For the concept of objects coming under this principle is only generally the pure concept of objects of possible empirical knowledge and involves nothing empirical. On the other hand, the principle of practical appropriateness, implied in the idea of the *determination* of a free *will*, would be a metaphysical principle, because the concept of a faculty of desire, as will, has to be given empirically; i.e., is not included among transcendental predicates. Nevertheless both these principles are not empirical, but *a priori* principles; because no further experience is required for synthesizing the predicate with the empirical concept of the subject of the judgments of these principles, but it may be apprehended quite *a priori*.

That the concept of nature as related to ends is a transcendental principle is abundantly evident from the maxims of judgment upon which we rely *a priori* in investigating nature, and which only deal with the possibility of experience, and consequently the possibility of the knowledge of nature—but not just nature generally, but nature as determined by a manifold of particular laws. These maxims crop up frequently enough in the course of this science, though only in a scattered way. They are aphorisms of metaphysical wisdom, making their appearance in a number of rules the necessity of which cannot be demonstrated from concepts: "Nature takes the shortest way (*lex parsimoniae*); yet it makes no leap, either in the sequence of its changes, or in the juxtaposition of specifically different forms (*lex continui in natura*); its vast variety in empirical laws is, for all that, unity under a few principles (*principia praeter necessitatem non sunt multiplicanda*)"; and so forth.

If we propose to assign an origin to these elementary rules, and attempt to do so on psychological lines, we fly right in the teeth of their sense. For they tell us, not what happens, that is, according to what rule our powers of judgment actually discharge their functions, and how we judge, but how we ought to judge; and we cannot find this logical objective necessity where the principles are merely empirical. Hence the appropriateness of nature for our thinking faculties and their employment which manifestly radiates from them is a transcendental principle of judgments, and so needs also transcendental deduction, by means of which the grounds for this way of judging must be traced to the *a priori* sources of knowledge.

Now, looking at the grounds for the possibility of an experience, 5:183 naturally the first thing that meets us is something necessary; namely, the universal laws apart from which nature in general as an object of sense cannot be conceived. These laws rest on the categories, applied to the formal conditions of all observation possible for us, so far as observation is also given *a priori*. Under these laws judgment is determinant; for it has nothing else to do than to subsume under given laws. For instance, the intellect says: all change has its cause (universal law of nature); transcendental judgment has nothing further to do than to furnish *a priori* the condition of subsumption under the concept of the intellect placed before it: this we get in the succession of the determinations of one and the same thing. Now for nature in general, as an object of possible experience, that law is understood as absolutely necessary. But besides this formal time-condition, the objects of empirical knowledge are determined, or so far as we can judge *a priori* are determinable, in diverse ways, so that specifically differentiated nature, over and above what they have in common as things of nature in general, are further capable of being causes in an infinite variety of ways; and each of these modes must, on the concept of a cause in general, have its rule which is a law and consequently imports necessity: although owing to the constitution and limitations of our faculties for knowledge we may entirely fail to see this necessity. Accordingly, in respect to nature's merely empirical laws, we must conceive in nature the possibility of an endless multiplicity of empirical laws, which are yet accidental so far as our insight goes; that is, they cannot be understood *a priori*. According to these laws we evaluate as accidental the unity of nature and the possibility of the unity of experience as a system of empirical laws. Such a unity must be presupposed and assumed as otherwise no thoroughgoing coherence of empirical knowledge would occur [and thus] experience [would not be] a whole. For the general laws of nature certainly provide for such coherence among things of nature generically but they do not provide it for particular things of nature. Hence, for its own use, judgment is compelled to adopt for an *a priori* principle: what appears accidental to human insight in the particular empirical laws of nature, nevertheless contains unity of

law in the synthesis of its manifold aspects in an intrinsically possi-
5:184 ble experience, unfathomable, though still conceivable, as such
unity may be for us. Consequently the unity of law in a synthesis is
understood by us according to a necessary intention or need of the
mind and, though recognized as accidental, is imagined as a fitness
of objects of nature. Therefore judgment merely reflects upon
things under possible and still to be discovered empirical laws, and
must think about nature in respect of the empirical laws according
to a *principle of appropriateness*. This principle then finds expression
in the above maxims of judgment. This transcendental concept of
appropriateness in nature is neither a concept of nature nor of
freedom, since it attributes nothing at all to the object: nature. This
concept only represents the unique manner in which we must
proceed in reflecting upon the objects of nature if we are to get a
thoroughly coherent experience. So this concept is a subjective
principle or maxim of judgment. Also for this reason, we rejoice as
though good fortune favored us when we meet with such systematic unity under merely empirical laws; although we must necessarily assume the presence of such a unity, apart from any ability
on our part to perceive or prove its existence.

In order to convince ourselves of the validity of this deduction
of the concept before us, and the necessity for assuming it as a transcendental principle of knowledge, let us just consider the magnitude of the task. We have to form a connected experience from
given perceptions of a nature containing a perhaps endless multiplicity of empirical laws, and this problem has its basis *a priori* in
our intellect. This intellect is no doubt *a priori* in possession of universal laws of nature, apart from which nature would be incapable
of being an object of experience at all. But beyond this there is
needed a certain order in the particular rules of nature which are
only capable of being brought to the knowledge of the intellect
empirically, and which are possible as far as the intellect is concerned. These rules, without which we would have no means for
advancing from the universal analogy of a possible general experience to a particular experience, must be regarded by the intellect as
5:185 laws, i.e., as necessary, for otherwise they would not form an order

of nature, even though intellect may be unable to comprehend or ever get an insight into their necessity. Although the intellect can determine nothing *a priori* in respect to these objects in pursuit of such empirical so-called laws, it must base all reflections upon them on an *a priori* principle, to the effect that a comprehensible order of nature is possible according to them. A principle of this kind is expressed in the following propositions: In nature there is a subordination of genera and species that we can understand. Each of these genera is approximated to the others on a common principle, so that a transition may be possible from one to the other, and thereby to a higher genus. While it seems unavoidable at the outset that our intellect assume, for the specific variety of natural operations, a like number of various kinds of causality, yet these may all be reduced to a small number of principles, the quest for which is our business. This adaptation of nature to our thinking faculties is presupposed *a priori* by judgment for reflecting upon this adaptation according to empirical laws. But all the while the intellect recognizes this adaptation objectively as accidental, and only judgment attributes it to nature as transcendental fitness, i.e., appropriate to the subject's faculty for knowing. Were it not for this presupposition, we should have no order of nature in accordance with these [principles of causality] in all their variety, or for an investigation of them.

Despite the uniformity of things of nature according to universal laws, without which we would have no form of general empirical knowledge at all, it is quite conceivable that the specific variety of the empirical laws of nature with their effects might still be so great as to make it impossible for our intellect to discover an intelligible order in nature; to divide its products into genera and species so as to avail ourselves of the principles for explaining and comprehending one in order to explain and interpret another, and to make a consistent context of experience out of the material resulting from such confusion, material that properly speaking is infinitely multiform and ill-adapted to our power of apprehension.

Thus judgment also possesses an *a priori* principle for the possibility of nature, but only in a subjective respect. By means of this it

5:186 prescribes a law, not to nature, but to itself to guide its reflection upon nature. This law may be called *the law of specification of nature* in respect of its empirical laws. It is not a law recognized *a priori* in nature. But judgment adopts such a law for the purpose of making a natural order understandable to our intellect when classifying nature's general laws and subordinating a variety of particular laws to them. So when it is said that nature specifies its universal laws on a principle appropriate to our thinking faculties, we are not thereby either prescribing a law to nature, or learning one from it by observation, although the principle in question may be confirmed by this means. For it is not a principle of the determinant but merely of the reflecting judgment. All that is intended is that, no matter what the order and disposition of nature is in respect to its universal laws, we must investigate the empirical laws throughout nature based on this principle and the maxims founded thereon, because only so far as that principle applies can we make any headway in using our intellect in experience or in gaining knowledge.

VI.

The Association of the Feeling of Pleasure with the Concept of the Appropriateness of Nature.

So far as our insight goes, the conceived harmony of nature in the manifold of its particular laws, as well as our need for finding universal principles for it, must be deemed contingent and must also be deemed indispensable for the requirements of our intellect and consequently a fitness by which nature is in accord with our aim, but only in so far as it is directed to knowledge. The universal laws of knowledge, which are equally laws of nature, are, though spontaneous, just as necessary to nature as are the laws of motion applicable to matter. Their origin does not presuppose any regard to our thinking faculties, since only by their means can we first have any concept of the meaning of a knowledge of things of nature and they must apply to nature as an object of our general understanding. But so far as we can see it is conditional upon the fact that the order of nature in its particular laws, with their potential wealth of variety and heterogeneity transcending all our powers of compre-

hension, should still actually be commensurate with these powers. 5:187
To find out this order of nature is an undertaking for our intellect,
which pursues it with a regard to a necessary end of its own; that of
introducing unity of principle into nature. This intention must be
attributed to nature by judgment, since no law can be prescribed to
it by the intellect.

The attainment of any aim is coupled with a feeling of pleasure.
Now wherever such attainment has *a priori* for its condition an
imagining, as it has here a principle for the reflecting judgment in
general, then the feeling of pleasure is also determined by grounds
which are *a priori* valid for all men, by merely referring the object to
our faculty of knowledge. As the concept of appropriateness (fitness) pays no attention whatever here to the faculty of desire, it differs entirely from all practical fitness of nature.

As a matter of fact we do not and cannot find in ourselves the
slightest feeling of pleasure from perceptions coinciding with the
laws in accordance with the universal concepts of nature, i.e.,
the Categories, since in their case the intellect necessarily follows
its own bent without ulterior aim. But while this is so, the discovery
that two or more empirical laws of nature are linked under one
principle embracing them both is the grounds for a very apprecia-
ble pleasure, often even for admiration, and is a kind that does not
diminish even though we are already familiar enough with its object. It is true that we no longer notice any decided pleasure in
comprehending nature, or in the unity of its classification into genera and species, without which the empirical concepts that afford
us our knowledge of nature and its particular laws would not be
possible. However, such pleasure certainly was experienced at one
time. Only because the most common experience would be impossible without comprehending nature, has such comprehension
gradually become fused with mere knowledge of any kind and is no
longer particularly noticed. Something is required to make us at-
tentive in our estimate of nature to its appropriateness for our understanding; to make us endeavor to bring, wherever possible,
nature's heterogeneous laws under higher, though still always em- 5:188
pirical laws in order that, on meeting with success, pleasure may be
felt in their accord with our thinking faculty, which accord is re-

garded by us as purely fortuitous. As against this, imagining nature would be altogether displeasing to us, were we to be forewarned that, on the slightest investigation carried beyond the commonest experience, we should come in contact with such a heterogeneity of nature's laws as would make uniting its particular laws under universal empirical laws impossible for our intellect. For this would conflict with the principle of the subjectively final specification of nature in its genera, and with our own reflecting judgment in respect thereof.

Yet this presupposition of judgment is so indeterminate on the question of the extent of the prevalence of that ideal fitness of nature for our thinking faculties, that if we are told that a more searching or enlarged knowledge of nature derived from observation must eventually bring us into contact with a multiplicity of laws that no human understanding could reduce to a principle, we can reconcile ourselves to the thought. But still we listen more gladly to others who hold out to us the hope that the more intimately we come to know the secrets of nature, or the better we are able to compare nature with other aspects as yet unknown to us, the more simple shall we find nature in its principles. The further our experience advances the more harmonious shall we find nature in the apparent heterogeneity of its empirical laws. For our judgment makes it imperative that we proceed on the principle of the conformity of nature to our faculty for knowing, so far as that principle extends, without deciding—for the rule is not given us by a determinant judgment—whether limits are anywhere set to it or not. For while limits may be definitely determined for the rational use of our thinking faculty, in the empirical field no such determination of limits is possible.

5:195

IX.

Joining the Laws of the Intellect and Reason by Means of Judgment.

The intellect prescribes laws *a priori* for nature as an object of the senses, so that we may have a theoretical knowledge of it in a possible experience. Reason prescribes laws *a priori* for freedom and its peculiar causality as the supersensible in the subject, so that we may have a purely practical knowledge. The realm of the concept of nature under the one law, and that of the concept of freedom under the other, are completely cut off from all mutual influence that each, according to its own principles, might exert upon the other, because of the broad gulf that divides the supersensible from phenomena. The concept of freedom determines nothing in respect of the theoretical knowledge of nature, and the concept of nature likewise determines nothing in respect of the practical laws of freedom. To that extent then it is not possible to throw a bridge from the one realm to the other. Although the determining grounds for causality according to the concept of freedom, and the practical rule that this contains, have no place in nature, and although the sensible cannot determine the supersensible in the subject, yet the converse is possible in respect of the consequences arising from the supersensible and bearing on the sensible, though not in respect of the knowledge of nature. Indeed, this much is implied in the concept of a causality by freedom whose *operation* is to take effect in the world in conformity with the formal laws of freedom. However, the word *cause*, when applied to the supersensible only signifies the *grounds* determining the causality of things of nature as an effect in conformity with their appropriate natural laws, and also in unison with the formal principle of the laws of reason—grounds which, while their possibility is impenetrable, may still be completely cleared of the charge of contradiction they allegedly involve.[1] In

5:196

1 One of the supposed contradictions in this radical distinction between the causality of nature and that of freedom is expressed in the objection that when I speak of *hindrances* opposed by nature to causality according to laws of freedom or moral laws, or of *assistance* lent it by nature, I am all the time admitting an *influence* of the former upon the latter. But the misinterpretation is easily avoided, if only attention is paid to the meaning of the statement. The resistance or furtherance is not between nature and freedom, but between the former as phenomenon and *the effects* of the latter as phenomena in the world of sense. Even the causality of freedom, that is, of pure and practical reason, is the causality of a natural cause subordinated to freedom, a causality of the subject regarded as man, and consequently as a phenomenon, and whose grounds for determination are contained in the intelligible; that is, thought under freedom, in a manner that is not further or otherwise explicable. . . .

5:195

5:196

accordance with the concept of freedom the effect is the final end which, or the manifestation of which in the sensible world, is to exist, and this presupposes the condition of the possibility of that end in nature; that is, in the nature of the subject as a being of the sensible world, or man. It is so presupposed *a priori*, and without regard to the practical, by judgment. This faculty, with the concept of the fitness of nature, provides us with the mediating concept between concepts of nature and the concept of freedom—a concept that makes possible the transition from the pure and theoretical (laws of the intellect) to the pure practical (laws of reason) and from conformity to law in accordance with the former to final ends according to the latter. For through that concept we conceive of the possibility of the final end that can only be actualized in nature and in harmony with nature's laws.

The intellect, by the possibility of its supplying *a priori* laws for nature, furnishes a proof of the fact that nature is understood by us only as a phenomenon, and in so doing points to nature's having a supersensible substratum; but the intellect leaves this substratum quite undetermined. Judgment by the *a priori* principle of its evaluation of nature according to its possible particular laws provides this supersensible substratum within, as well as without, us with *determinability through the intellectual faculty.* But reason gives *determination* to the same substratum *a priori* by its practical law. Thus judgment makes possible the transition from the realm of the concept of nature to that of the concept of freedom.

In respect of the faculties of the soul generally, regarded as higher faculties, i.e., as autonomous faculties, intellect is that containing the *constitutive a priori* principles for the faculty of knowledge; that is, the theoretical knowledge of nature. The *feeling of pleasure and displeasure* is provided for by the judgment in its independence from concepts and from sensations that refer to the determination of the faculty of desire and would thus be capable of being immediately practical. For the *faculty of desire* there is reason, which is practical without mediation of any pleasure of whatsoever origin. Reason as a higher faculty determines for the faculty of desire the final end accompanied by pure intellectual delight in the ob-

5:197

ject. Judgment's concept of the fitness of nature falls under the head of natural concepts, but only as a regulative principle for the thinking faculties, although the aesthetic judgment regarding certain objects of nature or of art occasioning that concept is a constitutive principle in respect of the feeling of pleasure or displeasure. The spontaneity in the play of the thinking faculties whose harmonious accord contains the grounds for this pleasure, makes the concept in question in its consequences a suitable mediating link connecting the realm of the concept of nature with that of the concept of freedom, as this accord at the same time promotes the receptivity of the mind for moral sentiments. The following table may facilitate the review of all the above faculties in their systematic unity.[2]

LIST OF MENTAL FACULTIES	COGNITIVE FACULTIES 5:198
Thinking faculties	Intellect
Feelings of pleasure and displeasure	Judgment
Faculty of desire	Reason

A PRIORI PRINCIPLES	APPLICATION
Conformity to law	Nature
Appropriateness [to an end]	Art
Final End [and purpose]	Freedom

---

2 It has been thought somewhat suspicious that my divisions in pure philosophy should almost always come out threefold. But it is due to the nature of the case. If a division is to be *a priori* it must be either analytic, according to the law of contradiction, and then it is always twofold, or else it is *synthetic*. If it is to be derived in the latter case from *a priori* concepts, and not, as in mathematics, from the *a priori* observation corresponding to the concept, then to meet the requirements of synthetic unity in general; namely, (1) a condition, (2) a conditioned, (3) the concept arising from the union of the conditioned with its conditioned, the classification must necessarily be threefold.

FIRST SECTION
ANALYTIC OF AESTHETIC JUDGMENT

FIRST BOOK
ANALYTIC OF THE BEAUTIFUL

FIRST ASPECT
OF THE JUDGMENT OF TASTE:[3] ASPECT OF QUALITY

§ 1.

The judgment of taste is aesthetic.

If we wish to discern whether anything is beautiful or not, we do not refer its image to the object by means of the intellect with a view to knowledge, but by means of the imagination acting perhaps in conjunction with the intellect we refer the image to the subject

3 The definition of taste here relied upon is that it is the faculty for estimating the beautiful. But the discovery of what is required for calling an object beautiful must be reserved for the analysis of judgments of taste. In my search for the aspects to which attention is paid by this judgment in its reflection, I have followed the guidance of the logical functions of judging, for a judgment of taste always involves a reference to the intellect. I have brought the aspect of quality first under review, because this is what the aesthetic judgment looks to in the first instance.

and its feeling of pleasure or displeasure. Therefore the judgment of taste is not an intellectual judgment and so not logical, but is aesthetic—which means that it is one whose determining ground *cannot be other than subjective.* Every reference of images is capable of being objective, even that of sensations (in which case it signifies the real in an empirical image). The one exception to this is the 5:204 feeling of pleasure or displeasure. This denotes nothing in the object, but is a feeling which the subject has by itself and in the manner in which it is affected by the image.

To apprehend a regular and appropriate building with one's thinking faculties, whether the manner of imaginings is clear or confused, is quite different from being conscious of this image with an accompanying sensation of delight. Here the image is referred wholly to the subject, and what is more, to its feeling of life—under the name of the feeling of pleasure or displeasure—and this forms the basis of a quite separate faculty for discriminating and estimating, that contributes nothing to knowledge. All it does is to compare the given image in the subject with the entire faculty for imagining of which the mind is conscious in the feeling of its state. Given images in a judgment may be empirical, and so aesthetic; but the judgment which is pronounced by their means is logical, provided it refers them to the object. Conversely, even if the given images are rational, but referred in a judgment solely to the subject (to its feeling), they are always aesthetic to that extent.

§ 2.

The delight which determines the judgment of taste is independent of all interest.

The delight which we connect with imagining the real existence of any object is called interest. Such a delight, therefore, always involves a reference to the faculty of desire, either as its determining ground, or else as necessarily implicated with its determining ground. Now, where the question is whether something is beautiful, we do not want to know whether we or anyone else are or even could be concerned in the real existence of the thing, but rather what estimate we form of it on mere contemplation (intuition or reflection). If anyone asks me whether I consider that the palace I see before me is beautiful, I may perhaps reply that I do not care for things that are merely made to be gaped at. Or I may reply in the same strain as that Iroquois *sachem* who said that nothing in Paris pleased him better than the eating-houses. I may even go a step further and inveigh with the vigor of a Rousseau against the vanity of the great who spend the sweat of the people on such superfluous things. Or finally, I may quite easily persuade myself that if I found myself on an uninhabited island without hope of ever again coming among men and could conjure such a palace into existence by a mere wish, I should still not trouble to do so as long as I had a hut there that was comfortable enough for me. All this may be admitted and approved; only it is not the point now at issue. All one wants to know is whether the mere image of the object is to my liking, no matter how indifferent I may be to the real existence of the object of this imagining. It is quite plain that in order to say that the object *is beautiful*, and to show that I have taste, everything turns on the meaning which I can give to this representation, and not on any factor which makes me dependent on the real existence of the object. Everyone must allow that a judgment on the beautiful which is tinged with the slightest interest is very partial and not a pure judgment of taste. One must not be in the least prepossessed in favor of the real existence of the thing, but must preserve complete indifference in this respect, in order to play the part of judge in matters of taste.

This proposition, which is of the utmost importance, cannot be better explained than by contrasting the pure disinterested[4] delight which appears in the judgment of taste with that allied to an interest—especially if we can also assure ourselves that there are not other kinds of interest beyond those presently to be mentioned.

---

4 A judgment upon an object of our delight may be wholly *disinterested* but withal very *interesting*, i.e., it relies on no interest, but it produces one. Of this kind are all pure moral judgments. But, of themselves, judgments of taste do not even set up any interest whatsoever. Only in society is it *interesting* to have taste—a point which will be explained in the sequel.

§ 3.

Delight IN THE AGREEABLE *is coupled with interest.*

That is AGREEABLE *which the senses find pleasing in sensation.* This at once affords a convenient opportunity for condemning and directing particular attention to a prevalent confusion of the double meaning of which the word "sensation" is capable. All delight (as is said or thought) is itself sensation (of a pleasure). Consequently everything that pleases, and for the very reason that it pleases, is agreeable—and according to its different degrees, or its relations to 5:206 other agreeable sensations, is attractive, charming, delicious, enjoyable, etc. But if this is conceded, then impressions of sense which determine inclination, or principles of reason which determine the will, or mere observed forms which determine judgment, are all on a par in everything relevant to their effect upon the feeling of pleasure, for this would be agreeableness in the sensation of one's state; and since, in the last resort, all the elaborate work of our faculties must issue in and unite in the practical as its goal, we could credit our faculties with no other appreciation of things and the worth of things than that consisting in the gratification which they promise. How this is attained is in the end immaterial; and as the choice of the means is here the only thing that can make a difference, men might indeed blame one another for folly or imprudence, but never for baseness or wickedness; for they are all, each according to his point of view, pursuing one goal, which for each is the gratification in question.

When a modification of the feeling of pleasure or displeasure is termed sensation, this expression is given quite a different meaning to that which it bears when I call the image of a thing (through sense as a receptivity pertaining to the faculty of knowledge) sensation. For in the latter case the image is referred to the object, but in the former it is referred solely to the subject and is not available for any knowledge, not even for that by which the subject understands itself.

Now in the above definition the word "sensation" is used to denote an objective image of sense; and to avoid continually running the risk of misinterpretation, we shall call that which must always remain purely subjective, and which is absolutely incapable of imagining an object, by the familiar name of feeling. The green color of the meadows belongs to *objective* sensation, as the perception of an object of sense; but its agreeableness to *subjective* sensation, by which no object is represented: i.e., to feeling, through which the object is regarded as an object of delight (which involves no knowledge of the object).

5:207   Now, that a judgment of an object by which its agreeableness is affirmed expresses an interest in it is evident from the fact that through sensation it provokes a desire for similar objects, consequently the delight presupposes, not the simple judgment about it, but the bearing its real existence has upon my state so far as affected by such an object. Hence we do not merely say of the agreeable that it *pleases,* but that it *gratifies.* I do not accord it a simple approval, but inclination is aroused by it, and where agreeableness is of the liveliest type a judgment on the character of the object is so entirely out of place, that those who are always intent only on enjoyment, for that is the word used to denote intensity of gratification, would fain dispense with all judgment.

§ 4.

Delight IN THE GOOD *is coupled with interest.*

That is *good* which by means of reason commends itself by its mere concept. We call useful that *good for something* which only pleases as a means; but that which pleases on its own account we call *good in itself.* In both cases the concept of an end is implied, and consequently the relation of reason to at least possible willing, and thus a delight in the *existence* of an object or action, i.e., some interest or other.

To deem something good, I must always know what sort of a thing the object is intended to be, i.e., I must have a concept of it. That is not necessary to enable me to see beauty in a thing. Flowers, free patterns, lines aimlessly intertwining—technically termed foliage—have no significance, depend upon no definite concept, and yet please. Delight in the beautiful must depend upon the reflection on an object precursory to some (not definitely determined) concept. It is thus also differentiated from the agreeable, which rests entirely upon sensation.

In many cases, no doubt, the agreeable and the good seem convertible terms. Thus it is commonly said that all (especially lasting) gratification is of itself good; which is almost equivalent to saying that to be permanently agreeable and to be good are identical. But it is readily apparent that this is merely a vicious confusion of words, for the concepts appropriate to these expressions are far 5:208 from interchangeable. The agreeable, which as such represents the object solely in relation to sense, must in the first instance be brought under principles of reason through the concept of an end, to be called good, as an object of will. But that the reference to delight is wholly different when what gratifies is at the same time called *good,* is evident from the fact that with the good the question always is whether it is mediately or immediately good, i.e., useful or good in itself; whereas with the agreeable this point can never arise, since the word always means what pleases immediately—and it is just the same with what I call beautiful.

Even in everyday parlance a distinction is drawn between the agreeable and the good. We do not scruple to say of a dish that stimulates the palate with spices and other condiments that it is agreeable—owing all the while that it is not good: because, while it immediately *satisfies* the senses, it is mediately displeasing, i.e., in the eye of reason that looks ahead to the consequences. Even in our estimate of health this same distinction may be traced. To all who possess it, it is immediately agreeable—at least negatively, i.e., as remoteness of all bodily pains. But if we are to say that it is good, we must further apply to reason to direct it to ends, that is, we must regard it as a state that puts us in a congenial mood for all we have to do. Finally, in respect of happiness every one believes that the greatest aggregate of the pleasures of life, taking duration as well as number into account, merits the name of a true, nay even of the highest, good. But reason sets its face against this too. Agreeableness is enjoyment. But if this is all that we are bent on, it would be foolish to be scrupulous about the means that procure it for us—whether it be obtained passively by the bounty of nature or actively by the work of our own hands. But the notion that there is any intrinsic worth in the real existence of a man who merely lives for *enjoyment*, however busy he may be in this respect, even when in so doing he serves others—all like him intent only on enjoyment—as an excellent means to that one end, and does so, moreover, because through sympathy he shares all their gratifications—this is a view to which reason will never let itself be brought round. Only by what a man does heedless of enjoyment, in complete freedom and independently of what he can produce passively from the hand of nature, does he give absolute worth to his existence, as the real existence of a person. Happiness, with all its plethora of pleasures, is far from being an unconditioned good.[5]

But, despite all this difference between the agreeable and the good, they both agree in being invariably coupled with an interest in their object. This is true, not alone of the agreeable (§ 3) and of the mediately good, i.e., the useful, which pleases as a means to some pleasure, but also is true of that which is good absolutely and from every point of view, namely the moral good which carries with it the highest interest. For the good as the object of will, and taking an interest in it, are identical.

§ 5.

Comparison of the three specifically different kinds of delight.

Both the Agreeable and the Good involve a reference to the faculty of desire, and are thus attended, the former with a delight psychologically conditioned by stimuli, the latter with a pure practical delight. Such delight is determined not merely by imagining the object, but also by the represented bond of connection between the

---

5 An obligation to enjoy is a patent absurdity. The same must also be said of a supposed obligation to actions that have merely enjoyment for their aim, no matter how spiritually this enjoyment may be refined in thought (or embellished), and even if it be a mystical, so-called heavenly, enjoyment.

subject and the real existence of the object. It is not only the object, but also its real existence that pleases. On the other hand the judgment of taste is simply *contemplative;* i.e., it is a judgment which is indifferent as to the existence of an object, and only decides how its character is related to the feeling of pleasure and displeasure. But this contemplation itself is not even directed to concepts; for the judgment of taste is not a judgment of either theoretical or practical thought, and hence it is not *grounded* on concepts either, nor *intentionally directed* to them.

The agreeable, the beautiful, and the good thus denote three different relations of the imagination to the feeling of pleasure and displeasure, a feeling by which we distinguish different objects or ways of imagining. Also, the corresponding expressions which indicate our satisfaction in them are different. The *agreeable* is what GRATIFIES a man; the *beautiful* what simply PLEASES him; the *good* what is ESTEEMED (approved); i.e., that on which he sets an objective worth. Agreeableness is a significant factor even with irrational animals; beauty has purport and significance only for human beings, both animal and rational but not merely for them as rational—intelligent beings—but only for them as at once animal and rational; whereas the good is good for every rational being in general; a proposition which can only receive its complete justification and explanation in the sequel. Of all these three kinds of delight, that of taste in the beautiful may be said to be the one and only disinterested and *free* delight; for with it no interest, whether of sense or reason, extorts approval. And so we may say that delight, in the three cases mentioned, is related to *inclination,* to *favor,* or to *respect.* For FAVOR is the only free liking. An object of inclination, and one which a law of reason imposes upon our desire, leaves us no freedom to turn anything into an object of pleasure. All interest presupposes a want, or calls one forth; and being a ground determining approval deprives the judgment on the object of its freedom.

So far as the interest or inclination in the case of the agreeable goes, everyone says: Hunger is the best sauce; and people with a healthy appetite relish everything, so long as it is something they can eat. Such delight, consequently, gives no indication of taste having anything to say as to the choice. Only when men have got all they want can we tell who among the crowd has taste or not. Similarly there may be correct habits (conduct) without virtue, politeness without good-will, propriety without honor, etc. For where the moral law dictates, there is no room left for free objective choice as to what one has to do; and to show taste in the way one carries out these dictates, or in estimating the way others do so, is a totally different matter from displaying the moral frame of one's mind. For the latter involves a command and produces a need of judgment.

Definition of the Beautiful Derived from the First Aspect

Taste is the faculty for estimating an object or a mode of representation by means of a delight or aversion *apart from any interest.* The object of such a delight is called *beautiful.*

SECOND ASPECT
OF THE JUDGMENT OF TASTE:
ASPECT OF QUANTITY

§ 6.

The beautiful is that which, apart from concepts, is represented as the Object of a UNIVERSAL *delight.*

This definition of the beautiful is deducible from the foregoing definition of it as an object of delight apart from any interest. For where anyone is conscious that he has delight in an object independent of interest, it is inevitable that he should look on the object as one containing a basis of delight for all men. For, since the delight is not based on any inclination of the subject (or on any deliberate interests), but the subject feels himself completely *free* in respect to the liking which he accords to the object, he can find as reasons for his delight no personal conditions to which his own subjective self might alone be party. Hence he must regard it as resting on what he may also presuppose in every other person; and therefore he must believe that he has reason for demanding a similar delight from everyone. Accordingly he will speak of the beautiful as if beauty were a quality of the object and the judgment logical (acquiring a knowledge of the object by concepts of it); although it is only aesthetic, and contains merely a reference of the image of the object to the subject; because it still bears this resemblance to the logical judgment, that it may be presupposed to be valid for all men. But this universality cannot spring from concepts. For from concepts there is no transition to the feeling of pleasure or displeasure (save in the case of pure practical laws, which, however, carry an interest with them; and such an interest does not attach to the pure judgment of taste). The result is that the judgment of taste, with its attendant consciousness of detachment from all interest, must involve a claim to validity for all men, and must do so apart from universality attached to objects; i.e., there must be coupled with it a claim to subjective universality. 5:212

§ 7.

Comparison of the beautiful with the agreeable and the good by means of the above characteristic.

As regards the *agreeable* every one concedes that his judgment, which he bases on a private feeling, and in which he declares that an object pleases him, is restricted merely to himself personally. Thus he does not take it amiss if, when he says that Canary-wine is agreeable, another corrects the expression and reminds him that he ought to say: It is agreeable to *me*. This applies not only to the taste of the tongue, the palate, and the throat, but to what may with anyone be agreeable to eye or ear. A violet color is to one soft and lovely: to another dull and faded. One man likes the tone of wind instruments, another prefers that of string instruments. To quarrel over such points with the idea of condemning another's judgment as incorrect when it differs from our own, as if the opposition between the two judgments were logical, would be folly. With the agreeable, therefore, the axiom holds good: *Everyone has his own taste* (that of the senses).

The beautiful stands on quite a different footing. It would, on the contrary, be ridiculous if anyone who plumed himself on his taste were to think of justifying himself by saying: This object (the building we see, the dress that person has on, the concert we hear, the poem submitted to our criticism) is beautiful *for me*. For if it merely pleases *him*, he must not call it *beautiful*. Many things may possess charm and agreeableness for him—no one cares about that; but when he puts a thing on a pedestal and calls it beautiful, he demands the same delight from others. He judges not merely for himself, but for all men, and then speaks of beauty as if it were a property of things. Thus he says the *thing* is beautiful; and it is not as if he counted on others agreeing in his judgment of liking owing to his having found them in such agreement on a number of occasions, but he *demands* this agreement of them. He blames them if they judge differently, and denies them taste, which he still requires of them as something they ought to have; and to this extent it is not open to men to say: Everyone has his own taste. This would be equivalent to saying that there is no such thing at all as taste, i.e., no aesthetic judgment capable of making a rightful claim upon the assent of all men.

Yet even in the case of the agreeable we find that the estimates men form do betray a prevalent agreement among them, which leads to our crediting some with taste and denying it to others, and that, too, not as an organic sense but as a critical faculty in respect of the agreeable generally. So of one who knows how to entertain his guests with pleasures of enjoyment through all the senses in such a way that one and all are pleased, we say that he has taste. But the universality here is only understood in a comparative sense; and the rules that apply are, like all empirical rules, *general* only, not *universal*—the latter being what the judgment of taste upon the beautiful deals or claims to deal in. The former is a judgment in respect of sociability so far resting on empirical rules. In respect of the good it is true that judgments also rightly assert a claim to validity for every one; but the good is only imagined as an object of universal delight *by means of a concept*, which is the case neither with the agreeable nor the beautiful.

Third Aspect of Judgments of Taste:
Aspect of the Relation of the Ends
Brought Under Review in such Judgments

§ 10.

Finality in general.

Let us define the meaning of "an end" in transcendental terms (i.e., without presupposing anything empirical, such as the feeling of pleasure). An end is the object of a concept so far as this concept is regarded as the cause of the object (the real ground of its possibil- ity); and the causality of a *concept* in respect of its *object* is finality (*forma finalis*). Then wherever, not merely the knowledge of an object, but the object itself (its form or real existence) as an effect, is thought to be possible only through a concept of it, there we imagine an end. The image of the effect is here the determining ground of its cause and takes the lead of it. The consciousness of the causality of imagining the state of the subject as one tending *to preserve a continuance* of that state, may be said here to denote in a general way what is called pleasure; whereas displeasure is that imagining which contains the ground for converting the state of the images into their opposite (for hindering or removing them). 5:220

The faculty of desire, so far as it is determinable only through concepts, i.e., so as to act in conformity with an imagined end, would be the will. But an object, or state of mind, or even an action may, although its possibility does not necessarily presuppose an imagined end, be called final simply on account of its possibility being only explicable and intelligible for us by virtue of an assumption on our part of a fundamental causality according to ends, i.e., a will that would have so ordained it according to a certain represented rule. Finality, therefore, may exist apart from an end, in so far as we do not locate the causes of this form in a will, but yet are able to render the explanation of its possibility intelligible to ourselves only by deriving it from a will. Now we are not always obliged to look with the eye of reason into what we observe (i.e., to consider it in its possibility). So we may at least observe a finality of form, and trace it in objects—though by reflection only—without resting it on an end (as the material of the *nexus finalis*).

§ 11.

The sole foundation of the judgment of taste is the FORM OF APPROPRIATENESS *of an object (or mode of imagining it).*

Whenever an end is regarded as a source of delight it always imports an interest as determining ground of the judgment on the object of pleasure. Hence the judgment of taste cannot rest on any subjective end as its ground. But neither can any image of an objective end, i.e., of the possibility of the object itself on principles of final connection, determine the judgment of taste, and, furthermore, neither can any concept of the good. For the judgment of taste is an aesthetic and not a thinking judgment, and so does not deal with any *concept* of the nature or of the internal or external possibility, by this or that cause, of the object, but simply with the relative bearing of the representative powers so far as they are determined by imagination.

Now this relation is present when an object is characterized as beautiful, coupled with the feeling of pleasure. This pleasure is by the judgment of taste pronounced valid for everyone; hence an agreeableness attending the imagining is just as incapable of containing the determining ground of the judgment as imagining the perfection of the object or the concept of the good. We are thus left with the subjective appropriateness in the imagined object, exclusive of any end (objective or subjective)—consequently the bare form of appropriateness in the image whereby an object is *given* to us, so far as we are conscious of it—as that which is alone capable of constituting the delight which, apart from any concept, we estimate as universally communicable, and so of forming the determining ground of the judgment of taste.

§ 12.

The judgment of taste rests upon a priori *grounds.*

To determine *a priori* the connection of the feeling of pleasure or displeasure as an effect, with some representation or other (sensa-

tion or concept) as its cause, is utterly impossible; for that would be 5:222
a causal relation which (with objects of experience) is always one
that can only be understood *a posteriori* and with the help of experience. True, in the *Critique of Practical Reason* we did actually derive
a priori from universal moral concepts the feeling of respect as a
particular and peculiar modification of this feeling which does not
strictly answer either to the pleasure or displeasure which we receive from empirical objects. But there we were further able to
cross the border of experience and call in aid a causality resting on
a supersensible attribute of the subject, namely that of freedom.
But even there it was not this *feeling* exactly that we deduced from
the idea of the moral as cause, but from this was derived simply the
determination of the will. But the mental state present in the determination of the will by any means is at once in itself a feeling of
pleasure and identical with it, and so does not issue from it as an effect. Such an effect must only be assumed where the concept of the
moral as a good precedes the determination of the will by the law;
for in that case it would be futile to derive the pleasure combined
with the concept from this concept as mere knowledge.

Now the pleasure in aesthetic judgments stands on a similar
footing: only that here it is merely contemplative and does not
bring about an interest in the object; whereas in the moral judgment it is practical. The consciousness of mere formal purpose in
the play of the thinking faculties of the subject with imagining an
object, is the pleasure itself, because it involves a determining
ground for the subject's activity in respect of the quickening of its
thinking powers, and thus an internal causality (which is final) in
respect of knowledge generally, but without being limited to definite knowledge, and consequently a mere form of the subjective fitness of an image in an aesthetic judgment. This pleasure is also in
no way practical, neither resembling that from the psychological
ground of agreeableness nor that from the intellectual ground of
the imagined good. But still it involves an inherent causality;
namely, that of *preserving a continuance* of the state of the image itself and the active engagement of the thinking powers without ulterior aim. We *dwell* on the contemplation of the beautiful because
this contemplation strengthens and reproduces itself. The case is

analogous (but analogous only) to the way we linger on the charm [we feel] in imagining an object which keeps arresting the attention, the mind all the while remaining passive.

5:244

SECOND BOOK
ANALYTIC OF THE SUBLIME

§ 23.

Transition from the faculty for estimating the beautiful to that for estimating the sublime.

The beautiful and the sublime agree in that they are pleasing on their own account. Further they agree in not presupposing either a reaction of the senses or a logical judgment, but reflection instead. Hence it follows that the delight does not depend upon a sensation, as with the agreeable, nor upon a definite concept, as does the delight in the good, although it has, for all that an indeterminate reference to concepts. Rather the delight is connected with the mere presentation or faculty of presentation, and is thus taken to express the accord, in a given thing seen (*Anschauung*), of the faculty of presentation, or the imagination, with the *faculty of conceiving* that belongs to understanding or reason, in the sense of the former assisting the latter. Hence both kinds of judgments are *singular,* and yet such as profess to be universally valid in respect of every subject, despite the fact that their claims are directed merely to the feeling of pleasure and not to any knowledge of the object.

There are, however, also important and striking differences between the two. The beautiful in nature relates to the form of the object, and this consists in limitation, whereas the sublime is to be found in an object even devoid of form, so far as it immediately involves, or else by its presence provokes, an image of *limitlessness,* yet with a super-added thought of its totality. Accordingly the beautiful seems to be regarded as a presentation of an indeterminate intellectual concept, the sublime as a presentation of an indeterminate concept of reason. Hence the delight is in the former case coupled with the image of *Quality,* but in this case with that of *Quantity.*

Moreover, the former delight is very different from the latter in 5:245 kind. For the beautiful is directly attended by a feeling of the fur-therance of life, and is thus compatible with charms and a playful imagination. On the other hand, the feeling of the sublime is a pleasure that only arises indirectly, being brought about by the feeling of a momentary check to the vital forces followed at once by a discharge all the more powerful, and so it is an emotion that seems to be no sport, but a dead earnest affair of the imagination. Hence charms are repugnant to it; and, since the mind is not simply attracted by the object but is also alternately repelled thereby, the delight in the sublime does not so much involve positive pleasure as admiration or respect; i.e., merits the name of a negative pleasure.

But the most important and vital distinction between the sub-lime and the beautiful is certainly this: that if, as is allowable, we here confine our attention in the first instance to the sublime in ob-jects of nature (that of art being always restricted by the conditions of an agreement with nature) we observe that whereas natural beauty (such as is self-subsisting) conveys a finality in its form mak-ing the object appear, as it were, preadapted to our power of judg-ment, so that it thus forms of itself an object of our delight, that which, without our indulging in any refinements of thought but simply in our apprehension of it excites the feeling of the sublime, may appear in point of form to contravene the ends of our power of judgment, to be ill-adapted to our faculty for imagining, and to be, as it were, an outrage on the imagination, yet it is judged all the more sublime on that account.

From this it may be seen at once that we express ourselves on the whole inaccurately if we term any *object of nature* sublime, although we may with perfect propriety call many such objects beautiful. For how can that which is apprehended as inherently contra-final be noted with an expression of approval? All that we can say is that the object lends itself to the presentation of a sublimity discoverable in the mind. For the sublime, in the strict sense of the word, cannot be contained in any sensuous form, but rather concerns rational ideas, which, although no adequate presentation of them is possible, may be excited and called into the mind by that very inadequacy itself which does not admit of presentation through the senses. The broad ocean agitated by storms cannot be called sublime. Its aspect is horrible, and one must have stored one's mind in advance with a rich stock of ideas, if such an intuition is to raise it to the pitch of a feeling which is itself sublime—sublime because the mind has been incited to go beyond the senses, and employ itself upon ideas involving higher ends.

5:246

Self-subsisting natural beauty reveals to us a technique of nature which shows it in the light of a system ordered in accordance with laws whose principle is not to be found within the range of our entire faculty of the intellect. This principle is that of a finality relative to the employment of judgment in respect of phenomena which have thus to be assigned, not merely to nature regarded after the analogy of art. Hence it gives a veritable extension, not of course to our knowledge of objects of nature, but to our concept of nature itself—nature as mere mechanism being enlarged to the concept of nature as art—an extension inviting profound inquiries as to the possibility of such a form. But in what we are wont to call sublime in nature there is such an absence of anything leading to particular objective principles and corresponding forms of nature, that it is rather in its chaos, or in its wildest and most irregular disorder and desolation, provided it gives signs of magnitude and power, that nature chiefly excites the ideas of the sublime. Hence we see that the concept of the sublime in nature is far less important and rich in consequences than that of its beauty. It gives on the whole no indication of any final purpose in nature itself, but only in the possible *employment* of our observation of it inducing a feeling in our own selves of appropriateness quite independent of nature. For the beautiful in nature we must seek a ground outside ourselves, but for the sublime merely one inside ourselves: the attitude of mind that introduces sublimity into the image of nature. This is a very needful preliminary remark. It entirely separates the ideas of the sublime from those of the appropriateness of *nature*, and makes the theory of the sublime a mere appendage to the aesthetic estimate of the appropriateness of nature, because it does not give an image of any particular form in nature, but involves no more than the development of a final employment by the imagination of its own image.

CRITIQUE OF AESTHETIC JUDGMENT
SECOND SECTION

§ 55.

Dialectic of Aesthetic Judgment.

For a power of judgment to be dialectical it must first of all be rationalizing; that is to say, its judgments must lay claim to universality,[6] and do so *a priori,* for it is in the antithesis of such judgments that dialectic consists. Hence there is nothing dialectical in the irreconcilability of aesthetic judgments based on sense (the agreeable and disagreeable). And in so far as each person appears merely to his own private taste even the conflict of judgments of taste does not form a dialectic of taste—for no one is proposing to make his own judgment into a universal rule. Hence the only concept left to us of a dialectic affecting taste is one of a dialectic of the *Critique* of taste (not of taste itself) in respect to its *principles:* for, on the question of the ground of the possibility of judgments of taste in general, mutually conflicting concepts naturally and unavoidably make their appearance. The transcendental *Critique* of taste will, therefore, only include a part capable of bearing the name of a dialectic of the aesthetic judgment if we find an antinomy of the principles of the faculty which throws doubt upon its conformity to law, and hence also upon its inner possibility.

§ 56.

Image of the antinomy of taste.

The first commonplace of taste is contained in the proposition under cover of which everyone devoid of taste thinks to shelter himself from reproach: *everyone has his own taste.* This is only an-

---

6 Any judgment which claims to be universal may be termed a rationalizing judgment (*iudicium ratiocinans*); for so far as it is universal it may serve as the major premise of a syllogism. On the other hand, only a judgment which is thought as the conclusion of a syllogism, and, therefore, as having an *a priori* foundation, can be called rational (*iudicium ratiocinatum*).

other way of saying that the determining ground of this judgment is merely subjective (gratification or pain), and that the judgment has no right to the necessary agreement of others.

Its second commonplace, to which even those resort who concede the right of the judgment of taste to pronounce with validity for everyone, is: *there is no disputing about taste.* This amounts to saying that even though the determining ground of a judgment of taste be objective, it is not reducible to definite concepts, so that in respect of the judgment itself no *decision* can be reached by proofs, although it is quite open to us to *contend* upon the matter, and to contend with right. For though *contention* and *dispute* have this point in common, that they aim at bringing judgments into accordance out of and by means of their mutual opposition; yet they differ in the latter hoping to effect this from definite concepts, as grounds of proof, and, consequently, adopting *objective concepts* as grounds of the judgment. But where this is considered impracticable, dispute is regarded as alike out of the question.

Between these two commonplaces an intermediate proposition is readily seen to be missing. It is one which has certainly not become proverbial, but yet it is at the back of everyone's mind. It is that *there may be contention about taste* (although not a dispute). This proposition, however, involves the contrary of the first one. For in a matter in which contention is to be allowed, there must be a hope of coming to terms. Hence one must be able to count on grounds of judgment that possess more than private validity and are thus not merely subjective. And yet the above principle, *everyone has his own taste,* is directly opposed to this.

The principle of taste, therefore, exhibits the following antinomy:

1. *Thesis.* The judgment of taste is not based upon concepts; for, if it were, it would be open to dispute (decision by means of proofs).

2. *Antithesis.* The judgment of taste is based on concepts; for otherwise, despite diversity of judgment, there could be no room even 5:339 for contention in the matter (a claim to the necessary agreement of others with this judgment).

§ 57.

Solution of the antinomy of taste.

There is no possibility of removing the conflict of the above principles, which underlie every judgment of taste (and which are only the two peculiarities of the judgment of taste previously set out in the Analytic) except by showing that the concept to which the object is made to refer in a judgment of this kind is not taken in the same sense in both maxims of the aesthetic judgment; that this double sense, or point of view, in our estimate, is necessary for our power of transcendental judgment; and that nevertheless the false appearance arising from the confusion of one with the other is a natural illusion, and so unavoidable.

The judgment of taste must have reference to some concept or other, as otherwise it would be absolutely impossible for it to lay claim to necessary validity for everyone. Yet it need not on that account be provable from a concept. For a concept may be either determinable, or else at once intrinsically undetermined and indeterminable. An intellectual concept, which is determinable by means of predicates borrowed from sensible looking-at-things and corresponding to it, is of the first kind. But of the second kind is the transcendental rational concept of the supersensible, which lies at the basis of all that sensible looking-at-things and is hence incapable of being further determined theoretically.

Now the judgment of taste applies to objects of sense, but not so as to determine a *concept* of them for the intellect; for it is not a logical judgment. Rather it is a singular image or observation referable to the feeling of pleasure, and, as such, only a private judgment. And to that extent it would be limited in its validity to the individual judging: the object is *for me* an object of delight, for others it may be otherwise—everyone according to his taste.

For all that, the judgment of taste contains beyond doubt an enlarged reference by imagining the object in such a way as to lay the foundation for an extension of judgments of this kind so as to make them binding for everyone. This must of necessity be founded upon some concept or other, but such a concept as does not admit of being determined by observation, and affords no knowledge of anything. Hence, too, it is a concept *which does not afford any proof* of the judgment of taste. But the mere pure rational concept of the supersensible lying at the basis of the object (and of the judging subject for that matter) as object of sense, and thus as phenomenon, is just such a concept. For unless such a point of view were adopted there would be no means of saving the claim to universal validity of the judgments of taste. And if the concept forming the required basis were an intellectual concept, though a mere confused one, as, let us say, of perfection, answering to which the sensible observation of the beautiful might be adduced, then it would be at least intrinsically possible to found the judgment of taste upon proofs, which contradicts the thesis.

All contradiction disappears, however, if I say: The judgment of taste does not depend upon a concept (namely that of a general ground of the subjective appropriateness of nature for the power of judgment), but one from which nothing can be known of the object, and nothing proved, because it is in itself indeterminable and useless for knowledge. Yet by means of this very concept the judgment acquires at the same time validity for everyone (but for each individual, no doubt, as a specific judgment immediately accompanying his observation): because its determining ground lies, perhaps, in the concept of what may be regarded as the supersensible substratum of humanity.

The solution of an antinomy turns solely on the possibility of two apparently conflicting propositions not being in fact contradictory, but rather being capable of consisting together, although the explanation of the possibility of their concept transcends our faculties for knowledge. That this illusion is also natural and for human reason unavoidable, as well as why it is so, and remains so, although upon the solution of the apparent contradiction it no longer misleads us, may be made intelligible from the above considerations.

For the concept which a judgment must have as a basis for its universal validity is taken in the same sense in both the conflicting judgments, yet two opposite predicates are asserted of it. The thesis should therefore read: The judgment of taste is not based on *determinate* concepts; but the antithesis: The judgment of taste does rest upon a concept, although an *indeterminate* one (namely, that of 5:341 the supersensible substratum of phenomena), and then there would be no conflict between them.

Beyond removing this conflict between the claims and counterclaims of taste we can do nothing. To supply determinate objective principles of taste in accordance with which its judgments might be derived, tested, and proved, is an absolute impossibility, for then it would not be a judgment of taste. The subjective principle—that is to say, the indeterminate idea of the supersensible within us—can only be indicated as the unique key to the riddle of this faculty, itself concealed from us in its sources; and there is no means of making it any more intelligible.

The antinomy here exhibited and resolved rests upon the proper concept of taste as a merely reflective aesthetic judgment, and the two seemingly conflicting principles are reconciled on the ground that *they may both be true,* and this is sufficient. If, on the other hand, owing to the fact that the image lying at the basis of the judgment of taste is singular, the determining ground of taste is taken, as by some it is, to be *agreeableness,* or, as others, looking to its universal validity, would have it, the principle of *perfection,* and if the definition of taste is framed accordingly, the result is an antinomy which is absolutely irresolvable unless we show *the falsity of both propositions* as contraries (not as simple contradictories). This would force the conclusion that the concept upon which each is founded is self-contradictory. Thus it is evident that the removal of the antinomy of the aesthetic judgment pursues a course similar to that followed by the Critique in the solution of the antinomies of pure theoretical reason; and that the antinomies, both here and in the *Critique of Practical Reason,* compel us, whether we like it or not, to look beyond the horizon of the sensible, and to seek in the supersensible the point of union of all our faculties *a priori:* for we are left with no other expedient to bring reason into harmony with itself.

PART II

CRITIQUE OF TELEOLOGICAL JUDGMENT

§ 61.

Objective appropriateness in nature [for its ends].

We do not need to look beyond the critical explanation of the possibility of knowledge to find ample reason for assuming a subjective appropriateness on the part of nature in its particular laws. This is a purpose relative to comprehensibility—man's power of judgment being such as it is—and to the possibility of uniting particular experiences into a connected system of nature. In this system, then, we may further anticipate the possible existence of some among the many products of nature that, as if put there with quite a special regard to our judgment, are of a form particularly adapted to that faculty. Forms of this kind are those which by their combination of unity and heterogeneity serve as it were to strengthen and entertain the mental powers that enter into play in the exercise of the faculty of judgment, and to them the name of *beautiful forms* is accordingly given.

But the universal idea of nature, as the complex of objects of sense, gives us no reason whatever for assuming that things of nature serve one another as means to ends, or that their very possibility is only made fully intelligible by a causality of this sort. For since, in the case of the beautiful forms above mentioned, imagining things is something in ourselves, it can quite readily be thought of even *a priori* as well-adapted and convenient for disposing our thinking faculties to an inward and final harmony. But where the ends are not ends of our own, and do not belong even to nature (which we do not take to be an intelligent being), there is no reason at all for presuming *a priori* that they may or ought nevertheless to constitute a special kind of causality or at least a quite peculiar order of nature. What is more, the actual existence of these ends cannot be proved by experience—save on the assumption of an antecedent process of mental jugglery that only reads the concept of an end into the nature of the things, and that, not deriving this concept from the objects and what it knows of them from experience, makes use of it more for the purpose of rendering nature intelligible to us by an analogy to a subjective ground upon which our imaginings are brought into inner connection, than for that of understanding nature from objective grounds. 5:360

Besides, objective appropriateness, as a principle upon which physical objects are possible, is so far from attaching *necessarily* to the concept of nature, that it is the stock example adduced to show the fortuitousness of nature and its form. So where the structure of a bird, for instance, the hollow formation of its bones, the position of its wings for producing motion and of its tail for steering, are cited, we are told that all this is in the highest degree accidental if we simply look to the *nexus effectivus* in nature, and do not call in aid a special kind of causality, namely, that of ends (*nexus finalis*). This means that nature, regarded as mere mechanism, could have fashioned itself in a thousand other different ways without lighting precisely on the unity based on a principle like this, and that, accordingly, it is only outside the conception of nature, and not in it, that we may hope to find some shadow of ground *a priori* for that unity.

We are right, however, in applying the teleological estimate, at least problematically, to the investigation of nature; but only with a view to bringing it under principles of observation and research by *analogy* to the causality that looks to ends, while not pretending to *explain* it by this means. Thus it is an estimate of the reflective, not of the determinant, judgment. Yet the concept of combinations and forms in nature that are determined by ends is at least *one more principle* for reducing its phenomena to rules in cases where the laws of its purely mechanical causality do not carry us sufficiently far. For we are bringing forward a teleological ground where we endow a concept of an object—as if that concept were to be found in nature instead of in ourselves—with causality in respect of the object, or rather where we picture to ourselves the possibility of the object on the analogy of a causality of this kind—a causality such as we experience in ourselves—and so regard nature as possessed of a capacity of its own for acting like a technician; if we did not ascribe such a mode of operation to nature its causality would have to be regarded as blind mechanism. But this is a different thing from crediting nature with causes acting *designedly,* to which it may be regarded as subjected in following its particular laws. The latter would mean that teleology is based, not merely on a *regulative* principle, directed to the simple *estimate* of phenomena, but is actually based on a *constitutive* principle available for *deriving* natural products from their causes; with the result that the concept of an end of nature now exists for the determinant, rather than the reflective judgment. But in that case the concept would not really be specially connected with the power of judgment, as is the concept of beauty as a formal subjective appropriateness. Natural ends would, on the contrary, be a concept of reason, and would introduce a new causality into science—one which we are borrowing all the time solely from ourselves and attributing to other beings, although we do not mean to assume that they and we are similarly constituted.

5:361

5:369

FIRST DIVISION
ANALYTIC OF TELEOLOGICAL JUDGMENT

§ 64.

The distinctive character of things considered as physical ends.

A thing is possible only as an end where the causality to which it owes its origin must not be sought in the mechanism of nature, but

370

in a cause whose capacity of acting is determined by concepts. What is required in order that we may perceive that a thing is only possible in this way is that its form is not possible on purely natural laws—that is to say, such laws as we may understand by means of unaided intellect applied to objects of sense—but that, on the contrary, even to know it empirically in respect of its cause and effect presupposes concepts of reason. Here we have, as far as any empirical laws of nature go, a *fortuitousness* of form of the thing in relation to reason. Now reason in every case insists on understanding the necessity of the form of a natural product, even where it only desires to perceive the conditions involved in its production. In the given form above mentioned, however, it cannot get this necessity. Hence the fortuitousness is itself a ground for making us look upon the origin of the thing as if, just because of that fortuitousness, it could only be possible through reason. But the causality, so construed, becomes the faculty of acting according to ends—that is to say, a will; and the object, which is represented as only deriving its possibility from such a will, will be represented as possible only as an end.

Suppose a person was in a country that seemed to him uninhabited and was to see a geometrical figure, say a regular hexagon, traced on the sand. As he reflected, and tried to get a concept of the figure, his reason would make him conscious, though perhaps obscurely, that in the production of this concept there was unity of principle. His reason would then forbid him to consider the sand, the neighboring sea, the winds, or even animals with their footprints, as causes familiar to him, or any other irrational cause, as the ground of the possibility of such a form. For the fortuitousness of coincidence with a concept like this, which is only possible in reason, would appear to him so infinitely great that there might just as well be no law of nature at all in the case. Hence it would seem that the cause of the production of such an effect could not be contained in the mere mechanical operation of nature, but that, on the contrary a conception of such an object, as a conception that only reason can give and compare the object with, must likewise be what alone contains that causality. On these grounds it would appear to him that this effect was one that might without reservation be regarded as an end, though not as a natural end. In other words he would regard it as a product of art—*vestigium hominis video*.

But when a thing is recognized to be a product of nature, then something more is required—unless, perhaps, our very estimate involves a contradiction—if, despite its being such a product, we are yet to estimate it as an end, and, consequently, as an *end of nature*. As a provisional statement I would say that a thing exists as an 5:371 end of nature *if it is* (in a double sense) *both cause and effect of itself.* For this involves a kind of causality that we cannot associate with the mere concept of a nature unless we make that nature rest on an underlying end, but which can then, though incomprehensible, be thought without contradiction. Before analysing the component factors of this idea of an end of nature or natural end, let us first illustrate its meaning by an example.

A tree produces, in the first place, another tree, according to a familiar law of nature. But the tree which it produces is of the same genus. Hence, in its *genus*, it produces itself. In the genus, now as effect, now as cause, continually generated from itself and likewise generating itself, it preserves itself generically.

Secondly, a tree produces itself even as an *individual.* It is true that we only call this kind of effect growth; but growth is here to be understood in a sense that makes it entirely different from any increase according to mechanical laws, and renders it equivalent, though under another name, to generation. The plant first prepares the matter that it assimilates and bestows upon it a specifically distinctive quality which the mechanism of nature outside it cannot supply, and it develops itself by means of a material which, in its composite character, is its own product. For, although in respect of the constituents that it derives from nature outside, it must be regarded as only a product, yet in the separation and recombination of this new material we find an original capacity of selection and construction on the part of natural beings of this kind such as infinitely outdistances all the efforts of art, when the latter attempts to reconstitute those products of the vegetable kingdom out of the elements which it obtains through their analysis, or else out of the material which nature supplies for their nourishment.

Thirdly, a part of a tree also generates itself in such a way that the preservation of one part is reciprocally dependent on the preservation of the other parts. An eye taken from the sprig of one tree and set in the branch of another produces in the alien stock a growth of its own species, and similarly a scion grafted on the body of a different tree. Hence even in the case of the same tree each branch or leaf may be regarded as engrafted or inoculated into it, and, consequently, as a tree with a separate existence of its own, and only attaching itself to another and living parasitically on it. At the same 5:372 time the leaves are certainly products of the tree, but they also maintain it in turn; for repeated defoliation would kill it, and its growth is dependent upon the action of the leaves on the trunk. The way nature comes, in these forms of life, to her own aid in the case of injury, where the want of one part necessary for the maintenance of the neighboring parts is made good by the rest; the abortions or malformations in growth, where, on account of some chance defect or obstacle, certain parts adopt a completely new formation, so as to preserve the existing growth, and thus produce an anomalous form: are matters which I only desire to mention here in passing, although they are among the most wonderful properties in the forms of organic life.

§ 65.

Things considered as physical ends are organisms.

Where a thing is a product of nature and yet, so regarded, has to be understood as possible only as a natural end, it must from its character, as set out in the preceding section, stand to itself reciprocally in the relation of cause and effect. This is, however, a somewhat inexact and indeterminate expression that needs derivation from a definite concept.

In so far as the causal connection is thought about merely by means of the intellect, it is a nexus constituting a series of causes and effects that is invariably progressive. The things that as effects presuppose others as their causes cannot themselves in turn be also causes of the latter. This causal connection is termed that of efficient causes (*nexus effectivus*). On the other hand, however, we are also able to think of a causal connection according to a rational concept, that of ends, which, if regarded as a series, would involve regressive as well as progressive dependency. It would be one in which a thing designated at first as an effect deserves none the less, if we take the series regressively, to be called the cause of the thing of which it was said to be the effect. In the domain of practical matters, such as in art, we readily find examples of a nexus of this kind. Thus a house is certainly the cause of the money that is received as rent, but yet, conversely, the imagining of this possible income was the cause of the building of the house. A causal nexus of this kind is termed that of final causes (*nexus finalis*). The former might, perhaps, more appropriately be called the nexus of real and the latter the nexus of ideal causes, because with this use of terms it would be understood at once that there cannot be more than these two kinds of causality.

5:373

Now the *first* requisite of a thing, considered as an end of nature, is that its parts, both as to their existence and form, are only possible by their relation to the whole. For the thing is itself an end, and is, therefore, comprehended under a concept or an idea that must determine *a priori* all that is to be contained in it. But so far as the possibility of a thing is only thought of in this way, it is simply a work of art. It is the product, in other words, of an intelligent cause, distinct from the matter, or parts, of the thing, and of one whose causality, in bringing together and combining the parts, is determined by its idea of a whole made possible through that idea, and, consequently, not by external nature.

But if a thing is a product of nature, and as such is necessarily to possess intrinsically and in its inner possibility a relation to ends, in other words, is to be possible only as an end of nature and independently of the causality of the concepts of external rational agents, then this *second* requisite is involved, namely, that the parts of the thing combine of themselves into the unity of a whole, being reciprocally cause and effect of their form. For this is the only way in which it is possible that the idea of the whole may conversely, or reciprocally, determine in its turn the form and combination of all parts, not as cause—for that would make it an art-product—but as the epistemological basis upon which the systematic unity of the form and combination of all the manifold contained in the given matter becomes understandable for the person studying it.

What we require, therefore, in the case of a body which in its intrinsic nature and inner possibility has to be considered as nature's end, is as follows. Its parts must in their collective unity reciprocally produce one another alike as to form and combination, and thus by their own causality produce a whole, the concept of which, conversely—in a being possessing the causality according to concepts that is adequate for such a product—could in turn be the cause of the whole according to a principle, so that, consequently, the nexus of *efficient causes* might as well be interpreted as an *operation brought about by final* [end-related] causes.

In such a natural product as this every part is thought as *owing* its presence to the *agency* of all the remaining parts, and also as existing *for the sake of the others* and of the whole, that is as an instrument, 5:374 or organ. But this is not enough—for it might be an instrument of art, and thus have no more than its general possibility referring to an end. On the contrary the part must be an organ *producing* the other parts—each, consequently reciprocally producing the others. No instrument of art can answer to this description, but only the instrument of that nature from whose resources the materials of every instrument are drawn—even the materials for instruments of art. Only under these conditions and upon these terms can such a product be an *organized* and *self-organized being*, and, as such, be called a *natural end*.

In a watch one part is the instrument by which the movement of the others is effected, but one wheel is not the efficient cause of the production of the other. One part is certainly present for the sake of another, but it does not owe its presence to the agency of that other. For this reason, also, the producing cause of the watch and its form is not contained in the nature of this material, but lies outside the watch in a being that can act according to ideas of a whole which its causality makes possible. Hence one wheel in the watch does not produce the other, and still less, does one watch produce other watches, by utilizing, or organizing, foreign material; hence it does not of itself replace parts of which it has been deprived, nor, if these are absent in the original construction, does it make good the deficiency by the support of the rest; nor does it, so to speak, repair its own casual disorders. Yet these are all things which we are justified in expecting from organized nature. An organized being is, therefore, not a mere machine. For a machine has solely *motive power*, whereas an organized being possesses inherent *formative* power, and such, moreover, as it can impart to material devoid of it—material which it organizes. This, therefore, is a self-propagating formative power, which cannot be explained by the capacity of movement alone, that is to say, by mechanism.

We do not say half enough of nature and her capacity in organized products when we speak of this capacity as being the *analogue of art*. For what is here present to our minds is an artist—a rational being—working from without. But nature, on the contrary, organizes itself, and does so in each species of its organized products—following a single pattern, certainly, as to general features, but nevertheless admitting deviations calculated to secure self-preservation under particular circumstances. We might perhaps come nearer to the description of this impenetrable property if we were to call it an analogue of life. But then either we should have to endow matter as mere matter with a property (hylozoism) that contradicts its essential nature; or else we should have to associate with it a foreign principle *being in communion* with it (a soul). But, if such a product is to be a natural product, then we have to adopt one or other of two courses in order to bring in a soul. Either we must presuppose organized matter as the instrument of such a soul, which makes organized matter no whit more intelligible, or else we must make the soul the artificer of this structure, in which case we must withdraw the product from (corporeal) nature. Strictly speaking, therefore, the organization of nature has nothing analogous to any causality known to us.[7] Natural beauty may justly

5:375

---

7 We may, on the other hand, make use of an analogy to the above-mentioned immediate physical ends to throw light on a certain union, which, however, is to be found more often in idea than in fact. Thus in the case of a complete transformation, recently undertaken, of a great people into a state, the word *organization* has frequently, and with much propriety, been

be termed the analogue of art, for it is only ascribed to the objects in respect of reflection upon the *external* view of them and, therefore, only on account of their superficial form. But *intrinsic natural perfection,* as possessed by things that are only possible as *ends of nature,* and that are therefore called organisms, is unthinkable and inexplicable on any analogy to any known physical, or natural, agency, not even excepting—since we ourselves are part of nature in the widest sense—the suggestion of any strictly apt analogy to human art.

The concept of a thing as intrinsically a natural end is, therefore, not a constitutive concept either by the intellect or by reason, but yet it may be used by reflective judgment as a regulative conception for guiding our investigation of objects of this kind by a remote analogy with our own causality according to ends generally, and as a basis of reflection upon their supreme source. But in the latter connection it cannot be used to promote our knowledge either of nature or of such original sources of those objects, but must on the contrary be confined to the service of just the same practical faculty of reason in analogy with which we considered the cause of this finality.

Organisms are, therefore, the only beings in nature that, considered in their separate existence and apart from any relation to other things, cannot be thought possible except as ends of nature. It 5:376 is they, then, that first provide objective reality to the concept of an *end* that is an end *of nature* and not a practical end. Thus they supply natural science with the basis for a teleology, or, in other words, a mode of estimating its objects on a special principle that it would otherwise be absolutely unjustifiable to introduce into that science—seeing that we are quite unable to perceive *a priori* the possibility of such a kind of causality.

---

used for the constitution of the legal authorities and even of the entire body politic. For in a whole of this kind certainly no member should be a mere means, but should also be an end, and, seeing that he contributes to the possibility of the entire body, should have his position and function in turn defined by the idea of the whole.

§ 66.

The principle on which the intrinsic finality [relation to ends] in organisms is estimated.

This principle, the statement of which serves to define what is meant by organisms, is as follows: *an organized natural product is one in which every part is reciprocally both end and means.* In such a product nothing is in vain, without an end, or to be ascribed to a blind mechanism of nature.

It is true that the occasion for adopting this principle must be derived from experience—namely, from such experience as is methodically arranged and is called observation. But owing to the universality and necessity which that principle predicates of such finality, it cannot rest merely on empirical grounds, but must have some underlying *a priori* principle. This principle, however, may be one that is merely regulative, and it may be that the ends in question only reside in the idea of the person forming the estimate and not in any efficient cause whatever. Hence the above-named principle may be called a *maxim* for estimating the intrinsic finality of organisms.

It is common knowledge that scientists who dissect plants and animals, seeking to investigate their structure and to see into the reasons why and the end for which they are provided with such and such parts, why the parts have such and such a position and interconnection, and why the internal form is precisely what it is, adopt the above maxim as absolutely necessary. So they say that nothing in such forms of life is in *vain,* and they put the maxim on the same footing of validity as the fundamental principle of all natural science, that *nothing* happens *by chance.* They are, in fact, quite as unable to free themselves from this teleological principle as from that of general physical science. For just as the abandonment of the latter without any experience at all, so the abandonment of the former would leave them with no clue to assist their observation of a type of natural things that have once come to be thought under the concept of natural ends.

Indeed this concept leads reason into an order of things entirely 5:377 different from that of a mere mechanism of nature, since *mere mechanism* no longer proves adequate in this domain. An idea has to underlie the possibility of the natural product. But this idea is an absolute unity of the representation, whereas the material is a plurality of things that of itself can afford no definite unity of composition. Hence, if that unity of the idea is actually to serve as the *a priori* determining ground of a natural law of the causality of such a form of the composite, the end of nature must be made to extend to *everything* contained in its product. For once we lift such an effect out of the sphere of the blind mechanism of nature and relate it *as a whole* to a supersensible ground of determination, we must then consider it entirely on this principle. We have no reason for assuming the form of such a thing to be still partly dependent on blind mechanism, for with such confusion of heterogeneous principles every reliable rule for estimating things would disappear.

No doubt in an animal body, for example, many parts might be explained as accretions resulting from simple mechanical laws (as skin, bone, hair). Yet the cause that accumulates the appropriate material, modifies and fashions it, and deposits it in its proper place, must always be estimated teleologically. Hence, everything in the body must be regarded as organized, and everything, also, in a certain relation to the thing is itself in turn an organ.

§ 67.

The principle on which nature in general is estimated teleologically as a system of ends.

We have said above that the *extrinsic* finality of natural things affords no adequate justification for taking them as ends of nature to explain the reason of their existence, or for treating their accidentally final effects as ideally the grounds for their existence on the principle of final causes. Thus we are not entitled to consider *rivers* as natural ends then and there, because they facilitate international intercourse in inland countries, or *mountains,* because they contain the sources of the rivers and hold stores of snow for the mainte-

5:378 nance of their flow in dry seasons, or, similarly, the *slope* of the land, that carries down these waters and leaves the country dry. For, although this configuration of the earth's surface is very necessary for the origination and sustenance of the vegetable and animal kingdoms, yet intrinsically it contains nothing the possibility of which should make us feel obliged to invoke a causality according to ends. The same applies to plants utilized or enjoyed by man; or to animals, as the camel, the ox, the horse, dog, etc., which are so variously employed, sometimes as servants of man, sometimes as food for him to live on, and mostly found quite indispensable. The external relationship of things that we have no reason to regard as ends in their own right can only be hypothetically estimated as related to ends.

There is an essential distinction between estimating a thing as a natural end in virtue of its intrinsic form and regarding the real existence of this thing as an end of nature. To maintain the latter view we require, not merely the concept of a possible end, but a knowledge of the final end (*scopus*) of nature. This involves our referring nature to something supersensible, a reference that far transcends any teleological knowledge we have of nature; for, to find the end of the real existence of nature itself, we must look beyond nature. That the origin of a simple blade of grass is only possible on the rule of ends is, to our human critical faculty, sufficiently proved by its internal form. But let us lay aside this consideration and look only to the use to which the thing is put by other natural beings—which means that we abandon the study of the internal organization and look only to external adaptations to ends. We see, then, that the grass is required as a means of existence by cattle, and cattle similarly, by man. But we do not see why after all it should be necessary that men should in fact exist (a question that might not be so easy to answer if the specimens of humanity that we had in mind were, say, the New Hollanders or Fuegians). We do not then arrive in this way at any categorical end. On the contrary all this adaptation is made to rest on a condition that has to be removed to an ever-retreating horizon. This condition is the unconditioned condition—the existence of a thing is not a natural end either, since it (or its entire genus) is not to be regarded as a product of nature.

Hence it is only in so far as matter is organized that it necessarily involves conceiving of it as an end of nature, because here it possesses a form that is at once specific and a product of nature. 5:379 But, brought so far, this concept necessarily leads us to the idea of aggregate nature as a system following the rule of ends, to which idea, again, the whole mechanism of nature has to be subordinated on principles of reason—at least for the purpose of testing phenomenal nature by this idea. The principle of reason is one which it is competent for reason to use as a merely subjective principle, that is as a maxim: everything in the world is good for something or other; nothing in it is in vain; we are entitled, nay incited, by the example that nature affords us in its organic products, to expect nothing from it and its laws but what is related to ends or final when things are viewed as a whole.

It is evident that this is a principle to be applied not by the determinant, but only by the reflective, judgment, that it is regulative and not constitutive, and that all that we obtain from it is a clue to guide us in the study of natural things. These things it leads us to consider in relation to a ground of determination already given, and in the light of a new uniformity, and it helps us to extend physical science according to another principle, namely, that of final causes, yet without interfering with the principle of the mechanism of physical causality. Furthermore, this principle is altogether silent on the point of whether anything considered according to it is, or is not, an end of nature *by design:* whether, that is, the grass exists for the sake of the ox or the sheep, and whether these and the other things of nature exist for the sake of man. We do well to consider even things that are unpleasant to us, and that in particular connections are contrafinal, from this point of view also. Thus, for example, one might say that the vermin which plague men in their clothes, hair, or beds, may, by a wise provision of nature, be an incitement toward cleanliness, which is of itself an important means for preserving health. Or the mosquitoes and other stinging insects that make the wilds of America so trying for the savages may be so many goads to urge these primitive men to drain the marshes and bring light into the dense forests that shut out the air, and, by so doing, as well as by the tillage of the soil, to render their abodes more sanitary. Even what appears to man to be contrary to nature in his internal organization affords, when treated on these lines, an interesting, and sometimes even instructive, outlook into a teleological order of things, to which mere unaided study from a physical point of view apart from such a principle would not lead us. Some persons say that men or animals that have a tapeworm receive it as a sort of compensation to make good some deficiency in their vital organs. Now, just in the same way, I would ask if dreams (from which our sleep is never free, although we rarely remember what we have dreamed) may not be a regulation of nature adapted to ends. For when all the muscular forces of the body are relaxed dreams serve the purpose of internally stimulating the vital organs by means of the imagination and the great activity which it exerts—an activity that in this state generally rises to psychophysical agitation. This seems to be why imagination is usually more actively at work in the sleep of those who have gone to bed at night with a loaded stomach, just when this stimulation is most needed. Hence, I would suggest that without this internal stimulating force and fatiguing unrest that makes us complain of our dreams, which in fact, however, are probably curative, sleep, even in a sound state of health, would amount to a complete extinction of life.

Once the teleological estimate of nature, supported by the natural ends actually presented to us in organic beings, has entitled us to form the idea of a vast system of natural ends we may regard even natural beauty from this point of view, such beauty being an accordance of nature with the free play of our thinking faculties as engaged in grasping and estimating its appearance. For then we may look upon it as an objective finality of nature in its entirety as a system of which man is a member. We may regard it as a favor[8] that nature has extended to us, that besides giving us what is useful

8 In the Part on Aesthetics the statement was made: *we regard nature with favor,* because we take a delight in its form that is altogether free (disinterested). For in this judgment of mere taste no account is taken of any end for which these natural beauties exist: whether to excite pleasure in us, or irrespective of us as ends. But in a teleological judgment we pay attention to this relation; and so we can *regard it as a favor of nature,* that it has been disposed to promote our culture by exhibiting so many beautiful forms.

it has dispensed beauty and charms in such abundance, and for this we may love it, just as we view it with respect because of its immensity, and feel ourselves ennobled by such contemplation—just as if nature had erected and decorated its splendid state with this precise purpose in mind.

The general purport of the present section is simply this: once we have discovered a capacity in nature for bringing forth products that can only be thought by us according to the concept of final causes, we advance a step farther. Even products which do not (either as to themselves or the relation, however final, in which they stand) make it necessarily incumbent upon us to go beyond the mechanism of blind efficient causes and seek out some other principle on which they are possible, may nevertheless be justly esti- 5:381 mated as forming part of a system of ends. For the idea from which we started is one which, when we consider its foundation, already leads beyond the world of sense, and then the unity of the supersensible principle must be treated, not as valid merely for certain species of natural beings, but as similarly valid for the whole of nature as a system.

SECOND DIVISION
DIALECTIC OF TELEOLOGICAL JUDGMENT

5:385

§ 69.

Nature of an antinomy of judgment.

The *determinant* judgment does not possess as its own separate property any principles upon which *concepts of objects* are founded. It is not autonomous; for it *subsumes* merely under given laws, or concepts, as principles. Just for this reason it is not exposed to any danger from inherent antinomy and does not run the risk of a conflict of its principles. Thus transcendental judgment, which was shown to contain the conditions of subsumption under categories, was not independently *nomothetic.* It only specified the conditions of visualizing by the senses upon which reality, that is, application, can be provided for a given concept as a law of the intellect. In doing this, judgment could never fall into a state of internal disunion, at least in the matter of principles.

But the *reflecting* judgment has to subsume under a law that is not yet given. It has, therefore, in fact only a principle of reflection upon objects for which we are objectively at a complete loss for a law, or concept of the object, sufficient to serve as a principle covering the particular cases as they come before us. Now as there is no permissible employment of the thinking faculties apart from principles, the reflecting judgment must in such cases be a principle to itself. As this principle is not objective and is unable to introduce any basis of knowledge of the object sufficient for the required purpose of subsumption, it must serve as a mere subjective principle for the employment of our thinking faculties in a final manner, namely, for reflecting upon objects of a particular kind. The reflecting judgment provides, therefore, maxims applicable to such cases—maxims that are in fact necessary for obtaining a knowledge of the natural laws to be found in experience, and which are directed to assist us in attaining to concepts, be these even concepts of reason, wherever such concepts are absolutely required for the mere purpose of getting to know nature's empirical laws. Between these necessary maxims of the reflecting judgment a conflict may arise, and consequently an antinomy. This antinomy provides the basis of a dialectic; and if each of the mutually conflicting maxims has its foundation in the nature of our thinking faculties, this dialectic may be called a natural dialectic, which creates an unavoidable illusion which it is the duty of critical philosophy to expose and to resolve lest it should deceive us.

§ 70.

Exposition of this Antinomy.

In dealing with nature as the complex of objects of external sense, reason is able to rely upon laws, some of which are prescribed by the mind itself *a priori* to nature, while others are capable of indefinite extension by means of the empirical determinations occurring in experience. For the application of the laws prescribed *a priori* by the intellect, that is, of the *universal* laws of material nature in general, judgment does not need any special principle of reflection; for there it is determinant, an objective principle being furnished to it by the intellect. But in respect of the particular laws with which we can become acquainted through experience alone, there is such a wide scope for diversity and heterogeneity that judgment must be a principle to itself, even for the mere purpose of searching for a law and tracing one in the phenomena of nature. For it needs such a principle as a guiding thread, if it is even to hope for a consistent body of empirical knowledge based on a thoroughgoing uniformity of nature— that is a unity of nature in its empirical laws. Now from the fact of this accidental unity of particular laws it may come to pass that judgment acts upon two maxims in its reflection, one of which it receives *a priori* from mere intellect, but the other of which is prompted by particular experiences that bring reason into play to institute an estimate of corporeal nature and its laws according to a particular principle. What happens then is that these two different maxims seem to all appearance unable to be harmonized, and a dialectic arises that throws judgment into great confusion as to the principle of its reflection.

5:387

The first maxim of such reflection is the *thesis:* All production of material things and their forms must be estimated as possible on mere mechanical laws.

The second maxim is the *antithesis:* Some products of material nature cannot be estimated as possible on mere mechanical laws (that is, for estimating them quite a different law of causality is required; namely, that of final causes).

If now these regulative principles of investigation were converted into constitutive principles of the possibility of the objects themselves, they would read thus:

Thesis: All production of material things is possible on mere mechanical laws.

Antithesis: Some production of such things is not possible on mere mechanical laws.

In this latter form, as objective principles for the determinant judgment, they would contradict one another, so that one of the pair would necessarily be false. They would then form an antinomy certainly, though not one of judgment, but rather a conflict in the laws of reason. But reason is unable to prove either one or the other of these principles: seeing that we can have no *a priori* determining principle of the possibility of things [based] on mere empirical laws of nature.

On the other hand, looking at the maxims of a reflecting judgment as first set out, we see that they do not in fact contain any contradiction at all. For if I say: I must inquire into the possibility of all events in material nature, and, consequently, also all forms considered as its products, as resulting from mechanical laws, I do not thereby assert that they *are solely possible in this way*, that is, to the exclusion of every other kind of causality. On the contrary this assertion is only intended to indicate that I *ought* at all times to *reflect* upon these things *according to the principle* of the simple mechanism of nature, and, consequently, push my investigation with it as far as I can, because unless I make it the basis of research there can be no knowledge of nature in the true sense of the term at all. Now this does not stand in the way of the second maxim when a proper occasion for its employment presents itself—that is to say, in the case of some natural forms (and, at their instance, in the case of entire nature), we may, in our reflection upon them, follow the trail of a principle which is radically different from explanation by the mechanism of nature, namely, the principle of final causes. For re-flection according to the first maxim is not in this way superseded. On the contrary we are directed to pursue it as far as we can. Further it is not asserted that those forms were not possible as the result of the mechanism of nature. It is only maintained that *human reason*, adhering to this maxim and proceeding on these lines, could never discover a particle of foundation for what constitutes the specific character of a natural end, whatever additions it might make in this way to its knowledge of natural laws. This leaves it an open question, whether in the unknown inner basis of nature itself the physicomechanical and the final nexus present in the same things may not cohere in a single principle; it being only our reason that is not in a position to unite them in such a principle, so that our judgment, consequently, remains *reflective*, not determinant, that is,

5:388

acts on a subjective ground, and not according to an objective principle of the possibility of things in their inherent nature, and, accordingly, is compelled to conceive a different principle from that of the mechanism of nature as a ground of the possibility of certain forms in nature.

§ 71.

Introduction to the solution of the above antinomy.

We are wholly unable to prove the impossibility of the production of organized natural products in accordance with the simple mechanism of nature. For we cannot see into the first and inner ground of the infinite multiplicity of the particular laws of nature, which, being only known empirically, are for us contingent, and so we are absolutely incapable of reaching the intrinsic and all-sufficient principle of the possibility of a nature—a principle which lies in the supersensible. But may not the productive capacity of nature be just as adequate for what we estimate to be formed or connected according to the idea of ends as it is for what we believe merely calls for mechanical functions on the part of nature? Or may it be that in fact things are genuine natural ends (as we must necessarily estimate them to be), and as such founded upon an original causality of a completely different kind, which cannot be an incident of material nature or of its intelligible substratum, but instead are caused by a constructing mind? What has been said shows that there are questions upon which our reason, very narrowly restricted to the specific *a priori*, can give absolutely no answer. But that, relatively to our thinking faculties, the mere mechanism of nature is also unable to furnish any explanation of the creation of organisms, is a matter just as indubitably certain. *For the reflective judgment*, therefore, this is a perfectly sound principle: that for the clearly manifest nexus of things according to final causes, we must think a causality distinct from mechanism, namely, a world-cause acting according to ends, that is, an intelligent cause—however rash and undemonstrable a principle this might be *for the determinant judgment*. In the first case the principle is a simple maxim of

5:389

judgment. The concept of causality which it involves is a mere idea to which we in no way undertake to concede reality, but only make use of it as a guide to reflection that still leaves the door open for any available mechanical explanation, and that never strays from the world of sense. In the second case the principle would be an objective principle. Reason would prescribe it and judgment would have to be subject to it and be determined accordingly. But in that case reflection wanders from the world of sense into transcendent regions, and possibly gets led astray.

All semblance of an antinomy between the maxims of the strictly physical or mechanical mode of explanation and the teleological or constructive, rests, therefore, on our confusing a principle of the reflective with one of the determinant judgment. The *autonomy* of the former, which is valid merely subjectively for the use of our reason in respect of particular empirical laws, is mistaken for the *heteronomy* of the second, which has to conform to the laws, either universal or particular, given by the mind.

5:395

§ 74.

The impossibility of treating the concept of a construction of nature dogmatically springs from the inexplicability of a natural end.

Even though a concept is to be placed under an empirical condition we deal dogmatically with it, if we regard it as contained under another concept of the object—this concept forming a principle of reason—and determine it in accordance with the latter. But we deal merely critically with the concept if we only regard it in relation to our thinking faculties, and consequently to the subjective conditions of thinking it, without undertaking to decide anything as to its object. Hence the dogmatic treatment of a concept is treatment which is authoritative for the determinant judgment: the critical treatment is such as is authoritative merely for the reflective judgment.

5:396 Now the concept of a thing as a natural end is one that subsumes nature under a causality that is only thinkable by the aid of reason, and so subsumes it for the purpose of letting us judge of what is given of the object in experience [on the basis of] this principle. But in order to make use of this concept dogmatically for the determinant judgment we should have first to be assured of its objective reality, as otherwise we could not subsume any natural thing under it. The concept of a thing as a natural end is, however, certainly one that is empirically conditioned, that is, is one only possible under certain conditions given in experience. Yet it is not one to be abstracted from these conditions, but, on the contrary, it is only possible [if based] on a rational principle in the estimating of the object. We have no insight into the objective reality of such a principle, that is to say, we cannot perceive that an object answering to it is possible. We cannot establish it dogmatically; and we do not know whether it is a mere logical fiction and an objectively empty concept (*conceptus ratiocinans*), or whether it is a rational concept, supplying a basis of knowledge and substantiated by reason (*conceptus ratiocinatus*). Hence it cannot be treated dogmatically on behalf of the determinant judgment. In other words, not only is it impossible to decide whether or not things of nature, considered as natural ends, require for their production a causality of a quite peculiar kind, namely, an intentional causality, but the very question is quite out of order. For the concept of a natural end cannot at all be proved by reason to have objective reality, which means that it is not constitutive for the determinant judgment, but merely regulative for the reflective judgment.

That a natural end is not provable is clear from the following considerations. Being a concept of a *natural product* it involves necessity. Yet it also involves in one and the same thing, considered as an end, an accompanying fortuitousness in the form of the object in respect of mere laws of nature. Hence, if it is to escape self-contradiction, besides containing a basis of the possibility of the thing in nature it must further contain a basis of the possibility of this nature itself and of its reference to something that is not an empirically understandable nature, namely to something supersensible, and, therefore, to what is not understandable by us at all. Otherwise in judging of its possibility, we should not have to estimate it in the light of a kind of causality different from that of natural mechanism. Accordingly the concept of a thing as a natural end is transcendent *for the determinant judgment* if its object is viewed by reason—albeit for the reflective judgment it may be immanent in respect of objects of experience. Objective reality, therefore, cannot be procured for it on behalf of the determinant judgment. Hence we can understand how it is that all systems that are devised with a view to the dogmatic treatment of the concept of natural ends or of nature as a whole as owing its consistency and coherence to final causes, fail to settle anything whatever either by their objective affirmations or by their objective denials. For, if things are subsumed under a concept that is merely problematic, the synthetic predicates attached to this concept—as, for example, in the present case, whether the natural end which we suppose for the production of the thing is designed or undesigned—must yield judgments about the object of a like problematic character, be they affirmative or negative, since one does not know whether one is judging about what is something or nothing. The concept of a causality through ends, that is, ends of art, has certainly objective reality, just as that of a causality according to the mechanism of nature has. But the concept of a natural causality following the rule of ends, and still more of such a Being as is utterly incapable of being given to us in experience—a Being regarded as the original creator of nature—while it may no doubt be thought without self-contradiction, is nevertheless useless for the purpose of dogmatic definitive assertions. For, since it is incapable of being extracted from experience, and besides is unnecessary for its possibility, there is nothing that can give any guarantee of its objective reality. But even if this could be assured, how can I count among products of nature things that are definitely posited as products of divine art, when it was the very incapacity of nature to produce such things according to its own laws that necessitated the appeal to a cause distinct from nature?

sible to encounter the appropriateness of nature along this road, but only on the ground that it is impossible *for us* as men. For in order to get results along this line of investigation we should require a capacity of looking-at-things different from our senses and a determinate knowledge of the intelligible substratum of nature from which we could show the reason of the very mechanism of phenomena and their particular laws. But this wholly surpasses our capacity.

So where it is established beyond question that the concept of a natural end applies to things, as in the case of organized beings, if the naturalist is not to throw his labor away, he must always in forming an estimate of them accept some original organization or other as fundamental. He must consider that this organization avails itself of the very mechanism above mentioned for the purpose of producing other organic forms, or for evolving new structures from those given—such new structures, however, always issuing from and in accordance with the end in question.

It is praiseworthy to employ a comparative anatomy and go through the vast creation of organized beings in order to see if there is not discoverable in it some trace of a system, and indeed of a system following a genetic principle. For otherwise we should be obliged to content ourselves with the mere critical principle—which tells us nothing that gives any insight into the production of such beings—and to abandon in despair all claim to *insight into nature* in this field. When we consider the agreement of so many genera of animals in a certain common schema, which apparently underlies not only the structure of their bones, but also the disposition of their remaining parts, and when we find here the wonderful simplicity of the original plan, which has been able to produce such an immense variety of species by the shortening of one member and the lengthening of another, by the involution of this part and the evolution of that, there gleams upon the mind a ray of hope, however faint, that the principle of the mechanism of nature, apart from which there can be no natural science at all, may yet enable us to arrive at some explanation in the course of organic life. This analogy of forms, which in all their differences seem to be produced in accordance with a common type, strengthens the suspicion that they have an actual kinship due to descent from a common parent. This we might trace in the gradual approximation of one animal species to another, from that in which the principle of 5:419 ends seems best authenticated, namely, from man, back to the polyp, and from this back even to mosses and lichens, and finally to the lowest perceptible stage of nature. Here we come to crude matter; and from this, and the forces which it exerts in accordance with mechanical laws (laws resembling those by which it acts in the formation of crystals) seems to be developed the whole construction of nature which, in the case of organized beings, is so incomprehensible to us that we feel obliged to imagine a different principle for its explanation.

Here the archaeologist of nature is at liberty to go back to the traces that remain of nature's earliest revolutions, and, appealing to all he knows of or can conjecture about its mechanism, to trace the genesis of that great family of living things (for it must be pictured as a family if there is to be any foundation for the consistently coherent affinity mentioned). He can suppose that the womb of mother earth as it first emerged, like a huge animal, from its chaotic state, gave birth to creatures whose form displayed less relation to ends, that these bore others which adapted themselves more perfectly to their native surroundings and their relations to each other, until this womb, becoming rigid and ossified, restricted its birth to definite species incapable of further modification, and the multiplicity of forms was fixed as it stood when the operation of that fruitful formative power had ceased. Yet, for all that, he is obliged eventually to attribute to this universal mother an organization suitably constituted with a view to all these forms of life, for unless he does so, the possibility of the final form of the products of the animal and plant kingdoms is quite unthinkable.[9] But when he does attribute all this to 5:420

9 An hypothesis of this kind may be called a daring venture on the part of reason; and 5:419 there are probably few even among the most acute scientists to whose minds it has not sometimes occurred. For it cannot be said to be absurd, like the *generatio aequivoca*, which means the generation of an organized being from crude inorganic matter. It never ceases to be *generatio univoca* in the widest acceptation of the word, as it only implies the generation of some-

nature he has only pushed the explanation a stage farther back. He cannot pretend to have made the genesis of those two kingdoms intelligible independently of the condition of final causes.

Even as regards the alteration which certain individuals of the organized genera contingently undergo, where we find that the character thus altered is transmitted and taken up into the generative power, we can form no other plausible estimate of it than that it is an occasional development of a purposive capacity originally present in the species with a view to the preservation of the race. For in the complete inner appropriateness of an organized being, the generation of its like is intimately associated with the condition that nothing shall be taken up into the generative force which does not also belong, in such a system of ends, to one of its undeveloped native capacities. Once we depart from this principle we cannot know with certainty whether many constituents of the form at present found in a species may not be of equally accidental and purposeless origin, and the principle of teleology, that nothing in an organized being which is preserved in the propagation of the species should be estimated as devoid of a relation to ends, would be made very unreliable and could only hold good for the parent stock, to which our knowledge does not go back.

In reply to those who feel obliged to adopt a teleological principle of critical judgment, that is of constructing intellect in the case of all such natural ends, Hume raises the objection that one might ask with equal justice how such an intellect is itself possible. By this he means that one may also ask how it is possible that there should be such a teleological coincidence in one being of the manifold

---

thing organic from something else that is also organic, although, within the class of organic beings, differing specifically from it. It would be as if we supposed that certain water animals transformed themselves by degrees into marsh animals, and from these after some generations into land animals. In the judgment of plain reason there is nothing *a priori* self-contradictory in this. But experience offers no example of it. On the contrary, as far as experience goes, all generation known to us is *generatio bomonyma*. It is not merely *univoca* in contradistinction to generation from an unorganized substance, but it brings forth a product which in its very organization is of like kind with that which produced it, and a *generatio beteronyma* is not met with anywhere within the range of our experience.

faculties and properties presupposed in the very concept of a mind possessing at once intellectual and executive capacity. But there is nothing in this point. For the whole difficulty that besets the question as to the genesis of a thing that involves ends (purposes) and that is solely comprehensible by their means rests upon the demand for unity in the source of the synthesis of the multiplicity of *externally existing* elements in this product. For, if this source is to be understood as a simple substance regarded as a productive cause, the above question, as a teleological problem, is abundantly answered, whereas if the cause is merely sought in matter, as an aggregate of many externally existing substances, the unity of principle requisite for the intrinsically end-related form of its complex structures is wholly absent. The *autocracy* of matter in productions that by our understanding are only conceivable as ends is a word with no meaning. 5:421

This is the reason why those who look for a supreme ground of the possibility of the objectively end-related forms of matter, and yet do not concede an intellect to this ground, choose nevertheless to make the universe either an all-embracing substance (Pantheism), or else—and this is only the preceding in more refined form—a complex of many determinations inhering in a single *simple substance* (Spinozism). Their object is to derive from this substance that *unity* which all relation to ends presupposes. And in fact, thanks to their purely ontological concept of a simple substance, they really do something to satisfy *one* condition of the problem—namely, that of the unity implied in the reference to an end. But they have nothing to say on the subject of the *other* condition, namely, the relation of the substance to its consequence regarded as an *end*, this relation being what gives to their ontological ground the more precise determination which the problem demands. The result is that they in no way answer the *entire* problem. For our intellect the problem is absolutely unanswerable except on the following terms. First, the original source of things must be pictured by us as a simple substance. Then its attribute, as a simple substance, in its relation to the specific character of the natural forms whose source it is, i.e., the character of unity through ends, must be pictured as the attribute of an intelligent substance. Lastly, the relation of this intelligent substance to the natural forms must, owing to the contingency which we find in everything which we imagine to be possible only as an end, be pictured as one of causality.

§ 81.

The association of mechanism with the teleological principle
which we apply to the explanation of an end of nature
considered as a product of nature.

5:422 We have seen from the preceding section that the mechanism of nature is not sufficient to enable us to conceive the possibility of an organized being, but that in its root origin it must be subordinated to a cause acting by design—or, at least, that the type of our thinking faculty is such that we must conceive it to be so subordinated. But just as little can the mere teleological source of a being of this kind enable us to consider and to estimate it as at once an end and a product of nature. With that teleological source we must further associate the mechanism of nature as a sort of instrumental cause acting by design and contemplating an end to which nature is subordinated even in its mechanical laws. The possibility of such a union of two completely different types of causality, namely, that of nature in its universal conformity to law and that of an idea which restricts nature to a particular from of which nature, as nature, is in no way the source, is something which our reason does not comprehend. For it resides in the supersensible substratum of nature, of which we are unable to make any definite affirmation, further than that it is the self-subsistent being of which we know merely the phenomenon. Yet, for all that, this principle remains in full and undiminished force, and everything which we assume to form part of phenomenal nature and to be its product must be thought as linked with nature by mechanical laws. For, apart from this type of causality, organized beings, although they are ends of nature, would not be natural products.

Now suppose we adopt the teleological principle of the production of organized beings, as indeed we cannot avoid doing, we may then base their internal form as related to ends either on the *occasionalism* or on the *pre-establishment* of the cause. According to occasionalism the Supreme Cause of the world would directly supply on the occasion of each impregnation the organic formation, stamped with the impress of His idea, to the commingling substances united in the generative process. On the premise of preestablishment the Supreme Cause would only endow the original products of His wisdom with the inherent capacity by means of which an organized being produces another after its own kind, and the species preserves its continuous existence, while the loss of individuals is ever being repaired through the agency of a nature that concurrently labors toward their destruction. If the occasionalism of the production of organized beings is assumed, all co-operation of nature in the process is entirely lost, and no room is left for the exercise of reason in judging of the possibility of products of this kind. So we may take it for granted that one will embrace this system who cares anything for philosophy.

Again the system of pre-establishment may take either of two forms. Thus it treats every organized being produced from one of 5:423 its own kind either as its *educt* or as its *product.* The system which regards the generations as educts is termed that of *individual preformation,* or, sometimes, the *theory of evolution;* that which regards them as products is called the system of *epigenesis.* The latter may also be called the system of *generic preformation,* inasmuch as it regards the productive capacity of the parents, in respect of the inner final tendency that would be part of their original stock, and, therefore, the specific form, as still having been *virtualiter* preformed. On this statement the opposite theory of individual preformation might also more appropriately be called the *theory of involution* (or *encasement*).

The advocates of the *theory of evolution* exclude all individuals from the formative force of nature, for the purpose of deriving them directly from the hand of the Creator. Yet they would not venture to describe the occurrence on the lines of the hypothesis of occasionalism, so as to make the impregnation an idle formality, which takes place whenever a supreme intelligent Cause of the world has made up His mind to form a foetus directly with His own hand and relegate to the mother the mere task of developing and nourishing it. They would avow adherence to the theory of preformation; as if it were not a matter of indifference whether a supernatural origin of such forms is allowed to take place at the start or in the course of the world-process. They fail to see that in fact a whole host of supernatural contrivances would be spared by acts of creation as occasion arose, which would be required if an embryo formed at the beginning of the world had to be preserved from the destructive forces of nature, and had to keep safe and sound all through the long ages till the day arrived for its development, and also that an incalculably greater number of such preformed entities would be created than would be destined ever to develop, and that all those would be so many creations thus rendered superfluous and in vain. Yet they would like to leave nature some role in these operations, so as not to lapse into an unmitigated hyperphysics that can dispense with all explanation on naturalistic lines. Of course they would still remain unshaken in their hyperphysics; so much so that they would discover even in abortions—which yet cannot possibly be deemed ends of nature—a marvelous appropriateness, even if directed to no better purpose than that of being a meaningless employment intended to put some chance anatomist at his wit's end, and make him fall on his knees with admiration. However, they would be absolutely unable to make the generation of hybrids fit in with the system of preformation, but would be compelled to allow to the seed of the male creature, to which in other cases they had denied all but the mechanical property of serving as the first means of nourishment for the embryo, a further and additional 5:424 formative force directed to ends. And yet they would not concede this force to either of the two parents when dealing with the complete product of two creatures of the same genus.

As against this, even supposing we failed to see the enormous advantage on the side of the advocate of *epigenesis* in the matter of empirical evidence in support of his theory, still we should at the outset be strongly prepossessed in favor of his line of explanation. For as regards things the possibility of whose origin can only be represented to the mind according to a causality of ends, epigenesis none the less regards nature as at least itself productive in respect of the continuation of the process, and not as merely unraveling something. Thus with the least possible expenditure of the supernatural it entrusts to nature the explanation of all steps subsequent to the original beginning, which is what baffles all the attempts of physics, no matter what chain of causes it adopts.

No one has rendered more valuable services in connection with this theory of epigenesis than Herr Hofrat Blumenbach. This is as true of what he has done toward establishing the correct principles of its application—partly by setting due bounds to an over-liberal employment of it—as it is of his contributions to its proof. He makes organic substance the starting point for physical explanations of these formations. For to suppose that crude matter, obeying mechanical laws, was originally its own architect, that life could have sprung up from the nature of what is void of life, and matter have spontaneously adopted the form of a self-maintaining finality, he justly declares to be contrary to reason. But at the same time he leaves to the mechanism of nature, in its subordination to this inscrutable *principle* of a primordial *organization,* an indeterminable yet also unmistakable function. The capacity of matter here required he terms—in contradistinction to the simply mechanical *formative force* universally residing in it—in the case of an organized body a *formative impulse,* standing, so to speak, under the higher guidance and direction of the above principle.

§ 82.

5:425

The teleological system in the extrinsic relations of organisms.

By extrinsic appropriateness I mean the appropriateness that exists where one thing in nature serves another as a means to an end. Now even things which do not possess any intrinsic relevancy, and whose possibility does not imply any, such as earth, air, water, and the like, may nevertheless be extrinsically, that is in relation to other beings, very well adapted to ends. But then those other beings must in all cases be organized, that is be nature's ends, for unless they are ends the former could not be considered means. Thus water, air, and earth cannot be regarded as means to the upgrowth of mountains. For intrinsically there is nothing in mountains that calls for their being a source of somehow possibly serving ends. Hence their cause can never be referred to such a source and represented under the predicate of a means subservient thereto.

Extrinsic appropriateness is an entirely different concept from that of intrinsic appropriateness, the latter being connected with the possibility of an object irrespective of whether its actuality is itself an end or not. In the case of an organism we may further inquire: For what end does it exist? But we can hardly do so in the case of things in which we recognize the simple effect of the mechanism of nature. The reason is that in the case of organisms we have already pictured to ourselves a causality according to ends—a creative intellect—to account for their intrinsic appropriateness, and have referred this active faculty to its determining ground, the design. There is one extrinsic appropriateness which is the single exception—and it is intimately bound up with the intrinsic purpose of an organization. This case does not leave open the question as to the end for which the nature so organized must have existed, and yet it is an extrinsic relation of a means to an end. This is the organization of the two sexes in their mutual relation with a view to the propagation of their species. For here we may always ask, just as in the case of an individual: Why was it necessary for such a pair to exist? The answer is: In this pair we have what first forms an *organizing* whole, though not an organized whole in a single body.

Now when it is asked to what end a thing exists, the answer may take one of two forms. It may be said that its existence and generation have no relation whatever to a cause acting designedly. Its origin is then understood to be always derived from the mechanism of nature. Or it may be said that its existence, being that of a contingent natural entity, has some ground or other involving design. And this is a thought which it is difficult for us to separate from the concept of a thing that is organized. For inasmuch as we are compelled to rest its intrinsic possibility on the causality of final causes and an idea underlying this causality, we cannot but think that the real ex-

5:426

istence of this product is also an end. For where the imagining of an effect is at the same time the ground determining an intelligent efficient cause to its production, the effect so imagined is termed an *end*. Here, therefore, we may either say that the end of the real existence of a natural being of this kind is inherent in itself, that is, that it is not merely an end, but also a *final end;* or we may say that the final end lies outside it in other natural beings, that is, that its real existence, which is adapted to ends, is not itself a final end, but is necessitated by its being at the same time a means.

But if we go through the whole of nature we do not find in it, as nature, any being capable of laying claim to the distinction of being the final end of creation. In fact it may even be proved *a priori,* that what might do perhaps as an *ultimate end* for nature, endowing it with any conceivable qualities or properties we choose, could nevertheless in its character of a natural thing never be a final end.

Looking to the vegetable kingdom we might at first be induced by the boundless fertility with which it spreads itself abroad upon almost every soil to think that it should be regarded as a mere product of the mechanism which nature displays in its formations in the mineral kingdom. But a more intimate knowledge of its indescribably wise organization precludes us from entertaining this view, and drives us to ask: For what purpose do these forms of life exist? Suppose we reply: For the animal kingdom, which is thus provided with the means of sustenance, so that it has been enabled to spread over the face of the earth in such a manifold variety of genera. The question again arises: For what purpose then do these herbivora exist? The answer would be something like this: For the carnivora, which are only able to live on what itself has animal life. At last we get down to the question: What is the end and purpose of these and all the preceding natural kingdoms? Man, we say, and the multifarious uses to which his intelligence teaches him to put all these forms of life. He is the ultimate end of creation here upon earth, because he is the one and only being upon it that is able to form a concept of ends, and from an aggregate of things purposively fash- 5:427 ioned is able to construct by the aid of his reason a system of ends.

We might also follow the Chevalier Linné and take the seemingly opposite course. Thus we might say: The herbivorous animals exist for the purpose of checking the profuse growth of the vegetable kingdom by which many species of that kingdom would be choked; the carnivora for the purpose of setting bounds to the voracity of the herbivora; and finally man exists so that by pursuing the latter and reducing their numbers a certain equilibrium between the productive and destructive forces of nature may be established. So, on this view, however much man might in a certain relation be esteemed as end, in a different relation he would in turn only rank as a means.

If we adopt the principle of an objective relation to ends in the manifold variety of the specific forms of terrestrial life and in their extrinsic relations to one another as beings with a structure adapted to ends, it is only reasonable to go on and imagine that in this extrinsic relation there is also a certain organization and a system of the whole kingdom of nature related to ends as causes. But experience seems here to give the lie to the maxim of reason more especially as regards an ultimate end of nature—an end which nevertheless is necessary to the possibility of such a system, and which we can only place in man. For, so far from making man, regarded as one of the many animal species, an ultimate end, nature has no more exempted him from its destructive than from its productive forces, nor has it made the smallest exception to its subjection of everything to a mechanism of forces devoid of an end.

The first thing that would have to be expressly arranged in a system ordered with a view to a final whole of natural beings upon the earth would be their habitat—the soil or the element upon or in which they are intended to thrive. But a more intimate knowledge of the nature of this basal condition of all organic production shows no trace of any causes but those acting altogether without design, and in fact tending toward destruction rather than calculated to promote genesis of forms, order, and ends. Land and sea not alone contain memorials of mighty primeval disasters that have overtaken both them and all their brood of living forms, but their entire structure—the strata of the land and the coast lines of the 5:428 sea—has all the appearance of being the outcome of the wild and all-subduing forces of a nature working in a state of chaos. However wisely the configuration, elevation and slope of the land may now seem to be adapted for the reception of water from the air, for the subterranean channels of the springs that well up between the diverse layers of earth (suitable for various products) and for the course of the rivers, yet a closer investigation of them shows that they have resulted simply as the effect partly of volcanic eruptions, partly of floods, or even invasions of the ocean. And this is not alone true as regards the genesis of this configuration, but more particularly of its subsequent transformation, attended with the disappearance of its primitive organic productions.[10] If now the abode for all these forms of life—the lap of the land and the bosom of the deep—points to none but a wholly undesigned mechanical generation, how can we, or what right have we to ask for or to maintain a different origin for these latter products? And even if man, as the most minute examination of the remains of those devastations of nature seems, in Camper's judgment, to prove, was not comprehended in such revolutions, yet his dependence upon the remaining forms of terrestrial life is such that, if a mechanism of nature whose power overrides these others is admitted, he must be regarded as included within its scope, although his intelligence, to a large extent at least, has been able to save him from its work of destruction.

But this argument seems to go beyond what it was directed to prove. For it would seem to show not merely that man could not be an ultimate end of nature, or, for the same reason, the aggregate of the organized things of terrestrial nature be a system of ends, but

10 If the name of *natural history*, now that it has once been adopted, is to continue to be used for the description of nature, we may give the name of *archaeology* of *nature*, as contrasted with art, to that which the former literally indicates, namely, an account of the bygone or *ancient* state of the earth—a matter on which, though we dare not hope for any certainty, we have good ground for conjecture. Fossil remains would be objects for the archaeology of nature, just as rudely cut stones, and things of that kind, would be for the archaeology of art. For, as work is actually being done in this department, under the name of a theory of the earth, steadily though, as we might expect, slowly, this name would not be given to a purely imaginary study of nature, but to one to which nature itself invites and summons us.

that even the products of nature previously deemed to be ends of nature could have no other origin than the mechanism of nature.

5:429   But, then, we must bear in mind the results of the solution above given of the antinomy of the principles of the mechanical and teleological generation of organic natural beings. These principles, as we there saw, are merely principles of reflective judgment in respect of formative nature and its particular laws, the key to whose systematic correlation is not in our possession. They tell us nothing definite as to the origin of the things in their own intrinsic nature. They only assert that by the constitution of our understanding and our reason we are unable to conceive the origin in the case of beings of this kind otherwise than in the light of end-related causes. The utmost persistence, nay even a boldness, is allowed us in our endeavors to explain them on mechanical lines. More than that, we are even summoned by reason to do so, albeit we know we can never complete such an explanation—not because there is an inherent inconsistency between the mechanical generation and an origin according to ends, but for subjective reasons involved in the particular type and limitations of our intellect. Lastly, we saw that the reconciliation of the two modes of picturing the possibility of nature might easily lie in the supersensible principle of nature, both external and internal. For the imagining based on end-related causes is only a subjective condition of the exercise of our reason in cases where reason is not merely seeking the proper estimate to be made of objects arranged as phenomena, but is bent rather on referring these phenomena, principles and all, to their supersensible substratum, for the purpose of recognizing the possibility of certain laws of their unity, which are capable of being figured by the mind only as means toward an end (of which reason also possesses examples of the supersensible type).

§ 83.

The ultimate end of nature as a teleological system.

We have shown in the preceding section that, looking to principles of reason, there is ample ground—for the reflective, though not of course for the determinant, judgment—to make us consider man as not merely an end of nature, such as all organized beings are, but as the being upon this earth who is the *ultimate end* of nature, and the one in relation to whom all other natural things constitute a system of ends. What now is the end in man, and the end which, as such, is intended to be promoted by means of his connection with nature? If this end is something which must be found in man himself, it must either be of such a kind that man himself may be satisfied as a result of nature and its beneficence, or else it is the aptitude and skill for all manner of ends for which he may employ nature both external and internal. The former end of nature would be the *happiness* of man, the latter his *culture*.

The concept of happiness is not one which man abstracts more or less from his instincts and so derives from his animal nature. It is, on the contrary, a mere *idea* of a state, and one to which he seeks to make his actual state of being adequate under purely empirical conditions—an impossible task. He projects this idea himself, and, thanks to his intellect and its complicated relations with imagination and sense, projects it in such different ways, and even alters his concept so often, that were nature a complete slave to his elective will, it would nevertheless be utterly unable to adopt any definite, universal and fixed law by which to accommodate itself to this fluctuating concept and so bring itself into accord with the end that each individual arbitrarily sets before himself. But even if we sought to reduce this concept to the level of the true wants of nature in which our species is in complete and fundamental accord, or, trying the other alternative, sought to increase to the highest level man's skill in reaching his imagined ends, nevertheless what man means by happiness, and what in fact constitutes his peculiar ultimate physical end, as opposed to the end of freedom, would never be attained by him. For his own nature is not so constituted as to rest or be satisfied in any possession or enjoyment whatever. Also external nature is far from having made a particular favorite of man or from having preferred him to all other animals as the object of its beneficence. For we see that in its destructive operations—plague, famine, flood, cold, attacks from animals great and small,

5:430

and all such things—it has as little spared him as any other animal. But, besides all this, the discord of inner *natural tendencies* betrays man into further misfortunes of his own invention, and reduces other members of his species, through the oppression of lordly power, the barbarism of wars, and the like, to such misery, while he himself does all he can to work ruin to his race, that, even with the 5:431 utmost goodwill on the part of external nature, its end, supposing it were directed to the happiness of our species, would never be attained in a system of terrestrial nature, because our own nature is not capable of it. Man, therefore, is ever but a link in the chain of nature's ends. True, he is a principle in respect of many ends to which nature seems to have predetermined him, seeing that he makes himself so; but, nevertheless, he is also a means toward the preservation of the appropriateness in the mechanism of the remaining members. As the single being upon earth that possesses intellect, and, consequently, a capacity for setting before himself ends of his deliberate choice, he is certainly titular lord of nature, and, supposing we regard nature as a teleological system, he is born to be its ultimate end [goal]. But this is always on condition that he has the intelligence and the will to give to nature and to himself such ends as can be self-sufficing independently of nature, and, consequently, [can constitute] a final end. Such an end, however, must not be sought in nature.

But where in man, at any rate, are we to place this *ultimate end* of nature? To discover this we must seek out what nature can supply for the purpose of preparing him for what he himself must do in order to be a final end, and we must segregate it from all ends whose possibility rest upon conditions that man can only expect at the hand of nature. Earthly happiness is an end of the latter kind. It is understood to mean the complex of all possible human ends attainable through nature whether in man or external to him. In other words it is the material substance of all his earthly ends and what, if he converts it into his sole end, renders him incapable of positing a final end [aim] for his own real existence and of harmonizing them. Therefore of all his ends in nature, we are left only with a formal, subjective condition, namely, that of the aptitude for setting goals before himself at all, and, independent of nature in his power of determining goals, of employing nature as a means in accordance with the maxims of his free goals generally. This alone remains of what nature can effect relative to the final end that lies outside it, and of what may therefore be regarded as its ultimate end. The development in a rational being of an aptitude for any ends whatever of his own choosing, consequently of being able to use his freedom, is *culture*. Hence it is only culture that can be the ultimate end which we have cause to attribute to nature in respect of the human race. His individual happiness on earth, and, we may say, the mere fact that he is the chief instrument for instituting order and harmony in irrational external nature, are ruled out.

But not every form of culture can fill the function of this ultimate end [purpose] of nature. *Skill* is a culture that is certainly the principal subjective condition of the aptitude for the furthering of ends of all kinds, yet it is incompetent for giving assistance to the 5:432 *will* in its determination and choice of its ends. But this is an essential factor, if an aptitude for ends [goals] is to have its full meaning. This latter condition of aptitude, involving what might be called culture by way of discipline, is negative. It consists in the liberation of the will from the despotism of desires whereby, in our attachment to certain natural things, we are rendered incapable of exercising a choice of our own. This happens when we allow ourselves to be enchained by impulses with which nature only provided us that they might serve as leading strings to prevent our neglecting, or even impairing, the animal element in our nature, while yet we are left free enough to tighten or slacken them, to lengthen or shorten them, as the ends of our reason may dictate.

Skill can hardly be developed in the human race otherwise than by means of inequality among men. For the majority, in a mechanical kind of way that calls for no special art, provide the necessaries of life for the ease and convenience of others who apply themselves to the less necessary branches of culture in science and art. These keep the masses in a state of oppression, with hard work and little enjoyment, though in the course of time much of the culture of the higher classes spreads to them also. But with the advance of this culture—the culminating point of which, where devotion to what is superfluous begins to be prejudicial to what is indispensable, is called luxury—misfortunes increase equally on both sides. With the lower classes they arise by force of domination from without, with the upper from seeds of discontent within. Yet this splendid misery is connected with the development of natural tendencies in the human race, and the end pursued by nature itself, though it be not our end, is thereby attained. The formal condition under which nature can alone attain this, its real end, is the existence of a constitution so regulating the mutual relations of men that the abuse of freedom by individuals striving one against another is opposed by a lawful authority centered in a whole, called a *civil community*. For it is only in such a constitution that the greatest development of natural tendencies can take place. In addition to this we should also need a *cosmopolitan* whole—had men but the ingenuity to discover

5:433   such a constitution and the wisdom voluntarily to submit themselves to its constraint. It would be a system of all states that are in danger of acting injuriously to one another. In its absence, and with the obstacles that ambition, love of power, and avarice, especially on the part of those who hold the reins of authority, put in the way even of the possibility of such a scheme, *war* is inevitable. Sometimes this results in states splitting up and resolving themselves into lesser states, sometimes one state absorbs other smaller states and endeavors to build up a larger unit. But if on the part of men war is a thoughtless undertaking, being stirred up by unbridled passions, it is nevertheless a deep-seated, maybe far-seeing, attempt on the part of supreme wisdom, ... to prepare the way for a rule of law governing the freedom of states, and thus bring about their unity in a system established on a moral basis. And, in spite of the terrible calamities which it inflicts on the human race, and the hardships, perhaps even greater, imposed by the constant preparation for it in time of peace, yet—as the prospect of the dawn of an abiding reign of national happiness keeps ever retreating farther into the distance—it is one further spur for developing to the highest pitch all talents that minister to culture.

We turn now to the discipline of inclinations. In respect of these our natural equipment is very purposively adapted to the performance of our essential functions as an animal species, but they are a great impediment to the development of our humanity. Yet here again, in respect of this second requisite for culture, we see nature striving on purposive lines to give us that education which opens the door to higher ends than it can itself afford. The preponderance of evil is indisputable which a taste refined to the extreme of idealization, and which even luxury in the sciences, considered as food for vanity, diffuses among us as the result of the mass of insatiable inclinations which they beget. But, while that is so, we cannot fail to recognize the end of nature—ever more and more to prevail over the rudeness and violence of inclinations that belong more to the animal part of our nature and are most inimical to an education that would fit us for our higher vocation (inclinations toward enjoyment), and to make way for the development of our humanity. Fine art and the sciences, if they do not make man morally better, yet, by conveying a pleasure that admits of universal communication and by introducing polish and refinement into society, make him civilized. Thus they do much to overcome the tyrannical propensities of sense, and so prepare man for a sovereignty in which reason alone shall have sway. Meanwhile the evils visited upon us, now by nature, now by the truculent egoism of man, evoke the energies of the soul, and give it strength and courage to submit to no such 5:434 force, and at the same time quicken in us a sense that in the depths of our nature there is an aptitude for higher ends.[11]

11 The value of life for us, measured simply by *what we enjoy* (by the natural end of the sum of all our inclinations, that is, by happiness), is easy to decide. It is less than nothing. For who would enter life afresh under the same conditions? Who would even do so according to a new, self-devised plan (which should, however, follow the course of nature), if it also were merely directed to enjoyment? We have shown above what value life receives from what it involves when lived according to the end with which nature is occupied in us, and which consists in *what we do*, not merely what we enjoy, we being, however, in that case always but a means to an undetermined final end. There remains then nothing but the worth which we ourselves assign to our life by what we not alone do, but do with a view to an end so independent of nature that the very existence of nature itself can only be an end subject to the condition so imposed.

§ 84.

The final end of the existence of a world, that is, of creation itself.

A *final end* [ultimate purpose] is an end that does not require any other end as condition of its possibility.

If the simple mechanism of nature is accepted as the explanation of the point of it all, it is not open to us to ask: For what end do the things in the world exist? For in such an imagined system we have only to reckon with the physical possibility of things—and things that it would be mere empty sophistry to imagine as ends. Whether we refer this form of things to chance, or whether we refer it to blind necessity, such a question would in either case be meaningless. But if we suppose the final nexus in the world to be real, and assume a special type of causality for it, namely, the activity of a cause *acting designedly,* we cannot then stop short at the question: What is the end for which things in the world, namely, organized beings, possess this or that form, or are placed by nature in this or that relation to other things? On the contrary, once we have conceived an intellect that must be regarded as the cause of the possibility of such forms as they are actually found in things, we must go on and seek in this intellect for an objective ground capable of determining such creative intellectual power for producing an effect of this kind. That ground is then the final end for which such things exist.

I have said above that the final end is not an end which nature would be competent to realize or produce in terms of its idea, because it is one that is unconditioned. For in nature, as a thing of sense, there is nothing whose determining ground, discoverable in nature itself, is not always in turn conditioned. This is not merely true of external or material nature, but also of internal or thinking nature—it being of course understood that I am only considering what in us is strictly nature. But a thing, which by virtue of its objective characterization is to exist necessarily as the final end of an intelligent cause, must be of such a kind that in the order of ends it

5:435

is dependent upon no further or other condition than simply its idea.

Now we have in the world beings of but one kind whose causality is teleological, or directed to ends, and which at the same time are beings of such a character that the law according to which they have to determine ends for themselves is imagined by them themselves as unconditioned and not dependent on anything in nature, but as necessary in itself. A being of this kind is man, but man regarded as noumenon. He is the only natural creature whose peculiar objective characterization is nevertheless such as to enable us to recognize in him a supersensible faculty—his *freedom*—and to perceive both the law of its causality and the object of freedom which that faculty is able to set before itself as the highest end—the supreme good in the world.

Now it is not open to us in the case of man, considered as a moral agent, or similarly in the case of any rational being in the world, to ask the further question: For what end (*quem in finem*) does he exist? His existence inherently involves the highest end—the end to which, as far as in him lies, he may subject the whole of nature, or contrary to which at least he must not deem himself subjected to any influence on its part. Now assuming that things in the world are beings that are dependent in point of their real existence and as such stand in need of a supreme cause acting according to ends, then man is the final end of creation. For without man the chain of mutually subordinated ends would have no ultimate point of attachment. Only in man, and only in him as the individual being to whom the moral law applies, do we find unconditional legislation in respect of ends. This legislation, therefore, is what alone 5:436 qualifies him to be a final end to which all of nature is teleologically subordinated.[12]

---

12 It would be possible for the happiness of the rational beings in the world to be an end of nature, and were it so, it would also be the *ultimate end of nature*. At least it is not obvious *a priori* why nature should not be so ordered, for, so far as we can see, happiness is an effect which it would be quite possible for nature to produce by means of its mechanism. But morality, or a causality according to ends that is subordinate to morality, is an absolutely impossible result of natural causes. For the principle that determines such causality of action is

§ 91.

The type of assurance produced by a practical faith.

If we look merely to the manner in which something can be an object of knowledge (*res cognoscibilis*) for us, that is having regard to the subjective nature of our powers of imagination, we do not in that case compare our concepts with the objects, but merely with our faculty for knowing and the use that it is able to make of the given image from a theoretical or practical point of view. So the question whether something is an understandable entity or not is a question which touches, not the possibility of the things themselves, but the possibility of our knowledge of them.

Understandable things are of three kinds: *matters of opinion, matters of fact, and matters of faith.*

1. The objects of mere ideas of reason, being wholly incapable of presentation on behalf of theoretical knowledge in any possible experience whatever, are to that extent also things altogether *unknowable*, and, consequently, we cannot even *form an opinion* about them. For to form an opinion *a priori* is absurd on the face of it and the straight road to pure figments of the brain. Either our *a priori* proposition is, therefore, certain or it involves no element of assurance at all. Hence, *matters of opinion* are always objects of an empirical knowledge that is at least intrinsically possible. They are, in

---

supersensible. In the order of ends, therefore, it is the sole principle possible which is absolutely unconditioned in respect to nature, and it is what alone qualifies the subject of such causality to be the *final end* of creation, and the one to which all of nature is subordinated. *Happiness,* on the other hand, as an appeal to the testimony of experience showed in the preceding section, so far from being a *final end of creation,* is not even an *end of nature* as regards man in preference to other creatures. It may ever be that individual men will make it their ultimate subjective end. But if, seeking for the final end of creation, I ask: For what end was it necessary that men should exist? my question then refers to an objective supreme end, such as the highest reason would demand for their creation. If we reply to this question: So that beings may exist upon whom that supreme Cause may exercise this beneficence, we then belie the condition to which the reason of man subjects even his own inmost wish for happiness, namely, harmony with his own inner moral laws. This proves that happiness can only be a conditional end and therefore that it is only as a moral being that man can be the final end of creation; while, as regards his state of being, happiness is only incident thereto as a consequence proportionate to the measure of his harmony with that end, as the end of his existence.

other words, objects belonging to the world of sense, but objects of which other than empirical knowledge is impossible because the degree of empirical knowledge we possess is as it is. Thus the ether of our modern physicists—an elastic fluid interpenetrating all other substances and completely permeating them—is a mere matter of opinion, yet it is in all respects of such a kind that it could be perceived if our external senses were sharpened to the highest degree, but its presentation can never be the subject of any observation or experiment. To assume rational inhabitants of other planets is a matter of opinion; for if we could get nearer the planets, which is intrinsically possible, experience would decide whether such inhabitants are there or not; but as we shall never get so near to them, the matter remains one of opinion. But to entertain an opinion that there exist in the material universe pure unembodied thinking spirits is mere romancing—supposing, I mean, that we dismiss from our notice, as well we may, certain phenomena that have been passed off for such. Such a notion is not a matter of opinion at all, but an idea pure and simple. It is what remains over when we take away from a thinking being all that is material and yet let it keep its thought. But whether, when we have taken away everything else, the thought—which we only know in man, that is, in connection with a body—would still remain, is a matter we are unable to decide. A thing like this is a *fictitious logical entity (ens rationis ratiocinantis)*, not a *rational entity (ens rationis ratiocinatae)*. With the latter it is anyway possible to substantiate the objective reality of its concept, at least in a manner sufficient for the practical use of reason, for this use, which has its peculiar and apodictically certain *a priori* principle, in fact demands and postulates that conception.

5:468

The objects that answer to concepts whose objective reality can be proved are *matters of fact*[13] (*res facti*). Such proof may be afforded by pure reason or by experience, and in the former case may be

13 I here extend the concept of a matter of fact beyond the usual meaning of the term, and, I think, rightly. For it is not necessary, and indeed not practicable, to restrict this expression to actual experience where we are speaking of the relation of things to our thinking faculties, as we do not need more than a merely possible experience to enable us to speak of things as objects of a definite kind of knowledge.

from theoretical or practical data of reason, but in all cases it must be effected by means of an observation corresponding to the concepts. Examples of matters of fact are the mathematical properties of geometrical magnitudes, for they admit of *a priori presentation* for the theoretical employment of reason. Further, things or qualities of things that are capable of being verified by experience, be it one's own personal experience or that of others (supported by evidence), are in the same way matters of fact—an idea which does not of itself admit of being visualized as an image, or, consequently, of any theoretical proof of its possibility. The idea in question is that of *freedom*. Its reality is the reality of a particular kind of causality (whose concept would be transcendent if considered theoretically), and as a causality of that kind it admits of verification by means of practical laws of pure reason and in the actual actions that take place in obedience to them, and, consequently, in experience. It is the only one of all the ideas of pure reason whose object is a matter of fact and must be included among them.

5:469   Objects that must be thought of *a priori*, either as consequences or as grounds, if pure practical reason is to be used as duty commands, but which are transcendent for the theoretical use of reason, are mere *matters of faith*. Such is the *summum bonum* which has to be realized in the world through freedom—a concept whose objective reality cannot be proved in any experience possible for us, or in any way so as to satisfy the requirements of the theoretical employment of reason. At the same time we are enjoined to use it for the purpose of realizing that end through pure practical reason in the best way possible, and, accordingly, its possibility must be assumed. This effect which is commanded, *together with the only conditions on which its possibility is conceivable by us*, namely, the existence of God and the immortality of the soul, are *matters of faith (res fidei)* and moreover, are of all objects the only ones that can be so called.[14]

14 Being a matter of faith does not make a thing an *article of faith*, if by articles of faith we mean such matters of faith as one can be bound to *acknowledge*, inwardly or outwardly—a kind therefore that does not enter into natural theology. For, being matters of faith, they cannot, like matters of fact, depend on theoretical proofs, and, therefore, the assurance is a free assurance, and it is only as such that it is compatible with the morality of the subject.

For although we have to believe that we can only learn by *testimony* from the experience of others, yet that does not make what is so believed in itself a matter of faith, for with *one* of those witnesses it was personal experience and matter of fact, or is assumed to have been so. In addition it must be possible to arrive at knowledge by this path—the path of historical belief; for the objects of history and geography, as, in general, everything that the nature of our thinking faculties makes at least a possible subject of knowledge are to be classed among matters of fact, not matters of faith. It is only objects of pure reason that can be matters of faith at all, and even they must then not be regarded as objects simply of pure speculative reason; for this does not enable them to be reckoned with any certainty whatever among matters, or objects, of that knowledge which is possible for us. They are ideas, that is, concepts, whose objective reality cannot be guaranteed theoretically. On the other hand, the supreme final purpose to be realized by us, which is all that can make us worthy of being ourselves the final purpose of a creation, is an idea that has objective reality for us in practical matters, and is a matter of faith. For since we cannot provide objective reality for this conception from a theoretical point of view, it is a mere matter of faith on the part of pure reason, as are also God and immortality, they being the sole conditions under which, owing to 5:470 the frame of our human reason, we are able to conceive the possibility of that effect of the use of our freedom according to law. But assurance in matters of faith is an assurance from a purely practical point of view. It is a moral faith that proves nothing for pure rational knowledge as theoretical, but only for it as practical and directed to the fulfilment of its obligations. It in no way extends either speculation or the practical rules of prudence actuated by the principle of self-love. If the supreme principle of all moral laws is a postulate, this involves the possibility of its supreme object, and, consequently, the condition under which we are able to conceive such possibility is also being postulated. This does not make knowing the postulate into any knowledge or opinion of the existence in nature of these conditions, as a mode of theoretical knowledge. The postulate is a mere assumption, confined to matters practical and commanded in practical interests, on behalf of the moral use of our reason.

Were we able with any plausibility to make the ends of nature which natural teleology sets before us in such abundance the basis of a *determinate* concept of an intelligent world-cause, the existence of this being would not then be a matter of faith. For as it would not be assumed on behalf of the performance of our duty, but only for the purpose of explaining nature, it would simply be the opinion and hypothesis best suited to our reason. Now the teleology in question does not lead in any way to a determinate concept of God. On the contrary such a concept can only be found in that of a moral author of the world, because this alone assigns the final end to which we can attach ourselves but only so far as we live in accordance with what the moral law prescribes to us as the final end, and, consequently imposes upon us as a duty. Hence, it is only by relation to the object of our duty, as the condition which makes its final end possible, that the concept of God acquires the position of figuring in our assurance as a matter of faith. On the other hand, this very same concept cannot make its object valid as a matter of fact, for although the necessity of duty is quite plain for a practical reason, yet the attainment of its final end, so far as it does not lie entirely in our own hands, is merely assumed in the interests of the practical employment of reason, and, therefore, is not practically necessary in the way duty itself is.[15]

5:471

5:471   15 The final end which we are enjoined by the moral law to pursue is not the foundation of duty. For duty lies in the moral law which, being a formal practical principle, directs categorically, irrespective of the objects of the faculty of desire—the subject-matter of volition—and, consequently, of any end whatever. This formal character of our actions—their subordination to the principle of universal validity—which alone constitutes their intrinsic moral worth, lies entirely in our own power; and we can quite easily make abstraction from the possibility or the impracticability of the ends that we are obliged to promote in accordance with that law—for they only form the extrinsic worth of our actions. Thus we put them out of consideration, as what does not lie altogether in our own power, in order to concentrate our attention on what rests in our own hands. But the object in view—the furthering of the final end of all rational beings, namely, happiness so far as consistent with duty—is nevertheless imposed upon us by the law of duty. But speculative reason does not in any way perceive the practicability of that object—whether we look at it from the standpoint of our own physical power or from that of the co-operation of nature. On the contrary, so far as we

Faith as *habitus*, not as *actus*, is the moral attitude of reason in its assurance of the truth of what is beyond the reach of theoretical knowledge. It is the steadfast principle of the mind, therefore, according to which the truth of what must necessarily be presupposed as the condition of the supreme final purpose being possible is assumed as true in consideration of the fact that we are under an obligation to pursue that end[16]—and assumed notwithstanding that we have no insight into its possibility, though likewise none into its impossibility. Faith, in the plain acceptation of the term, is a confidence of attaining a purpose the furthering of which is a duty, but whose achievement is a thing of which we are unable to *perceive* the possibility—or, consequently, the possibility of what we can alone conceive to be its conditions. Thus the faith that has reference to particular objects is entirely a matter of morality, provided such objects are not objects of possible knowledge or opinion, in which latter case, and above all in matters of history, it must be called

5:472

---

are able to form a rational judgment on the point, speculative reason must, apart from the assumption of the existence of God and immortality, regard it as a baseless and idle, though well-intentioned, expectation, to hope that mere nature, internal or external, will from such causes bring about such a result of our good conduct, and could it have perfect certainty as to the truth of this judgment, it would have to look on the moral law itself as a mere delusion of our reason in respect of practical matters. But speculative reason is fully convinced that the latter can never happen, whereas those ideas whose object lies beyond nature may be thought without contradiction. Hence for the sake of its own practical law and the task which it imposes, and, therefore, in respect of moral concerns, it must recognize those ideas to be real, in order not to fall into self-contradiction.

16 It is a confidence in the promise of the moral law. But this promise is not regarded as one involved in the moral law itself, but rather as one which we import into it, and so import on morally adequate grounds. For a final end cannot be commanded by any law of reason, unless reason, though it be with uncertain voice, also promises its attainability, and at the same time authorizes assurance as to the sole conditions under which our reason can imagine such attainability. The very word *fides* expresses this; and it must seem suspicious how this expression and this particular idea get a place in moral philosophy, since it was first introduced by Christianity, and its acceptance might perhaps seem only a flattering imitation of the language of the latter. But this is not the only case in which this wonderful religion has in the great simplicity of its statement enriched philosophy with far more definite and purer conceptions of morality than morality itself could have previously supplied. But once these concepts are found, they are *freely* approved by reason, which adopts them as concepts at which it could quite well have arrived itself and which it might and ought to have introduced.

credulity and not faith. It is a free assurance, not of any matter for which conclusive proofs can be found for the theoretical determinant judgment, nor of what we consider a matter of obligation, but of that which we assume in the interests of a purpose which we set before ourselves in accordance with laws of freedom. But this does not mean that it is adopted like an opinion formed on inadequate grounds. On the contrary it is something that has a foundation in reason (though only in relation to its practical employment), and *a foundation that satisfies the purpose of reason*. For without it, when the moral attitude comes into collision with theoretical reason and fails to satisfy its demand for a proof of the possibility of the object of morality, it loses all its stability, and wavers between practical commands and theoretical doubts. To be *incredulous* is to adhere to the maxim of placing no reliance on testimony; but a person is *unbelieving* who denies all validity to the above ideas of reason because their reality has no theoretical foundation. Hence, such a person judges dogmatically. But a dogmatic *unbelief* cannot stand side by side with a moral maxim governing the attitude of the mind—for reason cannot command one to pursue an end that is recognized to be nothing but a fiction of the brain. But the case is different with a *doubting faith*. For such a faith the want of conviction on grounds of speculative reason is only an obstacle—one which a critical insight into the limits of this faculty can deprive of any influence upon conduct and for which it can make amends by a paramount practical assurance.

5:473

———

If we desire to replace certain mistaken efforts in philosophy, and to introduce a different principle, and gain influence for it, it gives great satisfaction to see just how and why such attempts were bound to miscarry.

God, freedom, and the *immortality of the soul* are the problems to whose solution, as their ultimate and unique goal, all the laborious preparations of metaphysics are directed. Now it was believed that the doctrine of freedom was only necessary as a negative condition for practical philosophy, whereas that of God and the nature of the soul, being part of theoretical philosophy had to be proved independently and separately. Then each of those two concepts was subsequently to be united with what is commanded by the moral law (which is only possible on terms of freedom) and a religion was to be arrived at in this way. But we perceive at once that such attempts were bound to miscarry. For from simple ontological conceptions of things in the abstract, or of the existence of a necessary being, we can form absolutely no concept of an original being determined by predicates which admit of being given in experience and which are therefore available for knowledge. But should the concept be founded on experience of the physical appropriateness of nature, it could then in turn supply no proof adequate for morality, or, consequently, the knowledge of a God. Just as little could knowledge of the soul drawn from experience—which we can only obtain in this life—furnish a concept of its spiritual and immortal nature, or, consequently, one that would satisfy morality. *Theology* and *pneumatology*, regarded as problems framed in the interests of sciences pursued by a speculative reason, are in their very implication transcending all our faculties of knowledge, and cannot, therefore, be established by means of any empirical data or predicates. These two concepts, both that of God and that of the soul (in respect to its immortality), can only be defined by means of predicates which, although they themselves derive their possibility entirely from a supersensible source, must, for all that, provide their reality in experience, for this is the only way in which they can make possible a knowledge of a wholly supersensible being. Now 5:474 the only concept of this kind to be found in human reason is that of the freedom of man subject to moral laws and, in conjunction therewith, to the final end which freedom prescribes by means of these laws. These laws and this final end enable us to ascribe, the former to the author of nature, the latter to man, as the properties which contain the necessary conditions for the possibility of both. Thus it is from this idea that an inference can be drawn to the real existence and the nature of both God and the soul—beings that otherwise would be entirely hidden from us.

Hence, the source of the failure of the attempt to attain to a proof of God and immortality by the merely theoretical route lies in the fact that no knowledge of the supersensible is possible if the path of natural concepts is followed. The reason why the proof succeeds, on the other hand, when the path of morals, that is of the concept of freedom, is followed, is because from the supersensible, which in morals is fundamental (i.e., as freedom), there issues a definite law of causality. By means of this law the supersensible here not only provides material for the knowledge of the supersensible, that is of the moral final end and the conditions of its practicability, but it also substantiates its own reality, as a matter of fact, in actions. For that very reason, however, it is unable to afford any valid argument other than from a practical point of view—which is also the only one needful for religion.

There is something very remarkable in the way this whole matter stands. Of the three ideas of pure reason, God, freedom, and immortality, that of freedom is the one and only concept of the supersensible which (owing to the causality implied in it) proves its objective reality in nature by its possible effect there. By this means it makes possible the connection of the two other ideas with nature, and the connection of all three to form a religion. We are thus ourselves in possession of a principle which is capable of determining the idea of the supersensible within us, and, in that way, also of the supersensible without us, so as to constitute knowledge—a knowledge, however, which is only possible from a practical point of view. This is something of which mere speculative philosophy—which can only give a simply negative concept even of freedom—must despair. Consequently the concept of freedom, as the root-concept of all unconditionally practical laws, can extend reason beyond the bounds to which every natural or theoretical concept must remain hopelessly restricted.

SELECTIONS FROM

RELIGION
WITHIN THE
LIMITS OF
REASON ALONE

[1793-1794]

Translated by Hoyt W. Hudson and
Theodore Greene

BOOK ONE

CONCERNING THE INDWELLING OF THE EVIL PRINCIPLE WITH THE GOOD, OR ON THE RADICAL EVIL IN HUMAN NATURE

That "the world lieth in evil" is a plaint as old as history, old even as the older art, poetry; indeed, as old as that oldest of all fictions, the religion of priestcraft. All agree that the world began in a good estate, whether in a Golden Age, a life in Eden, or a yet more happy community with celestial beings. But they represent that this happiness vanished like a dream and that a fall into evil (moral evil, with which physical evil ever went hand in hand) presently hurried mankind from bad to worse with accelerated descent;[1] so that now (this "now" is also as old as history) we live in the final age, with the Last Day and the destruction of the world at hand. In some parts of India the Judge and Destroyer of the world, Rudra (sometimes called Siwa or Siva), already is worshipped as the reigning God—

---

1 *Aetas parentum peior avis tulit*
Nos nequiores, mox daturos
Progeniem vitiosorem.
                HORACE

Vishnu, the Sustainer of the world, having some centuries ago grown weary and renounced the supreme authority which he inherited from Brahma, the Creator.

More modern, though far less prevalent, is the contrasted optimistic belief, which indeed has gained a following solely among philosophers and, of late, especially among those interested in education—the belief that the world steadily (though almost imperceptibly) forges in the other direction, to wit, from bad to better; at least that the predisposition to such a movement is discoverable in human nature. If this belief, however, is meant to apply to *moral* goodness and badness (not simply to the process of civilization), it has certainly not been deduced from experience; the history of all times cries too loudly against it. The belief, we may presume, is a well-intentioned assumption of the moralists, from Seneca to Rousseau, designed to encourage the sedulous cultivation of that seed of goodness which perhaps lies in us—if, indeed, we can count on any such natural basis of goodness in man. We may note that since we take for granted that man is by nature sound of body (as at birth he usually is), no reason appears why, by nature, his soul should not be deemed similarly healthy and free from evil. Is not nature herself, then, inclined to lend her aid to developing in us this moral predisposition to goodness? In the words of Seneca: *Sanabilibus aegrotamus malis, nosque in rectum genitos natura, si sanari velimus, adiuvat.*

But since it well may be that both sides have erred in their reading of experience, the question arises whether a middle ground may not at least be possible, namely, that man as a species is neither good nor bad, or at all events that he is as much the one as the other, partly good, partly bad. We call a man evil, however, not because he performs actions that are evil (contrary to law) but because these actions are of such a nature that we may infer from them the presence in him of evil maxims. In and through experience we can observe actions contrary to law, and we can observe (at least in ourselves) that they are performed in the consciousness that they are unlawful; but a man's maxims, even his own, are not thus observable; consequently the judgment that the agent is an evil man cannot be made with certainty if grounded on experience. In order, then, to call a man evil, it would have to be possible *a priori* to infer from several evil acts done with consciousness of their evil, or from one such act, an underlying evil maxim; and further, from this maxim to infer the presence in the agent of an underlying common ground, itself a maxim, of all particularly morally evil maxims.

Lest difficulty at once be encountered in the expression *nature,* which, if it meant (as it usually does) the opposite of *freedom* as a basis of action, would flatly contradict the predicates *morally* good or evil, let it be noted that by "nature of man" we here intend only [to imply] the subjective ground of the exercise (under objective moral laws) of man's freedom in general; this ground—whatever may be its character—is necessarily antecedent of every act apparent to the senses. But this subjective ground, again, must itself always be an expression of freedom (for otherwise the use or abuse of man's power of choice in respect of the moral law could not be imputed to him nor could the good or bad in him be called moral). Hence the source of evil cannot lie in an object *determining* the will through inclination, nor yet in a natural impulse; it can lie only in a rule made by the will for the use of its freedom, that is, in a maxim. But now it must not be considered permissible to inquire into the subjective ground in man of the adoption of this maxim rather than of its opposite. If this ground itself were not ultimately a maxim, but a mere natural impulse, it would be possible to trace the use of our freedom wholly to determination by natural causes; this, however, is contradictory to the very notion of freedom. When we say, then, Man is by nature good, or, Man is by nature evil, this means only that there is in him an ultimate ground (inscrutable to us)[2] of

6:21

---

2 That the ultimate subjective ground of the adoption of moral maxims is inscrutable is indeed already evident from this, that since this adoption is free, its ground (why, for example, I have chosen an evil and not a good maxim) must not be sought in any natural impulse, but always again in a maxim. Now since this maxim also must have its ground, and since apart from maxims no *determining ground* of free choice can or ought to be adduced, we are referred back endlessly in the series of subjective determining grounds, without ever being able to reach the ultimate ground.

the adoption of good maxims or of evil maxims (i.e., those contrary to law), and this option he has, being a man; and hence he thereby expresses the character of his species.

We shall say, therefore, of the character (good or evil) distinguishing man from other possible rational beings, that it is *innate* in him. Yet in doing so we shall ever take the position that nature is not to bear the blame (if it is evil) or take the credit (if it is good), but that man himself is its author. But since the ultimate ground of the adoption of our maxims, which must itself lie in free choice, 6:22 cannot be a fact revealed in experience, it follows that the good or evil in man (as the ultimate subjective ground of the adoption of this or that maxim with reference to the moral law) is termed innate only in *this* sense, that it is posited as the ground antecedent to every use of freedom in experience (in earliest youth as far back as birth) and is thus conceived of as present in man at birth—though birth need not be the cause of it.

OBSERVATION

The conflict between the two hypotheses presented above is based on a disjunctive proposition: *Man is* (by nature) *either morally good or morally evil.* It might easily occur to anyone, however, to ask whether this disjunction is valid, and whether some might not assert that man is by nature neither of the two, others, that man is at once both, in some respects good, in other respects evil. Experience actually seems to substantiate the middle ground between the two extremes.

It is, however, of great consequence to ethics in general to avoid admitting, so long as it is possible, of anything morally intermediate, whether in actions (*adiophora*) or in human characters; for with such ambiguity all maxims are in danger of forfeiting their precision and stability. Those who are partial to this strict mode of thinking are usually called *rigorists* (a name which is intended to carry reproach, but which actually praises); their opposites may be called *latitudinarians.* These latter, again, are either latitudinarians of neutrality, whom we may call *indifferentists,* or else latitudinarians of combination, whom we may call *syncretists.*[3]

A morally indifferent action (*adiaphoron morale*) would be one resulting merely from natural laws, and hence standing in no relation whatsoever to the moral law, which is the law of freedom; for such action is not a morally significant fact at all and regarding it neither *command,* nor *prohibition,* nor *permission* (legal *privilege*) occurs or is necessary.

According to the rigoristic diagnosis,[4] the answer to the question 6:23

---

3 If the good = a, then its diametric opposite, the not-good is the result either of a mere absence of a basis of goodness, = o, or of a positive ground of the opposite of good, = – a. In the second case the not-good may also be called positive evil. (As regards pleasure and pain there is a similar middle term, whereby pleasure = a, pain = – a, and the state in which neither is to be found, indifference, = o.) Now if the moral law in us were not a motivating force of the will, the morally good (the agreement of the will with the law) would = a, and the not-good would = o; but the latter, as merely the result of the absence of a moral motivating force, would = a × o. In us, however, the law is a motivating force, = a; hence the absence of agreement of the will with this law (= o) is possible only as a consequence of a real and contrary determination of the will, i.e., of an *opposition* to the law, = – a, i.e., of an evil will. Between a good and an evil disposition (inner principle of maxims), according to which the morality of an action must be judged, there is therefore no middle ground.

A morally indifferent action (*adiaphoron morale*) would be one resulting merely from natural laws, and hence standing in no relation whasoever to the moral law, which is the law of freedom; for such action is not a morally significant fact at all and regarding it neither *command,* nor *prohibition,* nor *permission* (legal *privilege*) occurs or is necessary.

4 Professor Schiller, in his masterly treatise (*Thalia,* 1793, Part III) on *grace* and *dignity* in morality, objects to this way of representing obligation as carrying with it a monastic cast of 6:23 mind. Since, however, we are at one upon the most important principles, I cannot admit that there is disagreement here, if only we can make ourselves clear to one another. I freely grant that by very reason of the dignity of the *idea of duty* I am unable to associate *grace* with it. For the idea of duty involves absolute necessity, to which grace stands in direct contradiction. The majesty of the moral law (as of the law on Sinai) instils awe (not dread, which repels, nor yet charm, which invites familiarity); and in this instance, since the ruler resides within us, this *respect,* as of a subject toward his ruler, awakens a *sense of the sublimity* of our own destiny which enraptures us more than any beauty. *Virtue,* also, i.e., the firmly grounded disposition strictly to fulfil our duty, is also *beneficent* in its results, beyond all that nature and art can accomplish in the world; and the august picture of humanity, as portrayed in this character, does indeed allow the attendance of the *graces.* But when duty alone is the theme, they keep a respectful distance. If we consider, further, the happy results which virtue, should she gain admittance everywhere, would spread throughout the world, [we see] morally directed reason (by means of the imagination) calling the sensibilities into play. Only after vanquishing monsters did Hercules become Musagetes, leader of the Muses—after labors from which

at issue rests upon the observation, of great importance to morality, that freedom of the will is of a wholly unique nature in that an incentive can determine the will to an action *only so far as the individual has incorporated it into his maxim* (has made it the general rule in accordance with which he will conduct himself); only thus can an incentive, whatever it may be, co-exist with the absolute spontaneity of the will (i.e., freedom). But the moral law, in the judgment of reason, is in itself an incentive, and whoever makes it his maxim is *morally* good. If, now, this law does not determine a person's will in the case of an action which has reference to the law, an incentive contrary to it must influence his choice; and since, by hypothesis, this can only happen when a man adopts this incentive (and thereby the deviation from the moral law) into his maxim (in which case he is an evil man) it follows that his disposition in respect to the moral law is never indifferent, never neither good nor evil.

Neither can a man be morally good in some ways and at the same time morally evil in others. His being good in one way means that he has incorporated the moral law into his maxim; were he, therefore, at the same time evil in another way, while his maxim would be universal as based on the moral law of obedience to duty, which is essentially single and universal, it would at the same time be only particular; but this is a contradiction.[5]

---

those worthy sisters, trembling, drew back. The attendants of Venus Urania become wantons in the train of Venus Dione as soon as they meddle in the business of determining duty and try to provide springs of action therefor.

Now if one asks, What is the *aesthetic character*, the *temperament*, so to speak, *of virtue*, whether courageous and hence *joyous* or fear-ridden and dejected, an answer is hardly necessary. This latter slavish frame of mind can never occur without a hidden *hatred* of the law. And a heart which is happy in the *performance* of its duty (not merely complacent in the *recognition* thereof) is a mark of genuineness in the virtuous spirit—of genuineness even in *piety*, which does not consist in the self-inflicted torment of a repentant sinner (a very ambiguous state of mind, which ordinarily is nothing but inward regret at having infringed upon the rules of prudence), but rather in the firm resolve to do better in the future. This resolve, then, encouraged by good progress, must needs beget a joyous frame of mind, without which man is never certain of having really *attained a love* for the good, i.e., of having incorporated it into his maxim.

5 The ancient moral philosophers, who pretty well exhausted all that can be said upon virtue, have not left untouched the two questions mentioned above. The first they expressed

To have a good or an evil disposition as an inborn natural constitution does not here mean that it has not been acquired by the man who harbors it, that he is not author of it, but rather, that it has not been acquired in time (that he has *always* been good, or evil, *from his youth up*). The disposition, i.e., the ultimate subjective ground of the adoption of maxims, can be one only and applies universally to the whole use of freedom. Yet this disposition itself must have been adopted by free choice, for otherwise it could not be imputed. But the subjective ground or cause of this adoption cannot further be known (though it is inevitable that we should inquire into it), since otherwise still another maxim would have to be adduced in which this disposition must have been incorporated, a maxim which itself in turn must have its ground. Since, therefore, we are unable to derive this disposition, or rather its ultimate ground, from any original act of the will in time, we call it a property of the will which belongs to it by nature (although actually the disposition is grounded in freedom). Further, the man of whom we say, "He is by nature good or evil," is to be understood not as the single individual (for then one man could be considered as good, by nature, another as evil), but as the entire race; that we are entitled so to do can only be proved when anthropological research shows that the evidence, which justifies us in attributing to a man of these characters as innate, is such that it gives no ground for excepting anyone, and that the attribution therefore holds for the race.

6:26

thus: Must virtue be learned? (Is man by nature indifferent as regards virtue and vice?) The second they put thus: Is there more than one virtue (so that man might be virtuous in some respects, in others vicious)? Both questions were answered by them, with rigoristic precision, in the negative and rightly so; for they were considering virtue *as such*, as it is in the idea of reason as that which man ought to be. If, however, we wish to pass moral judgment on this moral being, man *as he appears*, i.e., as experience reveals him to us, we can answer both questions in the affirmative; for in this case we judge him not according to the standard of pure reason (at a divine tribunal) but by an empirical standard (before a human judge). This subject will be treated further in what follows.

I. Concerning the Original Predisposition to Good in Human Nature

We may conveniently divide this predisposition, with respect to function, into three divisions, to be considered as elements in the fixed character and destiny of man.

(1) The predisposition to *animality* in man, taken as a *living* being.
(2) The predisposition to *humanity* in man, taken as a living and at the same time a *rational* being.
(3) The predisposition to *personality* in man, taken as a rational and at the same time an *accountable* being.[6]

1. The predisposition to *animality* in mankind may be brought under the general title of physical and purely *mechanical* self-love, wherein no reason is demanded. It is threefold: first, for self-preservation; second, for the propagation of the species, through the sexual impulse, and for the care of offspring so begotten; and third, for community with other men, i.e., the social impulse. On these three stems can be grafted all kinds of vices (which, however, do not spring from this predisposition itself as a root). They may be termed vices of the coarseness of nature, and in their greatest deviation from natural purposes are called the *beastly* vices of *gluttony*

6:27

---

6 We cannot regard this as included in the concept of the preceding, but necessarily must treat it as a special predisposition. For from the fact that a being has reason it by no means follows that this reason, by the merely imagining its maxims as fit to be laid down as general laws, is thereby rendered capable of determining the will unconditionally, so as to be "practical" of itself; at least, not so far as we can see. The most rational mortal being in the world might still stand in need of certain incentives, originating in objects of desire, to determine his choice. He might, indeed, bestow the most rational reflection on all that concerns not only the greatest sum of these incentives in him but also the means of attaining the end thereby determined, without ever suspecting the possibility of such a thing as the absolutely imperative moral law which proclaims that it is itself an incentive, and indeed, the highest. Were it not given us from within, we should never by any ratiocination subtilize it into existence or win over our will to it; yet this law is the only law which informs us of the independence of our will from determination by all other incentives (of our freedom) and at the same time of the accountability of all our actions.

and *drunkenness, lasciviousness,* and wild lawlessness (in relation to other men).

2. The predisposition to humanity can be brought under the general titles of a self-love which is physical and yet *compares* (for which reason is required); that is to say, we judge ourselves happy or unhappy only by making comparison with others. Out of this self-love springs the desire *to acquire value in the opinion of others.* This is originally a desire merely for *equality,* to allow no one superiority above oneself, bound up with a constant care lest others strive to attain such superiority; but from this arises gradually the unjustifiable craving to win such superiority for oneself over others. Upon this twin stem of *jealousy* and *rivalry* may be grafted the very great vices of secret and open animosity against all whom we look upon as not belonging to us—vices, however, which really do not sprout of themselves from nature as their root; rather are they desires, aroused in us by the anxious endeavors of others to attain a hated superiority over us, to attain for ourselves as a measure of precaution and for the sake of safety such a position over others. For nature, indeed, wanted to use the idea of such rivalry (which in itself does not exclude mutual love) only as a spur to culture. Hence the vices which are grafted upon this desire might be termed vices of *culture,* in their highest degree of malignancy, as, for example, in *envy, ingratitude, spitefulness,* etc. (where they are simply the idea of a maximum of evil going beyond what is human), they can be called the *diabolical vices.*

3. The predisposition to *personality* is the capacity for respect for the moral law *as in itself a sufficient incentive of the will.* This capacity simply to respect the moral law within us would thus be moral sentiment, which in and through itself does not constitute an end of the natural predisposition except so far as it is the motivating force of the will. Since this is possible only when the free will incorporates such moral sentiment into its maxim, the character of the free will is something which can only be acquired; its possibility, however, demands the presence in our nature of a predisposition on which it is absolutely impossible to graft anything evil. We cannot 6:28 rightly call the idea of the moral law, and the respect which is in-

separable from it, *a predisposition to personality;* it is [the essence of] personality itself (the idea of humanity considered quite intellectually). But the subjective ground for the adoption into our maxims of this respect as a motivating force seems to be an adjunct to our personality, and thus to deserve the name of a predisposition to its furtherance.

If we consider the three predispositions named, in terms of the conditions of their possibility, we find that the first requires no reason, the second is based on practical reason, but a reason thereby subservient to other incentives, while the third alone is rooted in reason which is practical in itself, that is, reason which dictates laws unconditionally. All of these predispositions are not only *good* in a negative way in that they do not contradict the moral law; they are also predispositions *toward good* enjoining the observance of the law. They are *original,* for they are bound up with the possibility of human nature. Man can indeed use the first two contrary to their ends, but he can extirpate none of them. By the predispositions of a being we understand not only its constituent elements which are necessary to it, but also the forms of their combination, by which the being is what it is. They are *original* if they are involved necessarily in the possibility of such a being, but *contingent* if it is possible for the being to exist of itself without them. Finally, let it be noted that here we treat only those predispositions which have immediate reference to the faculty of desire and the exercise of the will.

II. Concerning the Propensity to Evil in Human Nature

6:29 By *propensity* (*propensio*) I understand the subjective ground of the possibility of an inclination (habitual craving, *concupiscentia*) so far as mankind in general is liable to it.[7] A propensity is distinguished

---

7 A *propensity* (*Hang*) is really only the *predisposition* to crave a delight which, when once experienced, arouses in the subject an *inclination* to it. Thus all savage peoples have a propensity for intoxicants; for though many of them are wholly ignorant of intoxication and in consequence have absolutely no craving for an intoxicant, let them but once sample it and there is aroused in them an almost inextinguishable craving for it.

from a predisposition by the fact that although it can indeed be innate, it *ought* not to be represented merely thus; for it can also be regarded as having been *acquired* (if it is good), or *brought* by man *upon himself* (if it is evil). Here, however, we are speaking only of the propensity to genuine, that is, moral evil; for since such evil is possible only as a determination of the free will, and since the will can be appraised as good or evil only by means of its maxims, this propensity to evil must consist in the subjective ground of the possibility of the deviation of the maxims from the moral law. If, then, this propensity can be considered as belonging to mankind in general and hence as part of the character of the race, it may be called a *natural* propensity in man to evil. We may add further that the will's capacity or incapacity, arising from this natural propensity, to adopt or not to adopt the moral law into its maxim, may be called *a good or an evil heart.*

In this capacity for evil there can be distinguished three distinct degrees. First, there is the weakness of the human heart in the general observance of adopted maxims, or in other words, the *frailty* of human nature; second, the propensity for mixing unmoral with moral motives which causes *impurity*, even when it is done with good intent and under maxims of the good, third, the propensity to adopt evil maxims, that is the *wickedness* of human nature or of the human heart.

First: the frailty (*fragilitas*) of human nature is expressed even in the complaint of an Apostle, "What I would, that I do not!" In other words, I adopt the good (the law) into the maxim of my will, but this good, which objectively, in its ideal conception (*in thesi*), is an irresistible incentive, is subjectively (*in hypothesi*), when the maxim is to be followed, the weaker (in comparison with inclination).

Second: the impurity (*impuritas, improbitas*) of the human heart 6:30

Between inclination, which presupposes acquaintance with the object of desire, and propensity there still is *instinct*, which is a felt want to do or to enjoy something of which one has as yet no conception such as the constructive impulse in animals, or the sexual impulse. Beyond inclination there is finally a further stage in the faculty of desire; not *emotion*, for this has to do with the feeling of pleasure and pain, but passion which is an inclination that excludes any mastery over oneself.

consists in this, that although the maxim is indeed good in respect of its object (the intended observance of the law) and perhaps even strong enough for practice, it is yet not purely moral; that is, it has not, as it should have, adopted the law *alone* as its *all-sufficient* objective: instead, it frequently (perhaps continually) stands in need of other incentives beyond this, in determining the will to do what duty demands; in other words, actions called for by duty are done not purely for duty's sake.

Third: the wickedness (*vitiositas, pravitas*) or, if you like, the *corruption* (*corruptio*) of the human heart is the propensity of the will to maxims which neglect the incentives springing from the moral law in favor of others which are not moral. It may also be called the *perversity* (*perversitas*) of the human heart, for it reverses the ethical order [of priority] among the incentives of a *free* will; and although conduct which is lawfully good (i.e., legal) may result from it, yet the cast of mind is thereby corrupted at its root so far as the moral disposition is concerned, and the man is hence designated as evil.

It will be remarked that this propensity to evil is here ascribed as regards conduct to men in general, even to the best of them; this must be the case if it is to be proved that the propensity to evil in mankind is universal, or, what here comes to the same thing, that it is woven into human nature.

There is no difference, however, as regards conformity of conduct to the moral law, between a man of good morals (*bene moratus*) and a morally good man (*moraliter bonus*)—at least there ought to be no difference, save that the conduct of the one has not always, perhaps has never, the law as its sole and supreme incentive while the conduct of the other has it *always*. Of the former it can be said: He obeys the law according to the *letter*, that is, his conduct conforms to what the law commands; but of the second: he obeys the law according to the *spirit*, the spirit of the moral law consisting in this, that the law is sufficient in itself as an incentive. *Whatever is not done out of such faith is sin*, as regards cast of mind. For when incentives other than the law itself, such as ambition, self-love in general, yes, even a kindly instinct such as sympathy, are necessary to bend the will to conduct which is *conformable to the law*, it is merely accidental

6:31

that these causes coincide with the law, for they could equally well impel a man to violate it. The maxim, then, in terms of whose goodness all moral worth of the individual must be appraised, is thus contrary to the law, and the man, despite all his good deeds, is nevertheless evil.

The following explanation is also necessary in order to define the concept of this propensity. Every propensity is either physical, i.e., pertaining to the will of man as a natural being, or moral, i.e., pertaining to his will as a moral being. In the first sense there is no propensity to moral evil, for such a propensity must spring from freedom; and a physical propensity grounded in sense impulses toward any use of freedom whatsoever—whether for good or bad—is a contradiction. Hence a propensity to evil can inhere only in the moral capacity of the will. But nothing is morally evil and capable of being so imputed but that which is our own *act*. On the other hand, by the concept of a propensity we understand a subjective determining ground of the will which *precedes all acts* and which, therefore, is itself not an act. Hence in the concept of a simple propensity to evil there would be a contradiction were it not possible to take the word "act" in two meanings, both of which are reconcilable with the concept of freedom. The term "act" can apply in general to that exercise of freedom whereby the supreme maxim in harmony with the law or contrary to it is adopted by the will, but also to the exercise of freedom whereby the actions themselves, considered substantively, that is with reference to the objects of volition, are performed in accordance with that maxim. The propensity to evil, then, is an act in the first sense (*peccatum originarium*), and at the same time the formal ground of all unlawful conduct in the second sense, which latter, considered substantively, violates the law and is termed vice (*peccatum derivatum*). The first offense remains, even though the second, from incentives which are not comprised by the law itself may be repeatedly avoided. The former is intelligible action, known by means of pure reason alone, apart from every temporal condition; the latter is sensible action, empirical, given in time (*factum phaenomenon*). The former, particularly when compared with the latter, is called a simple propensity and

innate, [first] because it cannot be eradicated, since for such eradication the highest maxim would have to be that of the good—
6:32 whereas in this propensity it already has been postulated as evil, but chiefly because we can no more assign a further cause for the corruption in us by evil of just this highest maxim, although this is our own action, than we can assign a cause for any fundamental attribute belonging to our nature. Now it can be understood, from what has just been said, why it was that in this section we sought, at the very first, the three sources of the morally evil solely in what, according to laws of freedom, touches the ultimate ground of the adoption or the observance of our maxims, and not in what touches sensibility when regarded as receptivity.

III. MAN IS EVIL BY NATURE

Vitiis nemo sine nascitur.
HORACE

In view of what has been said above, the proposition, Man is *evil*, can mean only, he is conscious of the moral law but has nevertheless adopted into his maxim the occasional deviation therefrom. He is evil *by nature* means but this, that evil can be predicated of man as a species; not that such a quality can be inferred from the concept of his species, that is, of man in general—for then it would be necessary. It rather means that from what we know of man through experience we cannot judge otherwise of him, or, (to put it another way) that we may presuppose evil to be subjectively necessary to every man, even to the best. Now this propensity must itself be considered as morally evil, yet not as a natural predisposition but rather as something that can be imputed to man. Consequently this propensity must consist in maxims of the will which are contrary to the (moral) law. Further, for the sake of freedom, these maxims must in themselves be considered contingent, a circumstance which, on the other hand, will not tally with the universality of this evil *unless* the ultimate subjective ground of all maxims somehow or other is entwined with and, as it were, rooted in humanity itself.

Hence we can call this a natural propensity to evil, and as we must, after all, ever hold man himself responsible for it, we can further call it a *radical* innate *evil* in human nature (yet none the less brought upon us by ourselves).

That such a corrupt propensity must indeed be rooted in man need not be formally proved in view of the multitude of crying examples which experience *of the actions* of men puts before our eyes. 6:33 If we wish to draw our examples from that state in which various philosophers hoped pre-eminently to discover the natural goodliness of human nature, namely, from the so-called *state of nature*, we need but compare with this hypothesis the scenes of unprovoked cruelty in the murderous scenes enacted in Tofoa, New Zealand, and in the Navigator Islands, and the unending cruelty of which Captain Hearne tells (occurring) in the wide deserts of northwestern America, from which, indeed, not a soul reaps the smallest benefit;[8] and we have vices of barbarity more than sufficient to (cause us to) abandon such an opinion. If, however, we incline to the opinion that human nature can better be known in the civilized state, in which its predispositions can more completely develop, we must listen to a long melancholy litany of indictments against humanity: of secret falsity even in the closest friendship, so that it is reckoned a universal maxim of prudence in intercourse to limit one's trust in the mutual confidences of even the best friends; of a propensity to hate him to whom one is indebted, for which a benefactor must always be prepared; of a hearty well-wishing which yet allows of the remark that "in the misfortunes of our best friends there is something which is not altogether displeasing to us"; and of many other

8 Thus the war ceaselessly waged between the Arathapescaw Indians and the Dog Rib Indians has no other object than mere slaughter. Bravery in war is, in the opinion of savages, the highest virtue. Even in a civilized state it is an object of admiration and a basis for the special regard commanded by that profession in which bravery is the sole merit; and this is not without rational cause. For that man should be able to possess a thing (i.e., honor) and make it an end to be valued more than life itself, and because of it renounce all self-interest, surely bespeaks a certain nobility in his natural disposition. Yet we recognize in the complacency with which victors boast their mighty deeds such as massacre, butchery without quarter, and the like that it is merely their own superiority and the destruction they can wreak, without any other objective, in which they really take satisfaction.

vices concealed under the appearance of virtue, to say nothing of the vices of those who do not conceal them, for we are content to call him good *who is a man bad in a way common to all;* and we shall have enough of the vices of *culture* and civilization which are the most offensive of all to make us rather turn away our eyes from the conduct of men lest we ourselves contract another vice, misan-

6:34 thropy. But if we are not yet content, we need but contemplate a state which is compounded in strange fashion of both the others, that is, the international situation. Here civilized nations stand toward each other in the relation obtaining in the barbarous state of nature, which is a state of continuous readiness for war; civilized nations seem to be firmly determined never to give up this state. We then become aware of the fundamental principles of the great societies called *states*[9]—principles which flatly contradict their public pronouncements but are never laid aside, and which no philosopher has yet been able to bring into agreement with morality. Nor, sad to say, has any philosopher been able to propose better principles which at the same time can be brought into harmony with human nature. The result is that the *philosophical utopianism,* which hopes for a state of perpetual peace based on a league of peoples as a world-republic, and the *theological utopianism,* which waits for the complete moral regeneration of the entire human race, is universally ridiculed as day-dreaming.

Now the ground of this evil (1) cannot be placed, as is so com-

---

9 When we survey the history of these, merely as the phenomenon of the inner predispositions of mankind which are for the most part concealed from us, we become aware of a certain machine-like movement of nature toward ends which are nature's own rather than those of the nations. Each separate state, so long as it has a neighboring state which it dares hope to conquer, strives to aggrandize itself through such a conquest, and thus to attain a world-empire, a polity wherein all freedom, and as a consequence virtue, taste, and learning, would necessarily expire. Yet this monster in which laws gradually lose their force, after it has swallowed all its neighbors, finally dissolves of itself, and through rebellion and disunion breaks up into many smaller states. These, instead of striving toward a league of nations, a republic of federated free nations, begin the same game over again, each for itself, so that war, the scourge of humankind, may not be allowed to cease. Although indeed war is not so incurably evil as that tomb, a universal autocracy (or even as a confederacy which exists to hasten the weakening of a despotism in any single state), yet, as one of the ancients put it, war creates more evil than it destroys.

monly done, in man's *senses* (*Sinnlichkeit*) and the natural inclina- 6:35
tions to evil (rather do they afford the occasion for what the moral
disposition in its power can manifest, namely, virtue); we cannot,
must not even be considered responsible for their existence since
they are implanted in us and we are not their authors. We are accountable, however, for the propensity to evil, which, as it affects
the morality of the subject, is to be found in him as a free-acting
being and for which it must be possible to hold him accountable as
the offender—this, too, despite the fact that this propensity is so
deeply rooted in the will that we are forced to say that it is to be
found in man by nature. Neither can the ground of this evil (2) be
placed in a *corruption* of the reason-giving moral laws—as if reason
could destroy the authority of the very law which is its own, or
deny the obligation arising therefrom; this is absolutely impossible.
To conceive of oneself as a freely acting being and yet as exempt
from the law which is appropriate to such a being (the moral law)
would be tantamount to conceiving a cause operating without any
laws whatsoever (for determination according to natural laws is excluded by the fact of freedom); this is a self-contradiction. In seeking, therefore, a ground of the morally-evil in man, (we find that)
the senses comprise too little, for when the incentives which can
spring from freedom are taken away, man is reduced to a mere *animal* being. On the other hand, a reason exempt from the moral law,
a *malignant reason* as it were, a thoroughly evil will, comprises too
much, for thereby opposition to the law would itself be set up as an
incentive since in the absence of all incentives the will cannot be
determined, and thus the subject would be made a *satanic* being.
Neither of these designations is applicable to man.

But even if the existence of this propensity to evil in human nature can be demonstrated by experiential proofs of the real opposition, in time, of man's will to the law, such proofs do not teach us
the essential character of that propensity or the ground of this opposition. Rather, because this character concerns a relation of the
will which is free and the concept of which is therefore not empirical to the moral law as an incentive the concept of which, likewise,
is purely intellectual, it must become known *a priori* through the

concept of evil, so far as evil is possible under the laws of freedom, of obligation and accountability. This concept may be developed in the following manner.

6:36   Man, even the most wicked, does not under any maxim whatsoever repudiate the moral law in the manner of a rebel who renounces obedience to it. The law rather forces itself upon him irresistibly by virtue of his moral predisposition. If no other incentive were working in opposition, he would adopt the law into his supreme maxim as the sufficient determining ground of his will, that is, he would be morally good. But by virtue of an equally innocent natural predisposition he depends upon the incentives of his senses and adopts them also in accordance with the subjective principle of self-love into his maxim. If he took the latter into his maxim *as in themselves wholly adequate* to the determination of the will, without troubling himself about the moral law which, after all, he does have in him, he would be morally evil. Now, since he naturally adopts *both* into his maxim, and since furthermore he would find either, if it were alone, adequate in itself for the determining of the will, it follows that if the difference between the maxims amounted merely to the difference between the two incentives, that is the substance of the maxims, in other words, if it were merely a question as to whether the law or the sense impulse were to furnish the incentive, man would be at once good and evil: this, however, as we saw in the Introduction, is a contradiction. Hence the distinction between a good man and one who is evil cannot lie in the difference between the incentives which they adopt into their maxim; that is not in the substance of the maxim, but rather must depend upon the *subordination* or the form of the maxim, in other words, *which of the two incentives he makes the condition of the other.* Consequently even the best man is evil, but only in that he reverses the moral order of the incentives when he adopts them into his maxim. He adopts, indeed, the moral law along with the law of self-love; yet when he becomes aware that they cannot remain on a par with each other but that one must be subordinated to the other as its supreme condition, he makes the incentive of self-love and its inclinations the condition of obedience to the moral law; whereas, on the contrary, the moral law, as the *supreme condition* of the satisfaction of self-love, ought to have been adopted into the universal maxim of the will as the sole incentive.

Yet, even with this reversal of the ethical order of the incentives in and through his maxim, a man's actions still may prove to be as much in conformity to the law as if they sprang from true basic principles. This happens when reason employs the unity of the 6:37 maxims in general, a unity which is inherent in the moral law, merely to bestow upon the incentives of desire, under the name of *happiness*, a unity of maxims which otherwise they cannot have. For example, truthfulness, if adopted as a basic principle, delivers us from the anxiety of making our lies agree with one another and of not being entangled by their serpent coils. The empirical character is then good, but the intelligible character is still evil.

Now if a propensity to this does lie in human nature, there is in man a natural propensity to evil; and since this very propensity must in the end be sought in a will which is free, and can therefore be imputed, it is morally evil. This evil is *radical*, because it corrupts the ground of all maxims; it is, moreover, as a natural propensity, *eradicable* by human effort, since eradication could occur only through good maxims, and cannot take place when the ultimate subjective ground of all maxims is postulated as corrupt; yet at the same time it must be possible to *overcome* it, since it is found in man, a being whose actions are free.

We are not, then, to call the depravity of human nature *wickedness*, taking the word in its strict sense as a subjective *principle* of the maxims or a disposition to adopt evil *as evil* into our maxims as an incentive, for that is satanic; we should rather term it the *perversity* of the heart, which then because of what follows from it is also called an *evil heart*. Such a heart may co-exist with a will which in general is good: it arises from the frailty of human nature, the lack of sufficient strength to follow out the principles it has chosen for itself, joined with its impurity, the failure to distinguish the incentives (even of well-intentioned actions) from each other by the gauge of morality; and so at last, if the extreme is reached, [it results] from looking only to the squaring of these actions with the [moral] law and not to the derivation of them from the law as the sole motivating spring. Now even though there does not always follow therefrom an unlawful act and a propensity thereto, namely, *vice,* yet the outlook which considers the absence of such vice as if it were virtue and such mentality to the [moral] law [imposed by] duty itself deserves to be called a radical perversity in the human heart—since in this case no attention whatever is being paid to the incentives involved in the maxim but only to the observance of the letter of the law.

6:38   This *innate* guilt (*reatus*), which is so denominated because it may be observed in man as early as the first manifestations of the exercise of freedom, but which, none the less, must have originated in freedom and hence can be imputed—this guilt may be judged in its first two stages (those of frailty and impurity) to be unintentional guilt (*culpa*), but in the third to be deliberate guilt (*dolus*). It displays the character [of this guilt] in a certain *insidiousness* of the human heart (*dolus malus*), which deceives itself in regard to its own good and evil convictions. If only its conduct has no evil consequences which it might well have, with such maxims, the human heart does not trouble itself about its convictions but rather considers itself justified before the law. Thence arises the peace of conscience of so many men, conscientious in their own estimation when, in the course of conduct concerning which they did not take the [moral] law into their counsel, or at least in which the [moral] law was not the supreme consideration, they merely eluded evil consequences by good fortune. They may even picture themselves as meritorious, feeling themselves guilty of no such offenses as they see others burdened with; nor do they ever inquire whether good luck should not have the credit, or whether by reason of the frame of mind which they could discover, if they only would, in their own inmost nature, they would not have practised similar vices, had not inability, temperament, training, and circumstances of time and place which serve to tempt one and for which a man is not responsible, kept them away from those vices. This dishonesty by which we "kid" ourselves and which thwarts the developing of genuine moral convictions, broadens itself into falsehood and deception of others. If this is not to be termed wickedness, it at least deserves the name of worthlessness, and is an element in the radical evil of human nature. Inasmuch as such evil puts out of commission the moral capacity to judge what a man is to be taken for, and renders wholly uncertain both internal and external attribution of responsibility, it constitutes the foul taint in our race. So long as we do not eradicate it, it prevents the seed of goodness from developing as it otherwise would.

A member of the British Parliament once exclaimed in the heat of debate, "Every man has his price, for which he sells himself." If this is true, a question to which each must make his own answer, if there is not virtue for which some temptation cannot be found capable of overthrowing it, and if whether the good or evil spirit wins us over to his party depends merely on which bids the most and pays us most promptly, then certainly it holds true of men universally, as the Apostle said: "They are all under sin—there is none righteous (in the spirit of the law), no, not one."[10]   6:39

IV. CONCERNING THE ORIGIN OF EVIL IN HUMAN NATURE

A first origin is the derivation of an effect from its first cause, that is, from that cause which is not in turn the effect of another cause of the same kind. It can be considered either as an *origin in reason* or as an *origin in time*. In the former sense, regard is had only to the *existence* of the effect; in the latter, to its *occurrence*, and hence it is related as an event to its *first cause in time*. If an effect is referred to a cause to

---

10 The special proof of this sentence of condemnation by morally judging reason is to be found in the preceding section rather than in this one, which contains only the confirmation of it by experience. Experience, however, never can reveal the root of evil in the supreme maxim of the free will relating to the law, a maxim which, as *intelligible act,* precedes all experience. Hence from the singleness of the supreme maxim, together with the singleness of the law to which it relates itself, we can also understand why, for the pure intellectual judgment of mankind, the rule of excluding a mean between good and evil must remain fundamental; yet for the empirical judgment based on *sensible conduct* (the actual performance or failure to act), the rule may be laid down that there *is* a mean between these extremes—on the one hand, a negative mean of indifference prior to all education, on the other hand, a positive, a mixture, partly good and partly evil. However, this latter is merely a judgment upon the morality of mankind as appearance, and must give place to the former in a final judgment.

which it is bound under the laws of freedom, as is true in the case of moral evil, then the determination of the will to the production of this effect is conceived of as bound up with its determining ground not in time but merely in rational image (*Vorstellung*); such an effect

6:40 cannot be derived from any *preceding* state whatsoever. Yet derivation of this sort is always necessary when an evil action, as an *event* in the world, is referred to its natural cause. To seek the temporal origin of free acts as such as though they were operations of nature is thus a contradiction. Hence it is also a contradiction to seek the temporal origin of man's moral character, so far as it is considered as contingent, since this character signifies the ground of the *exercise* of freedom; this ground like the determining ground of the free will generally must be sought in purely rational images.

Whatever the origin of moral evil in man may be like, surely of all the explanations of the spread and propagation of this evil through all members and generations of our race, the most inept describes it as descending to us as an *inheritance* from our first parents; for one can say of moral evil precisely what the poet said of good: *genus, et proavos, et quae non fecimus ipsi, vix ea nostra puto.*[11] Yet we should note that, in our search for the origin of this evil, we do not deal first of all with the propensity thereto (as *peccatum in potentia*); rather do we direct our attention to the actual evil of given ac-

---

11 The three so-called "higher faculties" (in the universities) would explain this transmission of evil each in terms of its own specialty, as *inherited disease, inherited debt,* or *inherited sin.* (1) The *faculty of medicine* would represent this hereditary evil somewhat as it represents the tapeworm, concerning which several naturalists actually believe that, since no specimens have been met with anywhere but in us, not even (of this particular type) in other animals, it must have existed in our first parents. (2) The *faculty of law* would regard this evil as the legitimate consequence of succeeding to the patrimony bequeathed us by our first parents, [an inheritance] encumbered, however, with heavy forfeitures (for to be born is no other than to inherit the use of the earthly goods so far as they are necessary to our continued existence). Thus we must fulfil payment (atone) and at the end still be dispossessed (by death) of the property. How just is legal justice! (3) The *theological faculty* would regard this evil as the personal participation by our first parents in the *fall* of a condemned rebel, maintaining either that we ourselves then participated (although now unconscious of having done so) or that even now, born under the rule of the rebel (as prince of this world), we prefer his favors to the supreme command of the heavenly Ruler, and do not possess enough faith to free ourselves; wherefore we must also eventually share his doom.

tions with respect to what [inner defeat] makes them possible—to 6:41
what must take place within the will if evil is to be performed.

In the search for the rational origin of evil actions, every such
action must be regarded as though the individual had fallen into it
directly from a state of innocence. For whatever his previous de-
portment may have been, whatever natural causes may have been
influencing him, and whether these causes were to be found within
him or outside him, his action is yet free and determined by none
of these causes; hence it can and must always be judged as an *original* use of his will. He should have refrained from that action, whatever his temporal circumstances and entanglements; for through no
cause in the world can he cease to be a freely acting being. Rightly
is it said that to a man's account are set down the *consequences* arising from his former free acts which were contrary to the law; but
this merely amounts to saying that man need not involve himself in
the evasion of seeking to establish whether or not these consequences are free, since there exists in the admittedly free action,
which was their cause, ground sufficient for holding him responsible. However evil a man has been up to the very moment of an im-
pending free act so that evil has actually become custom or second
nature it was not only his duty to have been better [in the past], it
is *now* still his duty to better himself. To do so must be within his
power, and if he does not do so, he is susceptible of, and subjected
to, being held responsible in the very moment of that action, just as
much as though, endowed with a predisposition to good which is
inseparable from freedom, he had stepped out of a state of innocence into evil. Hence we cannot inquire into the temporal origin
of this deed, but solely into its rational origin, if we are thereby to
determine and, wherever possible, to elucidate the propensity, if it
exists, i.e., the general subjective ground of the adoption of transgression into our maxim.

The foregoing agrees well with that manner of presentation
which the Scriptures use, whereby the origin of evil in the human
race is depicted as having a [temporal] *beginning*, this beginning
being presented in a narrative, wherein what in its essence must be
considered as primary (without regard to the element of time) ap-

pears as coming first in time. According to this account, evil does not start from a propensity thereto as its underlying basis, for otherwise the beginning of evil would not have its source of freedom; 6:42 rather does it start from *sin* (by which is meant the transgressing of the moral law as a *divine command*). The state of man prior to all propensity to evil is called the state of *innocence*. The moral law became known to mankind, as it must to any being not pure but tempted by desires, in the form of a *prohibition* (Genesis II, 16–17). Now instead of straightway following this law as an adequate incentive (the only incentive which is unconditionally good and regarding which there is no further doubt), man looked about for other incentives (Genesis III, 6) such as can be good only conditionally (namely, so far as they involve no infringement of the law). He then made it his maxim—if one thinks of his action as consciously springing from freedom—to follow the law of duty, not as duty, but, if need be, with regard to other aims. Thereupon he began to call in question the severity of the commandment which excludes the influence of all other incentives; then by sophistry he reduced[12] obedience to the law to the merely conditional character of a means, subject to the principle of self-love; and finally he adopted into his maxim of conduct the ascendancy of the sense impulse over the incentive which springs from the law—and thus occurred sin (Genesis III, 6). *Mutato nomine de te fabula narratur.* From all this it is clear that we daily act in the same way, and that therefore "in Adam all have sinned" and still sin; except that in us there is presupposed an innate propensity to transgression, whereas in the first man, from the point of view of time, there is presupposed no such propensity but rather innocence; hence transgression on his part is called a *fall into sin;* but with us sin is represented as resulting from

---

12 All homage paid to the moral law is an act of hypocrisy, if, in one's maxim, ascendancy is not at the same time granted to the law as an incentive sufficient in itself and higher than all other determining grounds of the will. The propensity to do this is inward deceit, that is, a tendency to deceive oneself in the interpretation of moral law, to its detriment (Genesis III, 5). Accordingly, the Christian portion of the Bible denominates the author of evil who is within us as the liar from the beginning, and thus characterizes man with respect to what seems to be the chief ground of evil in him.

an already innate wickedness in our nature. This propensity, however, signifies no more than this, that if we wish to address ourselves to the explanation of evil in terms of its *beginning in time*, we must search for the causes of each deliberate transgression in a previous period of our lives, far back to that period wherein the use of reason had not yet developed, and thus back to a propensity to evil as a natural ground which is therefore called innate—the source of evil. But to trace the causes of evil in the instance of the first man, who is depicted as already in full command of the use of his reason, is neither necessary nor feasible, since otherwise this, the evil propensity, would have had to be created in him; therefore his sin is set forth as engendered directly from innocence. We must not, however, look for an origin in time of a moral character for which we are to be held responsible; though to do so is inevitable if we wish to *explain* the contingent existence of this character, and perhaps it is for this reason that Scripture, in conformity with this weakness of ours, has thus pictured the temporal origin of evil.

6:43

But the rational origin of this perversion of our will whereby it makes lower incentives supreme among its maxims, that is, of the propensity to evil, remains inscrutable to us, because this propensity itself must be set down to our account and because, as a result, that ultimate ground of all maxims would in turn involve the adoption of an evil maxim [as a basis]. Evil could have sprung only from the morally evil, not from mere limitation in our nature; and yet the original predisposition which no one other than man himself could have corrupted, if he is to be held responsible for this corruption, is a predisposition to good; there is then for us no conceivable ground from which the moral evil in us could originally have come. This inconceivability, together with a more accurate specification of the wickedness of our race, the Bible expresses in the historical narrative as follows.[13] It finds a place for evil at the creation

---

13 What is written here must not be read as though intended for Scriptural exegesis, which lies beyond the limits of the domain of bare reason alone. It is possible to explain how an historical account is to be put to moral use without deciding whether this is the intention of the author or merely our interpretation, provided this meaning is true in itself, apart from all historical proof. Moreover this moral use is the only one whereby we can derive

BOOK TWO

CONCERNING THE CONFLICT OF THE
GOOD WITH THE EVIL PRINCIPLE FOR
RULE OVER MAN

To become morally good it is not enough merely to allow the seed of goodness implanted in our species to develop without hindrance; there is also present in us an active and opposing cause of evil to be combatted. Among the ancient moralists it was preeminently the Stoics who called attention to this fact by their watchword *virtue*, which in Greek as well as in Latin signifies courage and valor and thus presupposes the presence of an enemy. In this regard the word *virtue* is a noble one, and that it has often been ostentatiously misused and derided, as has of late the word "Enlightenment," can do it no harm. For simply to make the demand for courage is to go half-way toward infusing it; on the other hand, the lazy and pusillanimous frame of mind in morality and religion which entirely mistrusts itself and hesitates waiting for help from without, is weakening to all a man's powers and makes him unworthy even of this assistance.

Yet those valiant men [the Stoics] mistook their enemy: for he is not to be sought merely in the undisciplined natural inclinations which present themselves so openly to everyone's consciousness; rather is he, as it were, an invisible foe who hides himself behind reason and is therefore all the more dangerous. They called out *wisdom* against *folly*, which allows itself to be deceived by the inclinations through mere carelessness, instead of summoning her against the *wickedness* of the human heart, which secretly undermines the convictions with soul-destroying principles.[14]

6:58   Natural inclinations, *considered in themselves*, are *good*, that is, not a matter of reproach, and it is not only futile to want to extirpate them but to do so would also be harmful and blameworthy. Rather, let them be tamed and instead of clashing with one another they can be brought into harmony in a wholeness which is called happiness. Now the reason which accomplishes this is termed *prudence*. But only what is opposed to the moral law is evil in itself, ab-

6:58   14 These Stoic philosophers derived their universal ethical principle from the dignity of human nature, that is, from its freedom regarded as an independence from the power of the inclinations, and they could not have used as their foundation a better or nobler principle. They then derived the moral laws directly from reason, which alone makes moral laws and whose command, through these laws, is absolute. Thus everything was quite correctly defined—objectively, with regard to the rule, and subjectively, with reference to the incentive—provided one ascribes to man an uncorrupted will to incorporate these laws unhesitatingly into his maxims. Now it was just in the latter presupposition that their error lay. For no matter how early we direct our attention to our moral state, we find that this state is no longer a *res integra*, but that we must start by dislodging from its stronghold the evil which has already entered in, and it could never have done so, had we not ourselves adopted it into our maxims; that is, the first really good act that a man can perform is to forsake the evil, which is to be sought not in his inclinations, but in his perverted maxim, and so in freedom itself. Those inclinations merely make difficult the *execution* of the good maxim which opposes them; whereas genuine evil consists in this, that a man does not *will* to withstand those inclinations when they tempt him to transgress—so it is really this disposition that is the true enemy. The inclinations are but the opponents of basic principles in general (be they good or evil); and so far that high-minded principle of morality [of the Stoics] is of value as an initiatory lesson and a general discipline of the inclinations in allowing oneself to be guided by basic principles. But so far as specific principles of moral *goodness* ought to be present but are not present, as maxims, we must assume the presence in the agent of some other opponent with whom virtue must join combat. In the absence of such an opponent all virtues would not, indeed, be *splendid vices*, as the Church Father has it; yet they would certainly be *splendid frailties*. For though it is true that thus the rebellion is often stilled, the rebel himself is not being conquered and exterminated.

solutely reprehensible, and must be completely eradicated; and only a reason which teaches this truth, and more especially one which puts it into actual practice, alone deserves the name of *wisdom*. The vice corresponding to this may indeed be termed *folly*, but again only when reason feels itself strong enough not merely to *hate* vice as something to be feared, and to arm itself against it, but to *scorn* vice with all its temptations.

So when the Stoic regarded man's moral struggle simply as a conflict with his inclinations, so far as these inherently innocent inclinations had to be overcome as hindrances to the fulfilment of his duty, he could locate the cause of transgression only in man's failure to combat these inclinations, for he admitted no special, positive principle such as evil in itself. Yet since this failure is itself contrary to duty and a transgression and no mere lapse of nature, and since the cause thereof cannot without arguing in a circle be sought once more in the inclinations but only in something which determines the will as a free will, that is, in the first and inmost ground of the maxims which accord with the inclinations, we can well understand how philosophers could mistake the real opponent of goodness.[15]

6:59

It is not surprising that an Apostle imagines this *invisible* enemy, who is known only through his effect upon us and who destroys basic principles, as being outside us and, indeed, as an evil *spirit*: "We wrestle not against flesh and blood (the natural inclinations) but against principalities and powers—against evil spirits." This is an expression which seems to have been used not to extend our

15 It is a very common assumption of moral philosophy that the existence of moral evil in man may easily be explained by the power of the incentives of his senses on the one hand, and the impotence of his rational impulses (his respect for the law) on the other, that is, by *weakness*. But then the moral goodness in him, his moral predisposition, would have to allow of a still easier explanation, for to comprehend the one apart from comprehending the other is quite unthinkable. Now reason's ability to master all opposing motivating forces through the bare idea of a [moral] law is utterly inexplicable; it is also inconceivable, therefore, how the incentives of the senses would be able to gain the ascendancy over a reason which commands with such authority. For if all the world were to proceed in conformity with the precepts of the [moral] law, we should say that everything came to pass according to natural order, and no one would so much as think to inquire after the cause.

knowledge beyond the world of sense but only to make clear *for practical use* the conception of what is for us unfathomable. Moreover, as far as its practical value is concerned, it is all one whether we place the seducer merely within ourselves or without, for guilt touches us not a whit less in the latter case than in the former, inasmuch as we would not be led astray by him at all were we not already in secret league with him.[16] We shall treat of this whole subject in two sections.

6:60

SECTION ONE

CONCERNING THE LAWFUL CLAIM OF THE GOOD PRINCIPLE TO RULE OVER MAN

A. THE PERSONIFIED IDEA OF THE GOOD PRINCIPLE

Mankind or rational earthly existence in general *in its complete moral perfection* is that which alone can render a world the object of a divine decree and the end of creation. With such perfection as the prime condition, happiness is the direct consequence, according to the will of the Supreme Being. Man so conceived, alone pleasing to God, "is in Him through eternity," the idea of him proceeds from God's very being; hence he is no created thing but His only-begotten Son, "the *Word* (the *Fiat!*) through which all other things are, and without which nothing is in existence that is made," since

---

16 It is a peculiarity of Christian ethics to represent moral goodness as differing from moral evil not as heaven from *earth* but as heaven from *hell*. Though this representation is figurative, and, as such, disturbing, it is none the less philosophically correct in meaning. That is, it serves to prevent us from regarding good and evil, the realm of light and the realm of darkness, as bordering on each other and as losing themselves in one another by gradual steps (of greater and lesser brightness); but rather to represent those realms as being separated from one another by an immeasurable gulf. The complete dissimilarity of the basic principles, by which one can become a subject of this realm or that, and the danger, too, which attends the notion of a close relationship between the characteristics which fit an individual for one or for the other, justify this manner of representation—which, though containing an element of horror, is none the less very exalting.

for him, that is, for rational existence in the world, so far as he may be regarded in the light of his moral destiny, all things were made. 6:61 "He is the brightness of His glory." "In him God loved the world," and only in him and through the adoption of his disposition can we hope "to become the sons of God," etc.

Now it is our common duty as men to *elevate* ourselves to this ideal of moral perfection, that is, to this archetype of the moral disposition in all its purity—and for this the idea itself, which reason presents to us for our zealous emulation, can give us power. But just because we are not the authors of this idea, and because it has established itself in man without our comprehending how human nature could have been capable of receiving it, it is more appropriate to say that this archetype has *come down* to us from heaven and has assumed our humanity; for it is less possible to conceive how man, by nature *evil*, should of himself lay aside evil and *raise* himself to the ideal of sanctity, than that the latter should *descend* to man and assume a *humanity* which is, in itself, not evil. Such union with us may therefore be regarded as a state of *humiliation* of the Son of God if we represent to ourselves this godly-minded person, regarded as our archetype, as assuming sorrows in fullest measure in order to further the world's good, though he himself is holy and therefore is bound to endure no sufferings whatsoever. Man, on the contrary, who is never free from guilt even though he has developed the very same disposition, can regard as truly merited the sufferings that may overtake him, how they come; consequently he must consider himself unworthy of having his character identified with the idea of God, even though this idea serves him as an archetype.

This ideal of a humanity pleasing to God and hence of such moral perfection as is possible to an earthly being who is subject to wants and inclinations we can imagine only as the idea of a person who would be willing not merely to discharge all human duties himself and to spread about him goodness as widely as possible by precept and example, but even, though tempted by the greatest allurements, to take upon himself every affliction, up to the most ignominious death, for the good of the world and even for his enemies. For man can frame to himself no concept of the degree and strength of a force like that of moral convictions except by picturing it as encompassed by obstacles, and yet, in the face of the fiercest onslaughts, victorious.

Man may then hope to become acceptable to God (and so be 6:62 saved) through *a practical faith in this Son of God,* so far as He is represented as having taken upon Himself man's nature. In other words, he, and he alone, is entitled to look upon himself as an object not unworthy of divine approval who is conscious of such moral convictions as enable him to have a well-grounded confidence in himself and to *believe* that, under like temptations and afflictions, so far as these are made the touchstone of that idea, he would be loyal unswervingly to the archetype of humanity and, by faithful imitation, remain true to his exemplar.

B. THE OBJECTIVE REALITY OF THIS IDEA

From the practical point of view this idea is completely existential in its own right, for it resides in our morally legislative reason. We *ought* to conform to it; consequently we must *be able* to do so. Did we have to prove in advance the possibility of man's conforming to this archetype, as is absolutely essential in the case of concepts of nature, if we are to avoid the danger of being deluded by empty notions, we should have to hesitate before allowing even to the moral law the authority of an unconditioned and yet sufficient determining ground of our will. For how it is possible that the mere idea of conformity to law, as such, should be a stronger incentive for the will than all the incentives conceivable whose source is personal gain, can neither be understood by reason nor yet proved by examples from experience. As regards the former, the law commands unqualifiedly; and as regards the latter, even though there had never existed an individual who yielded unqualified obedience to this law, the objective necessity of being such an one would yet be undiminished and self-evident. We need, therefore, no empirical example to make the idea of a person morally well-pleasing to God our pattern; this idea as a pattern is already present in our reason. Moreover, if anyone, in order to acknowledge, for his imitation, a particular individual as such an example which conforms to that idea, and therefore demands more than what he sees, more, that is, than a course of life entirely blameless and as meritorious as one could wish; and if he goes on to require, as credentials requisite to belief, that this individual should have performed miracles or had them performed for him—he who demands this thereby confesses to his own moral *unbelief,* that is, to his lack of faith in virtue. This is a lack which no belief that rests upon miracles and is therefore merely historical can repair. For only a faith in the practical validity of that idea which lies in our reason has moral value. Only this idea, to be sure, can establish the truth of miracles as possible effects of the good principle; but it can never itself derive from them its own verification. 6:63

Just for this reason an experience must be possible in which the example of such a [morally perfect] human being is presented (so far, at least, as we can expect or demand from any merely external experience the evidences of an inner moral disposition). According to the [moral] law, each man ought really to furnish an example of this idea in his own person. To this end does the archetype always reside in the reason: and this just because no example in outer experience is adequate to it; for outer experience does not disclose the inner nature of the character but merely allows of an inference about it though not one of strict certainty. For not even does a man's inner experience with regard to himself enable him so to fathom the depths of his own heart as to obtain, through self-observation, quite certain knowledge of the basis of the maxims which he professes, or of their purity and stability.

Now if it were indeed a fact that such a truly godly-minded man at some particular time had descended, as it were, from heaven to earth and had given men in his own person through his teachings, his conduct, and his sufferings as perfect an *example* of a man well-pleasing to God as one can expect to find in external experience (for be it remembered that the *archetype* of such a person is to be sought nowhere but in our own reason), and if he had, through all this, produced immeasurably great good upon earth by effecting a revolution in the human race—even then we should have no cause for supposing him other than a man naturally begotten. Indeed, the naturally begotten man feels himself under obligation to furnish himself just such an example. This is not, to be sure, absolutely to deny that he might be a man supernaturally begotten. But to suppose this can in no way benefit us practically, inasmuch as the ar-

6:64 chetype which we find embodied in this manifestation must, after all, be sought in ourselves, even though we are but natural men. And the presence of this archetype in the human soul is in itself sufficiently incomprehensible without our adding to its supernatural origin the assumption that it is hypostasized in a particular individual. The elevation of such a holy person above all the frailties of human nature would rather, so far as we can see, hinder the adoption of the idea of such a person for our imitation. For let the nature of this individual pleasing to God be regarded as human in the sense of being encumbered with the very same inclinations [as man], hence with the same temptations to transgress [the moral law]; let him, however, be regarded as superhuman to the degree that his unchanging purity of will, not achieved with effort but innate, makes all transgression on his part utterly impossible: his distance from the natural man would then be so infinitely great that such a divine person could no longer be held up as an *example to* him. Man would say: If I too had a perfectly sanctified will, all temptations to evil would of themselves be thwarted in me; if I too had the most complete inner assurance that, after a short life on earth, I should by virtue of this sanctity become at once a partaker in all the eternal glory of the kingdom of heaven, I too should take upon myself not only willingly but joyfully all sorrows, however bitter they might be, even to the point of a most ignominious death, since I would see before my eyes the glorious and imminent sequel. To be sure, the thought that this divine person was in actual possession of this eminence and this bliss from all eternity and needed not first of all to earn them through such afflictions, and that he willingly renounced them for the sake of those absolutely unworthy, even for the sake of his enemies, to save them from everlasting perdition— this thought must inspire our hearts to admiration, love, and gratitude. Similarly the idea of a demeanor in accordance with so perfect a standard of morality would no doubt be valid for us, as a model for us to copy. Yet he himself could *not* be presented to us an *example* for our imitation, nor, consequently, as a proof of the feasibility and attainability *for us* of so pure and exalted a moral goodness.[17]

6:65

Now such a godly-minded teacher, even though he was com-

17 It is indeed a limitation of human reason, and one which is ever inseparable from it, that we can conceive of no considerable moral worth in the actions of a personal being without representing that person, or his manifestation, in human guise. This is not to assert that such value is in itself and in truth so conditioned, but merely that we must always resort to some analogy to natural existences to render supersensible qualities intelligible to ourselves. Thus a philosophical poet assigns a higher place in the moral gradation of beings to man, so far as he has to fight a propensity to evil within himself, nay, just in consequence of this fact, if only he is able to master the propensity, than to the inhabitants of heaven themselves who, by reason of the holiness of their nature, are placed above the possibility of going astray:

6:65

"The world with all its faults
Is better than a realm of will-less angels." (Haller)

The Scriptures too accommodate themselves to this mode of representing [God] when, in order to make us comprehend the degree of His love for the human race, they ascribe to Him the very highest sacrifice which a loving being can make, a sacrifice performed in order that even those who are unworthy may be made happy ("For God so loved the world . . ."); though we cannot indeed rationally conceive how an all-sufficient Being could sacrifice a part of what belongs to His state of bliss or rob Himself of a possession. Such is the *schema of analogy* [pattern of reason], with which as a means of explanation we cannot dispense. But to transform it into a *schema of objective determination* for the extension of our knowledge is *anthropomorphism*, which has, from the moral point of view (in religion), most injurious consequences.

At this point let me remark incidentally that while, in proceeding from the sensible to the supersensible it is indeed allowable to *schematize*, that is, to render a concept intelligible by the help of an analogy to something sensible, it is on no account permitted to *infer* and thus to *extend* our concept by this analogy, so that what holds of the former must also be attributed to the latter. Such an inference is not possible, for the simple reason that it would run *directly counter* to all analogy to conclude that, because we absolutely need a schema to render a concept intelligible to ourselves, it therefore follows that this schema must necessarily belong to the object itself as its predicate. Thus, I cannot say: I can *make comprehensible* to myself the cause of a plant or of any organic creature, or indeed of the whole purposive world only by attributing intelligence to it, on the analogy of an artificer in his relation to his work, say a watch; therefore the cause of the plant and of the world in general must itself *possess* intelligence. That is, I cannot say that this postulated intelligence of the cause conditions not merely my comprehending it but also conditions the possibility of its being a cause. On the contrary, between the relation of a schema to its concept and the relation of this same schema of a concept to the objective fact itself there is no analogy, but rather a chasm, the overleaping of which leads us at once to anthropomorphism. The proof of this I have given elsewhere.

6:66 pletely human, might nevertheless truthfully speak of himself as though the ideal of goodness were displayed incarnate in his teachings and conduct. In speaking thus he would be alluding only to the convictions which he makes the rule of his actions. Since he cannot make these convictions visible, as an example for others, by and through themselves, he places them before their eyes only through his teachings and actions: "Which of you convinceth me of sin?" For in the absence of proofs to the contrary it is no more than right to ascribe the faultless example which a teacher furnishes of his teaching—when, moreover, this is a matter of duty for all—to the supremely pure moral character of the man himself. When a character such as this, together with all the afflictions assumed for the sake of the world's highest good, is taken as the ideal of mankind, it is, by standards of supreme righteousness, a perfectly valid ideal for all men, at all times and in all places, whenever man moulds his own character to be like it, as he ought to do. To be sure, such an attainment will ever remain a righteousness not our own, inasmuch as it would have to consist of a course of life completely and faultlessly harmonious with that perfect character. Yet an appropriation of this righteousness for the sake of our own must be possible when our own character is made similar to that of the archetype. However, the greatest difficulties will stand in the way of our rendering this act of appropriation comprehensible.

6:93

BOOK THREE

THE VICTORY OF THE GOOD OVER THE EVIL PRINCIPLE, AND THE FOUNDING OF A KINGDOM OF GOD ON EARTH

The combat which every morally well-disposed man must sustain in this life, under the leadership of the good principle, against the attacks of the evil principle, can procure him, however much he exerts himself, no greater advantage than freedom from the *rule* of evil. To become *free*, "to be freed from bondage under the law of sin, to live for righteousness"—this is the highest prize he can win. He continues to be exposed, none the less, to the assaults of the evil principle; and in order to assert his freedom, which is perpetually being attacked, he must ever remain armed for the fray.

Now man is in this perilous state through his own fault; hence he is *bound* at the very least to strive with all his might to extricate himself from it. But how? That is the question. When he looks around for the causes and circumstances which expose him to this danger and keep him in it, he can easily convince himself that he is subject to these not because of his own gross nature, so far as he is here a separate individual, but because of mankind to whom he is related and bound. It is not at the instigation of the former that what should properly be called the *passions,* which cause such havoc in his original good predisposition, are aroused. His needs are but few and his frame of mind in providing for them is temperate and tranquil. He is poor (or considers himself so) only in his anxiety lest other men consider him poor and despise him on that account. Envy, the lust for power, greed, and the malignant inclinations bound up with these, besiege his nature, contented within itself, *directly he is among* 6:94 *men.* And it is not even necessary to assume that these are men sunk in evil and examples to lead him astray; it suffices that they are at hand, that they surround him, and that they are men, for them mutually to corrupt each other's predispositions and make one another evil. If no means could be discovered for the forming of an alliance uniquely designed as a protection against this evil and for the furtherance of goodness in man—of a society, enduring, ever extending itself, aiming solely at the maintenance of morality, and counteracting evil with united forces—this association with others would keep man constantly in danger of falling again under its dominion, however much he may have done as a single individual to throw off the sovereignty of evil. As far as we can see, therefore, the sovereignty of the good principle is attainable, so far as men can work toward it, only through the establishment and spread of a society in accordance with, and [established] for the sake of, the laws of virtue, a society whose task and duty it is rationally to impress these laws in all their scope upon the entire human race. For only thus can we hope for a victory of the good over the evil principle. In addition to prescribing laws to each individual, morally legislative reason when giving moral laws also unfurls a banner of virtue as a rallying point for all who love the good, that they may gather beneath it and thus at the very start gain the upper hand over the evil which is attacking them without interruption.

A union of men under merely moral laws, patterned on the above idea, may be called an *ethical* society, and so far as these laws are public, an ethico-civil, in contrast to a juridico-civil, society; or [it may be called] an *ethical* commonwealth. It can exist within a political commonwealth and may even be made up of all its members; indeed, unless it is based upon such a commonwealth it can never be brought into existence by man. It has, however, a special and unique principle of union, virtue, and hence a form and constitution which fundamentally distinguish it from the political commonwealth. At the same time there is a certain analogy between these two kinds of commonwealths, in view of which the former may also be called an *ethical state, i.e.,* a *realm* of virtue, or of the good 6:95 principle. The idea of such a state possesses a thoroughly well-grounded objective existence in human reason and in man's duty to join such a state, even though, subjectively, we can never hope that man's good will may lead mankind to decide to work with unanimity toward this goal.

DIVISION ONE

PHILOSOPHICAL ACCOUNT OF THE VICTORY OF THE GOOD PRINCIPLE IN THE FOUNDING OF A KINGDOM OF GOD ON EARTH

I. CONCERNING THE ETHICAL STATE OF NATURE

A *juridico-civil* (political) *state* is the relation of men to each other in which they all alike stand socially under *public juridical laws* (which are, as a class, laws of coercion). An *ethico-civil* state is that in which they are united under non-coercive laws, that is, *laws of virtue* alone.

Now just as the rightful but not therefore always righteous, or *juridical state of* NATURE is opposed to the first, *the ethical state of* NATURE is distinguished from the second. In both, each individual is his own judge, and there exists no powerful *public* authority to determine with legal power, according to laws, what is each man's duty in every situation that arises, and to bring about the universal performance of duty.

In an already existing political commonwealth all the political citizens, as such, are in an *ethical state of nature* and are entitled to remain therein; for it would be a contradiction (in terms) for the political commonwealth to compel its citizens to enter into an ethical commonwealth, since the very concept of the latter involves freedom from coercion. Every political commonwealth may indeed wish to be able to rule, according to laws of virtue, over the 6:96 spirits [of its citizens]; for then, when its methods of compulsion do not avail, for the human judge cannot penetrate into the depths of other men, their convictions about virtue would bring about what was required. But woe to the legislator who wishes to establish through force a polity directed to ethical ends! For in so doing he would not merely achieve the very opposite of an ethical polity but also undermine his political state and make it insecure. The citizen of the political commonwealth remains therefore, so far as its legislative function is concerned, completely free to enter with his fellow-citizens into an ethical association or group in addition [to the political] or to remain in this kind of state of nature, as he may wish. Only so far as an ethical commonwealth must rest on *public* laws and possess a constitution based on these laws are those who freely pledge themselves to enter into this ethical state bound, not [indeed] to accept orders from the political power as to how they shall or shall not fashion this ethical constitution internally, but to agree to limitations. Namely, to the condition that this constitution shall contain nothing which contradicts the duty of its members as *citizens of the state*—although when the ethical pledge is of the genuine sort the political limitation need cause no anxiety.

Further, because the duties of virtue apply to the entire human race, the concept of an ethical commonwealth is extended ideally to the whole of mankind, and thereby distinguishes itself from the concept of a political commonwealth. Hence even a large number of men united in that purpose can be called not the ethical commonwealth itself but only a particular society which strives toward harmony with all men, finally even with all rational beings in order to form an absolute ethical whole of which every partial society is only a representation or schema; for each of these societies in turn, in its relation to others of the same kind, can be represented as in the ethical state of nature and subject to all the defects thereof. This is precisely the situation of separate political states which are not united through a public international law.

II. MAN OUGHT TO LEAVE HIS ETHICAL STATE OF NATURE IN ORDER TO BECOME A MEMBER OF AN ETHICAL *COMMONWEALTH*

Just as the juridical state of nature is one of war of every man against every other, so too is the ethical state of nature one in which the good principle, which resides in each man, is continually attacked by the evil which is found in him and also in everyone else. Men as was noted above mutually corrupt one another's moral predispositions. Despite the good will of each individual, because they lack a principle which unites them, men abandon, through their dissensions, the common goal of goodness and, just as though they were *instruments of evil,* expose one another to the risk of falling once again under the rule of the evil principle. Again, just as the state of a lawless external and brutish freedom and independence from coercive laws is a state of injustice and of war, everyone against everyone, which a man ought to leave in order to enter into a politico-civil state: so is the ethical state of nature one of *open* conflict between principles of virtue and a state of inner immorality which the natural man ought to bestir himself to leave as soon as possible.

Now here we have a duty which is *sui generis,* not of men toward men, but of the human race toward itself. For the species of rational beings is objectively, through the idea of reason, destined for a social goal, namely, the promotion of the highest good as a social good. But because the highest moral good cannot be achieved merely by the exertions of the single individual toward his own moral perfection, but requires such individuals to unite into a whole directed toward the same goal, that is into a system of well- 6:98 disposed men, in which and through whose unity alone the highest moral good can be achieved, the idea of such a whole as a universal republic based on laws of virtue is an idea sharply distinguished from all moral laws which concern what we know to lie in our own power. It involves working toward a union of which we do not know whether, as such, it lies in our power or not. Hence this duty is distinguished from all others both in kind and in principle. We can already foresee that this duty will require the presupposition of another idea, namely, that of a higher moral Being through whose universal dispensation the forces of separate individuals, insufficient in themselves, are united for a common end. First of all, however, we must follow up the clue of that moral need [for social union] and see whither this will lead us.

III. THE CONCEPT OF AN ETHICAL COMMONWEALTH IS THE CONCEPT OF A *PEOPLE OF GOD* UNDER ETHICAL LAWS

If an ethical commonwealth is to come into being, all single individuals must be subject to public legislation, and all the laws which bind them must be capable of being regarded as commands of a common lawgiver. Now if the commonwealth to be established is to be *juridical,* the mass of people uniting itself into a whole would itself have to be the lawgiver, of constitutional laws, because legislation proceeds from the principle of *limiting the freedom of each to those conditions under which it can be consistent with the freedom of everyone else according to a common law,* and because, as a result, the general will sets up an external legal control. But if the commonwealth is to be *ethical,* the people as a people cannot itself be regarded as the lawgiver. For in such a commonwealth all the laws are expressly designed to promote the *morality* of actions, which is something *inner*

6:99 and hence cannot be subject to public human laws, whereas, in contrast, these public laws are directed only toward the *legality* of actions, which meets the eye, and not toward inner morality, which alone is in question here. There must therefore be someone other than the populace capable of being specified as the public lawgiver for an ethical commonwealth. And yet, ethical laws cannot be thought of as emanating *originally* merely from the will of this superior being as statutes, which, had he not first commanded them, would perhaps not be binding, for then they would not be ethical laws and the duty proper to them would not be the free duty of virtue but the coercive duty of law. Hence only he can be thought of as highest lawgiver of an ethical commonwealth with respect to whom all *true duties,* hence also the ethical, only must be represented as *at the same time* his commands. He must therefore also be "one who knows the heart," in order to see into the innermost parts of the convictions of each individual and, as is necessary in every commonwealth, to bring it about that each receives whatever his actions are worth. But this is the concept of God as moral ruler of the world. Hence an ethical commonwealth can be thought of only as a people under divine commands, i.e., as *a people of God,* and indeed *under laws of virtue.*

We might indeed conceive of a people of God under *statutory laws,* under such laws that obedience to them would concern not the morality but merely the legality of acts. This would be a juridical commonwealth, of which, indeed, God would be the lawgiver. Hence the *constitution* of this state would be theocratic. But men as

6:100 priests receiving His behests from Him directly, would build up an aristocratic *government.* Such a constitution however, whose existence and form rest wholly on an historical basis, cannot settle the problem of the morally-legislative reason giving moral laws. It is this problem the solution of which alone we are to effect. An institution under politico-civil laws whose lawgiver through God is yet external and therefore will come under review in the historical section. Here we have to do only with an institution whose laws are purely inward—a republic under laws of virtue, that is, a people of God "zealous of good works."

IV. THE IDEA OF A PEOPLE OF GOD CAN BE REALIZED THROUGH HUMAN ORGANIZATION ONLY IN THE FORM OF A CHURCH

The sublime, yet never wholly attainable, idea of an ethical commonwealth dwindles markedly under men's hands. It becomes an institution which, at best capable of representing only the pure form of such a commonwealth, is by the conditions created by man being a creature of senses, greatly circumscribed in its means for establishing such a whole. How indeed can one expect something perfectly straight to be fashioned out of such crooked wood?

To found a moral people of God is therefore a task whose consummation can be looked for not from men but only from God Himself. Yet man is not entitled on this account to be idle in this business and to let Providence rule, as though each could apply himself exclusively to his own private moral affairs and relinquish to a higher wisdom all the affairs of the human race as regards its moral destiny. Rather must man proceed as though everything depended upon him; only on this condition dare he hope that higher wisdom will grant the completion of his well-intentioned endeavors. 6:101

The wish of all well-disposed people is, therefore, "that the kingdom of God come, that His will be done on earth." But what preparations must they now make that it shall come to pass?

An ethical commonwealth under divine moral legislation is a *church* which, so far as it is not an object of possible experience, is called the *church invisible*, a mere idea of the union of all the righteous under direct and moral divine world-government, an idea serving all as the archetype of what is to be established by men. The *visible Church* is the actual union of men into a whole which harmonizes with that ideal. So far as each separate society maintains under public laws an order among its members in the relation of those who obey its laws to those who direct their obedience, the group, united into a whole, the church, is a *congregation* under authorities, who while called teachers or shepherds of souls, merely administer the affairs of the invisible supreme head thereof. In this function they are all called *servants* of the church, just as in the political commonwealth the visible ruler occasionally calls himself the highest servant of the state even though he recognizes no single individual over him and ordinarily not even the people as a whole. The true visible church is that which exhibits the moral kingdom of God on earth so far as it can be brought into existence by men. The requirements upon and, hence the tokens, of the true church are the following:

1. *Universality*, and hence its numerical oneness; for which it must possess this characteristic, that although divided and at variance in unessential opinions it is none the less with respect to its fundamental intention founded upon such basic principles as must necessarily lead to a general unification in a single church, hence no sectarian divisions.

2. Its *nature* or quality is *purity*, that is, a union under no motivating forces other than *moral* ones purified [and freed from] the stupidity of superstition and the madness of fanaticism.

3. Its *relation* under the principle of *freedom*; both the internal relation of its members to one another, and the external relation of the church to political power—both relations as in a *republic*. Hence neither a *hierarchy*, nor an *illuminatism*, which is a kind of *democracy* through special inspiration, where the inspiration of one man can differ from that of another, according to the whim of each.

4. Its *modality*, the *unchangeableness* of its *constitution*, yet with the reservation that incidental regulations concerning merely its *administration* may be changed according to time and circumstance; to this end, however, it must already contain within itself *a priori* settled principles in the idea of its purpose. (Thus [it operates] under primordial laws, once [for all]) laid down, as it were out of a book of laws, for guidance; not under arbitrary symbols which, since they lack authenticity, are fortuitous, exposed to contradiction, and changeable.

An ethical commonwealth, then, in the form of a church, that is as a mere *representative* of a city of God, really has, as regards its basic principles nothing resembling a political constitution. For its constitution is neither *monarchical* under a pope or patriarch, nor *aristocratic* under bishops and prelates, nor *democratic* (as of sectar-

6:102

ian *illuminati*). It could best of all be likened to that of a household or family under a common, though invisible, moral Father, whose holy Son, knowing His will and yet standing in blood relation with all members of the household, takes His place in making His will better known to them; these accordingly honor the Father in him and so enter with one another into a voluntary, universal, and enduring union of hearts.

SELECTIONS FROM

CONCERNING THE

COMMON SAYING:

THIS MAY BE TRUE

IN THEORY

BUT DOES NOT

APPLY TO PRACTICE

[1793]

Translated by Carl J. Friedrich

We call a synthesis (even a synthesis of practical rules) a theory if the rules concerned are principles of a certain generality, and if in that condition we abstract them from many conditions, which necessarily have an influence in the application of such principles. Conversely, not every activity can be called a practice but only a realization of that end which is conceived as a result of following certain general principles of procedure. It is evident that a link and transition is needed between theory and practice no matter how complete a theory may be. An act of judgment must be added to the rational concept which contains a rule and it is by this act of judgment that the practitioner can decide whether something is to be subsumed under the rule or not. Since there cannot again be rules for judgment on how a subsumption is to be achieved, for this would go on into the infinite, there will be theoreticians who, in their whole lives, can never become practical because they lack judgment. For example, there are doctors and lawyers who, although they did well in school, do not know what to do when they are called upon to give counsel.

But even where a natural gift [of judgment] is encountered there may be a lack of premises. That is to say, the theory may be incomplete and must be supplemented, perhaps by additional experiments and experience from which a doctor, an agriculturalist, a cameralist could derive new rules and thus complete this theory. In such cases, theory is of little practical use, not because of theory as such, but because there is not enough theory that an experienced man could have used, and what theory there is, is true theory even though it may not be systematically teachable. . . .

No man has the right to pretend that he is practically expert in a science and yet show contempt for theory without revealing that he is an ignoramus in his field. Apparently such a man believes that he can get further than he can by using theory, by groping about in experience on experiments without developing certain principles which constitute what I call theory and without having thought out an integrated approach to his work which, when it is developed according to method, is called a system.

However, it is more nearly permissible that an ignoramus should declare theory to be unnecessary and dispensable for his imagined peace than that a smart aleck could concede the value of theory for academic purposes, perhaps as an exercise of the mind, but then at the same time assert that things work quite differently in practice; that when one goes from school out into the world one will discover that one has pursued empty ideals and philosophic dreams.

Everyone would ridicule an empirical machinist who denounced general mechanics or an artilleryman who denounced the mathematical doctrine of ballistics, by declaring that the theory might be skillfully conceived but that it did not apply to practice because the execution [of these tasks] produced very different results from what the theory suggested. For, if the theory of friction were added to the knowledge of general mechanics and the theory of the resistance of air were added to the doctrine of ballistics; if, in other words, some more theory were added, these theories would indeed coincide with experience. Still, [it might be urged] that a theory which is concerned with objects of observation is quite different from a theory in which these objects are only present through concepts, as in the case with objects of mathematics and philosophy. The objects of mathematics and philosophy may be *thought of* quite well and without objection by reason but perhaps they can never be *given* but [will remain] only empty ideas. In practice, such ideas could be used either not at all or with disadvantage. If this were true, the common saying would yet be right in such cases. But in a theory which is founded on the *concept of duty*, the concern over the empty ideality of that concept is eliminated, for it would not be a duty to pursue a certain effect of our will if this effect were not possible in experience, even if experience is imagined as complete or approaching completion. In the present discussion we are only dealing with this kind of theory....

This maxim about theory and practice which has become com- 6:277
mon in our wordy and deedless times causes very great damage if it
is applied to moral questions; i.e., moral or legal duty. For the canon
of practical reason is involved in this realm. Here the value of [a
given] practice depends upon its appropriateness to the theory
upon which it is based. All is lost if empirical, and consequently accidental, conditions of the execution of the law are made the conditions of the law itself. Then a practice which is calculated in relation
to the probable result of previous experience is accorded the right
of determining the theory itself. The following essay is divided according to three standpoints: first, that of the private individual or
businessman; second, the statesman; third, the cosmopolitan or
world citizen.

II.

OF THE RELATION OF THEORY TO PRACTICE   8:289
IN CONSTITUTIONAL LAW
(Contra Hobbes)

Of all the compacts by which a number of people join themselves
into a society (*pactum sociale*), the compact for the establishment of
a *civic constitution* (*pactum unionis civilis*) is of such a particular kind
that this compact is intrinsically distinct from all other compacts in
the principle of its constitution (*constitutionis civilis*). . . . The joining
of many persons for some common end which they all share is an
element in all social compacts. But a joining of many is an end in itself which every one of them *ought to have.* In other words, a joining
which is an absolute and first duty in any external relations among
human beings who cannot avoid having mutual influence, such a
union is only to be encountered in a society which has reached the
civic state; that is, the state constituting a commonwealth (*gemeines
Wesen*). The end which is a duty in itself in such external relations
and which is itself the supreme formal condition of all other external duties, is the *right* of human beings [to live] *under public-coercive
laws* by which every man's [right] is determined and secured
against the interference of every other man.

The concept of an external right is derived from the concept of freedom in the external relation of human beings to each other. This concept has nothing at all to do with the purpose which all human beings naturally have; namely, a desire for happiness, nor has it anything to do with the means of achieving such happiness. Thus the desire for happiness must not be included as a ground for 8:290 determining laws of external right. *Right* is the limitation of every man's freedom so that it harmonizes with the freedom of every other man in so far as harmonization is possible according to a general law. *Public Law* is the totality of external laws which makes such a general consonance possible, since every limitation of freedom by the will of another is called coercion. It follows that the civic constitution is a relationship of *free* men who, despite their freedom for joining with others, are nevertheless placed under coercive laws. This is so because it is so willed by pure *a priori* legislating reason which has no regard for empirical purposes such as are comprised under the general name of happiness. For men have many different ideas about happiness and what can be conceived as constituting it. Therefore, if happiness is adopted as a basic criterion for what ought to be law, men's will cannot be brought under a common principle nor under an external law which harmonizes with every man's freedom.

The civic state, considered merely as a legal state, is based on the following *a priori* principles:

1. The freedom of each member of society as a *man*.
2. The *equality* of each member with every other as a *subject*.
3. The autonomy of each member of a commonwealth as a *citizen*.

These principles are not laws given by a constituted state; they are rather the only principles according to which a state could be constituted, [and be in keeping with] the rational principles of the external law of man. Therefore; (1) I will state the *freedom* of man as man as a principle for the constitution of the commonwealth in the following formula: No one may force anyone to be happy according to his manner of imagining the well-being of other men; instead, everyone may seek his happiness in the way that seems good to him as long as he does not infringe on the freedom of others to pursue a similar purpose, when such freedom may coexist with the freedom of every other man according to a possible and general law.

A government might be constituted on the principle of benevolence, with an attitude toward the people such as a father has toward his children, that is, a paternal government under which the subjects are obliged to behave merely passively like minor children who cannot distinguish between what is truly useful or noxious, the idea being that they are to learn how to be happy according to the judgment of the head of the state, depending entirely upon his kindness. But such a government is the greatest conceivable *despotism,* having a constitution which suspends all the freedom of the subjects who thereby have no rights whatsoever. Not a *paternal* but only a *patriotic* government can be concerned with men who are capable of [enjoying their rights] even in relation to the benevolence of the ruler. For a patriotic attitude influences everyone in the state, including its head, to regard the commonwealth as his maternal womb, or the country as the paternal soil from which he has sprung and which he must leave as a beloved token to his descendants. [To put it another way; a patriotic attitude is one] which makes the citizens consider themselves authorized to protect the rights of the commonwealth by laws, but not authorized to subject the commonwealth to the absolute discretion [of the head] for his purposes. This right of freedom belongs to man as the member of a commonwealth in so far as he is a being who is capable of having rights.

(2)[We may state the principle of] the *equality* [of each member of society] as a subject in the following formula: Every member of the commonwealth has a right of coercion against every other member and the head of the state is exempted from that right only because he is not a member but the creator and maintainer of the commonwealth. The head of the state alone has the authority to coerce without being himself subject to coercion.... For if he could also be coerced he would not be the head of the state and the se-

8:291

quence of authority would go upward into the infinite. If there were two persons free from coercion neither would be subject to coercive laws and neither could do to the other anything contrary to right, all of which is impossible. The general equality of men as subjects in a state coexists quite readily with the greatest inequality in degrees of the possessions men have, whether the possessions 8:292 consist of corporeal or spiritual superiority or in material possession besides. Hence the general equality of men also coexists with great inequality of specific rights of which there may be many. Thus it follows that the welfare of one man may depend to a very great extent on the will of another man, just as the poor are dependent on the rich and the one who is dependent must obey the other as a child obeys his parents or the wife her husband or again, just as one man has command over another, as one man serves and another pays, etc. Nevertheless, all subjects are equal to each other before the law which, as a pronouncement of the general will, can only be one. This law concerns the form and not the matter of the object regarding which I may possess a right. For no man can coerce another [under constitutional government] except through publicly-known law and through its executor, the head of the state, and by this same law every man may resist to the same degree. No one can lose this right to coerce others except through a crime. In other words, no one can make an agreement or other legal transaction to the effect that he has no rights but only duties. By such a contract he would deprive himself of [the right to] make a contract, and thus the contract would nullify itself.

From this concept of the equality of men as subjects in a commonwealth the following formula is derived: Every member of a commonwealth must be able to reach every level of status in the commonwealth which can belong to a subject and which [he can achieve] by his talent, his industry or his good fortune. No subject 8:293 may stand in his way as a result of hereditary privilege and thus keep him and his descendants down forever.

The birth is no deed of him who is born. Therefore no inequality of legal status and no subjection under coercive laws can come through birth except that which a man has in common with all others as subjects under the sole supreme legislative power. ... No one can pass on to his descendants the privileged status which he occupies in a commonwealth. To put it another way: A man cannot forcibly prevent his descendants from reaching a superior status by their own merit by qualifying them for such status through their birth. He may bequeath everything else because material things do not concern the personality and can be acquired as property and disposed of again. In a line of succession this may cause a considerable inequality of wealth among members of the commonwealth (such as the inequality between the mercenary and his employer, the estate-owner and the hired man). ... No man can lose the equality [he has in a commonwealth as a subject] except through his own crime and especially he cannot lose that equality through a contract or as a result of military occupation. For he cannot cease, by any legal act, either his own or another's, to be master of himself. No man may enter into the class of domestic animals, which can be used for all services the master pleases and which are maintained in service without their consent as long as the master wishes, even though he is subject to the restriction not to cripple or kill them (which may, as with the Indians, be sanctioned by religion). Man may be considered happy in any condition if he is conscious that his condition is due to himself, his ability, or his earnest effort or to circumstances for which others cannot be blamed. But [he may not be considered happy] if his condition is due to the irresistible will of another and if he does not rise to the same status as others who, 8:294 as his co-subjects, have no advantage over him as far as his rights are concerned.

(3) [The principle of] the autonomy (*sibisufficientia*) or self-sufficiency of a member of a commonwealth as a citizen; that is, as a co-legislator may be stated as follows: As regards legislation, all who are free and equal under pre-existing public laws must be considered equal, but not as concerns the right to give these laws. Those who are not capable of exercising that right are nevertheless, as members of the commonwealth, obliged to obey these laws and are thereby entitled to the protection of the law, but not as citizens.

All right depends upon laws. A publicly-known law determining what everyone shall be legally permitted or forbidden [to do] is an act of the public will from which all right proceeds and which cannot itself act contrary to right. For this purpose no other will is possible but the will of the entire people because [through this will] all men decide about all men and hence everyone decides about himself. For no one can be considered unjust to himself. This basic law which originates only in the general and united will of the people is called the *original contract.*

He who has the right to vote on basic legislation is called a citizen (*citoyen,* i.e., *Staatsbürger,* not *Stadtbürger,* i.e., *bourgeois*). The requisite quality for this [status], apart from the natural one that the person not be a child nor a woman, is only this: that such a person be *his own master* (*sui iuris*) and hence that he have some property (under which we may include any art, craft, or science) that would provide him with sustenance. [To put this another way, he must be] a man who, when he must earn a livelihood from others, acquires property only by selling what is his own and not by conceding to others the right to make use of his strength. Consequently he *serves* no one, in the strict sense of the word, but the commonweal. In this respect artisans and great or small property-owners are all equal and each is entitled to only one vote. Regarding large property owners we leave aside the question of how a man might rightfully come into possession of more land than he can himself work, for acquisition by military conquest is no first acquisition. We also leave aside how it happened that many men who otherwise might have acquired permanent property have thus been reduced merely to serve others in order to live. In any case it would be contrary to the principle of equality if a law established the privileged status for those large estate owners so that their descendants would always remain large estate owners as under feudalism without there being any possibility that the estates would be sold or divided by inheritance and thus made useful for more people. Nor is it proper that only certain arbitrarily selected classes acquire some of these divided properties. Thus the big estate owner destroys the many smaller owners and their voice [in the commonwealth] who might be occupying his place. He does not vote in their stead for he has

8:296

only *one* vote.... Not the amount of property, but merely the number of those owning any property, should serve as a basis for the number of voters.

All who possess the right to vote must agree on this basic law of how to arrive at public justice; [for if they did not] there would be a conflict of law between those who agree to it and those who do not, which would necessitate a still higher legal principle to decide the issue. Since such general agreement cannot be expected of an entire people, only a majority of the votes must be considered to be the best that can be attained. In a large nation even this majority will not be that of the voters, but merely that of delegates representing the people. But then this principle of being satisfied by a majority will have to be presumed as having been accepted by general agreement; that is, through a contract, and hence [this principle will have to be presumed to be] the supreme reason for constituting a civic constitution. 8:297

CONCLUSION

In the foregoing we have an original contract upon which alone can a civic, and therefore completely legal, constitution among men be established. But this contract, which is called *contractus originarius* or *pactum sociale* ... need not be assumed to be a fact, indeed it is not [even possible as such. To suppose that would be like insisting] that before anyone would be bound to respect such a civic constitution, that it be proved first of all from history that a people, whose rights and obligations we have entered into as their descendants, had *once upon a time* executed such an act and had left a reliable document or instrument, either orally or in writing, concerning this contract. Instead, this contract is a *mere idea* of reason which has undoubted practical reality; namely, to oblige every legislator to give us laws in such a manner that the laws *could* have originated from the united will of the entire people and to regard every subject in so far as he is a citizen as though he had consented to such [an expression of the general] will. This is the testing stone of the rightness of every publicly-known law, for if a law were such that it was impossible for an entire people to give consent to it (as for example a law that a certain class of subjects, by inheritance, should have the privilege of the *status of lords*), then such a law is unjust. On the other hand, if there is a mere *possibility* that a people might consent to a (certain) law, then it is a duty to consider that the law is just, even though at the moment the people might be in such a position or have a point of view that would result in their refusing to give their consent to it if asked.[1]

8:298 But this limitation is evidently valid only for the judgment of the legislator, not for that of the subject. Therefore if a people should judge that they will probably lose their happiness from certain actual legislation, then what should they do? Should they not resist? The answer can only be that they can do nothing but obey. We are not interested here in the happiness of the subjects supposedly resulting from the institutions or the administration of the commonwealth but are interested only [in the law which is to be secured] for everyone by this institution and administration. This is the supreme principle with which all maxims concerning the commonwealth must begin and which is not restricted by any other. With regard to happiness no generally valid principle can be offered for legislation. For the conditions of the time as well as the very contradictory and constantly changing illusions as to what constitutes happiness—and no one can prescribe for anyone wherein he should seek happiness—render impossible all fixed principles and make the idea of happiness by itself unfit to be a principle of legislation. The proposition: *salus publica suprema civitatis lex est* remains unreduced in value and authority but the public weal which must be considered first is precisely that legal constitution which secures

1 For example, if a war tax, proportional for all subjects, were imposed, the subjects cannot, because the tax is onerous, claim that the tax is unjust because the war is unnecessary in their opinion. On that question they are not entitled to judge, as it is always possible that the war was inevitable and hence the tax is indispensable and so must be considered rightful in the judgment of the subjects. But if, in such a war, certain estate owners were bothered with requisitions which others in the same position were spared, then it is easy to see that an entire people could never consent to such a law. The people are therefore entitled at least to make representations against the law because they could not consider so uneven a distribution of burdens.

freedom for each man under the law. At the same time each man is free to seek his happiness in any way that seems best to him as long as he does not infringe upon the general lawful freedom and thereby on the rights of his fellow-citizens . . .

———

From this it follows that all resistance against the supreme legisla- 8:299 tive power, all instigation to rebellion, is the worst and most punishable crime in a commonwealth because this destroys the foundation of a commonwealth. The prohibition (of rebellion) is absolute. Even when the [supreme legislative] power, or its agent, the head of the state, has violated the original contract and he thereby, in the opinion of the subject, loses the right to legislate because the supreme power has authorized the government to be run thoroughly tyrannically, even in this case no assistance is allowed the subject for a countermeasure. The reason is that under an al- 8:300 ready existing civic constitution the people have no lawful judgment as to how the constitution should be administered. For, if one assumes that the people have such a power of judgment and have exercised it contrary to that of the real head of the state, who is to decide which one is right? Neither can do so, being judge in his own cause. Therefore there would have to be a head above the head of the state to decide between the people and the head of the state, which is self-contradictory.

Nor can some kind of emergency law, having a presumed right to do what is unlawful in the most extreme crisis, be introduced here and provide the key for closing the gate to restrict the power of the people. The head of the state may believe that he can justify his harsh procedure by the insubordination of his subjects, as readily as the subjects can justify their rebellion from complaints regarding their exceptional suffering. Who then shall decide? Only he who controls the supreme enforcement of the law can do this, and that is precisely the head of the state and hence there cannot be anyone in a commonwealth with the right to deny him this power.

Nevertheless I know respected men who assert this right of the 8:301 subject to resist his superior under certain circumstances. Among these I will mention here only Achenwall who is very cautious, definite and modest in his doctrines concerning natural law. He says: "If the danger which threatens a commonwealth as a result of the continued endurance of injustice from its head is greater than the danger which may be feared from using arms against him, then may the people resist him and on behalf of this right may they deviate from their part of submission and dethrone him as a tyrant." Then he concludes: "The people thus return into a state of nature."

I can well believe that in any actual case neither Achenwall nor any of the other honest men who, agreeing with him have reasoned concerning this matter, would have ever given counsel or assent to such dangerous undertakings. It cannot be doubted that if the rebellions, by which Switzerland, the United Netherlands and Great Britain have achieved their highly praised constitutions, had failed, the readers of the history of those rebellions would regard the execution of their celebrated originators as nothing more than the well-earned punishment of great criminals. For, concerning the grounds of legality [for such a venture] our judgment is usually affected by the outcome, although the outcome was uncertain at a time when the grounds of legality were certain. But it is clear that, even granting that no injustice is done through such a rebellion to a prince who violates a real contract with the people such as the *Joyeuse Entrée*, nevertheless the people have acted highly illegally by seeking their rights in this manner ...

8:302   I can see here what damage [is caused in public law by] the principle of happiness, which is actually incapable of forming a distinct principle just as [that principle causes difficulties] in ethics even when those who teach this doctrine have the best intentions. The sovereign makes the people happy according to his own ideas and becomes a despot; the people do not want to surrender the general human desire for seeking their own happiness and become rebels. If one had first of all asked what is right (for these principles which are certain *a priori* cannot be upset by empiricists), the idea of the social contract would remain in indisputable authority, not as a fact ... but merely as a rational principle for evaluating every public legal constitution. [If one knew what was right] then one would understand that until there is a general will the people have no coercive right against their lord because they can only legally coerce through him. But if there is a general will there still can be no force exercised against it because then the people themselves are the supreme authority. In short, people are never entitled to use force against the head of the state or to obstruct him in work or deed.

In practice, we see this theory quite adequately confirmed by the constitution of Great Britain where the people are as proud of their constitution as though it were the matrix of the whole world. We find that the constitution is silent regarding any authority of the people [to resist] in case the monarch should violate the contract of 1688. Does this mean that, because there is no law concerning this aspect, there is reserved the secret right of rebellion? For, a constitution which would contain a law authorizing anyone to overthrow the existing constitution upon which all specific laws rest, involves a clear contradiction because then the constitution would have to contain a *publicly constituted* counter-force.[2] This would mean having a second head of the state who would protect the rights of the people against the first head and then in turn a third to decide between the two. 8:303

Those leaders of the [British] people, or if you wish, guardians, being worried over such an accusation in case their enterprise should fail, invented a voluntary abandonment of the government by the monarch whom they scared away and they did this instead of claiming the right to depose him whereby they would have brought the constitution into contradiction with itself. Since no one, I trust, will accuse me of flattering the princes too much by asserting their inviolability, I also hope that I will be spared the accusation that I assert too much on the part of the people when I say that they likewise have inalienable rights against the head of the state even though those rights cannot be coercive.

Hobbes is of the opposite opinion. According to him (*de Cive*,

---

2 No right in a state can be kept under cover by a secret mental reservation, least of all the right [of revolution] which the people claim as belonging to the constitution, because all laws derived from it must be considered to have sprung from a public will. Therefore the constitution would, if it permitted revolution, have to declare this right publicly as well as the procedure by which to make use of it.

Chap. 7, 14) the head of the state is not obliged to anything by contract and he can act contrary to law and right against the citizen in whatever way he might decide regarding him. This proposition would be correct if that which is contrary to law and right were understood to mean a kind of injury providing the injured with a right against him who has acted contrary to law and right. But stated generally as Hobbes does, the proposition is terrifying. The non-resisting subject must be able to assume that his ruler does not want to do him injustice, for every man has his inalienable rights which he cannot give up even should he want to and concerning which he is entitled to form his own judgments. But the injustice, which in his opinion he is suffering occurs according to the above assumption only because of error and ignorance of certain (unforseen) consequences of the law the supreme power has made. Therefore the citizen must have the privilege of making public his opinion on the ordinances of the supreme power when it seems to him that they constitute an injustice against the commonwealth. Indeed, this privilege should be supported by the ruler himself, for to assume that the ruler could not err sometimes or be unaware of things would mean that we imagine him to be gifted with divine intuition and to be superior to mankind. As a result, the freedom of the pen is the sole shield of the rights of the people. Of course, this [freedom] should be kept within the limits of respect and loyalty for the constitution under which one lives, [and it should be used in the spirit of] the liberal frame of mind which that constitution inspires in the subjects. To some extent this sort of limitation is imposed by writers on each other so they do not lose their freedom. Denying the subject this freedom does not only mean, as in Hobbes, depriving him of all claim to justice before a sovereign; it also means depriving the sovereign of all knowledge of those matters which he himself would change if he knew the views of the subject and thus he would be put into self-contradiction. [In this connection it must be remembered that] the will of the sovereign only gives commands to the subject merely as a citizen because he represents the general will of the people. Insinuating to the sovereign that he should be worried about disturbances being created in the state by such thoughts and speeches would arouse an awakening in him and make him distrust his own power and come to hate the people. To sum up: the general principle according to which a people may judge negatively what is not ordered by the supreme legislative power in accordance with the best will of the people is contained in the proposition: *What a people cannot decide concerning themselves, the legislator cannot decide concerning the people.*

———

Nowhere do people engaged in practical pursuits speak with more 8:305
pretentiousness derogatively of theory and neglecting all pure rational principles, than on the question of what is required for a good constitution. This is because a legal constitution which has existed a long time accustoms people to its rule by and by and makes them inclined to evaluate their happiness as well as their rights in the light of the conditions under which everything has been quietly going forward. Men fail to do the opposite; namely, to evaluate the existing constitution according to concepts [stan- 8:306
dards] provided by reason in regard to both happiness and right. As a result, men prefer this passive state to the dangerous task of seeking a better one. They are following the maxim which Hippocrates urges doctors to keep in mind: *Judgment is uncertain and experiment dangerous. (Judicium anceps, experimentum pericolosum.)* In spite of their differences, all constitutions which have existed a long time, whatever their faults, produce one and the same result; namely, that people become satisfied with what they have. It follows from this that in considering people's welfare, theory is apparently not valued but all depends upon practices derived from experience.

[Against this I assert that] in reason there exists a concept which may be expressed by the words constitutional law (or constitutional justice—*Staatsrecht*). If this concept has binding force for men who are pitched against each other through the antagonism of their freedom, [perhaps we can further assume that] this concept has objective practical reality without our considering what good or ill may result; for knowledge of these results is based purely on experience. If this be so then constitutional law is based upon principles *a priori*, since what is right cannot be taught by experience. A theory of constitutional law exists with which practice must agree in order to be valid [from a moral standpoint].

Nothing can be brought forward against this proposition except [the fact] that human beings, even though they have a concept of their rights, are incapable and unworthy of being treated according to their rights because of their refractoriness and therefore a supreme power must proceed to keep them in order according to rules of prudence. However, this desperate conclusion (*salto mortale*) implies that, since there no longer is any mention of right but only of force, then people may also try their own power and thus endanger every legal constitution. For, if there is nothing which compels immediate respect through reason, such as basic human rights, then all attempts to influence men's arbitrary will cannot restrain their [arbitrary] freedom. On the other hand, if in addition to benevolence, right (law—*Recht*) speaks loudly, then human nature does not appear so corrupted that it does not hear this voice with respect. . . .

TO ETERNAL PEACE

[1795]

Translated by Carl J. Friedrich

Whether the above satirical inscription, once put by a certain Dutch innkeeper on his signboard on which a graveyard was painted, holds of men in general, or particularly of the heads of states who are never sated with war, or perhaps only of those philosophers who are dreaming that sweet dream of peace, may remain undecided. However, in presenting his ideas, the author of the present essay makes one condition. The practical statesman should not, in case of a controversy with the political theorist, suspect that any danger to the state lurks behind the opinions which such a theorist ventures honestly and openly to express. Consistency demands this of the practical statesman, for he assumes a haughty air and looks down upon the theorist with great self-satisfaction as a mere theorizer whose impractical ideas can bring no danger to the state, since the state must be founded on principles derived from experience. The worldly-wise statesman may therefore, without giving himself great concern, allow the theorizer to throw his eleven bowling balls all at once. By this "saving clause" the author of this essay knows himself protected in the best manner possible against all malicious interpretation.

FIRST SECTION

Which Contains the Preliminary Articles of an Eternal Peace Between States

1. *"No treaty of peace shall be held to be such, which is made with the secret reservation of the material for a future war."*

For, in that event, it would be a mere truce, a postponement of hostilities, not *peace*. Peace means the end of all hostilities, and to attach to it the adjective "eternal" is a pleonasm which at once arouses suspicion. The pre-existing reasons for a future war, including those not at the time known even to the contracting parties, are all of them obliterated by a genuine treaty of peace; no search of documents, no matter how acute, shall resurrect them from the archives. It is Jesuitical casuistry to make a mental reservation that there might be old claims to be brought forward in the future, of which neither party at the time cares to make mention, because both are too much exhausted to continue the war, but which they intend to assert at the first favorable opportunity. Such a procedure, when looked at in its true character, must be considered beneath the dignity of rulers; and so must the willingness to attempt such legal claims be held unworthy of a minister of state.

8:344

But, if enlightened notions of political wisdom assume the true honor of the state to consist in the continual increase of power by any and every means, such a judgment will, of course, evidently seem academic and pedantic.

2. *"No state having an independent existence, whether it be small or great, may be acquired by another state through inheritance, exchange, purchase or gift."*

A state is not a possession (*patrimonium*) like the soil on which it has a seat. It is a society of men, which no one but they themselves is called upon to command or to dispose of. Since, like a tree, such a state has its own roots, to incorporate it as a graft into another state is to take away its existence as a moral person and to make of it a thing. This contradicts the idea of the original contract, without which no right over a people can even be conceived.[1] Everybody knows into what danger, even in the most recent times the supposed right of thus acquiring states has brought Europe. Other parts of the world have never known such a practice. But in Europe states can even marry each other. On the one hand, this is a new

---

1 An hereditary monarchy is not a state which can be inherited by another state. Only the right to govern it may be transferred by heredity to another person. Thus the state acquires a ruler, not the ruler a state.

kind of industry, a way of making oneself predominant through family connections without any special effort; on the other, it is a way of extending territorial possessions. The letting out of troops of one state to another against an enemy not common to the two is in the same class. The subjects are thus used and consumed like things to be handled at will.

3. *"Standing armies shall gradually disappear."*   8:345

Standing armies incessantly threaten other states with war by their readiness to be prepared for war. States are thus stimulated to outdo one another in number of armed men without limit. Through the expense thus occasioned peace finally becomes more burdensome than a brief war. These armies are thus the cause of wars of aggression, undertaken in order that this burden may be thrown off. In addition to this, the hiring of men to kill and be killed, an employment of them as mere machines and tools in the hands of another (the state), cannot be reconciled with the rights of humanity as represented in our own person. The case is entirely different where the citizens of a state voluntarily drill themselves and their fatherland against attacks from without. It would be exactly the same with the accumulation of a war fund if the difficulty of ascertaining the amount of the fund accumulated did not work a counter effect. Looked upon by other states as a threat of war, a big fund would lead to their anticipating such a war by making an attack themselves, because of the three powers—the power of the army, the power of alliance, and the power of money—the last might well be considered the most reliable instrument of war.

4. *"No debts shall be contracted in connection with the foreign affairs of the state."*

The obtaining of money, either from without or from within the state, for purposes of internal development—the improvement of highways, the establishment of new settlements, the storing of surplus for years of crop failure, etc.—need create no suspicion. Foreign debts may be contracted for this purpose. But, as an instrument of the struggle between the powers, a credit system of debts endlessly growing though always safe against immediate demand (the demand for payment not being made by all the creditors at the same time)—such a system, the ingenious invention of a trading people in this century, constitutes a dangerous money power. It is a resource for carrying on war which surpasses the resources of all other states taken together. It can only be exhausted through a possible deficit of the taxes, which may be long kept off through the increase in commerce brought about by the stimulating influence of the loans on industry and trade. The facility thus afforded of making war, coupled with the apparently innate inclination thereto of those possessing power, is a great obstacle in the way of eternal peace. Such loans, therefore, must be forbidden by a preliminary article—all the more because the finally unavoidable bankruptcy of such a state must involve many other states without their responsibility in the disaster, thus inflicting upon them a public injury. Consequently, other states are at least justified in entering into an alliance against such a state and its pretensions.

8:346

5. *"No state shall interfere by force in the constitution and government of another state."*

For what could justify it in taking such action? Could perhaps some offense do it which that state gives to the subjects of another? Such a state ought rather to serve as a warning, because of the example of the evils which a people brings upon itself by its lawlessness. In general, the bad example given by one free person to another (as a *scandalum acceptum*) is no violation of the latter's rights. The case would be different if a state because of internal dissension should be split into two parts, each of which, while constituting a separate state, should lay claim to the whole. An outside state, if it should render assistance to one of these, could not be charged with interfering in the constitution of another state, as that state would then be in a condition of anarchy. But as long as this inner strife was not decided, the interference of outside powers would be a trespass on the rights of an independent people struggling only with its own inner weakness. This interference would be an actual offense which would so far tend to render the autonomy of all states insecure.

6. *"No state at war with another shall permit such acts of warfare as must make mutual confidence impossible in time of future peace: such as the employment of assassins, of poisoners, the violation of articles of surrender, the instigation of treason in the state against which it is making war, etc."*

These are dishonorable stratagems. Some sort of confidence in an enemy's frame of mind must remain even in time of war, for otherwise no peace could be concluded, and the conflict would become a war of extermination. For after all, war is only the regrettable instrument of asserting one's right by force in the primitive state of nature where there exists no court to decide in accordance with law. In this state neither party can be declared an unjust enemy, for this presupposes a court decision. The outcome of the fight, as in the case of a so-called "judgment of God," decides on whose side 8:347 the right is. Between states no war of punishment can be conceived, because between them there is no relation of superior and subordinate.

From this it follows that a war of extermination, in which destruction may come to both parties at the same time, and thus to all rights too, would allow eternal peace only upon the graveyard of the whole human race. Such a war, therefore, as well as the use of the means which might be employed in it, is wholly forbidden.

But that the methods of war mentioned above inevitably lead to such a result is clear from the fact that such hellish arts, which are in themselves degrading, when once brought into use do not continue long within the limits of war but are continued in time of peace, and thus the purpose of the peace is completely frustrated. A good example is furnished by the employment of spies, in which only the dishonorableness of others (which unfortunately cannot be exterminated) is taken advantage of.

Although all the laws above laid down would objectively—that 8:348 is, in the intention of the powers, be negative laws, (*leges prohibitiae*) yet some of them are strict laws, which are valid without consideration of the circumstances. They insist that the abuse complained of be abolished at once. Such are our rules number 1, 5, and 6. The others, namely rules number 2, 3, and 4, though not meant to be permitting exception from the "rule of law," yet allow for a good deal of subjective discretion in respect to the application of the rules. They permit delay in execution without their purpose being lost sight of. The purpose, however, does not admit of delay till doomsday—"to the Greek Calends," as Augustus was wont to say. The restitution, for example, to certain states of the freedom of which they have been deprived, contrary to our second article, must not be indefinitely put off. The delay is not meant to prevent restitution, but to avoid undue haste which might be contrary to the intrinsic purpose. For the prohibition laid down by the article relates only to the mode of acquisition, which is not to be allowed to continue, but it does not relate to the present state of possessions. This present state, though not providing the needed just title, yet was held to be legitimate at the time of the supposed acquisition, according to the then current public opinion.

SECOND SECTION

Which Contains the Definitive Articles for Eternal Peace Among States

The state of peace among men who live alongside each other is no state of nature (*status naturalis*). Rather it is a state of war which 8:349 constantly threatens even if it is not actually in progress. Therefore the state of peace must be *founded;* for the mere omission of the threat of war is no security of peace, and consequently a neighbor may treat his neighbor as an enemy unless he has guaranteed such security to him, which can only happen within a state of law.[2]

8:349   2 It is often assumed that one is not permitted to proceed with hostility against anyone unless he has already actively hurt him, and this is indeed very true if both live in a civic state under law, for by entering into this state one man proffers the necessary security to another through the superior authority which has power over both.—But man (or the nation) in a mere state of nature deprives me of this security and hurts me by this very state, simply by being near me, even though not actively (*facto*). He hurts me by the lawlessness of his state (*statu iniusto*) by which I am constantly threatened, and therefore I can compel him either to enter into a communal state under law with me or to leave my vicinity.—Hence the postu-

First Definitive Article of the Eternal Peace

The civil constitution in each state should be republican.

A republican constitution is a constitution which is founded upon three principles. First, the principle of the *freedom* of all members of a society as men. Second, the principle of the *dependence* of all upon a single common legislation as subjects, and third, the principle of the *equality* of all as *citizens.* This is the only constitution which is derived from the idea of an original contract upon which all rightful legislation of a nation must be based.[3]

8:350

---

late which underlies all the following articles in this: all men who can mutually affect each other should belong under a joint civic constitution.

There are three kinds of constitution under law as far as concerns the persons who belong under it: (1) the constitution according to the law of national citizenship of all men belonging to a nation (*ius civitatis*); (2) the constitution according to international law regulating the relation of states with each other (*ius gentium*); (3) the constitution according to the law of world citizenship which prevails insofar as men and states standing in a relationship of mutual influence may be viewed as citizens of a universal state of all mankind (*ius cosmopoliticum*).

This classification is not arbitrary but necessary in relation to the idea of eternal peace. For if even one of these were in a relation of physical influence upon the other and yet in a state of nature, the state of war would be connected with it, and to be relieved of this state is our very purpose.

3External lawful *freedom* may be defined as follows: it is the authority [*Befugnis*] not to obey any external laws except those which I have consented to.—Likewise, external (lawful) *equality* in a state is the relationship of the citizens according to which no one can obligate another legally without at the same time subjecting himself to the law of being obligated by the other in the same manner. (We do not explain the principle of lawful dependence since this principle is implied in the conception of any kind of constitution.)—The validity of these innate and inalienable rights which are implied in his very humanity is confirmed by the principle of the lawful relations of man to higher beings (in case he believes in them). For he imagines himself, according to these very same principles, as the citizen of a natural world.—For so far as my freedom is concerned, I have no obligation even with regard to the divine laws which I recognize by pure reason except insofar as I have given my own consent (for only in terms of the law of freedom of my own reason can I form a conception of the divine will). [Kant then argues that the principle of equality cannot be similarly confirmed because God has no equals.] Concerning the right of all citizens to be equal in their subjection to the law, the only thing which matters in regard to the question of the admissibility of a hereditary nobility is the following: whether the superior rank of one subject to another precedes merit or the latter the former, it seems obvious that it is most uncertain whether merit (ability and loyalty in one's office) will follow. Hence it is as if rank were attributed without

8:350

This republican constitution is therefore, as far as law is concerned, the one which underlies every kind of civil constitution, 8:351 and the question which we are now facing is, whether this is also the only one which can lead to eternal peace.

The answer is that the republican constitution does offer the 8:352 prospect of the desired purpose, that is to say, eternal peace, and the reason is as follows: If, as is necessarily the case under the constitution, the consent of the citizens is required in order to decide whether there should be war or not, nothing is more natural than that those who would have to decide to undergo all the deprivations of war will very much hesitate to start such an evil game. For the deprivations are many, such as fighting oneself, paying for the cost of the war out of one's own possessions, and repairing the devastation which it costs, and to top all the evils there remains a burden of debts which embitters the peace and can never be paid off on account of approaching new wars. By contrast, under a constitution where the subject is not a citizen and which is therefore not republican, it is the easiest thing in the world to start a war. The head of the state is not a fellow citizen but owner of the state, who loses none of his banquets, hunting parties, pleasure castles, festivities, etc. Hence he will resolve upon war as a kind of amusement on very insignificant grounds and will leave the justification to his diplomats, who are always ready to lend it an air of propriety.

It is important not to confuse the republican constitution with the democratic one as is commonly done. The following may be noted. The forms of a state (*civitas*) may be classified according to the difference of the persons who possess the highest authority, or they may be classified according to the method by which the people are governed by their rulers, whoever they may be. The first method is

---

merit to the most favored (to be commander). Clearly the general will of the people would never adopt such a provision in its original contract, which is the basis of all right, and in short a nobleman [*Edelmann*] is not necessarily a *noble* man [*edler Mann*]. As far as nobility derived from *office* [*Amtsadel*] is concerned, rank in that case does not attach as a position to the person but is connected with the post, and therefore the principle of equality is not violated, for when a man quits his office, he resigns his rank and returns to the people.

properly called the form of rulership (*forma imperii*). Only three such forms are conceivable; for either *one*, or a *few* associated with each other, or all who together constitute civil society possess the power to rule (*autocracy*, *aristocracy*, and *democracy*—the power of princes, of the nobility, and of the people).

The second method is the form of government (*forma regiminis*) and relates to the way in which the state employs its sovereign power—the constitution, which is an act of the general will by which a mass becomes a nation. The form of government in this case is either *republican* or *despotic*. Republicanism means the constitutional principle according to which the executive power (the government [*Regierung*]) is separated from the legislative power. *Despotism* exists when the state arbitrarily executes the laws which it has itself made; in other words, where the public will is treated by the prince as if it were his private will.

Among the three forms of state (or rulership), that of *democracy* is necessarily a *despotism* in the specific meaning of the word, because it establishes an executive power where all may decide regarding one and hence against one who does not agree, so that all are nevertheless not all—a situation which implies a contradiction of the general will with itself and with freedom. For all forms of government which are not *representative* are essentially *without form*, because the legislative cannot at the same time and in the same person be the executor of the legislative will; just as the general proposition in logical reasoning cannot at the same time be the specific judgment which falls under the general rule. The other two forms of rulership [*Staatsverfassung*] are defective also insofar as they give a chance to this (despotic) form of government. But it is at least possible that they provide a method of governing which is in accord with the *spirit* of representative system. Frederick II *said* at least that he was merely the highest servant of the state—while the democratic system makes this impossible, because all want to be ruler.[4]

It is therefore possible to say that the smallest number of truly

4 Many have criticized the high-sounding titles which are often given a ruler, such as "divinely anointed," "executor of God's will on earth," "God's representative," calling them

8:353

representative rulers approximates most closely to the possibility of a republicanism and may be expected to reach it eventually by gradual reforms. Such an evolution is harder in an aristocracy than in a monarchy, while in a democracy it is impossible to achieve this kind of constitution—which is the only constitution perfectly in accord with law and right [*Recht*]—except through a revolution.[5]

The people are very much more concerned with the form of government in this sense than with the form of rulership [*Staatsform*], although a good deal depends upon the latter's adequacy to realize the former's end. But if the form of government is to be appropriate to the idea of law and right, it requires the representative system. For only in this system is a republican form of government possible. Without it the form of government is despotic and violent, whatever the constitution may be.

None of the ancient, so-called republics knew this representative system, and hence they were bound to dissolve into despotism, which is the more bearable under the rule of a single man.

8:354

SECOND DEFINITIVE ARTICLE OF THE ETERNAL PEACE

The law of nations (Völkerrecht) should be based upon a *federalism* of free states.

Nations may be considered like individual men which hurt each

---

coarse and flattering, but it seems to me without reason. Far from making the prince conceited, they should make him humble, if he has brains (which surely one must assume) and therefore is conscious that he has assumed an office which is too big for a man: to administer man's law, the most sacred thing that God has on earth, to hurt this prized possession of God in any way must surely worry any man.

5 Mallet du Pan claims in his profound-sounding, yet hollow and empty language that after many years' experience he had come to accept the truth of Pope's well-known saying: "O'er forms of government let fools contest; that which is best administered is best." If that is to mean that the best-led government is the best led, then, to use a phrase of Swift, he has cracked a nut which rewarded him with a worm. If it is to mean that the best-led government is the best form of government, i.e., constitution, then it is very false; examples of good governing do not prove anything about the form of government. Who has governed better than a *Titus* or a *Marcus Aurelius?* Yet the one was succeeded by a *Domitian*, the other by a *Commodus*. This would have been impossible under a good constitution, since their incapacity to govern was known soon enough.

other in the state of nature, when they are not subject to laws, by their very propinquity. Therefore each, for the sake of security, may demand and should demand of the other to enter with him into a constitution similar to the civil one where the right of each may be secured. This would be a *union of nations* [*Völkerbund*] which would not necessarily have to be a *state of nations* [*Völkerstaat*]. A state of nations contains a contradiction, for every state involves the relation of a superior (legislature) to a subordinate (the subject people), and many nations would, in a single state, constitute only one nation, which is contradictory since we are here considering the right of nations toward each other as long as they constitute different states and are not joined together into one.

We look with deep aversion upon the way primitive peoples are attached to their lawless liberty—a liberty which enables them to fight incessantly rather than subject themselves to the restraint of the law to be established by themselves; in short, to prefer wild freedom to a reasonable one. We look upon such an attitude as raw, uncivilized, and an animalic degradation of humanity. Therefore, one should think, civilized peoples (each united in a state) would hasten to get away from such a depraved state as soon as possible. Instead, each *state* insists upon seeing the essence of its majesty (for popular majesty is a paradox) in this, that it is not subject to any external coercion. The luster of its ruler consists in this, that many thousands are at his disposal to be sacrificed for a cause which is of no concern to them, while he himself is not exposed to any danger. Thus a Bulgarian Prince answered the Emperor who good naturedly wanted to settle their quarrel by a duel: "A smith who has prongs won't get the hot iron out of the fire with his bare hands." The difference between the European savages and those in America is primarily this, that while some of the latter eat their enemies, the former know how better to employ their defeated foe than to feast on them—the Europeans rather increase the number of sub- 8:355 jects, that is, the number of tools for more extended wars.

In view of the evil nature of man, which can be observed clearly in the free relation between nations (while in a civil and legal state it is covered by governmental coercion), it is surprising that the word *law* [*Recht*] has not been entirely banned from the politics of war as pedantic, and that no state has been bold enough to declare itself publicly as of this opinion. For people in *justifying* an aggressive war still cite HUGO GROTIUS, PUFENDORF, VATTEL, and others (all of them miserable consolers). This is done, although their code of norms, whether stated philosophically or juristically, does not have the least *legal* force; nor can it have such force, since states as such are not subject to a common external coercion. There is not a single case known in which a state has been persuaded by arguments reinforced by the testimony of such weighty men to desist from its aggressive design.

This homage which every state renders the concept of law (at least in words) seems to prove that there exists in man a greater moral quality (although at present a dormant one), to try and master the evil element in him (which he cannot deny), and to hope for this in others. Otherwise the words *law* and *right* would never occur to states which intend to fight with each other, unless it were for the purpose of mocking them, like the Gallic prince who declared: "It is the advantage which nature has given the stronger over the weaker that the latter ought to obey the former."

In short, the manner in which states seek their rights can never be a suit before a court, but only war. However, war and its successful conclusion, *victory*, does not decide what is law and what right. A *peace treaty* puts an end to a particular war, but not to the state of war which consists in finding ever new pretexts for starting a new one. Nor can this be declared strictly unjust because in this condition each is the judge in his own cause. Yet it cannot be maintained that states under the law of nations are subject to the same rule that is valid for individual men in the lawless state of nature: "that they ought to leave this state." For states have internally a legal constitution and hence [their citizens] have outgrown the coercion of others who might desire to put them under a broadened legal constitution conceived in terms of their own legal norms. Nevertheless, reason 8:356 speaking from the throne of the highest legislative power condemns war as a method of finding what is right. Reason makes [the achievement of] the state of peace a direct duty, and such a state of peace cannot be established or maintained without a treaty of the nations among themselves. Therefore there must exist a union of a particular kind which we may call the *pacific union* (*foedus pacificum*) which would be distinguished from a *peace treaty* (*pactum pacis*) by the fact that the latter tries to end merely *one* war, while the former tries to end *all* wars forever. This union is not directed toward the securing of some additional power of the state, but merely toward maintaining and making secure the *freedom* of each state by and for itself and at the same time of the other states thus allied with each other. And yet, these states will not subject themselves (as do men in the state of nature) to laws and to the enforcement of such laws.

It can be demonstrated that this idea of *federalization* possesses objective reality, that it can be realized by a gradual extension to all states, leading to eternal peace. For if good fortune brings it to pass that a powerful and enlightened people develops a republican form of government which by nature is inclined toward peace, then such a republic will provide the central core for the federal union of other states. For they can join this republic and can thus make secure among themselves the state of peace according to the idea of a law of nations, and can gradually extend themselves by additional connections of this sort.

It is possible to imagine that a people says: "There shall be no war amongst us; for we want to form a state, i.e., to establish for ourselves a highest legislative, executive, and juridical power which peacefully settles our conflicts." But if this state says: "There shall be no war between myself and other states, although I do not recognize a highest legislative authority which secures my right for me and for which I secure its right," it is not easy to comprehend upon what ground I should place my confidence in my right, unless it be a substitute [*Surrogat*] for the civil social contracts, namely, a free federation. Reason must necessarily connect such a federation with the concept of a law of nations, if authority is to be conceived in such terms.

On the other hand, a concept of the law of nations as a right *to make* war is meaningless; for it is supposed to be a right to determine what is right not according to external laws limiting the freedom of 8:357

each individual, but by force and according to one-sided maxims, unless we are ready to accept this meaning: that it serves people who have such views quite right if they exhaust each other and thus find eternal peace in the wide grave which covers all the atrocities of violence together with its perpetrators. For states in their relation to each other there cannot, according to reason, be any other way to get away from the lawless state which contains nothing but war than to give up (just like individual men) their wild and lawless freedom, to accept public and enforceable laws, and thus to form a constantly growing world *state of all nations* (*civitas gentium*) which finally would comprise all nations. But states do not want this, as not in keeping with their idea of a law of nations, and thus they reject in fact what is true in theory.[6] Therefore, unless all is to be lost, the positive idea of a *world republic* must be replaced by the negative substitute of a *union* of nations which maintains itself, prevents wars, and steadily expands. Only such a union may under existing conditions stem the tide of the law-evading, bellicose propensities in man, but unfortunately subject to the constant danger of their eruption (*furor impius intus—fremit horridus ore cruento.* VIRGIL).

THIRD DEFINITIVE ARTICLE OF THE ETERNAL PEACE

"The Cosmopolitan or World Law shall be limited to conditions of universal hospitality."

We are speaking in this as well as in the other articles not of philanthropy, but of *law*. Therefore *hospitality* (good neighborliness) means the right of a foreigner not to be treated with hostility when he arrives upon the soil of another. The native may reject the for-

6 After the end of a war, at the conclusion of a peace, it would not be improper for a people to set a day of atonement after the day of thanks so as to pray to heaven asking forgiveness for the heavy guilt which mankind is under, because it will not adapt itself to a legal constitution in its relation to other nations. Proud of its independence, each nation will rather employ the barbaric means of war by which that which is being sought, namely the right of each state, cannot be discovered. The celebrations of victory, the hymns which in good Old Testament style are sung to the Lord of Hosts, contrast equally sharply with the moral idea of the father of mankind; because besides the indifference concerning the manner in which people seek their mutual right, which is lamentable enough, they rejoice over having destroyed many people and their happiness.

eigner if it can be done without his perishing, but as long as he stays peaceful, he must not treat him hostilely. It is not the right of becoming a permanent guest [*Gastrecht*] which the foreigner may request, for a special beneficial treaty would be required to make him a fellow inhabitant [*Hausgenosse*] for a certain period. But it is the right to visit [*Besuchsrecht*] which belongs to all men—the right belonging to all men to offer their society on account of the common possession of the surface of the earth. Since it is a globe, they cannot disperse infinitely, but must tolerate each other. No man has a greater fundamental right to occupy a particular spot than any other.

Uninhabitable parts of the earth's surface, the oceans and deserts, divide this community. But *ship* or *camel* (the ship of the desert) enable men to approach each other across these no-man's regions, and thus to use the right of the common *surface* which belongs to all men together, as a basis of possible intercourse. The inhospitable ways of coastal regions, such as the Barbary Coast, where they rob ships in adjoining seas or make stranded seamen into slaves, is contrary to natural law, as are the similarly inhospitable ways of the deserts and their Bedouins who look upon the approach (of a foreigner) as giving them a right to plunder him. But the right of hospitality, the right, that is, of foreign guests, does not extend further than to the conditions which enable them to attempt the developing of intercourse with the old inhabitants.

In this way, remote parts of the world can enter into relationships which eventually become public and legal and thereby may bring mankind ever nearer to an eventual world constitution.

If one compares with this requirement the *inhospitable* conduct of the civilized, especially of the trading nations of our continent, the injustice which they display in their *visits* to foreign countries and peoples goes terribly far. They simply identify visiting with *conquest*. America, the lands of the Negroes, the Spice Islands, the Cape of South Africa, etc., were countries that belonged to nobody, for the inhabitants counted for nothing. In East India (Hindustan) they brought in foreign mercenaries, under the pretense of merely establishing trading ports. These mercenary troops brought suppression of the natives, inciting the several states of India to extended wars against each other. They brought famine, sedition, 8:359 treason, and the rest of the evils which weigh down mankind.

China and Japan, who had made an attempt to get along with such guests, have wisely allowed only contact, but not settlement—and Japan has further wisely restricted this privilege to the Dutch only, whom they exclude, like prisoners, from community with the natives. The worst (or viewed from the standpoint of a moral judge the best) is that the European nations are not even able to enjoy this violence. All these trading companies are on the point of an approaching collapse; the sugar islands, which are the seat of the most cruel and systematic slavery, do not produce a yield—except in the form of raising recruits for navies; thus they in turn serve the conduct of war—wars of powers which make much ado about their piety and who want themselves to be considered among the morally elect, while in fact they consume [the fruits of] injustice like water.

The narrower or wider community of all nations on earth has in 8:360 fact progressed so far that a violation of law and right in one place is felt in *all* others. Hence the idea of a cosmopolitan or world law is not a fantastic and utopian way of looking at law, but a necessary completion of the unwritten code of constitutional and international law to make it a public law of mankind. Only under this condition can we flatter ourselves that we are continually approaching eternal peace.

FIRST ADDITION
On the Guarantee of Eternal Peace

No one less than the great artist *nature* (*natura daedala rerum*) offers such a *guarantee*. Nature's mechanical course evidently reveals a 8:361 teleology: to produce harmony from the very disharmony of men even against their will. If this teleology and the laws that effect it is believed to be like an unknown cause compelling us, it is called *fate*. But if it is considered in the light of its usefulness for the evolution of the world, it will be called *providence*—a cause which, responding to a deep wisdom, is directed toward a higher goal, the objective final end [*Endzweck*] of mankind which predetermines this evolution. We do not really *observe* this providence in the artifices of nature, nor can we *deduce* it from them. But we can and must *add this thought* (as in all relations of the form of things to ends in general), in order to form any kind of conception of its possibility. We do this in analogy to human artifices. The relation and integration of these factors into the end (the moral one) which reason directly prescribes is very sublime in *theory,* but is axiomatic and well-founded in practice, e.g., in regard to the concept of a duty toward eternal peace which that mechanism promotes.

When one is dealing as at present with theory (and not with religion), the use of the word *nature* is more appropriate in view of the limits of human reason which must stay within the limits of possible experience as far as the relation of effects to their causes is concerned. It is also *more modest* than the expression *providence,* especially a providence understandable to us; for by talking of providence we are arrogantly putting the wings of Icarus on our shoulders as if to get closer to the secret of its unfathomable purpose.

But before we ascertain more specifically how the guarantee is worked out, it is necessary to explore the situation which nature has 8:363 created for those who are actors upon its great stage, and which in the last analysis necessitates its guarantee of peace. Only after that can we see how nature provides this guarantee.

Nature's provisional arrangement consists in the following: (1) she has seen to it that human beings can live in all the regions where they are settled; (2) she has by war driven them everywhere, even into the most inhospitable regions, in order to populate them; (3) she has forced them by war to enter into more or less legal relationships. It is marvellous to notice that in the cold wastes of the Arctic Sea some mosses grow which the *Reindeer* scratches out of the snow thus being enabled to serve as food or as a draft animal for the Samoyeds. Such ends become even more apparent when one discovers that furred animals on the shores of the Arctic Sea, walruses and whales provide food through their meat and heat through their fat for the inhabitants. But nature's care causes the greatest admiration when we find that driftwood, the origin of which is not well known, is carried to these regions, since without this material the inhabitants could neither build boats and weapons, nor huts in which to dwell. In that situation they seem to be sufficiently occupied with war against the animals to live peacefully with each other.

But it was probably war which *drove* the inhabitants to these places. The first *instrument of warfare* among all the animals which man during the time of populating the earth learned to tame and to domesticate was the *horse;* for the elephant belongs to a later time, when established states made greater luxury possible. The same is true of the culture of certain kinds of grasses, now called *grain,* the original form of which we no longer know, as well as of multiplying and refining of fruit trees by transplanting and grafting—in Europe perhaps only two species, the wild apples and wild pears. Such achievements could take place only in established states with fixed property in real estate. Before this men had progressed from the lawless freedom of *hunting,*[7] fishing, and sheepherding to cultivating the land. After that *salt* and *iron* were discovered, perhaps the first articles of trade between nations which were in demand everywhere, through which they were first brought into a *peaceful relationship* with each other. This in turn brought them into understanding, community, and peaceful relations with the more remote nations.

Nature, by providing that men *can* live everywhere on earth, has at the same time despotically wanted that they *should* live everywhere, even against their inclination. This "should" does not presuppose a duty which obliged them to do it by a moral law. Instead, nature chose war to bring this about.

8:364

7 Among all the ways of living the hunting life is unquestionably most at variance with a civilized constitution: because the families which are separated from each other soon become alien, and soon thereafter, dispersed in extended forests, hostile to each other, since each requires much room for its feeding and clothing. The Mosaic law forbidding the eating of blood, Genesis 9:4–6, appears to have been originally nothing else but an attempt to forbid people to live as hunters; because in this life there often occur situations where meat must be eaten raw, and hence to forbid the eating of blood means forbidding a hunting life. This law, several times reenacted, was later, with a quite different purpose, imposed by the Jewish Christians as a condition upon the newly accepted heathen Christians.

We observe peoples which by their common language reveal their common ancestry, such as the *Samoyeds* on the Arctic Sea and a people of similar language, about two hundred miles away, in the Altaic Mountains. Between those two a Mongolian, horse-riding and hence belligerent, tribe have wedged themselves in, driving one part of these people far away, and the rest into the most inhospitable regions of ice and snow, where they surely would not have gone by choice.[8]

In the same manner the Finns in the northernmost part of Europe, called the Lapps, were separated from the Hungarians to whom they are related in their language by intruding Gothic and Sarmatian tribes. And what could have driven the Eskimos in the North, and the Pescheras in the South of America as far as it did, except war which nature uses everywhere as a means for populating the earth? War itself does not require a special motivation, since it appears to be grafted upon human nature. It is even considered something noble for which man is inspired by the love of honor, without selfish motives. This martial courage is judged by American savages, and European ones in feudal times, to be of great intrinsic value not only *when* there is a *war* (which is equitable), but also so *that* there may be war. Consequently war is started merely to show martial courage, and war itself invested with an inner *dignity*. Even philosophers will praise war as enobling mankind, forgetting the Greek who said: "War is bad in that it begets more evil people than it kills." This much about what nature does in pursuit of its own purpose in regard to mankind as a species of animal.

Now we face the question which concerns the essential point in accomplishing eternal peace: what does nature do in relation to the end which man's reason imposes as a duty, in order to favor thus his

8:365

8 Someone might ask: if nature did not intend these icy shores to remain uninhabited, what will happen to their inhabitants when no more driftwood comes to them (as may be expected)? For it may be assumed that the inhabitants of the more temperate regions will, as culture progresses, utilize their wood better, and will not allow it to drop into the river and drift into the sea. I answer: the inhabitants of those regions, of the Ob, the Yenisei, the Lena, etc., will barter for it the products of animal life which the sea provides so plentifully in the Arctic—when nature has forced the establishment of peace among them.

moral intent? In other words: how does nature guarantee that what man ought to do according to the laws of freedom, but does not do, will be made secure regardless of this freedom by a compulsion of nature which forces him to do it? The question presents itself in all three relations: *constitutional* law, *international* law, and cosmopolitan or world law.—And if I say of nature: she wants this or that to take place, it does not mean that she imposes a *duty* to do it—for that only the noncompulsory practical reason can do—but it means that nature itself does it, whether we want it or not (*fata volentem ducunt, nolentem trabunt*).

1. If internal conflicts did not compel a people to submit itself to the compulsion of public laws, external wars would do it. According to the previously mentioned arrangement of nature, a people discovers a neighboring people who are pushing it, against which it 8:366 must form itself into a *state* in order to be prepared as a *power* against its enemy. Now the *republican* constitution is the only one which is fully adequate to the right of man, but it is also the hardest to establish, and even harder to maintain. Therefore many insist that it would have to be a state of angels, because men with their selfish propensities are incapable of so sublime a constitution. But now nature comes to the aid of this revered, but practically ineffectual general will which is founded in reason. It does this by the selfish propensities themselves, so that it is only necessary to organize the state well (which is indeed within the ability of man), and to direct these forces against each other in such wise that one balances the other in its devastating effect, or even suspends it. Consequently the result for reason is as if both selfish forces were nonexistent. Thus man, although not a morally good man, is compelled to be a good citizen. The problem of establishing a state is solvable even for a people of devils, if only they have intelligence, though this may sound harsh. The problem may be stated thus: "To organize a group of rational beings who demand general laws for their survival, but of whom each inclines toward exempting himself, and to establish their constitution in such a way that, in spite of the fact that their private attitudes are opposed, these private attitudes mutually impede each other in such a manner that the public

behavior [of the rational beings] is the same as if they did not have such evil attitudes." Such a problem *must* be solvable. For it is not the moral perfection of mankind, but merely the mechanism of nature, which this task seeks to know how to use in order to arrange the conflict of unpacific attitudes in a given people in such a way that they impel each other to submit themselves to compulsory laws and thus bring about the state of peace in which such laws are enforced. It is possible to observe this in the actually existing, although imperfectly organized states. They approach in external conduct closely to what the idea of law prescribes, although an inner morality is certainly not the cause of it (just as we should not expect good constitution from such morality, but rather from such a constitution the good moral development of a people). These existing states show that the mechanism of nature, with its selfish 8:367 propensities which naturally counteract each other, can be employed by reason as a means. Thus reason's real purpose may be realized, namely, to provide a field for the operation of legal rules whereby to make secure internal and external peace, as far as the state is concerned.—In short, we can say that nature *wants* irresistibly that law achieve superior force. If one neglects to do this, it will be accomplished anyhow, albeit with much inconvenience. "If you bend the stick too much, it breaks; and he who wants too much, wants nothing" (Bouterwek).

2. The idea of a law of nations presupposes the separate existence of many states which are independent of each other. Such a situation constitutes in and by itself a state of war, unless a federative union of these states prevents the outbreak of hostilities. Yet such a situation is from the standpoint of reason better than the complete merging of all these states in one of them which overpowers them and is thereby in turn transformed into a universal monarchy. This is so, because the laws lose more and more of their effectiveness as the government increases in size, and the resulting soulless despotism is plunged into anarchy after having exterminated all the germs of good [in man]. Still, it is the desire of every state (or of its ruler) to enter into a permanent state of peace by ruling if possible the entire world. But *nature* has decreed differ-

ently.—Nature employs two means to keep peoples from being mixed and to differentiate them, the difference of *language* and of *religion*.[9] These differences occasion the inclination toward mutual hatred and the excuse for war; yet at the same time they lead, as culture increases and men gradually come closer together, toward a greater agreement on principles for peace and understanding. Such peace and understanding is not brought about and made secure by the weakening of all other forces (as it would be under the aforementioned despotism and its graveyard of freedom), but by balancing these forces in a lively competition.

8:368   3. Just as nature wisely separates the nations which the will of each state would like to unite under its sway either by cunning or by force, and even in keeping with the reasoning of the law of nations, so also nature unites nations which the concept of a cosmopolitan or world law would not have protected from violence and war, and it does this by mutual self-interest. It is the *spirit of commerce* which cannot coexist with war, and which sooner or later takes hold of every nation. For, since the money power is perhaps the most reliable among all the powers subordinate to the state's power, states find themselves impelled (though hardly by moral compulsion) to promote the noble peace and to try to avert war by mediation whenever it threatens to break out anywhere in the world. It is as if states were constantly leagued for this purpose; for great leagues *for* the purpose of making war can only come about very rarely and can succeed even more rarely.—In this way nature guarantees lasting peace by the mechanism of human inclinations; however the certainty [that this will come to pass] is not sufficient to *predict* such a future (theoretically). But for practical purposes the certainty suffices and makes it one's duty to work toward this (not simply chimerical) state.

9 Difference of religion: a strange expression! as if one were to speak of different *morals*. There may be different *kinds of faith* which are historical and which hence belong to history and not to religion and are part of the means in the field of learning. Likewise there may be different *religious books* (Zendavesta, Vedam, Koran, etc.). But there can only be one *religion* valid for all men and for all times. Those other matters are nothing but a vehicle of religion, accidental and different according to the difference of time and place.

SECOND ADDITION

A Secret Article Concerning Eternal Peace

A secret article in negotiations pertaining to *public* law is a contradiction objectively, i.e., as regards its substance or content; subjectively, however, i.e., as regards the quality of the person which formulates the article, secrecy may occur when such a person hesitates to declare himself publicly as the author thereof.

The sole article of this kind [in the treaty on eternal peace] is contained in the following sentence: *The maxims of the philosophers concerning the conditions of the possibility of public peace shall be consulted by the states which are ready to go to war.* Perhaps it would seem like belittling the legislative authority of a state to which one should attribute the greatest wisdom to suggest that it should seek instruction regarding the principles of its conduct from its *subjects* (the philosophers); nevertheless this is highly advisable. Hence the state will *solicit* the latter *silently* (by making it a secret) which means that it will 8:369 *let them talk* freely and publicly about the general maxims of the conduct of war and the establishment of peace (for they will do it of their own accord, if only they are not forbidden to do so). The agreement of the states among themselves regarding this point does not require any special stipulation but is founded upon an obligation posited by general morality legislating for human reason. This does not mean that the state must concede that the principles of the philosopher have priority over the rulings of the jurist (the representative of governmental power); it only means that the philosopher be *given a hearing.* The jurist who has made the *scales* of law and right his symbol, as well as the *sword* of justice, commonly employs the sword not only to ward off all outside influence from the scales, but also to put it into one of the scales if it will not go down (*vae victis*). A jurist who is not at the same time a philosopher (morally speaking) has the greatest temptation to do this, because it is only his job to apply existing laws, and not to inquire whether these laws need improvement. In fact he counts this lower order of his faculty to be the higher, simply because it is the concomitant of power (as is also the case of the other two faculties).—The philosophical faculty occupies a low place when confronted by all this power. Thus, for example, it is said of philosophy that she is the *handmaiden* of theology (and something like that is said regarding the other two). It is not very clear however "whether she carries the torch in front of her gracious lady or the train of her dress behind."

It is not to be expected that kings philosophize or that philosophers become kings, nor is it to be desired because the possession of power corrupts the free judgment of reason inevitably. But kings or self-governing nations will not allow the class of philosophers to disappear or to become silent, but will let them speak publicly, because this is indispensable for both in order to clarify their business. And since this class of people are by their very nature incapable of forming gangs or clubs they need not be suspected of carrying on *propaganda*.

8:370

APPENDIX

I.

On the Disagreement Between Morals and Politics in Relation to Eternal Peace

Morals, when conceived as the totality of absolutely binding laws according to which we *ought* to act, is in itself practice in an objective sense. It is therefore an apparent paradox to say that one *cannot* do [what one ought to do] once the authoritativeness of this concept of duty is acknowledged. For in that case this concept [of duty] would be eliminated from morals since *ultra posse nemo obligatur*. Hence there cannot occur any conflict between politics as an applied doctrine of right [*Rechtslehre*] and law [doctrine of right and law]. Hence there can be no conflict between theory and practice, unless theory were taken to mean a general *doctrine of expediency* [*Klugheitslehre*], that is to say a theory of the maxims as to how to choose the most appropriate means for the realization of self-interested purposes; in other words, altogether to deny that morals exist.

Politics says: "Be ye therefore wise as serpents"; but morals adds as a limiting condition: "and innocent as doves." If the two cannot coexist in one commandment, there would be a conflict of politics with morals. But if the two are to be combined, the idea of a contrast is absurd, and it is not even possible to present as a task the problem as to how to resolve the conflict. Although the sentence *Honesty is the best policy* contains a theory which practice unfortunately (!) often contradicts, yet the equally theoretical sentence *Honesty is better than all politics* is completely above all objections; indeed, it is the inescapable condition of all politics. The god who guards the boundaries of morals does not yield to Jove who guards the boundaries of force; for the latter is yet subject to destiny. That is to say, reason is not sufficiently inspired to comprehend the range of predetermining causes which would permit it to predict with certainty and in accordance with the mechanism of nature the happy or bad result of the doings or omissions of men (although it may well hope for a result according with what is intended). But what needs to be done in order to remain within the groove of duty according to the rules of wisdom, and thus our final end reason, shows us quite clearly enough.

The practical man to whom morals is mere theory bases his cheerless rejection of our kind-hearted hope upon the notion that we never *want* to do what is necessary in order to realize the end leading to eternal peace, even when he concedes both that we *ought* and that we *can* do [what we should]. Of course the will of *all individual* men to live under a lawful constitution in accordance with the principles of liberty (which constitutes the *distributive* unity of the will of *all*) is not sufficient for this end. In addition it is necessary that *all jointly* will this state (which constitutes the *collective* unity of the united [general] will) which is the solution of a difficult problem. Only thus can the totality of a civil society be created. Since therefore there must come into existence, over and above the variety of the particular will of all, such a uniting cause of a civil society in order to bring forth a common will—something which no one of all of them can do—the *execution* of the idea [of an eternal peace] in practice and the beginning of a lawful state can-

8:371

not be counted upon except by *force* upon the compulsion of which the public law is afterwards based. This fact would lead one to expect beforehand in practical experience great deviations from the original idea of the theory, since one can count little anyway upon the moral conviction of the legislator so that he would after he has united a wild multitude into a people leave it to them to establish a lawful constitution by their common will.

Therefore it is said: "He who has the power in his hands, will not let the people prescribe laws for himself. A state which is in possession of [the power of] not being subject to any external laws will not make itself dependent upon their judgments as far as concerns the manner of its seeking its right against such other states. Even a continent if it feels itself superior to another one, which may not actually be in its way, will not leave unutilized the opportunity of increasing its power by plundering or even dominating the other. Thus all theoretical plans for constitutional, international, and worldwide law dissolve into empty, unworkable ideals, whereas a practice which is based upon the empirical principles of human nature may hope to find a secure foundation for its structure of political prudence, inasmuch as such a practice does not consider it too mean to derive instruction for its maxims from the way in which the world is actually run."

8:372   Admittedly, if there exists no freedom and hence no moral law based upon it, and if everything which happens or may happen is simply part of the mechanism of nature, then politics as the art to use [the mechanism of nature] for the governing of men is the complete content of practical prudence, and the concept of right and law is an empty phrase. But should one find it absolutely necessary to combine the concept of law and right with politics, indeed to make it a limiting condition of politics, then the compatibility of the two must be conceded. I can imagine a *moral politician*—that is, a man who employs the principles of political prudence in such a way that they can coexist with morals—but I cannot imagine a *political moralist*, who would concoct a system of morals such as the advantage of the statesman may find convenient.

The moral politician will adopt the principle that if defects appear in the constitution or in the relations with other states which could not be prevented then it is one's duty, especially for the heads of states, to seek to remedy them as soon as possible; that is to say, to make such a constitution once again commensurate with the law of nature as it is presented to us as a model in the idea of reason. He will do this even though it cost him sacrifices of selfish interests. It would be unreasonable to demand that such a defect be eliminated immediately and with impetuosity, since the tearing apart of a [constitutional] bond of national or world-wide community, before a better constitution is available to take its place, is contrary to all morals, which in this respect agrees with political prudence. But we may properly demand that the necessity of such a change be intimately appreciated by those in power so that they may continue to approach the final end of a constitution which is best in accordance with right and law. A state may be *governed* as a republic even while it possesses despotic *power to rule* [*Herrschermacht*] according to the existing constitution, until gradually the people become capable of realizing the influence of the mere idea of the authority of law (as if it possessed physical force) and thus are found able to legislate for themselves. But should the violence of a *revolution* which was caused by a bad constitution have achieved illegitimately a more lawful one, then it should not be held permissible to bring the people back to the old one, even though during such a revolution everyone who got himself involved by acts of violence or intrigue would rightfully be subject to the penalties of a seditionist. As far as the external relation between states is concerned, it cannot be demanded of a state that it divest itself of its despotic constitution (which is after all the stronger in dealing with external enemies) as long as it runs the risk of being devoured by other states; thus even in this respect the delaying of the execution must be permitted until a better opportunity presents itself.[10]

8:373

10 These are permissive laws of reason which allow a state of public law which is affected by injustice to continue until everything is ready for a complete revolution or has been made ripe for it by peaceful means: since a *legal*, even though only to a small degree lawful, constitution is better than none, and a premature change would lead to anarchy. Political prudence will therefore, in the state in which things are at the present time, make it its duty

It may well be true that despotic moralists who make mistakes in executing their ideas violate political prudence in many ways by prematurely adopting or advocating various measures, yet experience will necessarily, in case of such offenses against nature, by and by get them into a better track. On the other hand, moralizing politicians *make* progress *impossible* and perpetuate the violation of right by glossing over political principles which are contrary to right by pretending that human nature is not *capable* of the Good according to the idea which reason prescribes.

Instead of the practice on which these clever politicos pride themselves they employ *tricks* in that they are only intent upon sacrificing the people and even the whole world by flattering the established powers in order not to miss their private profit. In this they follow the manner of true lawyers—of the trade, not legislators—when they get into politics. For since it is not their business to argue, themselves, concerning legislation, but rather to carry out the present commands of the law of the land [*Landrecht*], therefore any presently existing legal constitution must seem the best to 8:374 them; or should this one be changed by the "higher authorities," then the one following will seem the best. Thus all is right and proper in a formal order. But if this skill of being fit for any task gives such lawyers the illusion of being able to judge the principles of a basic constitution in accordance with concepts of law and right—that is, *a priori* and not empirically—they cannot make this transition except in a spirit of trickery. Likewise, if they boast of their knowledge of *men* (which may be expected, since they have plenty of dealings with them) without knowing *man* and what may be made of him (for which a higher standpoint of anthropological observation is required), and if they then, equipped with such principles, approach constitutional and international law as prescribed

---

to effect reforms which are in keeping with the ideals of public law and right. At the same time it will utilize revolutions where nature produces them of itself, not for the purpose of camouflaging an even greater suppression, but rather consider it a call of nature to bring about by thorough reforms a legal constitution which is based upon the principles of freedom and therefore the only lasting one.

by reason, they cannot make that transition either, except in a spirit of trickery. For they follow their usual method [of reasoning according to] despotically adopted compulsory laws even where the concepts of reason will permit only a compulsion which is lawful within the principles of freedom, since only such compulsion will make possible a constitution according to right and law. The pretended practitioner believes he can solve this problem empirically—from experience, that is—with hitherto existing, largely unlawful constitutions which have worked best, while by-passing the basic idea [of basic principles of freedom]. The maxims which he employs for this purpose (though he does not pronounce them) are roughly the following sophistical ones:

1. *Fac et excusa.* Seize every favorable opportunity for arbitrary appropriation of a right of the government [state] over its people, or over a neighboring nation. The justification will be formulated and the use of violence glossed over much more easily and more decoratively *after the accomplished deed* than if one tried first to think up convincing reasons and await the counter reasons. This is especially true in the first of these cases where the higher authority becomes at once the legislative authority which must be obeyed without arguing. Such boldness itself produces a certain appearance of inner conviction of the righteousness of the deed, and the God *bonus eventus* is afterwards the best legal representative.

2. *Si fecisti, nega.* Whatever [evil] you have committed—for example driving your own people to despair and into sedition—that you must deny and declare not to be your guilt. Instead you insist that what is to blame is the unruliness of the subjects. Or if it is a case of seizing a neighboring people, then blame it on human nature, since one can count with certainty upon being seized [by one's neighbor] if one does not forestall him in the use of force.

3. *Divide et impera.* This means: if there are certain privileged persons among your people who have merely elected you as their head as *primus inter pares,* then disunite them among themselves and set them at variance with the people; if then you will support the latter by pretending to favor greater liberties for them, all will depend upon your absolute will. Or, if it is a situation involving for-

8:375

eign countries, the creation of dissension among them is a relatively certain means to subject one after the other on the pretense of protecting the weaker.

No one is deceived by these political maxims, for they all are generally known. Nor is it a case of being too embarrassed, as if the injustice were too apparent. Great powers never worry about the judgment of the common crowd, but only about each other, and hence what embarrasses them is not that these principles become public, but merely that they *failed to work*, since they are all agreed among themselves on the morality of the maxims. What remains is the *political honor* which they can count upon, namely the *enlarging of their power* by whatever means are available.[11]

8:376 From all these serpentine turnings of an amoral prudential doctrine which seeks to derive the condition of peace among men from the warlike state of nature, one thing at least becomes clear: human beings cannot escape from the concept of right and law either in their private or in their public affairs, and they do not dare to base politics merely upon the manipulations of prudence and thus re-

---

11 If there may still be some doubt concerning the wickedness of *men* who live together in a state as rooted in human nature, and if instead the shortcomings of an as yet not sufficiently advanced culture may be cited as the cause of the lawless aspects of their frame of mind, this wickedness becomes quite obviously and unmistakably apparent in the external
8:376 relation of *states* with each other. At home in each state it is veiled by the compulsion of the civil laws, because a greater power, namely that of the government, strongly counteracts the inclination of the citizens to employ force against each other. This not only gives to the whole a moral lacquer (*causae non causae*), but by putting a stop to the outbreak of lawless proclivities provides a real alleviation for the development of the moral predisposition for directly respecting right and law.—For everyone now believes of himself that he would honor and obey the concept of right and law if only he could expect the same from everyone else, and this latter the government secures for him to some extent; thus a great step (though not a moral step yet) is taken toward a morality when this concept of duty is accepted for its own sake and without regard to reciprocity.—Since everyone in spite of his good opinion of himself presupposes a bad character in all others, men mutually pronounce judgment upon themselves to the effect that they all as a matter of *fact* are not worth much (why this is so, considering that the *nature* of man, as a free being, cannot be blamed for it, we will leave undiscussed). But since the respect for the concept of right and law which man cannot abandon most solemnly sanctions the theory of an ability to measure to such a concept, every one can see for himself that he must act in accordance with right and law, whatever others may do.

ject all obedience to a concept of public law—something which is particularly surprising in regard to the concept of a law of nations. Instead they show it all the honor that is due it, even if they think up a hundred excuses and camouflages in order to evade this concept in practice and to impute to a crafty force the genuine authority of being the origin and bond of all right and law.

In order to end this sophistry (although by no means the injustice which this sophistry glosses over) and to bring the deceitful *representatives* of the mighty of this world to confess that it is not right and law but force which they defend (and the tone of which they adopt as if they themselves had something to command in this connection), it will be well to uncover the fraud with which such persons deceive themselves and others, to discover the highest principle from which the purpose of eternal peace is derived and to show that all the evil which stands in the way of eternal peace results from the fact that the political moralist starts where the moral politician equitably ends. In short, the political moralist subordinates his principles to the end, i.e., puts the wagon before the horse, and thereby thwarts his own purpose of bringing politics into agreement with morals.

In order to harmonize practical philosophy within itself, it is necessary first to decide the question whether in tasks of practical reason we should start from its *material* [i.e., substantive] principle, 8:377 from its end (as object of the will), or from its *formal* one, i.e., from the principle which relates to freedom in one's relation to the outside world which states: act in such a way that you could want your maxim to become a general law (whatever its purpose may be). Without a doubt, the latter principle must take precedence; for as a principle of right it possesses absolute necessity, whereas the material principle is compelling only on condition that the empirical conditions for its realization exist. Thus even if this purpose (e.g., eternal peace) were a duty, this latter would have had to be deduced from the formal principle of the maxims of external action.

The first principle, that of the *political moralist* (the problem of constitutional, international, and world law), is a mere *technical task* (*problema technicum*); the second, which is the principle of the *moral*

politician, as an *ethical task* (*problema morale*) is therefore vastly different in its procedure for bringing about the eternal peace which is
now desired not only as a mere physical good, but also as a condition resulting from the recognition of duty.

Much knowledge of nature is required for the solution of the
first problem of political prudence, in order to utilize its mechanism for this purpose, and yet it is all rather uncertain as far as the
result, eternal peace, is concerned, whichever of the sections of the
public one considers. It is quite uncertain whether the people can
better be kept in obedience and at the same time in prosperity for
any length of time by severity or by flattery, whether by a single
ruler or by several, or by an aristocracy which devotes itself to the
public service, or by popular government. History offers examples
of the opposite happening under all forms of government, excepting the one truly republican form which, however, can only occur
to a moral politician. Even more uncertain is an *international law*
based upon a statute drafted by several ministries which is merely a
word without a reality corresponding to it [*ein Wort ohne Sache*],
since it would rest upon treaties which contain in the very act of
their conclusion the secret reservation of being violated.

8:378   By contrast, the solution of the second *problem of political wisdom*
readily presents itself, is evident to everyone, confounds all artifices, and leads directly to its end; yet with the remainder of prudence not to force it precipitately, but to approach it steadily as
favorable opportunities offer.

Therefore it is said: "Seek ye first the kingdom of pure practical
reason and of its *righteousness*, and your end (the well-being of eternal peace) will be added unto you." For that is the peculiar feature
of morals concerning its principles of public law and hence concerning a politics which is *a priori* knowable, that it harmonizes the
more with an intended objective, a physical or moral advantage
sought, the less it allows its behavior to depend upon it. The reason
for this is that the *a priori* given general will (within a nation or in
the relation between nations) alone determines what is right
amongst men. At the same time this union of the will of all, if only
the execution of it is carried out consistently, can be the cause

within the mechanism of nature which produces the intended effect and thus effectuates the idea of law.

Thus it is a principle of moral politics that a people should unite into a state solely according to the natural-law concepts of freedom and equality. This principle is based upon duty, and not upon prudence. Political moralists may argue ever so much concerning the natural mechanism of a mass of people entering into society which (according to them) invalidates those principles and prevents their purpose from being realized. They may likewise try to prove their contention against those principles by giving examples of badly organized constitutions of old and new times (e.g., of democracies with a system of representation). They do not deserve to be listened to—the less so, since such a pernicious doctrine may even cause the evil which it predicts. For man is thereby put into the same class with the other living machines, and man then needs only to possess the conscious knowledge that he is not a free being to make him in his own judgment the most miserable of all creatures.

Fiat justitia, pereat mundus is a proverbial saying which sounds a bit 8:379 pompous, yet it is true, and it means in simple language: "Justice shall prevail, even though all the rascals in the world should perish as a result." This is a sound principle of right and law which cuts off all the crooked paths of cunning and violence. However, care must be taken not to misunderstand this sentence as a permission to claim one's own right with the greatest severity, for that would conflict with one's ethical duty. Rather should it be understood to mean an obligation of those who have the power not to refuse or to infringe someone's right out of ill will or sympathy for others. [In order to achieve this result] there is required first of all an internal constitution of the state which is organized according to the pure principles of right and law, but then also the union of such a state with other states, either neighboring or more remote, for the purpose of settling their controversies legally (in analogy to what a universal state might do).

This sentence really does not intend to say anything more than that political maxims must not proceed from considering the welfare and happiness to be expected from their being followed, that is to say they must not proceed from the end which each of these maxims makes its object, nor from the will as the highest (but empirical) principle of political prudence. Rather such maxims must be derived from the pure principle of duty under natural law (from the Ought the principle of which is given *a priori* by pure reason) regardless of what might be the physical consequences thereof. The world will not perish because there are fewer bad men. The morally bad has a quality which is inseparable from its nature: it is self-contradictory and self-destructive in its purposes, especially in its relation to others who are like-minded. Therefore it yields to the moral principle of the good, though in a slow progression.

———

No conflict exists *objectively* (in theory) between morals and politics. Only *subjectively*, in the selfish disposition of men—which need not be called practice, however, since it is not based upon maxims of reason—such a conflict may remain [which is all right] since it serves as a whetstone for virtue. Virtue's true courage as expressed in the maxim *tu ne cede malis, sed contra audentior ito* consists in the present case not so much in standing up firmly against the evils and sacrifices which must be borne, but in facing the evil principle in ourselves and defeating its cunning. This principle is much more dangerous because it is deceitful and treacherous in arguing the weakness of human nature as a justification for all transgressions.

8:380   Indeed, the political moralist may say: ruler and people, or people and people are not doing *each other* an injustice when they fight each other with violence or cunning, even though they are committing an injustice by denying all respect to right and law. For while one violates his duty toward the other, who is just as lawless in his view toward him, it serves them both right if they exhaust themselves, as long as there remains enough of this species to continue this game till very distant times, so that a later generation may take them as a warning example. Providence [so they say] is justified in thus arranging the course of events; for the moral principle in man never is extinguished, and reason, which is capable pragmatically of executing the ideas of natural law according to this principle, is steadily on the increase because of the progress in culture; but so also is the guilt of such transgressions. It seems impossible to justify by any kind of theodicy the creation of such a species of corrupted beings upon this earth, if we are to assume that mankind never will be in a better state. But this standpoint of judging things is much too lofty for us—as if we could theoretically impute our notions (of wisdom) to the most supreme, inscrutable power.

We are inevitably pushed to such desperate consequences if we do not assume that the pure principles of right and law have objective reality in the sense that they can be realized, and hence that the people within the state and the states toward each other must act accordingly, whatever may be the objections of an empirical politics. True politics cannot take a single step without first paying homage to morals, and while politics by itself is a difficult art, its combination with morals is no art at all; for morals cuts the Gordian knot which politics cannot solve as soon as the two are in conflict.

The (natural) right of men must be held sacred, regardless of how much sacrifice is required of the powers that be. It is impossible to figure out a middle road, such as a pragmatically conditional right, between right and utility. All politics must bend its knee before the (natural) rights of men, but may hope in return to arrive, though slowly, on the level where it may continually shine.

II.

8:381

On the Agreement between Politics and Morals According to the Transcendental Idea of Public Right and Law

If I abstract right and law from all the *substance* [*Materie*] of public law (as it exists in keeping with the various empirically given relations of men within the state or the relations between states, and as it is customarily considered by jurists) there remains the *formal quality of publicity.* For each law and rightful claim [*Rechtsanspruch*] carries with it the possibility of such publicity, since without publicity there cannot be justice (which can only be thought of as capable of being *made public*) and hence also no right, since that is only attributed by justice.

This capacity of publicity every law and rightful claim [*Recht-*

sanspruch] must have. Therefore this quality provides a criterion which is easily applied and *a priori* discoverable through reason, because it is quite easy to determine whether it is present in a given case, i.e., whether it can be combined with the principles of him who is acting or not. If not, we can recognize the falsity (unlawfulness) [*Rechtswidrigkeit*] of the pretended claim (*praetensio juris*) quite readily and as by an experiment of pure reason.

After thus abstracting from all the empirical [substance] which the idea of constitutional and international law includes (of this order is the evil in human nature which necessitates coercion), it is possible to call the following statement the *transcendental formula* of public law: "All actions which relate to the right of other men are contrary to right and law, the maxim of which does not permit publicity." This principle should not only be considered as *ethically* relevant (belonging to the theory of virtue or ethics), but also as *juridically* relevant (concerning the right of men). For a maxim which I cannot permit to become *known* without at the same time defeating my own purpose, which must be *kept secret* in order to succeed, and which I cannot *profess publicly* without inevitably arousing the resistance of all against my purpose, such a maxim cannot have acquired this necessary and universal, and hence *a priori* recognizable, opposition of all from any other quality than its injustice, with which it threatens everyone.

8:382 Furthermore, this [standard] is merely *negative*, that is, it only serves to recognize what is *not right* toward others. Like any axiom it is unprovably certain and easy to apply, as may be seen from the following examples of public law.

1. A question occurs in *constitutional law* (*jus civitatis*) which many believe to be difficult to answer, but which the transcendental principle of publicity easily resolves: "Is rebellion a right and lawful means for a people to overthrow the oppressive power of a so-called tyrant (*non titulo, sed exercitio talis*)?" The rights of the people are violated, and no injustice (*Unrecht*) is done to the tyrant by the deposition; there can be no doubt of that. In spite of that, it is nevertheless in the highest degree contrary to right and law (*unrecht*) to seek their right in this manner, and they cannot complain of injus-

tice if after being defeated in such a conflict they have to submit to the most severe punishment.

Much can be argued both pro and contra in this matter, if one tries to settle the matter by a dogmatic deduction of the reasons in right and law [*Rechtsgründe*]; only the transcendental principle of the publicity of all public right and law can save itself this prolixity. According to this principle, the people ask themselves before the establishment of the civic contract whether they dare make public the maxim of allowing an occasional rebellion. It is easy to see that if one were to make it a condition of the establishment of a constitution to use force against the head of the government [*Oberhaupt*] in certain cases, the people would have to claim a right and lawful power over the head of the government. In that case the head would not be the head, or, if both [his being a head and the exercise of force against him] were to be made conditions of the establishment of the state, such establishment would not be possible, which was after all the objective of the people. The unrightfulness [*Unrecht*] of rebellion becomes evident by the fact that its maxim would vitiate its own purpose, if one *professed it publicly*. One would have to keep it secret.

Such secrecy would not be necessary for the head of the government. He could openly declare that he would punish every rebellion with the death of its ringleaders, even though these believe that he had violated the fundamental law first. For if the head of the government is convinced that he possesses the *irresistible* superior force (which must be assumed to be the case even under every civic constitution, because he who does not have enough power to protect each one among the people against the others, does not have the right to command them either), then he does not need to worry about vitiating his own purpose by letting his maxim become public. This conclusion is connected with another, namely, that in case of a successful rebellion such a head of government would return to the status of a subject, and hence he must not begin a rebellion to get himself restored, nor would he have to fear that he would be brought to account for his previous conduct of government. 8:383

2. *Concerning international law.* Only if we assume some kind of lawful state (i.e., the kind of external condition under which a man can secure his right), can there be talk of international law, because as a public law it contains in its very concept the publication of a general will which determines for each man what is his own. Such a *status juridicus* must result from some kind of treaty which cannot (like the one establishing a state) be based upon compulsory laws, but at most can be a state of *continuous free* association, like the above-mentioned one of a federalism of different states. For without some kind of *lawful state* which actively links the various physical and moral persons (i.e., in the state of nature) there can only be a private law [and rights of individual persons]. In these cases [of international law] a conflict between politics and morals (morals in this case meaning theory of law or jurisprudence) occurs again, but the criterion of publicity of the maxims [of prospective actions] likewise is easily applied [to resolve it]. There is this restriction, however, that a treaty binds the states only as concerns their intent of maintaining peace among themselves and toward other states, but not for the purpose of making conquests.

The following instances [which we shall outline] of an antinomy between politics and morals may present themselves, together with their solution. (a) "If one of these states has promised something to another, whether it be assistance or the cession of a certain territory, or subsidies, etc., it may be asked whether such a state can free itself of keeping its word in a case where the state's safety depends upon it by [its head] declaring that he must be considered as a dual person, namely first as a *sovereign* who is not responsible to anyone in his state, and second merely as the highest *servant of the state* (*Staatsbeamte*) who must give an account to his state: wherefrom it is concluded that he is absolved in his second capacity from what he has promised in his first." But if a state (or its head) were to make public such a maxim, every other state would avoid it, or would unite with others in order to resist such pretensions. This proves that politics, with all its cunning, would upon such a footing [of candor] vitiate its own purpose; hence such a maxim must be contrary to right [*unrecht*].

8:384

(b) "If a neighboring power having grown to tremendous size (*potentia tremenda*) causes anxiety, may one assume that such a power will *want* to oppress, because she *can* do it, and does that give the less powerful a right to make a united attack upon such a power, even without preceding insult?" A state which would publicize such a maxim affirmatively would merely bring about the evil more certainly and rapidly. For the greater power would forestall the smaller ones, and as for the uniting of the latter, this would prove a weak reed against him who knows how to use the *divide et impera*. This maxim of political prudence, if publicly declared, vitiates its own purpose and is therefore contrary to justice [*ungerecht*].

(c) "If a smaller state, by its location, divides the territory of a larger one which this larger one requires for its security, is the larger one justified in subjecting the smaller one and incorporating it into its territory?" It is easily seen that the larger should certainly not publicize such a maxim; for either the smaller ones would soon unite, or other powerful ones would fight over this prize. Therefore such publicizing is inadvisable, which is a sign that the maxim is contrary to justice and may be so in a very high degree. For a small object of injustice does not prevent the injustice from being very large.

3. As concerns the *world* law, I pass it over with silence: because its analogy with international law makes it easy to state and appreciate its corresponding maxims.

———

The fact that the maxims of international law are not compatible in principle with publicity constitutes a good sign that politics and morals (as jurisprudence) *do not agree*. But one needs to be informed which is the condition under which its maxims agree with the law 8:385 of nations. For it is not possible to conclude the reverse: that those maxims which permit publicity are for that reason alone also just, simply because he who has the decided superiority need not conceal his maxims. For the basic condition of the possibility of a [true] law of nations is that there should exist a *lawful state*. For [as we have pointed out] without such a state there can be no public law, rather all law and right [*Recht*] which one can imagine outside such a state (in the state of the nature, that is) is merely private right. We have seen above that a federative state among the states which has merely the purpose of eliminating war is the only *lawful* [*rechtliche*] state which can be combined with the *freedom* of these states. Therefore the agreement of politics with morals is possible only within a federative union (which therefore is according to principles of law and right *a priori* given and necessary). All political prudence has only one lawful ground upon which to proceed, namely to establish such a union upon the most comprehensive basis possible. Without this purpose, all its arguments are unwisdom and camouflaged injustice.

This sort of false politics has its own *casuistry* in spite of the best teaching of the Jesuit [*sic*]. There is first the *reservatio mentalis:* to word public treaties in such terms as may be interpreted in one's interest as one sees fit, e.g., the distinction between the *status quo de fait* and the *status quo de droit;* secondly, there is guessing at *probabilities* [*Probabilismus*]: to think up evil intentions of others, or to make the probability of their possible predominance the legal ground for undermining other peaceful states, finally there is the *peccatum philosophicum* (*pecatillum, bagatelle*): the absorption of a *small* state, if by that a much *larger* one gains in the pretended interest of the world at large.

This argument is favored by the duplicity of politics in regard to morals, and its use of one branch of morals or another for its own purposes. Both charity for other men [*Menschenliebe*] and respect for the *right* of others is a duty. But charity is only a *conditional* duty, whereas respect for the right of others is an *unconditional*, and hence absolutely commanding duty. He who wishes to enjoy the sweet sense of being a benefactor must first make sure that he has not 8:386 transgressed this duty. With morals in the first sense (as ethics) politics is readily agreed, in order to sacrifice the rights of men to their superiors. But with morals in the second sense (as a theory of right and law or jurisprudence [*Rechtslehre*], to which politics should bend its knee) politics prefers not to have any dealings at all, and prefers to deny it all reality and to interpret all its duties as mere charities. This cunning device of a secretive politics could easily be thwarted by philosophy through publicizing its maxims, if only politics would dare allow the philosopher to publicize his own maxims.

To this end I propose another transcendental and affirmative principle of public law the formula of which would be this: "All maxims which *require* publicity in order not to miss their purpose agree with right, law, and politics."

For if they can only achieve their purpose by such publicity, they must be in accord with the general purpose of the public, namely happiness, and it is the essential task of politics to agree with this—that is, to make the public satisfied with its state. But if this purpose can *only* be achieved by publicity—that is, by removing all mistrust of its maxims—such maxims must be in accord with the rights of such a public; for only in this right can the purposes of all be united. I must, however, leave the further elaboration and discussion of this principle to another occasion. But it is recognizable that this principle is a transcendental formula, [since it can be stated] by abstracting from all empirical conditions of happiness [*Glückseligkeitslehre*] as affecting the substance of law, and by merely taking into account the form of universal legality [*Gesetzmässigkeit*].

———

If it is a duty, and if at the same time there is well-founded hope that we make real a state of public law, even if only in an infinitely gradual approximation, then the *eternal peace* which will take the place of the peacemakings, falsely so-called because really just truces, is no empty idea, but a task which, gradually solved, steadily approaches its end, since it is to be hoped that the periods within which equal progress is achieved will become shorter and shorter.

SUGGESTIONS FOR
FURTHER READING

WRITINGS OF KANT IN ENGLISH

The Cambridge Edition of the Works of Immanuel Kant is a comprehensive, fifteen-volume edition of Kant's writings in English translation, under the general editorship of Paul Guyer and Allen W. Wood. It includes all of Kant's published works, plus selections from unpublished notes, fragments and essays, transcriptions of lectures, and correspondence.

BOOKS ABOUT KANT'S PHILOSOPHY

Following is a selected bibliography of recently published secondary sources (in English) on aspects of Kant's philosophy covered by the readings in this volume.

Allison, Henry E. *Kant's Transcendental Idealism.* New Haven: Yale University Press, 1983.

———. *Kant's Theory of Freedom.* New York: Cambridge University Press, 1990.

Ameriks, Karl. *Kant's Theory of Mind.* 2nd edition. Oxford: Clarendon Press, 2000.

Baron, Marcia. *Kantian Ethics (Almost) Without Apology.* Ithaca: Cornell University Press, 1995.

Friedman, Michael. *Kant and the Exact Sciences.* Cambridge, MA: Harvard University Press, 1992.

Guyer, Paul. *Kant and the Claims of Knowledge.* New York: Cambridge University Press, 1987.

———. *Kant and the Experience of Freedom.* New York: Cambridge University Press, 1993.

———. *Kant and the Claims of Taste.* 2nd edition. New York: Cambridge University Press, 1997.

———. *Kant on Freedom, Law and Happiness.* New York: Cambridge University Press, 1999.

———. (ed.) *The Cambridge Companion to Kant.* Cambridge: Cambridge University Press, 1992.

———. (ed.) *Kant's Groundwork of the Metaphysics of Morals: Critical Essays.* Lanham, MD: Rowman and Littlefield, 1998.

Keller, Pierre. *Kant and the Demands of Self-Consciousness.* New York: Cambridge University Press, 1998.

Kitcher, Patricia. *Kant's Transcendental Psychology.* New York: Oxford University Press, 1990.

———. (ed.) *Kant's Critique of Pure Reason: Critical Essays.* Lanham, MD: Rowman and Littlefield, 1998.

Korsgaard, Christine. *Creating the Kingdom of Ends.* New York: Cambridge University Press, 1996.

Longuenesse, Béatrice. *Kant and the Capacity to Judge.* Princeton: Princeton University Press, 1996.

Louden, Robert B. *Kant's Impure Ethics.* New York: Oxford University Press, 2000.

Rosen, Allen D. *Kant's Theory of Justice.* Ithaca: Cornell University Press, 1993.

Wood, Allen W. *Kant's Moral Religion.* Ithaca: Cornell University Press, 1970.

———. *Kant's Rational Theology.* Ithaca: Cornell University Press, 1978.

———. *Kant's Ethical Thought.* New York: Cambridge University Press, 1999.

———. (ed.) *Self and Nature in Kant's Philosophy.* Ithaca: Cornell University Press, 1984.

Yovel, Yirmiyahu. *Kant and the Philosophy of History.* Princeton: Princeton University Press, 1980.

A NOTE ON THE TYPE

The principal text of this Modern Library edition
was set in a digitized version of Janson,
a typeface that dates from about 1690 and was cut by Nicholas Kis,
a Hungarian working in Amsterdam. The original matrices have
survived and are held by the Stempel foundry in Germany.
Hermann Zapf redesigned some of the weights and sizes for Stempel,
basing his revisions on the original design.

MODERN LIBRARY IS ONLINE AT
WWW.MODERNLIBRARY.COM

MODERN LIBRARY ONLINE IS YOUR GUIDE
TO CLASSIC LITERATURE ON THE WEB

THE MODERN LIBRARY E-NEWSLETTER

Our free e-mail newsletter is sent to subscribers, and features sample chapters, interviews with and essays by our authors, upcoming books, special promotions, announcements, and news.

To subscribe to the Modern Library e-newsletter, send a blank e-mail to: **sub_modernlibrary@info.randomhouse.com** or visit **www.modernlibrary.com**

THE MODERN LIBRARY WEBSITE

Check out the Modern Library website at
www.modernlibrary.com for:

- The Modern Library e-newsletter
- A list of our current and upcoming titles and series
- Reading Group Guides and exclusive author spotlights
- Special features with information on the classics and other paperback series
- Excerpts from new releases and other titles
- A list of our e-books and information on where to buy them
- The Modern Library Editorial Board's 100 Best Novels and 100 Best Nonfiction Books of the Twentieth Century written in the English language
- News and announcements

Questions? E-mail us at **modernlibrary@randomhouse.com**.
For questions about examination or desk copies, please visit
the Random House Academic Resources site at
www.randomhouse.com/academic